Praise for *Search*

Carrabis knocks another one right out of the park!

Once again Carrabis takes us on a wild ride wondering how he'll bring it all together. Never fear, he does and in grand style.

Gio's soliloquy about the use of power is something every industrialist, every government official, every religious leader needs to read.

Carrabis pens a gritty paranormal psychological thriller that keeps you in your seat until you've turned the last page.

Go ahead, pick a genre. Carrabis covers them all: paranormal, fantasy, thriller, true crime, magic realism, … If you know the world is more than you can see, you'll love this one.

Characters intertwine and grow in unexpected ways, especially ways that show a balance in all things; Great Gifts often bring Great Loss. It hurts you as a reader to see it happen on the page. That's good storytelling.

Carrabis poses great philosophical questions in the guise of understandable, believable characters. Amazing!

Carrabis' Search proves that power need not corrupt, and absolute power need not corrupt absolutely.

Joseph Carrabis

SEARCH
The First John Chance Mystery

Northern Lights Publishing

Nashua, NH

ISBN 979-8-9878048-7-2

Library of Congress Control Number

Editing by Jennifer Day, Susan Carrabis
Cover by John Bernard Scullin
            http://skolenimation.com/
Book design by Jennifer Day

Printed and bound in the United States of America
First printing December 2023

Published by Northern Lights Publishing
www.northernlightspublishing.com

For Susan

(because everything should be)

And AJ

(who said I could)

A special thanks to Susan

for helping me through this project.
Princess, you are a gem.

To my Grandfather John

with whom all things were possible
I miss you, Buppa

Thanks to

Casey Della Rosa, Lisa Melanson, Amy Doyle, Matthew Roscoe,
Rox Burkey, Lynnette Curran, Jennifer Day, Sienna Day, Dr. Archie
W. Robinson, MD; Grandmother Running Water,

And of course,

Raven

for their help with this story.

Also by Joseph Carrabis

Fiction

Search
The Shaman
The Inheritors
Empty Sky
Tales Told 'Round Celestial Campfires
The Augmented Man

Non-Fiction

Reading Virtual Minds Volume I: Science and History
Reading Virtual Minds Volume II: Experience and Expectation
Reading Virtual Minds Volume III: Fair-Exchange and Social Networks
That Th!nk You Do: 60 Ways to Be Healthy, Happy & Hold Off Harm

Contents

SEARCH

x

Author's Note

The language used in this book may offend some readers. My goal is to use all the tools at an author's disposal and all the tools in my author's toolbag to create as exacting a sensory experience for the reader and to be as accurate to my creation as possible. Sometimes that means language which may offend some is used to create such exacting sensory images.

I've learned to accept my limitations and hope you'll do the same.

Characters, events, places, and things described, depicted, or referred to in this work are fictitious. Any similarity to actual persons, events, places, or things is purely coincidental

\\\\\\\\\

Content Advisory: *Search* contains graphic scenes of sex and violence.

Here is what you asked me to bring you; you little know what it has cost. - Beauty's father to Beauty in 'Beauty and the Beast'

The universe is full of magical things, patiently waiting for our wits to grow sharper. - Eden Phillpotts

There are those who would rather shake the Devil by the tail than me by the hand. - Brother Theodore

The patterns we see are the ones we're trained to see. Only madmen and geniuses see patterns where none existed before. If we're lucky, they teach us. If we're unlucky, we kill them.

Friday, 30 November 1973

John Chance's hair rose on his arms as if reaching for the wind. The air around him shimmered.

He paused raking the hillside between Ramsey College's Finance and Admin buildings and flattened the hairs with a gloved hand.

It would happen again, and soon, but if he just kept about his work no one would notice, he could ignore it and it would go away.

He focused on what was happening around him, locked himself to what was immediate, what was here and now, and let the slope of the hill guide his rake: lost himself in the feel of the wooden handle, the tines pulling crinkling leaves, the smell of freshly mowed grass. Down the hill and across the service road was a lake. A bigger-than -average pond, really. In the summer, with little rains, it became briny due to the proximity of the Atlantic a few miles away. Now it was full and clear, and lily pads formed little traveling islands. More and more often there'd be a glaze of ice rimming the edges of the pond, along the shore where the trees, sedges, and rushes drank deep before the late autumn warmth yielded to the cold of winter.

He remembered his grandfather's stories about the seasons. "*Sta arrivando l'Uomo d'Inverno, Gio. Sta seguendo le mandrie verso sud. In primavera li seguirà a nord.*" WinterMan's coming, Gio. He's following the herds south. Come Spring, he'll follow them back north.

He snorted. "Yeah, right."

The air carried a hint of salt water. Sometimes it mixed with a whiff of diesel and gasoline exhaust from trucks and cars traveling north and south on Rte. 128. The trucks supplied Manchester-By-the-Sea, Magnolia, Gloucester, and Rockport. Some, the refrigeration units, backhauled today's catch from Gloucester, Essex, and Ipswich.

His grandfather called raking "combing Grandmother's hair" and he remembered working with the old man in his garden.

"*Gio, pettiniamo i capelli della nonna.*" Gio, we comb Grandmother's hair.

His grandfather always called him *Gio*, an abbreviation of his given name, Giovanni Fortuna. John Chance in English, but whenever anybody asked his name he replied "Gio."

He shook his head to scatter the memories and pulled on the rake.

The scent of his grandfather's clove aftershave surrounded him like a mist rising from the sea.

Pay attention, Gio. *Ascolta!* Listen.

Blue jays, wrens, and starlings gathered in the branches over his head. He isolated each's song, heard each separate from the others. Chickadees and crows hopped along the rake's path and pecked the freshly turned grass for seeds and grubs. Blue jays mocked him. Robins landed and turned their ears to the ground as they listened for worms.

"Shouldn't you guys have migrated south by now?"

One robin looked straight at him as it turned its head. "*Ascolta, Gio. Ascolta!*"

Gio blinked.

He felt his grandfather's strong hands, hands not felt since a child, lift him, felt himself sitting in the old man's lap, saw the bright, shining birthday paper on the box his grandmother held out to him. "*Cos'è questo, Giò? Cosa ti ha regalato la nonna?*" What's this, Gio? What's Grandma got for you?

He heard his grandparents sharing his delight as he tore open the paper, saw the picture on the box.

A pink View-Master, beside it several picture disks. He couldn't read the writing but Grandpa - his Buppa - could.

"*Parchi nazionali. Preferiti Disney. Animali selvatici.*" National Parks. Disney Favorites. Wildlife.

"*Grazie*, Buppa. *Grazie, nonna.*" Thank you, Buppa. Thank you, Grandma.

He remembered the old man helping him hold the viewer up to his eyes. His grandfather took out one of the disks, looked at its label. "*Parchi nazionali. Bene!*"

Then he'd hear his Buppa's calm, sure voice in his head, in his heart. "*Trova un posto dove vuoi andare; ti insegnerò come arrivarci..*" Find a place you want to go; I'll teach you how to get there.

And they'd never leave Gio's bedroom, never set foot outside his grandparents' house.

"Is what we do magic, Buppa?"

The old man hugged him close. "*Magia del cuore, Gio. Magia del cuore.*" Magic of the heart, Gio. Magic of the heart.

He remembered the plastic-muted metal click as you advanced the slides.

Click!

A new slide snapped into place.

Gio slipped off his grandfather's lap.

This wasn't a slide he remembered. The slides were 3D, not sound, not movement.

The slide showed two young boys racing through dense, ground-level foliage. Someone followed them, someone older. Late teens, early twenties? "Ed, Harry, watch where you go. Remember what I taught you. Be watchful for bear sign and coyote. 'Cat, too. You know what your mom will do to me if anything happens to you?"

The boys laughed and moved faster, ducking and dodging as if avoiding pursuit.

Gio smelled the musk of damp earth and rotting stumps, not the scents of the Ramsey College pond, the mix of fallen leaves and raked earth, the pines, elms, and oaks around him.

He sweated in the heat of the woods. The young man popped the second and third buttons on his shirt and flapped his lapels to get some air across a hairless chest. A small, silver Cross dropped out. Its chain caught on one of the buttons and jiggled bright, reflected sunlight.

Click!

One of the boys ducked behind a tree. "Can't find me, Dave! Can't find me!"

The man adjusted a backpack. "Oh, you can't hide from me, Harry Thompson!"

Gio blinked, pulled his head back as if pulling free of the viewer.

In the campus trees overhead chickadees took flight, their wings *phht-a-phht-a-phht*ing from branch to branch only to return a moment later when they realized it was safe.

Crows nodded at him and waited for his rake to turn grass over.

Click!

The young man, Dave, moved carefully, applied woodcraft, didn't leave a trail. The pack weighed heavy on his back and slid onto his left hip every twenty or thirty steps. Dave'd adjust the straps and the pack'd slip again.

Gio focused, confused. He has good woodcraft but doesn't know how to load a pack?

Dave looked up at him from the slide and pointed towards the two boys. "Bill, their father, doesn't know how to load properly."

He took a few steps, stopped, adjusted his pack, and looked up at Gio again. "Doesn't matter. It's just an overnight." He pointed. "You can see where we'll be camping, right at the end of the thumb."

Gio looked where Dave pointed. Water glistened through the trees, lake-small waves lapped an unseen shore.

"We'll be home tomorrow. I'll repack for the trip back."

Blackbirds, grackles, and woodcock flushed as the boys trampled through the undergrowth and shrieked challenges to each other.

Dave's gaze went after his two charges. "You boys are making this too easy."

Gio pulled back a second time, back to the present, back to the here and now.

A single *caw* caught his ear. A largish raven peered down at him from a pine branch overhead. It pranced back and forth, pacing, as if it had asked a question and waited for Gio to make up his mind.

Frogs croaked at Ramsey's pond. The late Fall, midafternoon sun's heat came through Gio's plaid flannel shirt and sweat trickled down his back and chest. Chickadees, wrens, and blackbirds chirped in the branches.

A work-weary Ramsey College pickup parked at the bottom of the hill. Somebody waved.

Click!

Dave's gaze fell back to the path to the river. Where were the boys?

"Boys?"

Silence.

"Ed? Harry? No games now. Come on out."

A puff of smoke floated beside an elm. A light wind rustled its leaves and dispersed the smoke towards Gio and Dave.

Dave called out, "Who's there?"

Another man, mid- to late-twenties, stepped out from behind the elm. Tall and sickly thin, he held each boy by the throat and tilted their heads back slightly as he flicked his wrists. "Kind of like puppets, aren't they?"

Dave's face reddened. A vein pulsed up the right side of his neck. "Let them go, Todd."

Gio's eyes went back and forth from Dave to the newcomer holding the two boys and back.

What am I seeing? Who is that?

Dave answered out of the side of his mouth. "Todd Anderson. I knew him. From before."

A large-brimmed, felt burgundy hat shaded Todd Anderson's face, revealed only a too-wide smile. His sleeves were rolled up and Dave glanced at his arms.

Gio heard the pickup door creak open and slam shut. Heavy, tired footsteps came up the hill towards him. "Gio?"

Todd Anderson nodded towards his arms but kept his eyes on Dave. "That's right, Dave. You look. No new marks. I'm clean now. Got a good business going. I could give you a job. Good income. Benefits. Learning the ropes from one of the best. May be able to offer a retirement plan next year some time."

"What are you going to do with them?"

Todd shook the boys slightly and they flopped like rag dolls. Their eyes bulged and their faces turned blue. "Didn't know they were this young, Dave."

The heavy footsteps stopped a few feet from Gio. "Gio? You okay?"

Dave took a step towards Anderson and the boys. "How did you know we'd be here, Todd?"

Anderson's grip tightened. The boys sagged. "So pretty and healthy. Nobody told me they were this beautiful."

"Please, Todd."

Todd released his grip. Ed and Harry shook and coughed as they fell to the ground.

Dave stepped forward slowly, his eyes on Todd as he helped the boys up. "You kids okay?"

Their faces reddened and they whimpered. Dave wiped tears from their eyes.

"What can I tell you? Like I said, I've got a growing business now. Expansion plans and everything. Probably have to get warehouse space before long. An office, too." Anderson's gaze went beyond Dave and the boys. "You'd like that, wouldn't you, Mason?"

Dave kept a hand on each boy's shoulder and his eyes on Todd. Behind him twigs cracked and brush crinkled. A muscular man, his dark brown hair cut short in a military crew, crossed thick arms over a chest stretching out a white, sleeveless t-shirt.

He ignored Dave and stared down at Harry and Ed. "Dick candy."

"It's nothing personal, Dave.

Dave pulled the boys close to him. "Come on, boys. We're going back to the wagon."

Todd took his hat off and fluttered it back and forth. "Hey, Dave? Like my hat?"

Dave turned back to Todd. His hat off, his long, blonde locks fell down to his shoulders.

He threw his hat into Dave's face.

Dave pulled back. He let go of the boys. A thick arm came over the pack frame and went around his throat.

Ed and Harry screamed. Dave reached for the arm at his throat.

Todd lifted the two boys by their throats again but kept his eyes on Dave. "Like I said, Dave. It's just business. Nothing personal."

Something hit the side of Dave's head.

"Gio!"

The View-Master fell out of his hands, faded into the leaf pile. He looked up. What happened to the raven?

Somebody grabbed his arm. "Gio! Gio!"

Gio turned his head slowly. Joe Radwel, Ramsey Head of Maintenance, stared intently into Gio's eyes.

Gio focused on what was near; the trickling sweat under his flannel shirt, the steamy scent of his body laboring under the sun, the motions of his muscles and tendons under his skin, the feel of the handle, the roughness of his calluses, Joe's work-roughened hand on his arm.

"I'm fine, Joe. Really, I'm fine."

"Don't give me that 'I'm fine, Joe' routine. This has happened before. I know. I watch you. This happens when you're driving a piece of equipment..." Joe let it hang for a moment. "You want to get yourself checked? The school insurance'll cover it if I say it happened while you were working - "

"My past is getting in the way of my present."

"Huh?"

"Sorry. I'm okay. Cafeteria food's not agreeing with me. That and I'm thinking about my next class. Got a final coming up."

Students emptied buildings and headed to other ones. Some walked silently, others chatted and laughed. Voices raised in safe mirth, good conduct, voices lowered in shared confidences, whispered gossip. Some stayed to the walkways, others took direct routes across the grass. Some waved.

Joe let go. "You know you're always welcome to our place for meals. And we got that spare room nobody's using. You can have the room rent free if - "

"Thanks, Joe. I'm good. Really."

"Cause I don't want to lose you, you know. You're my best worker. I lose you and I got to get back in the field. I'm good at pushing papers and writing up maintenance logs. Nobody wants me driving a plow or a backhoe anymore."

Gio laughed. "I'm okay. Really. I swear."

The maintenance chief leaned into him. "Gio, the wife and I worry about you. You're too world-smart to be one of these Boys-for-Jesus. What are you doing here? I'd say you came here to be near your girl but you met her here, didn't you?"

Gio half-heartedly raked the slope. "I don't know what I'm doing here either, Joe. And yeah, I met Jess at the start of this term. But right now I'm supposed to be here. Don't ask me why, all I know is I'm supposed to be here for some reason."

Joe grimaced. "Yeah, like you know where the fuel line's blocked or when a bearing's about to go." He handed the truck keys to Gio. "I got to check on the other crews. You load up the truck and get it back to the barn. You'll have time to do that before your next class?"

"Sure."

Joe gave him one more good long look. "Don't let anybody else catch you staring off into space like that, you hear? These people'll think you're possessed and perform an exorcism on you."

"I'll tell them I have mild epilepsy. *Petite mals.*"

Joe walked off shaking his head. "Petty malice? Never heard of it. Get the truck back to the barn and call it a day."

"Yes, sir."

The hair on Gio's arms rose, the sky shimmered. Harry and Ed screamed. Dave flopped on the ground. Gio's nose wrinkled with the scent of clove.

He spoke head lowered, under his breath. "Leave me alone, Grandpa."

Sunday, 30 September 1973

Raised in northern Maine trailer-trash poverty, petite, dark complexioned, wide-eyed Pam Rigaux met tall, strapping, nordic blond Bill Thompson in an UMO freshman English class and visited his family once to make sure his claims were true. She quickly got herself pregnant because she realized he, a good Christian boy, would do the right thing. Marrying into the upper-middle class, she quit school and insisted on a small home on French Island, just ten minutes away from classes if he hurried, so she could raise their daughter, Stephanie, while he completed his MBA, which he did in double-quick time, three years.

Now in Gardiner, Pam Thompson spread herself onto her living room settee as if spreading her robes when ascending her throne. Pam made it a point to fill whatever space she could find; she appropriated church committees, civic groups, PTA, tennis, and golf clubs whether she was chair or not, and did it graciously, with a smile, assuming entitlements she did not possess and keeping track of who was with her and who wasn't in a tiny black book she kept in her petite, tightly held purse.

A pair of long knitting needles waved like some monstrous insect's antennae in her hands. Balls of yarn jostled around her like chicks ready to hatch. She glanced up at Bill as he pulled a straight-backed, hardwood kitchen chair into the living room. He set it by the big picture window overlooking their two-hundred-foot long front yard, the two lane driveway beside it, the white picket fence demarcating the Thompson's land from the rest of the world and the country road beyond.

A bit too tall for the chair, he slid forward no matter how he sat. He got a throw-pillow from the couch and used it as a chair pad to keep himself seated. It didn't work. He gave up and stood by the window, arms folded, leaning into it every time a car came down the road.

He checked his watch, checked the shadows of their house and backyard elms as they stretched across their lawn driven by the setting sun, checked the grandfather clock standing opposite their wall-broad fireplace, checked the clock pendulum's slow swing back and forth.

Tick. Tick. Tick.

"We should call the police."

Pam focused on the knitting in her hands. A slight French accent emerged when she tensed. "No, they're fine." She snapped the needles. The balls of yarn twitched around her.

"I'm calling the police."

"No. They stayed late. They got good fishing. Wait."

Bill went into the kitchen and picked up the phone.

"You made me drop a stitch. I have to rip the entire thing out now."

Bill shook his head and dialed the Gardiner Police.

"My boys are fine."

\\\\\\\\

Sergeant Alan Dykstra placed a bulging paper bag on the stained and scattered police reports covering his desk. He shrugged off his dark blue patrolman's winter jacket and draped it over his chair, took off his cap and placed it in a bottom drawer, shook off the early Fall chill clinging to him like melting snow, and looked out a station window into the Gardiner, Maine, night.

Winter soon.

His mind wandered to someplace warm. Girls in hula skirts. Retirement. Someplace far away. He nodded. Yeah, I'll take some of that.

He sat, placed thick arms on either side of the paper bag, and surveyed his desk.

"Coffee."

He ran a hand through red hair cut so short it disappeared against the color of his scalp. After a heavy sigh, he rose, went into the hall, came back with a cup of steaming black coffee, and sat again, his arms once again protectively placed on either side of the paper bag.

One more look at his desk.

He nodded and opened the bag. The smell of a Vagabond Village Sub Shop "Special" masked the scents of *Old Spice* the older patrol wore and *Musk for Men* which seemed to be the go-to of the recruits. Dykstra's mouth watered as he unwrapped the sub, placed napkins on the oily wax paper, and took a sizable bite.

His phone rang. He chewed, watched a red light on the phone blink in time to the ringing, and took another bite. Swallowing, he wiped a hand on an already damp napkin and loosened his tie. A ring of flesh hurried back under his collar.

The red light continued blinking. He took another bite. He sipped some coffee.

Somewhere past the twentieth ring he put the "Special" down, wiped his hands, lifted the phone and pressed the red button. "Gardiner Police Department." His last bite slurred his speech and he swallowed. "Sergeant Dykstra speaking. How may I help you?"

"Hello, Sergeant? I would like to report some missing people."

Dykstra rolled his eyes. The tone of the voice, the careful pronunciation of his name. This would be kids not home on time, out drinking on Swans Island or Nehumkeag or The Sands or in the woods. How many of these do we get in a year? They lost their canoe or forgot where they parked. He tore the heal off the subroll and sopped up the splay of tomatoes, pickles, onions, oil, and hot toppings from the wax paper. "Who's talking, please."

"This is Bill Thompson. On Meredith Drive." Pause. "Next to the Interstate?"

"You said something about missing people?"

A female voice, away from the phone. "Give me the phone. You don't know what you're doing."

The man's voice, muffled. Probably had his hand over the receiver. Dykstra couldn't make out the words.

The voice came back to him more controlled than before. "Our two boys, Harry and Ed, are a day late from their camping trip."

"How old are they?"

"Ten and Eight. Why?"

"Did they have adult supervision?"

"Their live-in's with them. Dave LaVerne. He's an adult. Nineteen."

Dykstra stopped sopping. LaVerne? "A day late? Have you checked the hospitals? Kennebec Valley? Augusta General?"

Dykstra heard a tussle. The woman's voice came on the phone. "Wouldn't the hospitals have contacted us?"

"Who's speaking, please?"

"I am Pam Thompson. The boys' mother."

Dykstra could almost hear "you idiot" at the end of her sentence. He wondered if Pam Thompson's eyes bulged when she spoke.

"Was anybody carrying any ID? Something would alert the authorities where they lived or who they were?"

"How should I know if they had any ID?"

Dykstra took a mouthful of subroll and talked around the tomatoes and pickles and onions. "I'll send a car out. It'll be there in ten, fifteen minutes."

The Thompsons hung up.

Dykstra sipped his coffee and kept his eyes on the phone.

It sat silent; no lights, no ringing.

He used the last of the roll to scoop up toppings from the wax paper and got a second cup of coffee.

After washing his hands, he called dispatch to send out a car.

\\\\\\\\

Bill kept his hand on the phone after hanging up. "Has David seen Todd recently?"

Pam emptied the remains of the morning's coffee into the sink. "I'm going to make some coffee."

Bill stood beside her at the sink. He placed his hands equidistant apart on the countertop and pushed slightly as if testing its resilience. "You told the deacons we could provide him a good Christian home. Teach him God's ways. Remember?"

"I can't find the sponge. What did you do with the sponge?"

Bill hung his head. He shook it and the shaking motion seemed to lift it until he gazed out the kitchen windows. "And it was your idea he take the boys camping this weekend."

Pam opened the cabinet under the sink to get a sponge.

Bill drove his knee into it and slammed it shut. "You wouldn't let up until I guilted him into taking them. Did you forget that?"

Pam rinsed out the pot without washing it. She shook it out over the sink, turned her back to Bill, and scooped coffee into the percolator basket. "You agreed he could stay with us. You and the deacons."

Bill's gaze returned to the scene out the window, the expansive backyard, the blanket of dusk stretching out from the mountains beyond. "I'll ask again, has David seen Todd recently?"

Pam plugged the pot in, crossed her arms tightly over her chest, and went back into the living room. "Pour me a cup, would you?"

Of his two boys, Ed, the younger one, had a good head on his shoulders. Ed had more patience and showed more skill. Harry was the tackler. He lowered his head and rushed in without thinking, always looking for the next thing, the next challenge, taking what he could get and making fun of Ed for holding back. Ed considered, evaluated, checked and rechecked, waited, checked again, moved cautiously. Ed helped Harry home when Harry hurt himself doing some stunt. Harry made sure anything that went wrong was Ed's fault.

Bill poured two cups and went back into the living room.

They drank half the pot before the patrol car arrived.

Bill watched moonlight fill the rooftop blues as two men exited. They looked around and talked to each other, adjusted their harnesses, put their nightsticks into their belt rings, checked their holsters, secured their weapons.

He opened the front door and cast a small shadow under the overhead light. "Hello, Officers. Thanks for coming by."

Their long shadows shrunk to human size as they approached. The closer one, the one with the tan, blue eyes, and pencil mustache, offered his hand. "Mr. Thompson? I'm Officer Sid Lyndon. This is my partner, Officer Harry Towne."

After half an hour of asking questions and taking notes, undrunk coffees cold and staining cups, Lyndon flipped his notepad closed. "I'll file this just to be safe, but to tell you the truth, they probably hit good fishing and stayed late. I wouldn't worry about it. But just in case, do you have any pictures of them? Photos, maybe? No keepsakes. Just something we could circulate. Just in case."

Pam didn't rise from her chair. Her eyes remained fixed on her intersecting needles as if gazing into the depths of time and space.

Bill headed for the stairs. "I've got some photos I keep. Take them once a year with the mountain out back as the backdrop."

Pam looked up. "You do?"

He hesitated, his foot on the first stair, as if a sudden weight fell upon him. "I tell them they're going to own that mountain some day. Have them stand in the same spot each year. To watch how they grow."

He came back a moment later with 8x10s in hand. "These do?"

Lyndon took the photos and handed them to Towne. "Thank you."

Bill waved as they drove away.

Pam stood by the kitchen sink washing everyone's cups. "I told you there was no need to worry."

"They're not home yet."

Monday, 3 December 1973

Todd shook out the white, double-bed sheet and reached up into the oak's lower branches. Behind him the Kennebec River's lower rapids splashed. He wrapped the sheet's end over the limb and clothespinned it so the sheet fell open like a film projector screen. He stepped back, made sure it was secure, then shook a spray can and sprayed a barely noticeable "2" on the sheet.

Leaves rustled at ground level and he lowered the can.

"What'd you do with the boys, Andersen?"

"Sergeant Dykstra, how good of you to come. What boys?"

"Don't bullshit me, you sick fuck. The Thompson boys. What'd you do with them?"

"Not a thing. Has something happened to them?"

"You drive the Hershey highway with Dave LaVerne, don't you?"

"Why whatever do what you mean, Sergeant Dykstra?"

Dykstra's hand went to his nightstick.

"Oh, Sergeant Dykstra. I had no idea you were into brutality. Doesn't surprise me, though. I've seen your wife. Or wait. No, that would be bestiality, wouldn't it?"

Dykstra pulled his nightstick. "I'm gonna - "

"Not get paid? Whatever you do to me, make sure you don't hurt my hands. It'd be horrible if I couldn't hand you your cut every month, don't you think? How could you afford that pretty little lady you visit up in Bangor?"

Dykstra's grip weakened. The nightstick slipped back into its belt ring. "How do you know about her?"

"I know about her because I, unlike you, make it a point to know everything I can about the people I do business with."

"What are you doing with those sheets?"

"Making highway markers. Would you like to help?"

Dykstra turned and walked up the path from the river to the picnic area.

"Don't go to far, Sergeant. You can help me put the rest of these up along both sides of the river."

Dykstra paused, his back to Andersen, and clenched his fists.

"Beat me if you must, but do it with a smile, that way I know we're both getting pleasure out of it."

\\\\\\\\

Stephanie Thompson sat in her red Monte Carlo in the Tylers' Windham, Mass, driveway, her hands tight at ten and two on the steering wheel. "God damn you, mother. If you weren't so goddamn afraid I'd turn out like you, I'd've been home and none of this would've happened."

She pounded the steering wheel with each sentence. "Fuck you. Fuck you. Fuck you."

Tears glistened her cheeks. "Yeah, and I still turned out worse than you." She glanced in the rearview and gave her reflection the finger. "*Phphttt!*"

Robbie and DJ, the Tylers' twins she nannied, ran out the front door to her Monte Carlo. Toddlers, they couldn't manage the door and she waved them back before she opened it. "Yes, Trouble One and Trouble Two?"

They chuckled and ran back into the house.

"Oh, who wants snugglebunnies? Bring me those bellies!"

She checked her makeup in the mirror. "Can't have me looking like this, can we, Donnie?"

Her hand slid over the Monte Carlo's plush, black passenger seat on the other side of the console. The twins' father, Donnie Tyler, loved to throw money around and this Monte Carlo was no exception. Ruby red exterior, black plush interior, wrap around instrument console, the bigger, 454 engine, and seats that reclined.

He especially wanted seats that reclined. He bought the car a week before Stephanie came to work for them, after everyone agreed her nannying for the Tylers would be a good thing for everyone involved.

A month earlier, Stephanie's parents put the word out through the church grapevine they wanted a good, safe, Christian home for their daughter, a place where she - just back from a summer at a Montana Christian ranch - could develop her godly womanhood and foster her motherly tendencies.

Not that Stephanie was a wild child. No, hardly that. She simply needed responsibilities to bring out her virtuosity. Nannying two toddler twins seemed an ideal opportunity for such. Mark, the younger twin by three minutes, needed some coaxing to come out of his shell. Nobody mentioned DJ's - Donald Junior - propensity to harass and hit his brother when no one was looking.

Don Tyler managed business lending at Boston's State Street Bank, Caroline Tyler's father was a diplomat to some small European country and she spoke with a subtle accent from studying in European schools all her life. They learned about Stephanie through a visiting missionary, made calls and soon introductions were made. Shortly after they spent a night in Gardiner and attended a prayer meeting at the Thompsons' church. Pam and Bill reciprocated, of course. Ministers and other elders were consulted on both sides. The Thompsons visited the Tylers' home. The twins took to Stephanie immediately, crawling in her lap, pulling her hair, plucking at her blouse and skirt. "See our room, Step'nie, see our room."

They tugged her upstairs while the Tylers and Thompsons sipped coffee and exchanged church stories in the living room. After a few minutes, Don excused himself. "Want to make sure they haven't tied Stephanie to a bedpost."

Everybody laughed.

He came back five minutes later a little flushed.

Caroline frowned. "Is everything okay?"

"Oh, fine. Just laughing. She's used to boys because of your sons and knows the things they'll pull better than I do."

"Where's Stephanie now?"

"Freshening up."

They continued sipping coffee and exchanging church stories.

Stephanie wanted more time. Pam decided it wasn't necessary. Dates were set. Donnie drove up special to bring her down, save the Thompsons the trip.

Stephanie gave Donnie his second blowjob at a little beach he knew in Kittery. Difficult to get to. One road in and one road out. Only two cars there. With tinted windows. Donnie shook his head. "Wish I thought of that."

He didn't take long. She didn't even have to take off her blouse.

He brought his seat back up from the reclined position. "This is going to work out really well, don't you think, Stephanie?"

She lowered her window, hung her head out, spit.

"No."

"Oh? You want me to tell all those good folks in Gardiner you seduced me?"

She laughed and leaned into him. "No, I want the car." A small silver Cross fell out of her blouse and swung slightly.

Donnie fixed his eyes on it. "Okay." A moment's hesitation. "But I still get to take you places."

She nodded, turned away, checked her reflection in her window, and placed a stray lock of blonde hair back where it belonged.

Is that the kind of virtuosity you meant, Mother?

Caroline looked around the tables at Windham Donut. This was the first time she'd been inside. She'd driven past any number of times. Once she counted the trucks, many in disrepair, driven by unshaven men in overalls, both men and overalls also in disrepair. Once one of them smiled and waved at her as she drove past. His bucktoothed grin caused her to slow. Something familiar.

Oh yes, their garbageman. Every other Thursday. She waved back as she drove on.

A thin young man, long blond hair flowing around his shoulders from under a felt burgundy hat, sat by himself in a corner, a cup of coffee and some kind of long donut in a napkin in front of him.

He stood and waved.

She walked over. He pulled out a seat for her. She looked down on it but didn't sit. "Who are you and what's this about?"

"Thanks for taking my call and agreeing to meet me. I know I didn't give you much to go on."

"You said you knew my father? In Europe?"

"We - you, me, your mom and dad - knew each other a long time ago. I'd be surprised if you remembered. I don't think we ever met face-to-face."

"Then how am I supposed to know you?"

He took off his hat. His widow's peak was a match for her father's. His nose, her nose. His eyes, her eyes. His smile. She remembered that smile.

She collapsed into the chair. "No." She focused on the tabletop as if inspecting for cockroaches.

"Ah, you remember me." He sat and lifted his pastry to his lips, licked the tip. "Have you ever tried these? It's a cream-filled cruller?" He bit into it. Pale cream oozed from his mouth. "Mmmm. Delicious. Like having a huge cock explode in your mouth."

"How did you find me?"

"Oh, mother! I've made you one of my life's ambitions. Grandpa did such a good job hiding his tracks but you'd be surprised what good Catholic priests will do for a willing little boy-butt."

Caroline felt her lunch making a break for it.

"And once you know a person's weaknesses, you own them. You can do whatever you want." He took another bite, let the cream linger on his lips before dragging his tongue over them, cleaning them off. "Everybody has a dirty little secret, Mother, and it rarely matters how little or how dirty, so long as they don't want someone else to find out. Learn their secret, learn who they don't want to know their secret, and your work is done."

"What do you want?"

"What does anybody want, Mother? Money. You have it, I need it."

"I - "

"Oh, not to worry, Mom. You're my mother, after all. I'm not going to bleed you dry. I love you, care about you."

Caroline bit her lip.

"Far more than you ever cared about me, it seems. I want enough to start a business, to buy a share, as it were. I'd go to Donnie - he's your husband, right? Donald Tyler, VP of Business Finance at State Street Bank in Boston? Your husband Donnie is that Donald Tyler? Yes? - and ask for a loan but he'd want some kind of collateral, references, and you don't get those things being shuttled around from orphanage to guardian to foster home to rectory to orphanage. Thank goodness for the Good Will school or I'd still be hustling tricks for donuts and sodas."

Caroline tongue touched blood inside her lip.

"But that's enough about me. And I've already done my homework about you. And no Earl Gray and crumpets here, so let's get down to business, shall we?"

Tuesday, 25 December 1973

Pam drove her silver Marquis Brougham down to the coast and touched a tissue to her eyes every time she passed a holiday wreath or a yard decorated with two-foot tall candles or mangers or Santa in his sleigh or shepherds or snowmen.

Christmas.

Where were her children?

A month and nothing. From her boys, nothing. From Dave, nothing. The church held prayer vigils and mentioned Harry and Ed each Sunday in the service, told her and Bill not to worry, God was in control, and nothing. Bill called the police daily and nothing except it gave him a daily excuse to tell her this was her fault and he would never forgive her.

She snorted and her hands tightened on the wheel. "You think I need you to forgive me? All of a sudden you're a big man who can tell me what to do? Hmph! I tell my Papa, we'll see what a big man you are." She turned onto US Route 1. "I showed you, Mr. Bill Thompson. you haven't shaved in three weeks and come in from the garage so drunk you can't walk straight and your eyes red from the booze? Ha! You stink of drink, Mr. Bill Thompson. More and more each day you stink of drink."

He staggered slightly and blinked until his eyes focused on her. "A man can't have a little drink while waiting for his boys to open their Christmas presents, O' Dear Wife o' Mine?"

She walked out and left him standing on the front walk screaming. "I smell of drink? Well you smell of bitch. How 'bout that, Pammy? I'm a drunk? Well you're a bitch. Come on, Pam, say 'em with me. Say 'em all: bitch, shit, and fuck. And here's to the good wife and mother you are, Pam." He lifted a flask from his pocket and held it up while she raced down the driveway. "Salut!" He tipped it back and fell backward onto the morning's fresh snow.

She cut down to 1A, to the seaside towns, looking for a place to forget things for a while, a coffee shop or knickyknacky tickytacky tourist shop open out of season, a place she could laugh at what brought people to Maine, people who summered here, the "Leave your money and go home" people.

She passed a small strip mall, three of the five stores closed for the season, and saw a blinking "Homemade Jelly Donuts!" sign. She turned around and pulled in. "I'll bet their coffee tastes like shit, Bill. Shit. See? I can say shit. I'll bet their coffee tastes like shit. Shit, shit, shit."

The sign stopped blinking as she got out of the car. "Damn." She laughed. "How about that, Bill? I can say shit, I can say damn. How about we throw in a couple of good old 'fucks' for good measure?"

"You can't get rid of your guilt by swearing it away."

Pam spun towards the voice and placed a hand over her heart.

A middle-aged woman, dark skin, long braided hair, wearing some kind of ceremonial costume complete with beaded earrings and necklace, held a coffee cup out to her.

"You startled me."

"Didn't want to interrupt you."

Pam looked at the coffee. The woman held it up to her. Pam took it hesitantly, her eyes dancing back and forth from the cup to the woman and back. "Thank you."

"No milk or sugar in it. Didn't know how you take it."

Pam nodded towards the coffee shop. "You work here?"

The woman pointed one store down. "I work there."

Pam turned and looked at a sign in the window: Running Water's Native Crafts and Keepsakes.

"Saw you pull up to the coffee shop. It's been closed a few weeks now. Damn sign has a short in it. Keeps flickering. I called the owner to fix it. They haven't done a thing yet. You got to stop swearing at your guilt. You got to own it to get rid of it."

Pam shook her head. "Sorry?"

"Your guilt. You blame yourself for your boys going missing. You say it's grief but it's not. It's guilt. You brought that boy into your house, bullied your husband and your church to let you have him. That's what you said, wasn't it? 'Let me have him. I'll put the love of God in him'? Now he's missing with your boys and it's your fault because you trusted where you shouldn't have and now you have no control of the situation. That's why you haven't asked your father to help. Haven't told him anything either. Every time he asks you say Bill's out with the boys. Funny he's never gotten suspicious, don't you think?"

"I have no idea what you're talking about."

The woman nodded. "Uh-huh." She smiled and walked past Pam back to her store. "Keep the cup. A gift. Someone needs to see it. You don't know them yet. To stir a memory." She locked the door behind her, switched the OPEN sign to CLOSED, turned off the lights, and was gone.

Pam peered through the windows. Nothing and no one. No sound of a car starting up and no second story for an apartment above the store. She tossed the rest of the coffee and looked for a trash can to get rid of the cup.

Running Water stood in the parking lot. "Keep it."

Pam looked at the cup. Handmade. "Ha. Native crafts." No writing, only a picture on the side of a stream in a wood. The stream burbled as she watched. She blinked and looked again. Just a picture of a stream in a wood. "How do you get the picture to do that?"

She looked up. The woman was gone. A raven walked back and forth in her place.

"Shoo. Ugly bird. Go away."

Bill sat at his kitchen table. He checked the clock, the calendar, then back to the clock again. Where was Pam? Just got in her car and disappeared. The way she took off, you'd think the police were after her.

He chuckled. "You wouldn't say shit if you had a mouthful, Pam. Why would the police be after you? Hell, you haven't wanted them involved from day one. You think Dave and the boys will magically turn up when we're not looking?"

He went to the refrigerator and touched his boys' refrigerator art.

"Where are you, boys?"

He opened the refrigerator and reached for a Pepsi. His fingers touched the cold can and he pulled his hand back empty. He went through the porch and shook his head as he passed Pam's empty flowerpots and vases on the table. "Spread yourself out everywhere, don't you, Pam? Or you planning to go in on your father's business?"

He continued to the garage, to his side, to his workbench and tool shelves, and brought down a power saw box. Once on the workbench, he opened the box and took out an unopened bottle of Dewars.

"Yeah, Pam, I'm a drunk. Happy? Congratulate yourself. You do good work."

He sat in his silver Ford F150 long bed pickup, broke the seal, pulled the cork, raised the bottle to his lips and let the dark gold liquid burn its way down his throat.

"You know, Pam, my parents warned me against you. Said you'd suck all the fun out of my life." He lifted the bottle again. "I remember laughing to myself, thinking 'Well, she sure knows how to suck, you're right about that.' Remember you telling me no, you were saving yourself, but this was okay because it wasn't really sex?" He took another hit. "Funny how all that changed once you saw my parents' house." He swigged another mouthful, coughed, swigged again. "The first few years were good. And Stephanie and the boys made it worthwhile." He looked at the bottle, swirled the dark gold it contained, took a long slow pull, licked his lips at the burn. "But then you brought that queer son-of-a-bitch into this house so you could show everyone how to save someone." More dark gold burn. "How's that working out for you, Pam? Huh? How's that working out?"

\\\\\\\

Pam saw a public telephone sign on her way home, pulled over and dug coins out of her purse. Her father answered on the second ring.

"Papa, what have you done with Ed and Harry?"

She listened. The lines on her face sagged. She hung her head, wiped her cheek with her free hand, and hung up without saying another word.

Monday, 7 January 1974

Jess Rosen watched the tall, thin girl in the long technicolor scarf, mittens, and matching knitted hat walk from a ruby red Monte Carlo into the Danvers Stop&Shop. "Couldn't be."

She grabbed a shopping list and her wallet from the passenger seat of the Iperia University van and followed. A couple of glances up and down the aisles revealed nothing so she went about her task: bulk buying tampons, pads, wipes, and related feminine hygiene products for her dorm mates. Once a week somebody drew the short straw and borrowed a college van to go shopping. If the trip was to nearby Liberty Tree Mall, the van would be full. But picking up tampons and pads at the Danvers Stop&Shop? She was on her own.

She swung her cart down the Health & Beauty aisle and got out her list.

"On the rag, Rosen?"

"Thompson? Stephanie?"

The tall, thin girl's head poked around the aisle's end cap. She pulled off her woolen hat and long, blonde hair fell down her shoulders and back. "Hey, Jess."

"I thought that was you in the parking lot. You were out west, weren't you? Working at a ranch? Something like that?"

"More like Camp Jesus for Wayward Daughters, but yeah." She glanced at the list in Jess's hand. "Heavy month?"

"Buying supplies for my dorm. I'm at Iperia now. What are you doing here?"

"I got a job nannying a couple of kids in Windham. How much time do you have? Want some lunch? My treat. You know about the Capri?"

"Heard about it during orientation. My boyfriend takes me there a lot."

Stephanie's right eyebrow lifted and she faked a German accent. "We have a boyfriend, do we? You will tell us everything. Everything, do you hear? Everything!"

Twenty minutes later they'd placed their order for a large, extra cheese, well done, and were sipping Tabs in a dark booth at the back of the Capri. Stephanie toyed with her napkin, the salt and pepper shakers, the Parmesan cheese holder, their straw wrappers. She arranged, rearranged, and put everything back in their original positions only to repeat the process again and again.

Her eyes down and not on Jess, she singsonged, "So what's his name, what's he like, does he roll over when he's done, show me his sex face."

"What's going on, Thompson?"

Stephanie placed a hand on her chest and affected a southern accent. "Why whatever do you mean, Ms. Rosen?"

"You're pale, you're breathing shallow, and you're twitchy. You start doing drugs since I saw you last?"

Stephanie affected a Boston accent. "When did you become a doctah?"

"Since I started dating Gio. He pays attention to things like that. So what's going on?"

"Gio, eh? The last boy you dated was a Javier. You got a thing for foreigners, Rosen?"

"He's not a foreigner. Everybody calls him Gio. His name's John Chance. And quit changing the subject. What's going on?"

"You haven't heard about my brothers?"

"Eddie and Harry? Are they okay?"

Stephanie's eyes watered and she hung her head. "They're missing."

Jess sat beside Stephanie and put an arm over her shoulder. "Sweet Jesus, Steph. When did this happen?"

Stephanie filled in the details in between gut shaking sobs. She clung to Jess like a child seeking its mother's breast.

"And the police know nothing?"

"Idiots haven't done a thing in three months."

The pizza arrived. Jess shook her head at the waitress and mouthed, "Can we get that to go?" The waitress nodded and carried the steaming pie away.

Jess held Stephanie and waited until her sobs were under control. "You mind if I tell Gio about this?"

Stephanie laughed through her tears. "I thought he was a doctah."

Jess watched the waitresses moving back and forth, other customers eating pizza, subs, pasta. She shook her head. "He's different."

\\\\\\\

Jess straddled Gio's hips on the backseat of his 1964 Mercury Comet which he affectionately referred to as "Bessie." The windows steamed except for a clear patch on the windshield revealing the near-full moon rising over Manchester-By-The-Sea's Singing Beach. They parked in the dark, in the unlit lot on the other side of the beach house, closed for the season and also lightless.

Maria Muldaur whispered over the radio.

> *Midnight at the Oasis*
> *send your camel to bed*
> *shadows painted on faces*
> *traces of romance in our heads…*

The moon lit Gio's face like a celestial spotlight. "What did you tell her?"

Jess reached down and unzipped his pants. "I asked if I could tell you about it. Is that a problem?"

"What do you expect me to do? I told you before, I'm a good guesser. That's it. You want me to guess what's happened?"

She leaned forward and bit his ear. "You know things."

"Knowing where you left your notebook and when the girls in your dorm are going to have their periods is not the same as knowing where bodies are buried."

She leaned back. "You think they're dead?"

"Did I say that?"

"When Candy was two months late you touched her and she started bleeding."

"God, that sounds disgusting."

"She did."

"She was tense. Nervous. And getting more nervous by the minute. And even she said she was never regular anyway."

"You touched her."

"This sounds like a scene from a bad movie. 'He touched me and everything changed.' All I did was help her relax so she could start her period."

She pulled violently on his penis. "Bullshit."

"That's supposed to convince me?"

"You know what people are thinking."

"Sometimes I'm wrong."

"You know when people lie. You said it yourself. Diane challenged you and you told her all about herself, way back to when her parents got divorced and she started doing drugs. She said you were wrong. You said she was lying."

"I said, 'Okay, I'm wrong.'"

"Yeah, and the next day she's expelled for selling drugs on campus. They found them under her mattress, for chrissake."

"And your dorm mother forbid me to come into the dorm ever again."

Jess pulled her rugby shirt over her head and tossed it beside them on the seat.

"No."

"Well, while I'm here…"

He focused on the rising crescent moon. It turned over and emptied moonlight into the sea as he watched. His grandfather made up stories about the moon, about walking on moonlight. Gio's legs twitched. Under Jess, behind her and down to the floor, he saw them shimmer, remembered walking into the sky, remembered the smell of clove always encircling his grandfather, remembered that weird View-Master… hallucination? Illusion? Phantasm? He remembered the boys' screaming around the time Ed and Harry Thompson went missing.

And whatever it was he experienced, he got their names right.

He shook his head quickly, forcing the memories away.

"Gio?"

"Do you really want me to help?"

"Can you help?"

"Is Stephanie willing to talk with me?"

"Do you want me to ask her?"

"Feel like visiting your folks this weekend?"

\\\\\\\\\

Sergeant Dykstra's phone rang. He finished eating, balled up the wax paper and tossed it in the basket across the room. He nodded in approval.

The phone kept ringing, the red light kept blinking. He wiped his hands on his pants and picked it up. "Gardiner Police Department. Sergeant Dykstra speaking. How may I help you?"

He listened. His eyes widened. He flipped over a page on the record book on his desk and lifted a pen from his shirt pocket. "Okay, slowly now. It's a station wagon? You're sure of that? And it's all burnt up? Was it in an accident? You think someone set it on fire, torched it? Where did you find it?" He scribbled notes. "Wait, don't hang up. What's your name? Wait! Hello? Hello?"

Tuesday, 8 January 1974

Dykstra drove to Norris Point on Cobbosseecontee Lake and stopped a few curves in. A Maine State Police car was visible on the side of the road blocking access to a recently walked path through the woods. The Point was shaped like a grasping hand and the path went out towards the thumb. A Maine State Police officer walked back up the thumb and over to his car.

"You're a little out of your jurisdiction, aren't you, sergeant?"

Dykstra read the officer's tag. "Morelli? We got a call about an abandoned car somewhere out here. What are you doing here?"

Morelli snorted little steam jets into the cold, Maine winter air. "Well, ain't that at tickler. We got the same call. Must be important for a desk sergeant to make the trek. You didn't send uniforms?"

"Do I know you?"

"You didn't answer my question and last time I checked, MSP outranks local authorities."

"Sorry, didn't expect to see anybody out here. Caught me by surprise. What did you find?"

A middle-aged man wearing wool pants, heavy, calf-high boots, and a parka sloshed up the path, three cameras tightly strapped to his parka and one with a telephoto so large it bashed against him like a loose tree limb in a storm. "Got all I need, Tony."

Dykstra looked past Morelli. "You're Harding, right? With the 'Journal, right? What pictures did you get?"

Morelli shook his head at Harding.

Harding shrugged and got in Morelli's state police cruiser.

Dykstra nodded towards him. "What's he doing here?"

"His job. You?"

"I don't want a pissing contest, Morelli."

"Good. Neither do I and I got this covered. Appreciate your help and all. Ask your chief to call Lieutenant Jamison out of Augusta if he wants to see the report."

Dykstra turned his squad around and drove off. Once he could no longer see Morelli, Harding, or the state cruiser in his rearview he grabbed his mike. "Yeah, I need you to make a call for me, and I need it to be a private conversation. Can you do that?"

\\\\\\\\

Morelli watched Dykstra drive off. Harding got out of the cruiser and Morelli held up his hand. He closed his eyes tight and bowed his head as if in prayer.

Harding waited then cleared his throat. "Funny time to get religion."

Morelli opened his eyes and chuckled. "Listening. Want to make sure he drove off and hasn't doubled back."

Harding gazed down the road. "You listen good, Kimosabe. Dykstra bad medicine."

"Yeah, but nobody's caught him doing anything."

"Keep looking. Something'll come up. Let me know when you do. Love to take the exclusives."

Morelli nodded up towards Norris Point's thumb. "The plates are missing and somebody pulled the vehicle ID. We've already had heavy snows and whoever called dug it out enough to know it was trouble."

Harding pulled a DayTimer out of a pocket and flipped some pages. "These camps closed in what, September? October the latest? Tires were on bare earth. When did we start getting ground cover? My guess is they towed it here after these camps were closed for the season. Otherwise the summerers would've seen this new trail all broken through and reported it. So what, Thanksgiving? Beginning of December, maybe?"

"Probably also means whoever torched it knew when people'd come back to open their camps in late May. Late Spring, anyway. Things'd be grown out by then, the trail gone and the car worthless for forensics. Whoever did this knew what they were doing."

"Yeah, but leaving this trail? Big mistake. Some kids or somebody hunting out of season would find this and report it."

Morelli nodded.

"Which begs the question, who reported it?"

Morelli shook his head. "No idea. I just follow orders. How long until we get pictures?"

"The black&whites you'll have by the end of the day. The coloreds'll take a while. Maybe two if I tell the lab to rush them."

"Tell the lab to rush them."

\\\\\\\\

Gio sat at his desk staring out the window at the marsh behind his dorm, a two-story house converted into student housing on the edge of campus. The snow remained in patches. This close to the ocean, even the heaviest snows melted away in a few days.

There was little backyard, room enough for a rotary clothesline and a picnic table. Close beyond that, bullrushes and swamp grasses dominated the view. Some elms and birches sheltered the dorm from nearby traffic. A light breeze rustled the few, brown leaves still on the trees. Two marsh rabbits cut across the yard, stopped halfway, stood up, sniffed, their short ears moving, listening, then hurried on. Swamp-sparrows and water-thrush chattered back and forth. A raven landed in the nearer elm. Its weight bobbed the limb and knocked the remaining snow off.

"Should you be here? Or am I the only one who thinks of being someplace warm in winter?"

The raven fluffed its wings, turned its head, and stared at him.

The raven shimmered. Gio heard his Grandfather. "*Guarda attraverso i suoi occhi. Prestito. Cosa vedi?*" See through its eyes. Borrow. What do you see?

Gio's focus went soft. He felt the wind lift him, carry him to the raven, enter it. His arms grew into wings. His feet transformed into talons, his hair into feathers.

"The precision of his eyesight is amazing, Grandpa."

"*Cosa vedi?*" What do you see?

The Gio-raven looked down. A plop in the water. A harlequin duck, male. It looked up at him and smiled.

The raven took to the air, flew over the harlequin, headed north.

The harlequin lifted from the pond and followed the raven. Gio watched until they were both out of sight, over the trees, beyond the campus. He stared out his window. The scent of clove cigarettes surrounded him.

But not aftershave? Not like his grandfather's.

"*Ascolta. Guadare. Aspetto. Stai attento. Ricorda.*" Listen. Watch. Look. Be careful. Remember.

\\\\\\\\\

Several students assembled across campus in Herder Hall North's third-floor corner room. Tall and lean Tim Annandale, deep voiced, auburn haired and pallid faced, sat in their center. He motioned to a student standing by the room's lone window. "Pull the drapes, Barry." The room darkened. The only light came from a banker's green-shaded lamp on the desk built into the prefab dorm room's structure. Annandale looked around him and nodded at familiar faces. "Is this it? Everyone here?"

Others looked around the small single dorm room. Some leaned against the closet, also built into the prefab structure, others against walls. Two boys stood on either side of an nonregulation bureau and rested an arm on its top, careful not to knock over makeup and a small jewelry box. A few sat cross-legged on the floor, their faces turned up to hear Annandale's words. Some sat on the bed, another prefab artifact built against a wall.

Petite, raven haired, and with eyes like liquid obsidian, Laurie Sánchez knocked on the door frame.

The boys in the room took a long look at Laurie, silhouetted in the doorway by the hall light, the purpose of their meeting lost for a moment. Girlfriends flared their nostrils, inhaled sharply, cleared their throats. The boys brought their attention back to the center of the room.

Annandale quickly stood and opened his mouth as if to speak. Instead he cleared his throat, brushed his pant legs, and slowly took his seat. "No thanks, Laurie. We don't need this room cleaned now."

"I'm not working, I'm curious."

Annandale stared at her and smiled. "Good. Would you please close the door, Laurie?"

She shook her head and crossed her arms. Long black hair gathered on her shoulders like storm clouds, her eyes sparked like lightning against dark, Costa Rican skin. "It's open dorm. You can't close the door. Or men can't be in here with the door closed. There's already too many people in this room. You know the rules."

Annandale's lips tightened. "I don't think the housemother will mind once she knows what we're doing. Besides, Ramsey is a Christian school and we're all good Christians here, aren't we?"

Some of the gathered students nodded, some grunted, some went "uh-huh", and some did a combination of all three. A few looked around nervously and rubbed their hands together as if cold.

"You're free to leave if you're uncomfortable, Laurie."

She shook her head again. "I want to hear what you have to say."

A frail boy with delicate, artists' hands, thick glasses, and a face reddened with acne pushed past Laurie and closed the door. He pushed past her again on his way back to get closer to Annandale and the center of the room. Laurie pulled away as if he rang a leper's bell.

Annandale stood up. "Merl. That was rude."

The frail, acne faced boy's face blanched as much as possible, almost looking as if it suffered from tiny impact craters. "What? What did I do?"

Laurie straightened her sleeves and brushed her blouse as if brushing away dinner crumbs. "Don't worry about it."

Annandale sat once again, looked around the room, and smiled. "Good. Now that we're all here, what are we going to do about the problem of John Chance?"

Friday, 11 Jan 1974

Gio drove north on I-95, Jess beside him. Stephanie, on Jess' right and by the passenger door, filled out the Comet's front seat. Jess caught Gio staring at the Sheraton Inn off Maine Mall Road in South Portland.

"Never been this far into Maine before?"

"My grandfather brought me up here sometimes. To visit friends."

"Most people coming to Maine on business never get further than Portland. They get as far as the Sheraton and have people meet them there."

"Looks like a satellite, doesn't it? Big cylinder, all black with silvery edges and lines, and antennae sticking out of it? Never saw a round building before. Except in pictures."

Stephanie chuckled. "Yeah. Maine's an education for everybody."

Jess pointed at the approaching four lane divide. "Take 295. It's quicker." She checked the speedometer. "About fifteen, twenty minutes."

"You drive this road a lot?"

Stephanie pointed at the mall on the right. "Maine Mall's the only real mall in the entire state. You want to go shopping, you shop there, and we know all the ways to get there."

"Don't tell me you two played hooky your senior year."

Stephanie brushed one hand over the passenger side dashboard. "It was either that or Pin-the-Tail on the bucktoothed moron." She checked her hand for dust. "I told my parents you're coming up this weekend."

The odometer clicked a mile.

"Do you think you can help? Jess said you could help."

"I said he might be able to help."

Stephanie sat forward, her eyes on Gio. "Well can you? Jess said you're some kind of psychic."

Jess spun towards Gio. "I never said that. I swear I never said that."

He patted her thigh. "I believe you, Sweetcheeks."

Stephanie slumped back in her seat. "I-95'll get you there, too. More buck-toothed morons that way, though."

Gio eased up on the accelerator. He sat up and moved his head back and forth slowly, a cow lowing in a field. A moment later he smiled and sat back.

Stephanie watched him over Jess's shoulders. "What's going on?"

Jess scanned the highway. "There's a police car up ahead somewhere."

A half-mile further a state police cruiser hid behind some trees off the side of the highway. A Statey stood out from the trees, his hat pulled forward and down so the brim sheltered his eyes, which were further protected by dark-tinted wraparounds. He held a radar gun in one hand and a mike in the other.

When the Statey was no longer visible in the rearview, Gio tromped the accelerator. "We can still make it in about forty-five, fifty minutes."

Jess looked at Stephanie out of the corner of her eye and smiled.

\\\\\\\

Gio pulled up to the Thompson's garage. Stephanie got out and grabbed her pack from the backseat. "You want to come in? Say hi? Lend me some support?"

"No thanks. It's Friday night. You know what that means."

"Yeah, Friday Night Fights at the Rosens'. Thanks for the ride."

Gio checked his rearview and side mirror as he backed out of the Thompsons' driveway. "Friday Night Fights?"

"You'll love it. My parents host open discussions at our house on Friday nights. Anything goes. It can get pretty intense but never hostile."

"Good to know."

"Sometimes Mom and Pop invite people over to take part."

"A regular *yeshiva*."

"Too Jewish. We discuss everything."

The Rosen's two-story saltbox stood at the top of a hill separated from the street by a long front lawn. On the other side of the street the slope of the hill continued down to Gardiner Regional High School. "Going to tell me you walked uphill to school in ten feet of snow in both directions year round?"

Jess flicked his ear. "Wise ass."

He pulled Bessie in behind a Suzuki GT750 motorcycle parked by the garage. "Does everybody in Maine have huge front yards?"

Jess opened her door and smiled at the motorcycle. "Hey, Steve's home. Nobody told me Steve would be home."

"You people name your motorcycles?"

A large German Shepherd ran out of the backyard and charged the car, snarling, growling, and hackles raised.

Jess yelled, "Bella, no!"

Gio got out of his Comet. The sky shimmered. He sat on the ground. "Bella? Is that your name? Come here, girl."

The shimmer coalesced on the dog and wrapped her in a twinkling rainbow.

Bella slowed, stopped, and cocked her head right and left.

"It's okay, Bella. I won't take your taco."

Bella's tail lifted, she bounded to Gio, knocked him over and licked his face. He gently pushed her away and she came right back at him, a pup with its master. She mawed his left hand and he ruffled her fur and scratched her side with his right.

The rainbow faded, the shimmer stopped.

A stentorian male voice sounded from around the house. "Bella! Here! Now!"

Bella ignored the command. She rolled onto her back, offered Gio belly, and he gave it a good scratch. Her legs kicked like she was swimming; right, left, right, left as he scratched one side of her belly then the other, back and forth and side to side. "Ohh, who's the dog? Who's the dog? You are, Bella! You are!"

"It's us, Pop."

Sam Rosen stopped as he rounded the house. He raised a hand and slowly waved to his daughter. "What's going on here?"

Gio stood and Bella followed, his hand still in her mouth. "It's okay. She's not hurting me. She's letting me know I'm part of her pack and accepts me as top dog."

"That's Gio, Pop."

Gio waved his free hand. "Hi, Pop."

Sam Rosen looked from Gio to Bella and back. "I've never seen Bella behave like that. She's a guard dog. How did you get her to behave like that?"

Gio looked at Bella. She gently gnawed his hand. He'd seen wolves, coyotes, and wild dogs gently gnaw each other in play, to show submission. A memory, old. Primitive.

It just happened. I didn't control it. I just knew to do it.

He petted Bella with his free hand. "It's how dogs play with each other."

"Gio has a way, Pop."

Gio reached into the backseat with his free hand and pulled out an overstuffed laundry bag. Half a bra flopped out the top.

"What are you doing with my daughter's underwear in your laundry?"

"It's my laundry, Pop."

Sam looked in Gio's backseat. "You didn't bring your laundry?"

"I was supposed to bring my laundry?"

Sam cocked an eyebrow at Jess. "Your last boyfriend brought his laundry."

"My last boyfriend was an exchange student from Mexico."

"You had boyfriends before me?"

Sam relieved Gio of Jess's laundry. "Oh, he's going to fit right in, isn't he?" He poked Jess's bra back into the bag. "You've done something to my dog. We're going to talk about that. Understand?"

"Anything you say, Sir."

"Sir?" Sam turned to Jess. "He's a fast learner, too. I like that. You found yourself a good one this time, Daughter."

The sun fell below the western mountains and the Rosens' outside lights came on. A breeze rustled trees behind the Rosens' home. The driveway flood above the garage doors caught Gio and Bella in a spotlight.

Jess came over and rubbed Bella's head. "How did you know Bella's favorite toy is a rawhide taco?"

"I said her favorite toy is a taco?"

"You told her you weren't going to steal her taco. How did you know about that?"

Gio put his hand on his chest and tapped with his middle and index fingers. He looked down at Bella for a moment then looked back at Jess. "Are you sure I said that?"

Jess put her hands on her hips and tilted her head slightly.

"Don't give me that 'Oh really?' look." Gio looked back at Bella. His fingers tapped his chest. "I don't know how I knew. It just seemed... right."

Bella turned her head towards the tree line up the backyard from the house. She still held Gio's hand in her mouth. She growled, low and quiet.

Gio followed her gaze. "It's okay, Bella. I know, and it's okay."

"You know what? Jesus Christ, Gio. You say you can't do anything one minute and the next minute you're communicating to my dog like you're George of the Jungle." Jess shook her head as she went into the house.

Bella followed Jess inside, Gio's hand still in her mouth. Every few steps she glanced over her shoulder at the tree line behind the house and growled quietly.

\\\\\\\\

Maine State Police Officer Tony Morelli held a pair of non-department night goggles to his eyes and scanned the Kennebec River from his tree stand high in an oak back from the river. The tallest tree on this side of the river for a mile in either direction, it provided clear viewing. He wore a pair of non-departmental headphones but only had his right ear covered. The headphone cable went to an equally non-departmental handheld multiband scanner. He periodically lifted it, tilted it, and turned it to make sure it worked. A Coast Guard buddy explained what wasn't covered in Morelli's 'Nam SERE training, which wasn't much.

Something shuffled far below at the water line and he adjusted the night goggles. A beautiful twelve-point buck and out of season. It looked up, flicked its ears forward to listen down river for a moment then walked away.

Morelli adjusted his goggles. A flotilla of drift boats. He focused. Looked like Rogue River dories. Powered, but small outboards. Probably just enough to keep them headed upstream. Five, ten horse at the most. He counted twenty, all running in line, all moving slow.

The lead boat flicked a bluish light and caught something on the shoreline.

He missed it.

The last one broke off and headed for the shore. Morelli watched them land and scanned the tree line.

A white sheet. A bed sheet. He smiled. Nice. Doesn't make any noise and can't be seen unless you know where to look and when. Moon's not up yet, make your drop, pull in the sheet, head home. Nice.

The blue light flicked again but this time Morelli caught it. A bed sheet with a "2" on it.

Smart. Black light. Nice.

A second boat broke off.

Morelli marveled. Why go high tech when low tech did the job, was cheaper, and more reliable?

He had what he needed. Time to head back.

He tied his gear in a sack and lowered it to the ground via rope, attached another line to his harness, checked his spurs, and got halfway down when he heard voices.

He measured his breathing and held his position.

A man. Dressed as he was, black on black with camouflage face paint. He carried a high-caliber hunting rifle with a night scope, relaxed but ready to use. He stopped every few yards, lifted the scope to his eye, and scanned up and down, back and forth, back through the woods, down to the water line, right and left, but never into the trees.

Morelli thought back over his own training.

Either he's really good or he's never been taught three-dimensional warfare.

Morelli watched him walk down to the water then south along the bank.

When he could no longer hear the man's footsteps, he finished his descent and jogged to his car.

\\\\\\\\\\\

Tim Annandale stood outside Gio's dorm room waiting for Gio's roommate to show up. "Let me in."

"Why?"

Annandale pulled back, his eyes narrowed. He shook his head slightly, as if not hearing correctly. "What?"

"Why should I let you in?"

"This is Gio Chance's room, isn't it?"

"So?"

Annandale studied the other boy's face. "Don't I know you? Aren't we in Early American Lit together?"

"Again, so?"

"Are you in league with the Devil?"

"What?"

"I know Chance took off with that Jewish harlot of his."

The other boy rolled his eyes.

"She's a harlot, a *Zonah*, and he's a keeper of harlots. Are you in league with him?"

The boy walked away. "Sorry, he's a good roommate. And I don't like your brand of Christianity. Don't involve me in your crusades. Find another way to get what you want done."

"Let me in this room!"

\\\\\\\\

Gio lay in the guest room bed, eyes open, listening. He left the window open a crack to let fresh air in. A dog nose pushed the door ajar and poked into the room.

"Come on, girl. No need to ask."

Bella pushed the door open, jumped on the bed and curled up beside him.

He didn't like the door open but Bella pinned his legs under the covers so he couldn't get up.

"How did I know about your taco, girl?"

Bella thumped the covers with her tail.

"How do I know anything people claim I know?"

Bella crawled up beside him and licked his face.

"Grandpa taught me to listen, pay attention. Is that it? I just pay more attention than most people? I pick up clues everybody else misses?"

Bella's nuzzled under his neck. He stroked her back. She closed her eyes and sighed.

"It just happens, Bella. You know that, right?"

Bella woofed little doggy woofs in her sleep.

"Coincidence, nothing else."

Bella's legs twitched. A quiet little growl and another twitch.

"Don't suppose you'd like to get up and close the door, would you?"

A quiet, sleepy Woof, woof, woof.

Gio stroked Bella's fur. "Get that rabbit, Bella. Get the bunny." He looked at the door. "Grandpa taught me how to do this. I remember him teaching me how to do this. How did he start it?"

He closed his eyes.

Lower-Center-Relax-Breathe.

Push.

The door moved slowly.

Push.

It stopped when the bolt hit the strike plate.

Push.

Nothing.

The curtain fluttered. The window was ajar. A slight breeze moved through the room. He heard the bolt bounce back from the strike plate and the door opened slightly.

Gio snorted and rolled over. "Yeah, Jess, right. I know things. Ha."

The curtain stilled. The door closed.

Bella chased something in her dreams.

Saturday, 12 January 1974

Stephanie sipped hot chocolate from a mug her mother left in the dish drainer by the sink. Cute little thing. Had a funny little stream image on it, the kind that changed as you moved the cup around. "Jess's coming over with a friend this morning."

Pam sipped coffee standing at the sink and looked out the back window. Their house's shadow outlined the demarcation of cold and warmth, frost and mist, on their back lawn. "That's nice."

Bill came in from the garage. "What's nice?"

Pam continued watching the line of cold and warmth change with the sun's ascent. "We're having guests."

"Jess's bringing over a friend. He may be able to help find Ed and Harry."

Bill, in the middle of pouring a cup of coffee, put his half-filled cup down and turned to her. Pam, cup clenched in her hands at chest level, spun to face her daughter. "You didn't say that."

"Who's the friend?"

"Gio. Gio Chance."

Pam turned back to the window. "What kind of name is that, Gio Chance?"

"His name's really John. Everybody calls him Gio. Jess thinks he can help."

Bill looked at his half-filled cup waiting on the counter. "What the hell do you care what his name is? Jess says he can help. She's a good kid. We've known her and her family for years. Do you think she's going to get some kind of fool involved?"

"He goes to Ramsey College, Ma."

Pam lowered her cup. "And he's dating a Jew?"

Bill glared at his wife. "Stephanie, What time will they be here?"

Stephanie gave the mug a quick quarter turn to see if she could catch the image in mid-transition. No luck. "Ten, ten-thirty, somewhere in there." She put the mug in the dishwasher.

Bill picked up the phone, dialed the police, and started talking as soon as someone picked up on the other end. "Sergeant Dykstra? Yes. Bill Thompson here. Yes, I understand, no news, of course. I have some news, though. We're getting someone to help us find our boys. Just letting you know as a courtesy. How do they say it? There's another dog in this hunt?"

Dykstra's voice increased in volume as Bill hung up the phone.

\\\\\\\\\\

Gio and Jess sat on the Thompsons' living room couch. Pam knitted in her chair, Bill stood with his back to the big picture window, and Stephanie shuffled between kitchen and living room keeping coffee cups full.

She handed Gio the stream image mug. He touched it and snapped his hand back as if hit by electricity.

"Oops, sorry. Just pulled it from the dishwasher. Still a little hot, I guess."

Bill put his hands in his pockets and rattled keys and coins. "What do you think you can do, Mr. Chance?"

Stephanie stood in the kitchen doorway, pot in hand. "He knows things. He knows where the police are."

Pam looked up. Bill frowned. "Huh?"

Gio nodded. "That's true. I know they're here now."

Pam dropped her knitting. "You can tell where the police are? How can you tell that? How far away can you tell where they are?"

Bill and Stephanie frowned at her.

Pam cleared her throat and picked up her knitting. "It's impossible for you to know those kinds of things."

Gio held up his hands palms out. "I'm facing the window, folks." He pointed. "A police car just pulled in your driveway."

Bill turned to see Lyndon and Towne in a patrol car easing their way towards the house, laughed, and turned back to his guests. "Good one, Mr. Chance."

Gio stood and watched the patrol car approach. His nose twitched a few times and he pulled on it as if stifling a sneeze. "Mind if I go check out your boys' room? And LaVerne's?"

Bill went to the door. "Stephanie, would you show him?"

Stephanie, Gio, and Jess went upstairs as Bill opened the door. He watched Lyndon and Towne sit and talk in their squad for several minutes. His hands went into his pockets to keep warm and his breath sent little gusts of warmth into the cold.

Lyndon and Towne exited their squad and Bill offered his still warm hand. "Officer...Lyndon?"

Lyndon took off his hat, smiled, and shook Bill's hand. "Good memory, Mr. Thompson."

"And you're Officer Towne, correct?"

Towne nodded. "Ten-four that."

Lyndon took his notepad from his jacket pocket. "Our sergeant said you hired someone to find your boys? Maybe we could talk with the investigator?"

Inside, Lyndon stood by the grandfather clock, Towne stayed by the door. He held his cap by the brim vertically in front of him and slowly rotated it like a safecracker rotating the dial on a safe, patiently waiting for the tumblers to fall. "Is that his Chrysler in your driveway?"

Lyndon lifted his pencil. "We could run the plates. Decided to ask first."

Gio and Jess came down and sat at the foot of the stairs. Gio cupped his hands in front of him. "Do both. You can determine people's veracity that way. Watch how they respond. Learn their tells."

Lyndon frowned. "You are?"

The hairs on Gio's arms lifted slightly. He kept his hands cupped but put his arms between his legs.

What now?

A shimmer formed around Lyndon and Towne. Gio blinked. Lyndon and Towne were replaced by a sika deer and a bobcat.

He focused on the Lyndon-deer. "You're from Virginia. What are you doing in Maine?"

Towne's eyes went from Gio to Lyndon. "You said you were from Montana. Minnesota. Some place like that."

Stephanie and Jess joined Gio on the stairs. "I spent last summer in Montana. What part you from?"

Gio blinked again. The sika deer got caught in a whirlwind. A harlequin replaced it. "And you're not what you seem."

Towne's eyes went back and forth, Lyndon to Gio to Lyndon and back. He put his hand on his holster. "Hey, what is this?"

Another blink. The whirlwind died, the sika deer returned. The bobcat unsheathed its claws, crouched behind it, prepared to strike it.

Gio nodded towards Towne-bobcat. "And this one. You can't trust this one. I'd be careful if I were you."

He blinked again and Lyndon and Towne were back, the shimmer gone, the hairs on his arms lifeless once again.

Bill, Pam, Stephanie, and Jess's eyes went from Gio to Towne and Lyndon.

Pam blurted out, "He's John Chance. Everybody calls him Gio. He goes to Ramsey College in Windham, Mass."

Gio kept his eyes down. *This shit has a mind of its own? It wants me dead? Is that it? I can't control it so it just pops up whenever it feels like it and drops me into the deep end? Thanks a fucking lot, Grandpa.*

Lyndon shook his head at Towne. "That your car out there, Mr. Chance?"

Jess leaned into Gio and addressed Lyndon and Towne. "Is there a problem with my pop's car?" She whispered out of the side of her mouth, "You okay?"

"Damned if I know."

Lyndon turned to the Thompsons. "Is this the man you hired to find Ed and Harry?"

Bill worked to take his eyes off Gio. He focused on Lyndon. "Has there been any news? Did you find something? Did you find my boys?"

Pam held her coffee cup in front of her. "We aren't hiring anyone to do anything. Especially not this one."

Towne walked over to the picture window, looked out to the road in both directions, turned back into the room, lowered his hand to his holster.

Another shimmer. It moved through the living room, through the wall, out to the driveway and rested on Lyndon and Towne's squad car.

Its siren bipped.

Towne turned back to the window. "What the - "

The radio squawked. A rollover on the highway.

Gio exhaled slowly. "Sounds important. Better see what it's about."

Lyndon looked at Towne and nodded towards the door. "We'll be back later, folks. If anything develops."

Gio spoke softly, his eyes closed, his head resting on Jess's shoulder. "If anything develops."

Bill waited until Lyndon and Towne cleared the Thompsons' driveway. "What the hell was that about?"

Gio fell forward, off the stairs and onto the floor. Jess was beside him and lifted his head in one move. Stephanie came down the stairs two at a time.

Gio sat up, shook his head, looked around. "What did I miss?"

Bill came back from the kitchen with a glass of water and held it out to him. "Are you epileptic, Mr. Chance?"

Gio took the glass. "No." He drank a mouthful. "Thanks."

Jess stared at him and he patted her thigh. "Don't worry. I'm fine. Just me being me."

Stephanie stood like a hero over a vanquished foe. "Ha! I told you he was psychic."

Gio stood up. "I'm not psychic. And before anybody asks, no, I'm not doing drugs. Just got a little excited. I'm a coward by nature. Ask anybody. And police scare me."

Bill took the glass from Gio's hand. "You sure rattled their cages."

Gio shrugged. "Yeah, well..."

"So can you help us, Mr. Chance?"

Pam stood up and marched into the kitchen. "He's just going to cause trouble. He's going to upset the police and their investigations. He - "

Bill spoke over her. "Do you think you can help find our boys, Mr. Chance?"

"Your sons disappeared at the end of November, correct?"

Pam smirked. "We already knew that." She snorted at her husband. "Some help we'll get from this one."

"And in all this time, you've not received any ransom notes?"

Bill shook his head. "No."

"No requests for communication. Nobody coming forward with information about your boys or David LaVerne?"

Pam turned to face him. "So?"

"The police haven't turned up anything in all this time? They haven't gotten the FBI involved? State? Nobody? Nothing?"

Bill sat in his chair by the window. "What are you telling us, Mr. Chance?"

"Gio's fine. 'Mr. Chance' sounds like the name of a comic book villain. Neither the boys themselves nor LaVerne have contacted you?"

Bill frowned, working through Gio's questions. "No."

"Then your boys aren't missing, they're being held. Hostage somewhere. Probably in a locked room or basement so they can't get to a phone or be seen by anybody stopping by. There's only one or two people involved for this not to have leaked to the police. Surely the cops up here must have informants."

Bill looked straight ahead. "You seem to understand this stuff pretty well, Mr. Chance."

"I..we...my grandfather. I probably overheard the police talking with my grandfather. He helped their investigations sometimes."

"Anything else you can remember from these conversations?"

"You sure you want to know?"

Pam went into the kitchen. "We don't want to know anything from you, John Chance."

Bill sighed. "Go ahead, Gio. What else can you tell us?"

"The focus is LaVerne. He doesn't seem the type to kidnap them and run off to start a family, and if something happened to him your boys are smart enough to get back to the car and lay on the horn until help arrives."

"Which means?"

"Which means LaVerne is dead or soon will be, and the boys are being held hostage. If LaVerne is alive then he's involved, and either the authorities know what's going on, are also in on it, or are somehow supporting it. No matter how you cut it, this isn't looking good for your two boys right now."

Pam stood in the kitchen doorway, her arms crossed over her chest. "I don't want him involved."

Bill nodded to her. "Best reason I can think of to get him involved. What do you charge for your services, Mr. Chance? Gio?"

"No charge. It doesn't work that way."

"You've done this before? You helped your grandfather?"

"Me? No, I...I just know there's no charge. There isn't supposed to be a charge. I might not be able to do anything, anyway."

"A charity, then? A donation to some place in your name?"

"No." Gio rubbed his forehead. "Sorry, folks. I have to go."

\\\\\\\\

Jess and Gio turned left out of the Thompsons' driveway heading back towards Gardiner proper. Jess looked over at Gio. "Jesus fuck what happened back there?"

Gio leaned against the passenger door, his eyes closed. "Nothing."

"Don't goddamn nothing me. I was scared. I was really fucking scared." She pulled onto the shoulder and turned off the ignition.

Gio opened his eyes and turned to her. "You're shaking."

She punched his arm and her voice rose to a quiet shriek. "The one thing I want in life is to not be scared and you goddamn scare me. I lose one set of grandparents to the Nazis and the other set fills my childhood with stories of fleeing from one town to the other, one step ahead of the Gestapo. Don't fucking scare me, understand? Don't do that to me."

"Do you know you have a habit of hitting people when you're nervous?"

She punched him again.

"See?"

"Don't change the subject."

"I'm sorry I scared you. I didn't mean to do that." He paused, looked away from her, out the window. "What happened, exactly?"

"Weren't you there? You goddamn did it and you don't know what you did?"

His head slowly turned to her. "No. Actually, I don't."

"How could you be there and not know what happened?"

"Because you and everybody else keeps thinking this is something I do, something I have control of. I don't. I wish to hell you'd all get it through your heads that it just happens. One minute I'm fun-loving John Chance and the next I'm Gio Fortuna, international man of mystery."

"You really don't know what happens? How you do it?"

"I get a hint. Right before it happens, I get a hint. It's like a part of me…"

"A part of you what?"

He frowned and looked out through the windows. His voice grew quiet. "Goes wide."

"Goes wide? What the hell does 'goes wide' mean?"

Gio lifted his eyebrows. "It's something my grandfather used to say. I just remembered it. He had me practice it every day."

"He had you practice this? He expected you to do this on command or something? So he expected you to control it?"

Gio rested his head on the back of the seat and sighed. "It would seem so, yes."

"Then Jesus Christ, Gio, why aren't you practicing it?"

Sunday, 13 January 1974

Gio sat on the cold, bare ground in the Rosens' backyard, the exposed grass brittle under him. Bella sat in front of him. They stared into each other's eyes. Bella kept offering to shake.

Sam watched from the den. "How did he get her to do that? I never got her to do that. You bring a Svengali into my house, Daughter?"

Jess came up beside him, a head shorter, holding a glass of orange juice. Sam put his arm around her, pulled her in, and kissed the top of her head.

"First, Pop, he's not Jewish. Second, …"

"Second?"

Jess shook her head and leaned into her father. "I don't know. There's a second but I don't know what it is. I couldn't imagine him being a Svengali. He spends too much time helping people."

"Helping them do what?"

"Silly things. Little things. He always knows when I'm going to have my period."

Sam pulled away from his daughter and looked at her. She snickered. "Don't worry. I'm on the pill."

"I'm feeling so much better."

"He knows where people lost things."

"That's useful? You lost this in Toledo. I have no idea where it is now, but I know you lost it in Toledo?"

She punched Sam's arm. "I mean he can find things people lost, okay?"

"I lost money in the stock market."

Jess ground her heel into her father's foot until he winced.

"Your mother keeps hiding my cigars."

"He knows when people are sick. Every time somebody in the dorm has bad cramps he just touches them and the cramps go away."

"He holds stock in Midol?"

Jess pushed her father away. "I'm serious, Pop."

Sam rubbed her back. "You like him?"

She looked at Gio and Bella sitting in the backyard. He rose up and Bella bounded around him, a puppy with her master. "Yes."

"So do I."

Jess's brother Steve came through the kitchen. "Pop, there's no room for my bike in the garage, not with yours and Mom's cars in there. Okay if I store it in the basement for the winter?"

"Put rags under it and drain the tanks before you bring it in."

Steve hurried downstairs. Sam and Jess heard Bella barking in the driveway as Steve pulled Sam's Chrysler out of the garage and pushed his motorcycle in. A stair's height separated the garage floor from the basement and the motorcycle was having none of it.

Gio put his finger to his lips and Bella quieted. "You need help?"

Steve, breathing hard and red faced, had the front wheel through the door but nothing else. "Love some."

Gio stood at the bike's rear. "What can I hold onto that won't break off when I lift?"

Steve stared at him and shook his head. The corner of his mouth crinkled into half a smile and he pointed to the wheel mounts on either side.

"You guide it in when I lift. Ready?"

Steve smiled, nodded, and rested his hands on the handlebars.

Gio squatted, grabbed the wheel mounts, and stood. He held the bike's rear end a foot off the ground for a minute and stared at Steve. "Any time you're ready."

Steve, his eyes bulging, grabbed the handlebars in earnest. "Yeah, right, right. Sorry." He pulled and Gio walked the bike into the basement.

"Here?"

"Yeah, here's good."

Gio put the bike down. "Come on, Bella. Upstairs." He took the stairs two at a time, rounded the bend, went up the second story and into the guestroom, Bella always at his heels.

Steve, sweating, came up and into the kitchen. He poured himself a long drink of water, guzzled it, took another.

Sam cocked his head. "You okay?"

"The man's fucking strong."

Sam nodded. Listened overhead to where Gio and Bella played in the guest room, and nodded again.

\\\\\\\\\

Sid Lyndon sat in his three room, downtown Augusta apartment. The building was the tallest in Augusta with apartments and he took the dingy, corner one on the top floor. The manager offered to lower the rent if Lyndon would clean it up - pull the linoleum off the floors (there was good hardwood underneath), paint the walls (he'd supply the paint), do some drywalling, ... - And if Lyndon was good with tools and wanted to be Super to the rest of the building, even more could be cut off the rent.

The manager said all this as they rode the elevator up to the sixth floor. He concluded with "Used to be manufacturing. You from Maine? Ever heard of Bates? Or Edwards?"

Lyndon smiled, shook his head. "Tell me about my neighbors."

"You don't have any. Not on this floor. The other apartments never got finished. Below you are mostly people from around the region who work for the state but don't have a car. It's quiet, if that's what you mean."

The manager unlocked the door and let Lyndon in. He walked to the window and checked the view. "I'll take it."

"I can throw in the utilities if - "

"I said I'll take it."

The manager stared at him. "I can't tell you how many people I've showed this place to and no takers. You haven't even checked the plumbing. It works, I'm just saying - "

"Comes with its own bath?"

"Full head, sink, and shower, yes." The manager opened an interior door in the living room and moved aside for Lyndon to enter.

"No need, I trust you."

"You do drugs?"

"I'm a policeman. Gardiner PD."

"You a drinker?"

"Never touched a drop."

"Women?"

"Don't have one. No plans for one. Don't want one."

The manager shook his head.

Lyndon opened his wallet, took out two hundred-dollar bills. "This month's and next. You want a security deposit?"

"A security deposit? You're not from around here, are you."

Lyndon shook his head. "Just moved from out of state. You want references?"

"Those bills in your hand are all the references I need. The pipes are going to bang a bit for the first day or two. Haven't had the heat on in here in a while."

"No problem."

"Want some help bringing up your stuff?"

"Got one bag. I can handle it. Keys?"

"They're in the door."

"Thanks."

Lyndon waited for the man to leave. He looked around, walked though the living room to the kitchen to the bedroom and came back to the view from the living room windows. Perfect.

It took him a day to put in his own phone lines. He had his own equipment. Trunked the junction box in the basement, snaked the lines floor by floor up the service way, made his first call that night.

"Hi, Ma."

A musical old woman's voice answered. "Oh, it's my darling baby boy! How are you, son? They exchanged pleasantries about folks back home, aunts, uncles, cousins, and upcoming holiday plans.

"And how's dad doing these days?"

"Oh, just fine. You know him. Always busy with something. Just a minute and I'll put him on the line."

Three clicks. A strong, baritone voice came on the line. "Go ahead."

This week's call ended differently. When the strong, baritone voice asked, "Anything else?" Lyndon replied, "Yeah. Do a background check on John Gio Chance, goes to Ramsey College in Windham, Mass."

"Problem?"

"He sniffed me out in about a second."

Silence, then "Keep me posted."

\\\\\\\\\

Short, stocky, and with a light brown crewcut going to gray, FBI SAC Mark Kagan sat in the agency's Boston office on his day off dressed for work. He separated reports on his desk into three piles: Shit, Maybe, and Something. The Shits he determined before the end of the first paragraph. The Maybes he read to the bottom of the first page. Sometimes not that far, but always beyond the first paragraph.

Every time he found a Something he read it through to the end. Except when he got to a paragraph - usually on the second page - that clearly said Shit or Maybe to him. Most times the Maybes ended up with the Shits as punishment for taking up his time with no clear resolution.

The Somethings, though. Co-workers knew how strong a report was by the number of times Kagan adjusted his tie or pulled down the sleeves on his starched, white dress shirt, always worn under his dark blue sport coat. Really strong reports were identified by Kagan brushing his cheeks and chin as if checking for whiskers. Only certain field agents and undercovers were allowed facial hair and Kagan kept himself clean.

Somebody stopped in the hall outside the shared office. "Kagan, boss wants to see you in his office, pronto."

Kagan closed the file in front of him and rose from his desk. "What's it about?"

"No idea, something about The Old Man wanting results."

"Hoover's dead."

"Not that Old Man, the new Old Man."

Kagan adjusted his tie and sleeves as he trotted down the hallway. "You wanted to see me, Sir?"

Kagan's boss motioned him to close the door then pointed at a seat. "I'm surprised you came in today, Mark. I know your schedule's tight. How are things, by the way? You sure you got time to be here?"

Kagan shrugged.

"I read your report. The Old Man wants New England tied up, and if I send it on up we'll both have our asses against the grindstone. Want to tell me what I'm missing?"

Kagan swallowed and held the arms of his chair. "I got a second informant. To see where their stories separate."

His boss nodded. "Not policy. Can you guarantee they don't talk to each other?"

"I know they talk to each other. At least once a month. I'm counting on it."

\\\\\\\\\\

Bill pulled the watch chain on the grandfather clock. "You're not going back with Gio and Jess?"

Stephanie held the running stream mug in her hand, moving it back and forth, into and out of the light, watching the changing pattern in the water. "No. Donnie's coming up to get me." She looked at the grandfather clock. "Should be here soon. Said he'd be here by five, the latest."

Pam, in her chair, knitting, looked out the big picture window. "Driving in the dark?"

"Oh, we'll probably stop along the way. He always has to stop and get some."

Bill kept at the clock. "Get some what?"

Stephanie cleared her throat. "Coffee, a sandwich, you know." She chuckled into the mug. A blowjob. If nobody else is around, he'll bend me over the hood or the trunk, lay me out flat on my belly, pull up my skirt, push aside my panties. Give me a moment to clean up then it's 'Okay, back in the car, let's go.' He's quick, dad. No bother. No trouble at all.

Pam focused on her knitting. "He goes to Ramsey College, this Gio boy?"

"Good Christian lad, he."

"You must know somebody there. From the Tylers' church. Ask around about him. I don't like him. I want to know more."

Stephanie nodded as Donnie Tyler's headlights turned into the Thompsons' driveway. Stephanie went into the kitchen, rinsed the mug and put it in the sink. She opened the utility drawer, took out a small package of tissues and put them in her skirt pocket.

Bill handed her her coat and gave her a hug. "You catching a cold? You've been dragging all weekend."

"Catching something."

Thursday, 17 January 1974

The raven stared at Gio from its branch across the freshly snowed lawn from his dorm room. Gio, sitting at his desk, scanned the titles of his course books and rubbed his eyes. Anthropology, Bible Studies, Economics, Linguistics, Mathematics, Philosophy, Physics, and the list went down to the Zs. He took such a variety of courses his advisor twice asked his dorm father if Gio was ever going to decide what he wanted to do when he grew up. An exam tomorrow and he would fail it. He already knew, why bother. Physics made no sense to him. Not all of it. Some of it was...wrong? Inaccurate? How to phrase it. Once he walked Singing Beach alone, a night early in the school year, before meeting Jess. Stars made a mosaic of the sky and the full moon shone like a quiet, nocturnal sun. It spoke to him. He fought not to listen.

Then the sky shimmered and he was high in the cosmos, the earth passing beneath him. The moon whispered, "This is how you make antigravity. This is how you make faster-than-light travel. This is how you make teleportation. This is how you make time-travel."

He watched, fascinated, unable to look away.

The moon showed him something, a small machine, like a circuit board but not, the pieces changing places as the moon spoke. "You see? They are all the same thing, just arranged differently."

Always the same pieces, just arranged differently.

All things modern science said couldn't be.

"That's how it is with all things. We are all the same, just arranged differently."

Then he was back on the beach wondering what happened.

The raven looked out to the marsh and Gio followed its gaze.

A figure stood in the water. A woman's shape. Female. Made of water. Standing, watching him.

He shook his head. It was gone. He looked back to the raven. It, too, was gone.

A dorm mate knocked on his open door. "You got a visitor downstairs in the lounge, Gio. Young lady. Quite the looker."

Jess? Jess wasn't supposed to come by.

\\\\\\\\

Tim Annandale sat in Gio's dorm lounge in a corner chair, out of the light and away from the windows so neither overhead nor sunlight reached him. His fingers pyramided in front of his face and he tapped the tips of his index fingers each time he nodded. He checked his watch. The dorm father would be back soon and Tim would demand access to Chance's room. Tim would explain his suspicions and findings and demand to be let into Chance's room before Chance's filth consumed the campus.

A young woman opened the door and came in. He looked up, she smiled, he ignored her and kept tapping the tips of his fingers.

Another student came in behind her and started up the stairs to the living quarters. She stopped him, said something. All Tim caught was "Gio." The student nodded and continued up the stairs.

Tim rose from the chair and approached her quietly, arms akimbo, a marionette controlled by invisible strings.

The woman pulled back when she realized he arched over her, stared down at her, Nosferatu enveloping its prey.

"Are you his *Zonah*?"

"Whose what?"

Annandale pulled himself up to his full height without taking his eyes from her face. "You're his whore. Whore! *Jüde*! You carry his child!"

He threw the door open, letting the cold January air fill the basement lounge. "Go. Get out." His voice rose. "Out." He shrieked. "Out!"

The woman fell back into a chair, curled into a ball, pulled her legs up to her chest. She wrapped her arms around them. clinched them to her, and cried.

Both looked up when the door at the top of the stairs opened.

Annandale ran out.

Gio stopped halfway down the stairs. "Stephanie. Hi. What's going on? Who were you talking with? What happened?"

Stephanie stood. She shimmered. Gio cocked his head, looked at her belly.

"Do you know you're pregnant?"

She ran out to the Monte Carlo and drove away.

\\\\\\\\\

Gio sat alone for most meals. He chose seats next to the cafeteria's windows which ran from three feet off the floor to the ceiling and looked out over the backwoods and lake. Sometimes people came by to ask him questions, sometimes for help. They always approached - that was the only word that fit their behavior to Gio: approached - him as if seeking a moment of his time would cause the earth to lie still in its orbit. An older dorm mate from Nebraska, a veteran using the GI Bill to get an education, told him, "Getting near you is like swimming uphill against the current in a river of molasses."

"Really? I don't do anything to give that impression, do I?"

"You've never noticed people get out of your way? Even when you walk up behind them, they move aside to let you pass. You're the only person I know who produces a bow wake like a whale."

Gio chuckled. "Maybe I don't shower enough?"

The dorm mate saw Gio practicing *san qin* breathing in their dorm's backyard one day and stood to the side until Gio finished. "Is that some kind of karate?"

"It's more a meditation."

"Can you teach me? I studied shorin ki ryu."

"Small forest temple style? Where'd you study?"

"Wow, you're the first person in the States to know what it means. I was stationed in Japan for a while. Where did you study?"

"My grandfather. And some of his friends. It was a long time ago. I really don't remember much."

They became friends and exchanged stories and techniques until campus security grew concerned by all the yelling. The dorm mate left school at the end of that quarter. "This place is too confining. They want to create missionaries but have no idea what the mission is."

The day before he left, Gio asked if he could show him one more technique. "Sure! What?"

"I want you to punch me square in the chest. I want to show you how to send the energy back into your attacker."

His dorm mate pulled back. "Gio, I don't know. What if you don't do it right?"

"Imagine the lesson that'll be for me!"

He stood relaxed while his friend struck. Gio's arms shot out, wound around his dorm mate's, his hands touched his dorm mate's chest, his dorm mate lifted off the ground and sailed in an arc, landing on his back six feet away.

Gio walked up and offered his hand. "You okay?"

The dorm mate rubbed his chest. "How did you do that?"

"Return to your teachers. They'll show you."

The dorm mate spent his remaining time telling people what Gio could do and practicing it on anybody willing.

He never approached Gio in the cafeteria as others did. He just walked up, sat, and enjoyed the quiet and the view with Gio.

Gio missed him as he looked at the people giving his table a wide berth. He chuckled. *All I need is a few guards sitting at the surrounding tables and I can call myself* Don Fortuna.

A skinny kid with bad acne and a 35mm SLR camera in his hands walked up to the end of Gio's table and cleared his throat.

Gio watched some crows dance around bread crumbs someone tossed onto the snow behind the cafeteria.

The skinny kid cleared his throat again.

Gio turned to face him. "Hello, help yourself. Plenty of space available."

"I'm taking pictures for the yearbook. I've been taking pictures of people in the Student Lounge all day. Okay if I take your picture?"

Gio offered his hand. "Go ahead. I'm John Chance, by the way, in case there's a caption."

The kid held out his hand. "Merl. Merlin Choate."

Gio shook. "Your hand's a little sweaty. You okay?"

Choate's eyes danced around. "Yeah."

"You've been taking pictures all day. Where's your camera bag? Where're your rolls of film?"

"Forget it. I don't need your picture."

Gio shrugged and went back to his meal.

He heard a shutter click and looked up.

Choate hurried through the cafeteria lines and out the doors.

Gio shook his head, finished his meal, deposited his tray et al at the washing line, and headed back to his dorm.

He heard footsteps behind him on his way across the campus and slowed. A moment later Laurie Sánchez put her arm through his and walked beside him. "Hello, Handsome. What did Moonface want with you?"

"Moonface?"

"Merlin Choate. Moonface."

Gio chuckled and shook his head. "That's not nice, *mi pequeña animadora latina*! Did I say that right? And you're not working tonight?"

"Finished the offices, nobody wants me to clean their room. Is it true?"

"Is what true?"

"Am I your *pequeña animadora latina*?"

"Don't you know I'm dangerous? Hasn't anybody told you being with me can get you in trouble?"

"You must believe the whole world's against you around here."

"Not true. I'm sure some of the smaller countries are neutral."

"I'm not neutral."

"Laurie, I *am* dangerous. Didn't your grandmother tell you that when she saw me at orientation, that I was dangerous to be around? What was it she called me?"

"*Un protector, un hombre mágico.* A protector, a magic man."

"And to stay away, that I was dangerous."

"No, she told me to go to you only if I needed to, if I was in trouble. She said you were *ponderoso.*"

"Yeah, that's me, just one of the Cartwrights."

"*Ponderoso* means powerful. *Peligroso* is dangerous. That's not the same thing, is it?"

"Are you in trouble?"

Laurie leaned into him, held his arm tight in hers. "I worry about you."

"Laurie, please. No. People…Things happen…I don't want you hurt and I'm worried you will be if you spend time with me."

"Because people are afraid of you?"

"Because I'm afraid of me."

She pulled his arm until he looked into her face. "I'm not afraid of you."

"You would never have reason to be afraid of me."

"Not you. Me. I'm afraid of me. I'm afraid I love you and I don't know where that's going to go. You know I love you, don't you? You can't be *un hombre mágico* and not know I love you, right?"

"Yes, I know you're in love with me, but - "

"I know you don't love me. Not that way, anyway. But I can love you anyway. It doesn't matter. You can't stop me. You may be *el hombre más poderoso del planeta* and never love me the way I want and it doesn't matter."

"It matters to me."

"It does? Then you do love me?"

"God, Laurie, if Satan had as beautiful a spirit as you there wouldn't be room enough for me in Hell. I'd sin every second I'm around you. I love you so much I won't risk you being harmed because you're with me."

She rested against his warmth. "You're always such a furnace. Why is that?"

He kissed her forehead. "Hot Mediterranean blood. What made you find me on my way back to my dorm? What have I done now?"

"It's Annandale. He's going all vigilante on you. He wants them to expel you."

"I'm still not sure why they recruited me. He wants me expelled because...?"

"He and some others got together and talked about you. About what you do. They're claiming you converse with Friendly Angels."

"Friendly Angels?"

"Demons disguised as angels to lead Christians astray."

Gio laughed. "Wow. I've never heard it described as that."

"Is that what you do?"

"You want the truth?"

"Can you lie?"

Gio shook his head. "No. Not without great difficulty. Or laughing my head off."

"You're not laughing. Are you telling me the truth?"

"The truth is I don't know what I do. I don't control it. Or I control it rarely. And even when I control it, I'm not sure I'm not imagining what's happening. I've told people before, I'm a good guesser, that's all."

"You make some pretty accurate guesses."

"I had good teachers. This is your dorm. I don't want you to walk to mine. It's too far out and this campus isn't as safe as it looks."

"Kiss me first."

"Laurie."

"Just once. I want to know what it's like to kiss *un hombre mágico*."

The hair on his arms lifted.

Go with it, Gio. Just let it happen.

He remembered his grandfather telling him "Lower-Center-Relax-Breathe."

His hands shimmered. The shimmer passed through her, revealed her in ways simultaneously exciting and sickening. He saw her, saw inside her, knew her, understood.

He held her close. "Just once. For you." Because I love you in ways you can't imagine.

He lifted her to him. The shimmer wrapped around her. He kissed her. Oceans formed on distant planets, life bloomed in ancient seas.

She slid from his arms and he supported her against him.

She blinked her eyes open. They wandered, not focusing on anything until they landed on his face. She swallowed softly. "Do you kiss everybody like that?"

"No, only the ones I..." he stopped. His eyes focused in her.

"Yes?"

He almost said "will help" and held the words back, not sure what they meant.

She placed a shaking hand over her heart. "What are you looking at?"

"You are beautiful, Laurie."

She moved closer. "You were about to say? Only the ones you... what?"

"Care about. Only the ones I care about."

He didn't laugh. It wasn't difficult. And he knew there would be one more kiss. When he was able. When it was time.

"Phone call for you, Gio."

"Hello?"

"What did you do to Stephanie?"

"I'm fine, Jess. How are you?"

"Quit the horseshit. What did you say to Stephanie?"

"I asked if she knew she was pregnant."

"Men. Why did you ask her that?"

"Didn't you ask me to practice whatever it is I do?"

"And this is the first thing you do?"

"No, not the first."

"Do I want to know what the first thing was?"

"She came by and I knew she's pregnant, alright?"

"Another good guess?"

"How did I get ugly all of a sudden?"

"She came over and was in hysterics. I thought somebody raped her."

"She wasn't raped. It was consensual."

"Jesus Christ, how do you know that?"

"I'm a good guesser?"

Silence.

"Go ahead. Ask."

"Ask what?"

"Ask what you really called about."

"Can you help her?"

"Can you be specific?"

"You know what I mean."

"No, I'm the village idiot. I don't know anything until people tell me."

"Ha ha ha."

"I have an exam tomorrow. Can we talk about this some other time?"

"Mom and Pop are hosting a *Kabbalah* scholar in a few weeks. Pop asked you to come. He thinks you'll enjoy it. Want to go?"

"Is this one of those Rosen *yeshiva* things?"

"Ha ha ha. Can I tell him we'll be up?"

"Do I get to see you before then?"

"Depends. What did you have in mind?"

"Oh, nothing nasty or dangerous."

"Then forget it."

"Tomorrow night? If I promise to be nasty and dangerous?"

"We're not through talking about this."

"Yes, ma'am."

She chuckled and hung up the phone.

Friday, 18 January 1974

Kagan read through the reports, sighed, and checked his watch against the office clock on the wall in the bullpen he shared with six other agents. Two minutes to go. He tapped his pencil on his ink blotter once for each second and counted down as he did so. He glanced at each of the other agents in the room, each at their desk, and wondered what kept them going. Already four years past retirement, the Bureau allowed him to stay on to close outstanding investigations. Done, done, and done.

Then his boss and his boss' boss and his boss' boss' boss shuffled assignments around. In the midst of finding something for him to do, this came in. They asked if he wanted it and he jumped.

It humbled him and he jumped. The most decorated investigator north of DC and east to Ohio and he jumped.

Janey, his wife of thirty-five years, had Stage 4 cancer. It looked like a goddamn plant on the pictures they showed him; the son-of-a-bitch had vines and roots all through Janey's body and flowers blossomed everywhere. His wife of thirty-five years, his beloved Janey, was slowly dying in Beth Israel hospital in Boston's Longwood area and the Bureau wanted him to have all his benefits for her sake.

Same as the folks at the synagogue. Really Janey's synagogue. But now he went and prayed regularly. They had to give him a *yarmulke*.

He didn't own one. Whatever the FBI didn't pick up the synagogue did. It was charity. He knew it was charity. Never in his life did he accept charity.

Now he accepted it. From both. For her sake.

He pulled out his wallet. Behind his license was a small leather patch labeled "Lee Jeans." It came from the rear pocket of the jeans she wore the first time they met. "This way I'll always have a piece of your ass in my pocket."

It was a joke. They both laughed. They both told the story.

He rubbed the patch.

The clock ticked. Time for his weekly call to a Windham, Mass, phonebooth to check in with his informant. If nobody picked up by ring three, go to plan B.

He counted the rings like Lily Tomlin as Ernestine the Phone Operator. "One ringy-dingy. Two ringy-dingies. Three ringy…"

"Hello?"

He put a pad of paper on his desk and took a pen from his shirt pocket. "How's the snowfall this time of year?"

"Not bad for a kid from Sabrosa."

Kagan clicked his pen. "Go ahead."

\\\\\\\\

Gio drove down Hind St and took the 128 North ramp towards Iperia. He needed Jess's brand of insanity, her controlled wildness, to ground him, guide him, advise him.

He neared the Haskell St turn, put on his blinker, checked his rear-view mirror, and his heart banged in his chest.

Something stared at him from his backseat. An ovoid head, wider at the crown than at the jawline, with skin various shades of gray. Pocked and blistered, it resembled the cratered, impacted surface of the moon seen through a child's telescope. Two tusks angled up from the mouth, ending just below and outside the eyes. Two smaller tusks - fangs, really - protruded straight down to the chin. The nose was two holes above the fangs. Two large eyes, a slightly lighter gray than the skin, with no lids and black pinpoint pupils, stared back at him.

Thoughts raced through Gio's mind -

If I can see it, it's reflecting light.

If it's reflecting light, it has mass.

If it has mass, I can hit it.

If I can hit it, I can hurt it.

Gio drew his arm over his chest and drove his elbow back over the seat.

An oncoming car blasted its horn. Gio swerved out of its path. Bessie missed a tree by inches. Her tires bounced off a curb.

The creature disappeared.

Gio slowed, pulled over.

Shaking, he looked in his rearview mirror again.

The creature returned, but not the same. It stared at him from an angle, as if its attention was somewhere else.

He took a deep breath, turned, lurched over the front seat, arms extended.

A dummy head. A gargoyle's head. On a small mount to sit on the backseat, looked up at his rear window. A reflection. He lifted it. Papier-mâché. A solenoid to make it light up when moved. It fell from its perch when Gio avoided the oncoming car.

He pulled out the battery pack and solenoid circuit. Edmunds Scientific.

"What do you see?"

Gio cocked his head. He knew that voice. A friend? "Hello?"

"You see through fearing eyes. Nothing in life is to be feared, only understood."

"I know that voice."

"Understand or fear. Decide."

A raven flew overhead.

Gio pulled into the parking lot at Jess's dorm. She waited wearing a too tight, low cut jersey revealing ample cleavage, a leather miniskirt, black fishnets, three inch CFMs, makeup highlighting her full lips and deep, brown eyes, and shivering in the cold.

He opened the door for her. "You must be freezing."

"Expect you'd be able to do something about that." Edgar Winter's *Frankenstein* came on the radio as she scooched over to him and she sang along. "Da Na da na Da Na Na DA Da Na Na da Na."

They drove up Rt 127 to Singing Beach. Two verses in, she lowered the volume. "Would you help me if I was pregnant?"

"You ask me that question dressed like that?"

"You want to see any more than this tonight?"

"You wouldn't get pregnant by me."

"Would you help me, yes or - what do you mean I wouldn't get pregnant by you? Did you have mumps as a kid?"

"First off, what do you mean by 'help'?"

"Oh, Jesus fuck. Are we going down that hole again? Remember Candy? Or Glenna? How about Mags? She missed her period, you touched her, and she can't get on the rag fast enough. Quit bullshitting me, okay?"

"Bullshitting you? None of them were pregnant, they were afraid and nervous and half scared out of their minds of what their parents would say if their good little daughters got abortions or came home pregnant. It's not like when we were born, Jess. Pregnant girls back then had three options: families with money sent their daughters away for a while, families without money sent their daughters to backyard or alley butchers, or if the guy was willing, he got roped into a marriage that should never have been in the first place.

"So now you're saying the only way you'd marry me is if you got roped into it?"

He pulled over to the side of the road, drew her to him, and gave her one, long kiss. "Jess, I would follow the scent of your shit for a mile just to find the ass it came out of."

"That is disgusting."

"So is this conversation. I came to you wanting some sanity." He reached into his backseat's floor and lifted up the demon's head.

"That's...creepy."

"Somebody left it in my car. It was supposed to scare me."

"Did it?"

"Damn near drove off the road and into a tree."

"Turn around."

"What?"

"Turn around. Take me back to my dorm. You don't need the happy hooker tonight. Let me get into some regular clothes. We can go to the Capri then come back here and talk."

"Can I watch you change?"

Two hours later they were under a waning crescent moon at Singing Beach.

"Wish you kept that other outfit."

"Use your imagination. Care to tell me what that thing's doing in the backseat of your car?"

Gio picked up the demon's head again and held it in front of him. The hair rose on his arms. The head shimmered. "Many hands."

"What?"

The head passes from hands to hands to hands to an arts room. Paints and canvases and clays and knives. Colored cellophane becomes the eyes, electronics are added. The surface is mottled by glue puckered tissues. Fangs and tusks are applied. It is tested. A mount, an anchor, is given.

Gio's head titled slightly left and gazed into the demon-head's eyes. "Tell me."

Jess looked at the demon-head and frowned. "Tell you what?"

Gio rotated. He saw himself through the demon's eyes, felt other hands holding its head up.

"Who made you."

"Gio?"

The demon looked back through time to its beginnings, to the delicate hands forming it, to the artist's hands holding it, to the heavily pockmarked face smiling down on it.

He knew the face. Another Ramsey student. Mal? Merl? Something like that. Mal/Merl turned it from side to side, smiled, and nodded. Mal/Merl looked up, smiled, rotated the head.

A tall form, not in the room, standing in the shadows of a hallway. Voices. Gio couldn't make out what was said. The head is put down, given time to set. The room's lights go out.

Gio shook, lowered the head slowly and rested it on his lap. He turned his head, slowly, mechanically. The shimmer tracked with him, moved from the demon's face to Jess, centered on her. "Do you know how important you are to me?"

"Well, a girl likes to think - "

"You are more radiant to me than all the summer suns."

She drew away from him without moving, as if seen through the wrong end of a telescope, each second growing more distant, smaller.

And older.

And beside her, someone else sharing her years.

"And for the time I have you, I burn like the stars in the heavens."

The shimmer faded. She sat beside him, young, vibrant, and his once again.

"You alright?"

"Yes. Thank you."

She lifted the papier-mâché horror from his lap. "This thing really got to you, huh?"

"And I repeat, do you know how important you are to me?"

She stared at it face to face. "Because I give head?" She stuck her tongue out at the fake demon and tossed it in the backseat.

Gio's head tilted back. Bessie rocked with his laughter. "Because we laugh. Do you know how important laughter is? It doesn't matter what troubles people go through, if they can hold onto each other and laugh, know whatever's happening it's only for a moment and not forever, that's an amazing gift, Jess. That's what's important in a relationship."

"But giving head doesn't hurt, right?"

"My grandparents always laughed. My parents never did."

"That...sucks." She slid over next to him and pulled his head down to her shoulder. "I'll make you laugh, Gio."

"I know." He sighed and nodded. "I know."

"Did I ever tell you the one about the rabbi and the priest getting drunk together?"

He tilted his head back and Bessie rocked with laughter again.

Saturday, 19 January 1974

Pam watched the grandfather clock tick. She taught Stephanie how to tell time with that clock. She taught her boys how to tell time with that clock.

She hated that clock. For years it stood in her living room, tall, proud, loudly ticking, afraid of nothing, never hiding, its round face looking down at her and constantly reminding her what time it was, how much time had passed, how long she'd have to wait.

Her biggest problem with the clock was Bill's pleasure in it. He found it and restored it. He already made plans to pass it on to Stephanie when it came time for her to marry.

She stood before it and spit on it. With any luck it'd stain and his repeated polishings wouldn't be able to get it off.

The clock's hands merged. Straight up twelve. It began to chime. Even that annoyed her. Bill found a clock with St. Michael's chimes. Not Westminster chimes, not the chimes everyone knew, not the chimes everyone recognized, said "how nice" once and never again.

No, Bill found a clock with St. Michael's chimes. Every time people came over they commented on the chimes. People who'd been over the house a hundred times still commented on the chimes. And Bill, like a proud father, would tell the story of the chimes and the clock and how the original bells were part of American history and he'd beam and stand beside his clock and run his hand on it and talk about the feel of the grain and the type of polish used and the size of the weights and how the left one powered the striker and the right one powered the chimes and how the center one actually powered the hands and drove the pendulum.

She opened the clock cabinet and adjusted the chain links just enough to upset the clock's delicate mechanism a few minutes each day. Not enough to be noticed when Bill wound the clock, just enough to frustrate him with their repeated minuscule inaccuracy.

She closed the cabinet and spit on the clock again.

It started the actual hour count when the phone rang. She hurried into the kitchen before Bill would hear it in the garage.

"Yes, Papa?"

She held the phone to her face with two hands like a little child, nodded and listened.

"So my boys are safe? You're sure of that?"

She listened again and sighed. "Okay, Papa. You know what's best."

\\\\\\\\

Sam Rosen took Bella for her final walk of the night, down the driveway to the street in front of their house and back up. Halfway to the street he heard a siren approaching. A police car sped by, its lights blazing. Another followed a minute or so later.

Halfway back up, Bella's hackles rose and she let out a low, warning growl.

Sam looked across his lawn, up and down his driveway, and into his backyard. Nothing.

"What is it, girl?"

Bella turned and looked down the road towards Gardiner proper. She bared her fangs, her growl grew more insistent.

Sam tightened his hold on the leash.

A tow-truck, its yellow dome light flashing, slowly drove past in the same direction as the police cars.

Bella lunged after it. Sam braced himself and she pulled him over. He pulled back on her leash. She raged, snarling as the tow-truck followed after the police cars.

"Bella. Stop. Now."

The big german shepherd stood still, her teeth still bared.

Sam got up. "What's got into you, girl?" He knelt down beside his dog. She turned and licked his face. "You alright, young lady?"

Another patrol car went down the road.

"Must be one hell of an accident on the interstate."

Bella trotted back up to the house, pulling Sam behind her.

Sunday, 20 January 1974

Harding met Morelli in the Augusta barracks parking lot. "Heard you had a busy night, Tobes."

"Rollover on the interstate. Tire blew, they lost control. Folks had their seatbelts on, though. They got out alive. End of the dinner hour so there wasn't much other traffic. And we got there quick. Passersby in both directions stopped at the next exits and made calls. Other folks put out flares."

"You got artwork?"

Harding pulled a folder out of his inside coat pocket. "Right here. Giving them to the accident investigation boys. Hey, want a laugh?"

Morelli frowned at him.

"Not the accident." He put that folder back in his coat pocket and pulled another folder from the other side. "The tow truck driver. He's a piece of work. Asked if this was going to be in the paper. Wanted to know if I could get a picture of him and his truck in with the story. Hounded me like a son-of-a-bitch until I said yes."

Morelli shrugged.

"Take a look."

Morelli's eyes popped. "He skivved down to his t-shirt in last night's cold?"

"He would've dropped his pants if I let him."

Morelli shuffled 8x10s. "Truck's not much to look at."

"He's registered with Gardiner. Something happens in the town limits, he gets a call, automatic."

"Is he posing?"

"Yeah, said he's a body builder or something like that. A regular Arnold Schwarzeneggar."

"Definitely looks like it."

Morelli tipped a photograph on its side. "You got a magnifier?"

Harding reached into an outer pocket and handed over a Sherlock Holmes style lens.

"Mother of Christ."

Harding stood beside Morelli and looked through the glass. "What? What is it?"

"His truck's got vehicle plates."

"Oh, yeah. He said he collects them from old cars, wrecks. Buys them from dealers through the mail. I didn't know there was a market for that kind of thing. He swaps them out every few days. His rear plate is regulation, though."

"Get his name?"

"On the back of each photo next to the date."

Morelli flipped the photo over. "How about an address."

"That's in my notes. Lives in West Gardiner somewhere with a roommate. Todd something. Want me to look it up?"

"Please."

\\\\\\\\\\

Stephanie gave Robbie and DJ lemon drops to keep them from fidgeting in the Tylers' pew. Donnie and Caroline kneeled at the altar with ten other parishioners receiving communion, their heads back, their mouths open, their hands cupped in front of them in supplication.

She focused on the back of Donnie's ventless, European cut suit. Bet you'd pray like a son-of-a-bitch if you knew, Donnie. Bet you would.

DJ and Robbie started flipping pages in the hymnals. More lemon drops came out.

Donnie and Caroline came back to their pew. Caroline smiled at her children and patted them as they scooted over. Donnie smiled at Stephanie.

We going to have to go for a ride, Donnie? Something we'll need for dinner you forgot to get? And we'll stop along the way, of course. Couldn't miss a Sunday afternoon ass-fucking, could we?

Donnie's needs were spiraling out of control. It was one thing for him to fuck her. Now he insisted she strap one on and go after him when he was done. Without lubrication.

She wondered how he could shit when she finished.

They said the Blessing and called the Recessional. People stood, smiled at each other, gathered in the church hall for refreshments and gossip.

Donnie and Caroline led the way. Stephanie herded DJ and Robbie behind them. This is where Donnie and Caroline would take all the credit for DJ and Robbie being such fine, robust, loving children, and people would nod at Stephanie without saying a word to her.

Did any of them know? Did any of them suspect?

She wondered how many of the good church ladies, how many members of the Altar Guild, fucked Donnie before he acquired her for his needs.

Acquired?

She laughed at her use of one of Donnie's words: Acquired.

I'm a commodity. And he'll get rid of me as soon as I no longer suit his needs.

Better make sure my tits stay perky.

Her bras already felt tight.

She couldn't be swelling this soon, could she?

Over to the side of the church hall the Ramsey College Hens huddled like football players strategizing the game. One regular member was missing.

Stephanie sidled over. Their gossip always amused her.

"...so then Rachel told the housemother everything."

"Did she know how many months along she was?"

"He touched her, you know. That's how he did it. He touched her."

"I heard he just looked at her. Looked at her belly and she miscarried. Right there in the entranceway lounge. People were all around, looking."

"How did he know? Nobody knew. She didn't even tell the father."

"Disgusting."

"He used those Devil eyes of his. That's how he did it."

Everybody nodded. "Devil eyes. Yes."

"He's a good talker, too. Convince you of anything when he talks to you. I cover my ears not to listen."

"Oh, yes. So do I." "So do I." "Me, too." "Yeah."

Stephanie leaned against the wall, styrofoam cup of Lipton's tea in her hand, smiling at this person then that one.

"Tim is doing something about him, you know. Going to get him kicked out. Make sure we're safe."

"Not everybody thinks he's evil, though. How can they not see?"

"That's the way the Devil is. He fools people into thinking he's not what he is."

"That's John Chance, alright. Always saying he just guesses. Tim says he speaks to Friendly Angels."

More nods among the cackling hens.

"Did Rachel leave school?"

"I understand he told her to sleep with him."

"No."

"Yes. Oh, he's got lots of people mesmerized. That little Latina bitch is always talking him up."

"Her people aren't really Christians. They're from South America, you know. Mexico, I think."

"They worship people like Gio down there."

Stephanie couldn't be sure she got everything, but hearing "Gio" and "John Chance" together in less than a minute, she made up her mind.

Caroline signaled her. She was through showing off her children. Time for Stephanie to do her job.

She took another drink. About half a cup left. One of the Hens held her cup up and out to the side, her arms folded over her chest, her cupless arm supporting the other at the elbow. Stephanie dropped her cup into the Hen's cup, stacking them as she walked past. "Thanks."

\\\\\\\\\\

Stephanie sat on the bed in Jess's dorm room and watched Jess shift into a pair of Dickies. A lone card stood on the dresser amid makeup and jewelry. The front of the card had a pencil and ink drawing of a wide-eyed man with an almost insane smile. The man, dressed all in black, wore a pointy red hat and held a rose. He was about to fall down a series of huge, steep steps. Under the picture was written "Romantic enters the world". Inside in tiny but precise script was "XOXOX, Gio."

"Must be great to sleep in until," she checked her watch. "Eleven thirty? Late night, Rosen? Wish I could sleep in like that. I've already been up for five hours." Her eyes focused on the artwork on the walls. "No rock groups? No TV or movie stars?" She got up to look more closely and walked from one framed item to the next. "Matisse? Van Gogh? Pollack? Any of these originals?"

"I wish. Gio loves to go to museums. He got them for me."

Stephanie pointed at one on the other side of the bed. "What's that? You didn't frame your Gardiner High diploma and bring it, did you?" Stephanie's eyes narrowed on it. "Wow. NRA? You're Annie Obramowitz?"

Jess chuckled.

"Did you tell Gio I'm pregnant?"

"I didn't know until you came by after you'd seen him, remember?"

"It was your idea I talk with him about my brothers. You told me he's different. He knew where the speed trap was when we drove home." Her eyes went from picture to picture as she spoke. "You've been dating him for how long and you never talked with him about being in league with the Devil?"

"What?"

"That's what everybody at church says."

"Thank god I'm Jewish."

"I'm going to ask him to get rid of it for me."

"This may not be the best time to ask him something like that. Some people at Ramsey are out to get him."

"But do you think he'll do it? You can make him do it, can't you? I saw how he looks at you. He loves you. Make him do it. Okay?"

"What am I supposed to do? You want me to go all Lysistrata on him?"

"Lysistrata? I never heard of that one before. Missionary, doggie, butterfly, spoon, cowgirl, ... What's lysistrata? Is that where you stand on your heads in a hammock? I heard about that one at a bar in Montana. Guy walked up to a friend and said he wanted her in the worst way possible. She said 'Worst way I know of is standing on our heads in a hammock. Care to try it?' You could just see the guy's dick shrivel in his pants when he walked away. What do you say?"

Jess shook her head and finished dressing. "No."

"C'mon. You can get him to do anything. Make him do this. For me, okay?"

"No."

Wednesday, 23 January 1974

Stephanie sat in Gio's dorm lounge and looked up as he came down the stairs. "Did Jess talk to you yet?"

"About what?"

Stephanie rolled her eyes. "You want me to say it?"

"Yes, in fact. That way we'll both know what we're talking about."

She whispered, "About me being pregnant."

"Are you sure you're pregnant?"

"Didn't you tell me I was pregnant?"

"I'm not you. Do you know you're pregnant?"

"Is two months late pregnant enough for you?"

"Are you regular?"

She looked at the worn carpet and shook her head. "Talk about conversations I never thought I'd have with my best friend's boyfriend. Yes. I'm regular."

"And what do you want to do about it?"

"I want to get rid of it. What do you think I want to do about it? Aren't you the voodoo man? Aren't you supposed to know these things?"

Something Gio's grandfather said echoed back at him. *Do not do what you're not asked to do*? Was that it? Something about asking people

three times? To make sure they understood what they were asking for?
"Let's go outside."

"Don't you want a jacket?"

"No need."

They stood in the damp, ocean-filled, mid-January cold.

"What do you want me to do? Specifically. Don't mince words, don't speak in metaphors, use clear, plain, direct English. Tell me exactly what you want me to do for you, okay?"

"I'm pregnant."

"Okay."

She closed her eyes and shivered. "Well, go ahead."

Wet, heavy snow fell. A flake, then two, then more. They brushed her shoulders like epaulets and gave her a white, crystalline crown.

"Go ahead and what?"

"I said I'm pregnant. Do something about it."

"What, specifically, do you want me to do?"

"Can you make me...you know...un-pregnant?"

"Un-pregnant? Never heard it called that before."

"Nobody knows. I haven't told anybody except you and Jess. Can you take care of it for me?"

He stood still and stared but his eyes wouldn't focus. He felt...he sensed...movement. Felt himself moving. Something. Something not sensed since childhood. Since Grandpa.

No, not moving. He stood still, his eyes on Stephanie. She moved.

He widened his gaze. Everything moved. Everything but him. He was the center? Everything happened around him?

He shook his head, no.

Too solipsistic, that.

No, he also moved. Differently.

But he stood still.

And moved faster than light.

Parts of him separated and flowed around Stephanie, whirled around her, ghosts made of wind.

He shimmered. He held it within.

I remember.

I remember.

Stephanie stared back at him. "What do you mean, no? You're not going to help me?"

The shimmer focused. The ghosts made of wind. It collected on them. They flew off, showed him things. He watched through their eyes.

"Donnie suspects."

"What?"

He looked at Stephanie through someone else's eyes. Saw not-his hand reach out, cup a breast, tweak a nipple.

"He's noticed your bras are filling out more."

"What?"

"Especially that black one with the nipples cut out."

Stephanie put her arms over her chest and mashed herself down. "How do you - "

Another ghost, another body. "Yeah, he even told some people at his club - he goes to the Olympia Hunt Club, right? - about it. Said your cups runneth over. They wanted to know if he was going to help you get rid of it. He laughed."

Her face reddened. She wrapped her arms around herself and shook as the cold penetrated her bones.

His head lowedfrom side to side.

"You did that before, when you found the speed trap on the way home. What's going on?"

His eyes closed. He swiveled his head, one ear forward then the other, a blind man seeking out the source of a sound.

"He said you might be interested in doing a party. Entertaining all six of them. He'd get a cut, of course. Something...a finder's fee?"

She shrieked.

"They have a standing suite at the Suisse Chalet in Danvers. Party there at least once a month. He said he thought you were ready."

She sat in the slush at her feet. "Ready?"

He felt himself slowing, returning to the earth, returning to the cold, returning to the wet, heavy snow falling, melting on him as soon as it touched, his ghost-bodies coming back to him. One entered him. He doubled over with the impact.

He heard his grandfather whisper to him. "*Lento.*" Slow.

He opened the shimmer, gave the bodies a point of entry.

His grandfather whispered. "*Esatto, Gio. Come quello.*" That's right, Gio. Like that.

The ghost-bodies entered him. Shared their information. Showed their travels. He focused on the red-faced woman-child before him.

"Something about being double-vagged? Not sure what that is, really. Seems to involve acrobatics or flexibility, something like that."

Stephanie screamed and ran.

Gio's legs folded under him. He sat in the snow. A raven landed in front of him, cocked its head right, left, right again, seemed to nod and flew off.

Two dorm mates found him curled into a ball quaking in the snow.

\\\\\\\\\\\\

Annandale waited for Laurie outside her dorm. She came out and headed towards the student center. He stepped into stride beside her. "Hello, Laurie."

"What do you want, Tim?"

"Did you hear what happened to Gio?"

She stopped. "What happened to him? Is he okay? Where is he?"

Annandale drew himself to his full height. He put his hands behind his back, looked into the distance, and smiled. "Collapsed in the snow. Talked to some girl and fell down. One of his dorm mates saw it all."

"Where is he now?"

He looked down at her and frowned. "How should I know?"

"You're only your brother's keeper when it suits your needs? Is that it?"

"Are you in love with him?"

"What business is it of yours who I'm in love with. You're your sister's keeper but not your brother's? Is that how it works with you, Tim?"

Annandale' face reddened. He slowed a step then regained his pace beside her. "I...I could..."

Laurie stopped. She put her hands on her hips and faced him. Walkway traffic moved around them, water rushing around a stone in a fast-flowing stream. "You could what?"

"He doesn't love you. He sees some *Zonah* from Iperia. A harlot. She sleeps with him."

Laurie rocked back and laughed. She clapped her hands and laughed a second time. "You're jealous. You're jealous of him. With who? Me?"

He looked down, his hands clasped behind his back, suddenly a little boy caught stealing cookies.

Laurie came close to him, stood in front of him, looked up at him, her eyes on his, her hands behind her back, doing slow quarter turns as she spoke as if each turn a breath. She whispered, "Is that it, Tim? You want me to be your *pequeña animadora latina*?"

Tim breathed heavily, sighed, veins stood out and pulsed on his neck. He looked down, his face reddened.

Laurie stopped her slow quarter turns. She faced him full on, her hands on her hips. "You want me? You're not worthy of me. Look at yourself. You wouldn't know what to do with me."

She stepped back and wagged her finger at him like a chastising schoolmarm. "You couldn't even tell me how you feel and you want to be with me?" She lifted his chin until his eyes met hers and gently stroked his cheek. "You want me, Tim? You want the touch of me?" She slapped him hard across the face. "Look at yourself. The man who touches me is going to have a pair."

She pulled back from him. "Did you know Gio kissed me once? His lips touched mine and my God the fire. Just one kiss and it was like drinking electricity."

Annandale closed his eyes. His face scrunched in disgust as he turned away. "But you? You're a backbiting little coward who won't do anything unless you have half the student body on your side. And you want people to look at everybody else, never at you. Look around you, Tim. Everybody's looking at you now."

She continued to the student center. He stood where she left him. Movement on the walkway stopped, the river frozen. People stared and whispered. Some chuckled. Others sniggered. He paled. Everyone watched him. Not her as she walked away, they watched him. All of them. Watching, staring, listening, waiting.

He searched the eyes in the crowd. He straightened himself, stood his full height, smiled. "Did you see that? Did you see what Gio made her do? John Chance made her do that. You're all witnesses."

He walked to his dorm.

\\\\\\\

Merl inspected a cut glass lampshade at his workbench in the art studio located in a rear basement room of Emerald Science Center. "Shouldn't we be praying for him, Tim?"

Annandale looked around at the easels, the palettes, the furnaces off to one side, the various paints and canvases. "What is this doing in a science center? Couldn't you people find your own building to put this stuff in?"

"Art's an elective. Don't change the subject. I've talked with lots of people since that first meeting, Tim. Three out of ten hate the guy, three love the guy, three don't care, and one says, 'Gio who?' We're in the minority."

"His devils shook him. They abandoned him and left him to freeze in the snow. People saw it. They told me."

"Maybe he had a seizure. Ever consider that? Maybe he's got real health problems."

"He's evil, Merlin. Look at the man. You know he bathes in fire when people aren't looking."

"Some students think he sprouts wings and returns to heaven when nobody's looking."

"They're fools. They don't know. I do. I know. And I'm the only one willing to do something about it."

"One of my dorm brothers was driving back from the beach that night you had me put the head in Chance's car. Did you know he almost went off the road? He could've killed himself. Or somebody else. Ever think of that, Tim?"

"At least I did something. I tried to stop him."

"By almost killing him?"

"He knows no fear. Now he does. He knows Hell is on him."

Merl sat back in his chair. "Who decides that, Tim? You? Me? That's not what Scripture says. A few of us are doing what Scripture says. We've formed a prayer group. We pray for him. We have most of the day covered and can always use more. Care to join us?"

"I already pray for him. I pray for everybody." Annandale walked over to Merlin's workbench. "Where's that other mask I asked you make up for me?"

"Sorry, Tim. I'm praying for him. That's the most I'm willing to do. I'm going to let God do the rest."

Annandale face tightened. He took a handkerchief from a front pocket and wiped spittle from the sides of his mouth.

"Make sure you close the door on your way out."

Friday, 25 January 1974

Gio woke, cold. He lay under his top bunk's covers shivering. His breath misted in little gray clouds above him. His roommate snored peacefully underneath.

His gaze went to the windows.

Dawn?

He listened to the pipes creak as hot water from the furnace circulated to heat the house. Otherwise the house cum dorm remained silent. His nose twitched.

What's that scent? An animal scent. Deep woods. Musky. Heavy.

Bear?

He got out of bed, moving slowly so as not to wake his room mate. At the window he looked right, left, right again. He looked out over the marsh.

Nothing.

He took a deep breath.

Yes. He remembered that smell. From when he and his grandfather walked through the woods. From when they talked...

Talked?

With the bears?

No.

When we walked through the woods and talked with them, with everything in the woods.

A deep growl.

A bear, female, a sow, waking up to feed her cubs, finding something that doesn't belong in her den, warning the intruders off.

Then nothing. No sounds, no scents, nothing. Gio sat at his desk, rested his head in his hands, closed his eyes.

Grandpa, what have you done to me?

\\\\\\\\\

Todd Andersen sat in a second-hand kitchen chair in the small apartment. He kept his coat on due to the lack of heat. The kitchen floor's linoleum pocked and blistered in the middle, as if someone started a fire on it. Probably for warmth. Two meters clicked on the wall. They looked like parking meters until you read the instructions. One kept the electricity running, the other the gas. A quarter in the electricity kept the lights on for two hours, a dollar's worth of quarters got you half a day's heat. Or cooking.

David LaVerne lay curled on the floor, his face bruised, his mouth and nose bleeding, his pants soaked with his own piss.

"David, David, David."

Todd nodded and the tow truck driver's heavy boot smashed into the base of LaVerne's spine.

"What am I going to do with you?"

The tow truck driver pulled his foot back. Andersen shook his head, no. "Wait for us outside, please, Mason. This won't take a minute."

The tow truck driver spit on LaVerne and slammed the door on his way out. It rattled in its frame.

"I compensated you handsomely for those two boys. You couldn't get a better place than this?"

LaVerne's chest rattled like the door.

"I'm sorry, David. I missed that."

LaVerne got out "How" and the rest of his words were lost in burbles of blood.

"How what, David? How did I find you? Oh, your own stupidity found you. You keep the piece-of-shit car we gave you once Mason torched the 'wagon? You knew Rene mules for me up 201 to Quebec. He stops at the only store in forty miles to get gas, sees the car and a minute later you come out with a bag of groceries? You thought that weasel-dick would keep quiet about it? You thought giving him whatever money you had would be enough? From a man who's said in more than one meeting 'I have no trouble lying to people'? From a man who shakes your hand with his right while he's stabbing you with his left? Christ, he ran home to Sterne, told him about it, and the two couldn't get on the phone to me fast enough."

LaVerne coughed. Blood spittled onto the floor.

"You should have gone to Boston. Or New York. Some big city where you could hide. But here? One small-as-shit grocery store and the only place to get supplies in forty miles? Did you learn nothing from me? Tell me this was a simple mistake. Please don't tell me I shared my bed with an idiot all those years."

"Why?"

"I'm sorry, David. Why what? What 'why' are we talking about?"

"Why. This?"

"Why did I have Mason exercise his frustration on you? Oh, I don't know. He hasn't had any real fun in a while. You should see how he gets when he hasn't had any...release? Shall we call it that, release? Sexual tension, I suppose. Why sometimes I can't sit down for days when he's through with me." Andersen's body tightened and trembled. "It's so exciting. It's almost like that scene in *Deliverance*." He threw his hands over his head, closed his eyes, and faced the ceiling. "Squeal like a piggy! Squeal!"

He nudged LaVerne with his boot.

No response.

He stepped on LaVerne's hand, slowly increasing his weight until LaVerne opened his eyes. "Good. I thought you left us for a moment. Where was I? Oh yes, frustration and release."

He checked his fingernails as if coming back from a good manicure.

"Can you believe those two munchkins escaped? The little imps! From our cellar. You do remember our cellar, don't you? I knew those handcuffs were too big for them. And naked! They must be freezing if not dead already out there somewhere. Mason is incensed. He misses them so. Talk about a square peg going in a round hole, I tell you, he so delighted in them."

LaVerne coughed. Andersen pulled him over to a wall and got him into a sitting position. "Here's my problem. I don't know them all that well, you do. I don't know if they could survive, perhaps you do. You might even know where they'd go, being all woodsy yourself." He stood and walked to the door. "So here's the deal. You're going to help us find them. You find them first, you get to keep one. Mason finds them first, he gets to keep you."

Andersen opened the door. "And I remember your tastes. You won't like it." He watched Mason quietly close the hood to Dave's car.

He dug into his pocket and threw a handful of dimes, quarters, nickels, and pennies on the floor. "Stay warm, okay?"

\\\\\\\\

Gio sat in his dorm's phonebooth and dialed Stephanie's number. The phonebooth use to be a hallway closet. They removed the hanger rod, added a small bench in the corner to serve as a seat, and put a door switch on the overhead light: close the door, the light comes on, open the door, the light goes off. Gio sometimes played with the door when he made calls. The light switch was an old contact type and not the best; it sparked with a crinkly sound as the contact engaged and disengaged. The light flickered when the contact sparked, neither fully on nor off. Gio practiced keeping the switch between the worlds of on and off. Today he caught the switch just right. The crinkling grew steady, like an old AM radio signal from a distant station, something you knew was there but couldn't quite tune in. The light flickered dimly. It reminded him of an idea half formed: it was there but you couldn't quite grasp it.

Stephanie picked up the phone. "Hello?"

"Your brothers are alive."

"Gio?" She stopped ironing toddler clothes and tilted the iron up on the ironing board. "How do you know?"

Silence.

"I said, how do you know?"

"I know because the bear growled."

"Not fucking funny." She hung up.

He closed the door so the light stayed on and dialed her again.

"Hello?"

"Do you care more about the fact your brothers are alive or who told me?"

"A bear told you my brothers are alive?"

"Didn't you come to me for help?"

"Yeah, to find my brothers. Who asked you to play Doctor Doolittle?"

"Do you want me to stop helping you?"

Silence.

"Do you want me to stop helping you? Tell me you don't want me involved and I'll go my merry way, trust me. You'll never see or hear from me again."

"Do you really think you've found them."

"I didn't say I found them, I said they're alive."

"Oh, holy Jesus Christ. You know they're alive but not where they are? How much good is that going to do anybody?"

"It's a start. One step at a time, okay?"

"Yeah, okay. Sure. Fine. How about you call me when you have something somebody can use to find them."

"Don't you think this will help your parents? Make them feel better? Give them some hope?"

"My mom didn't want you involved in the first place."

Gio, sat in the makeshift phonebooth and played with the light. "Yeah. I remember. Seemed odd to me at the time. A mother not wanting help finding her children. Didn't that seem odd to you?"

"She was raised a Roman Catholic then became a Born-Again when she met my dad. She's got a lot of training against psychics, witch doctors, voodoo men..." She paused.

"Go on."

"And people like you."

"Your mom has a problem with everybody. Your dad didn't have any trouble with me being involved."

Silence.

"I said - "

"I heard what you said. I'll call my parents. Let them know. You're going to keep looking? Or whatever it is you do?"

"Of course."

Stephanie picked up the iron and blasted a pair of toddler pants with steam.

Caroline stood in the doorway. "Didn't sound like a good call, Stephanie. You alright?"

Stephanie stepped back from the ironing board. Her hand went to her chest and she flushed. "Caroline. I didn't know you were standing there."

"Did you say somebody found your brothers?"

Stephanie focused on her ironing. She shook her head. "Just my friend's screwy boyfriend. He talks to bears. Pay no attention."

"So long as you're okay. I have to step out for a bit. You'll keep your eye on the boys?"

"Of course."

\\\\\\\\

Stephanie put neatly folded pants in the twins' bureaus. She suggested dressing them differently would make life easier all around and Caroline agreed, went on a shopping spree at the North Shore Mall's Jordan Marsh, and came back with completely different outfits for the two boys. Now the only problem was remembering whose pants were whose, whose shirts were whose, whose...finally she put name tags in their clothes without telling anybody. Caroline saw them one day and went ecstatic. "My god but you're clever, Stephanie."

"Thank you, Caroline." Your husband said the same thing when I showed him the ice cube trick.

By the time Stephanie got to the third pair of pants, she shoved them into Robbie's drawer, slammed it shut, and tossed the rest of the ironed clothing on DJ's bed. "Shit."

DJ once again pissed his bed in the night, not told anybody, and pulled his covers up to hide the splotch.

She put the clothes on Robbie's bed and pulled the covers back on DJ's to get to the rubber sheet she secretly placed there to save the mattress. Thank god Donnie didn't know about it. She couldn't imagine what he'd use it for.

She got as far as the fitted sheet, saw her hands shake at the thought of Donnie touching her again, clenched them tight, and gritted her teeth. "This too shall pass."

It wouldn't.

"Fuck it." She marched into her room, closed the door, and dialed Jess's dorm. "Rosen, tell me your man's not a flake."

"My man's not a flake."

"Okay, C'mon now. Serious. Is he on something? Does he do drugs? Does he hallucinate? He almost passed out that time you came over to my parents' house. Is he epileptic? Wait a second, he's Christian, right? He gets visions from God, is that it? Talks to the Holy Spirit? Something like that?"

"What are we talking about?"

"He called me about half an hour ago. Said he knows Harry and Ed are alive. You know anything about that?"

"That's a good thing, isn't it, their being alive?"

"Your man talks to bears, does he? Is that how he works?"

"Okay, wait a minute. He said a bear told him Harry and Ed are alive and okay?"

"Oh, no. Nothing except they're alive. And yes, he said a bear told him. So does he do drugs, hallucinate, talk to God, have seizures? Give me a reason to write this schmuck off, okay?"

"I know he's awfully good with animals. Bella took to him immediately. Listens to him more than she listens to my dad."

"Oh holy Jesus Christ." She slammed the phone down on its cradle and stared at it. "Holy Jesus fuck. Will somebody please tell me what to do?"

A soft tap came from low on her door. "Yes?"

She heard one of the twins fumbling to reach the doorknob. She opened it and DJ stood there looking up at her with an opened matchbook in his hand. Little puffs of smoke rose between them. She looked down to see the plush, thick pile carpet smoldering. "You okay, Step'nie? I made hot hot for you."

His habit of starting fires was getting troublesome. That and hiding knives.

And Donnie was no help. He took DJ and only DJ into the woods with that rifle - what people back home considered a squirrel gun, really - of his. So proud when they came back with some small, bloodied squirrel, rabbit, or chipmunk still twitching.

Stephanie's eyes went from DJ to the smoldering carpet and back. How 'bout I hold your little hands in the fire? Think you'll learn what hot hot it is then, Donald Junior? They named you right when they named you after your father.

She closed her eyes, took a deep breath.

Get it together, girl. One set of missing kids is enough.

She picked him up and raspberried his neck while stamping out the smoking embers. "Thank you, DJ. No more hot hots, okay? Promise?"

Donald Junior looked away. She tickled his belly until he relented. "'Kay." He looked around her room. "Who talking to?"

"Just myself. Did I scare you?"

"Who's Holes Geezee Fuck?"

"Oh, I was praying. You know, Jesus like at church? In the Bible? That's Holy Jesus."

"Who's fuck?"

She put DJ down and steered him downstairs. "I'll tell you all about him tomorrow but only if you're a good boy. Okay? It's our secret."

"Get ice cream."

My but aren't you your father's son. "Sure, we can get you some ice cream. I need to make a phone call first. Go play with your cars and I'll be down in a minute. Okay?"

He held the railing in two hands as he went down the stairs one toddling step at a time.

Stephanie went back in her room, closed the door, sat on her bed, and sighed. "Watch your mouth, girl."

She picked up the phone and dialed her parents' number. Pam answered.

"Hi, Ma. Is Dad around?"

"He's out back. He got that woodchipper he always wanted and is clearing out some dead trees. Why?"

"Gio said he knows Harry and Ed are alive."

"Does he know where they are?"

"Not yet. He's looking."

"He's looking? He's up here?"

"Not that I know of. I think he called me from his dorm."

"Then how does he know they're alive?"

"I don't know, Mom. Give me a break, okay? I'm just relaying the message."

"Why do you call me with things like this. You think this is helping? You and your little Jew friend find this Gio guy under a rock and all of a sudden he's god to you?"

Stephanie pulled the phone away from herself, stared at it, brought it back to talk again. "You want to get Dad on the line so we can talk about this?"

"Where are you now?"

"I'm at the Tylers'. Why?"

"I'm going to have your uncles come down. You take them to see this Gio, alright?"

"Uncles Meville and Xavier? I haven't seen them in years. They're going to drive down from way up north? That's what, a sixteen hour trip?"

"They're down here for the day. Making deliveries. People like fresh berries and herbs. Won't take them more than three and a half, four hours to make the trip. I'll send them down, okay?"

"Yeah, sure, but what good do you think it'll do?"

"They want to talk to your friend Gio, find out what he knows and how he knows it. You'll take them to him?"

"He said a bear told him."

Pam snorted. "Yeah, and pigeons shit on the fly."

"That's the first time I've heard you swear, Mom. Everything okay?"

"You take your uncles to see this Gio. Find out what he knows. You do that, okay?"

"Yeah. Sure. Of course. Yes."

\\\\\\\\

"How's the snowfall this time of year?"

"Not bad for a kid from Sabrosa."

Kagan clicked his pen. "Go ahead."

Routine routine routine and then, "Do you have anything to do with the Thompson boys? We never talked about them."

"Go ahead and talk about them."

"Have you ever heard of a John Chance? Goes to Ramsey College, right down the road from me. People call him Gio, no idea why."

"Should I have heard of him?"

"He said he knows where the Thompson boys are."

Kagan cradled the phone on his shoulder freeing his hands to take notes. "He said what? You're sure? Are they safe? Does he know where they are?"

"That's all I have. Nothing else." The phone went dead.

Kagan contemplated and clicked his pen with each thought. He said, "Yeah, okay," to no one in particular, then pushed a button for an open line to call his wife. "How you feeling, Princess?"

She wheezed an answer, air pushed up and out from rotting lungs through a throat constricted by growths the size of fists.

Her own body's strangling her and there's nothing I can do about it.

Kagan didn't know what he hated more: his inability, her disease, or the future they planned being eaten away by a disease nobody could cure.

She used to sing. I'd love to hear you sing again.

"They did more tests? Any results?"

He held the phone away while his wife coughed her way through an answer.

"I may be a little late tonight. I need to check on some things."

She laughed and mumbled something.

"There's never been anybody else, you know that. You're joking, aren't you? Please don't even think that. I could never do that."

She sighed.

"I'll be down as soon as I can. Promise. And I'll be there all day tomorrow. I'll clear my schedule. No matter what. Okay?"

He nodded.

"Love you, too."

He heard a dial tone. He looked at the receiver in his hand. His lip curled and a bitter taste filled his mouth. He wanted to strangle that receiver. It never brought good news.

\\\\\\\\

Morelli sat in an unmarked Ford in the West Gardiner service plaza just off both I-95 and 295. Big city skiers flocked to the north country and the West Gardiner service plaza served as a shopping mall for everything beyond food, beverage, and gas.

A beat but serviceable 1970 green, International D-series Bonus Load half-ton pickup rumbled into the parking lot and backed into a spot by the outdoor payphone. The front held a plow blade. Somebody painted two eyes on either side of the blade, a nose, and what looked like a wolf's open mouth complete with red tongue and sharp teeth underneath. Two men sat in the cab, either brothers or close cousins, smoking cigarettes and dressed for heavy winter. The passenger door had a brightly painted cornucopia on the side with "Rigaux Farms" on top and a phone number underneath. Once in a while steam rose from the tarp covering the pickup's bed.

Morelli frowned at the phone number's exchange. "From way up north. Must have a gas heater back there to keep their produce warm."

He sipped his coffee. From where he parked, he could hear the payphone ring. Every time it did, one of the men got out of the pickup, took the call, and anywhere from ten minutes to half an hour later a car pulled up, the driver got out, the men got out, money was exchanged, a box of produce was retrieved from the pickup's bed, everybody shook hands, the car drove off and the men - Morelli decided they were brothers - got back in their cab.

"Nice way to beat grocery licensing. Bet this gets past paying state taxes, too. Plowing's probably a front for their produce business. They can hide their earnings that way so long as everything's a cash transaction."

The phone rang yet again. A brother answered it.

Morelli was turning away when the brother closed the phonebooth door. "That's different."

The brother waved his hands. His face flushed. He stamped his feet, yelled into the receiver. The one or two words Morelli could make out were in French. The brother hung up the phone, jumped into the pickup, and the two brothers held a very animated conversation.

Half an hour later a silver Marquis Brougham pulled in beside them. A petite, well-dressed woman got out. The brothers got out of their truck. The three of them argued. She threw her hands up in the air. One brother turned away, shaking his head, obviously disgusted with something. The other grabbed the first one's arm. More French. They kissed the woman's cheeks, got in their pickup and took off. She left a minute or so later.

He lifted a long-range walkie-talkie from the passenger floorboard, keyed it, identified himself, waited for a response, then, "Yeah, I need you to run a plate for me."

Meville and Xavier Rigaux towered over Stephanie like two trees over a sapling in the Tylers' kitchen. Xavier handed her a cellophane wrapped peppermint. "Oh, Uncle Xavier. Thank you. But I'm not a twelve-year-old girl anymore."

"That I can see. You see this little girl, Brother? She all grown up."

"So long she don't bite the watermelon seed."

Stephanie frowned at her Uncle Meville. "Bite the watermelon seed? What's that mean?"

"It means your belly swell, get pregnant. You bite the watermelon seed and you get all blown up. Sounds better in French."

"You think I'm pregnant?"

Meville held his hands up in front of him. "Hey, no, Little Girl. But you're a looker. The boys, they come sniffing around. You be careful."

She nodded slowly, her eyes going from one to the other. "I will. Thanks."

"So you tell this Gio to meet us?"

She lied. "I haven't been able to get in touch with him."

Xavier looked down at her. "Oh?"

"Okay, I haven't tried. I'm afraid of him. He scares me."

Meville stood on her other side. "How he scare our Little Girl?"

"Oh, no, nothing like that. He's just...you know. Different."

"You can find him now?"

"He'll be somewhere on campus, either his dorm or the student lounge probably."

"You call him now. Tell him we're coming."

Stephanie headed for her bedroom. Xavier blocked her path. "Where you going?"

"To my bedroom. I have my own phone there."

He pointed to the kitchen phone, its long blue cord reaching the floor before looping backup. "Use that phone there."

"I just thought - "

"Use that phone there."

\\\\\\\\\

Gio played with the phonebooth's light while listening to Stephanie. "You sound tense. Everything okay?"

"Of course everything's okay. Why shouldn't everything be okay? Are you willing to meet me or not?"

"Happy to meet you. How come you can't come to my dorm?"

"I'm hungry. I want to get something at the snackshop."

Gio Lowered-Centered-Relaxed-Breathed.

Nothing.

Oh, come on. I know something's going on. How come this never works when I want it to?

"Okay. What time?"

"Half an hour. Eight o'clock. You'll be there?"

"Sure. I'll be there."

Gio got to Lane Student Center early. He sat in a lounge chair in the corner of the glass walled hallway, in the dark, out of the lights of the hallway, the outside floods, and headlights coming into the parking lot.

A pickup pulled in as a car drove out. The car's headlights showed the pickup's passengers in bold relief; Stephanie sat between two middle-aged, heavily bearded men, dark haired and dressed for the weather. Something glittered in the cab's rear window as the car's headlights passed.

"You didn't tell me you were bringing friends, Stephanie."

Stephanie and the two men backed into a parking space across from the student center next to Ramsey's student service vans. They left the engine running. They could see people approaching from three sides. Behind them was a snow-covered bowl rimmed with elm and pine trees. The bottom of the bowl held two tennis courts in warmer weather, and behind the bowl sat the nurse's building.

They sat in the pickup. Two other cars came and went while Gio watched. Each time, Stephanie and the two men were caught in headlights. Each time they all sat still, not talking. One of the men lit a cigarette. "Smoking's not allowed on campus, Stephanie. Better tell your friends before you get in trouble."

He stayed in the shadows and went out the student center's rear door nearest the nurse's building. He circled around behind them, stayed on the rim of the bowl and approached the pickup, always staying in their blind spot. Another car drove past and caught them all in a rear-window silhouette.

"A gunrack?" Gio felt his throat thicken. His words came out halfway a growl. "You bring hunters to me?" His hair rose but not like before. It rose, thickened, changed. His nose and mouth stretched out from his face. His eyes saw different colors, different hues, revealed more. He blinked and realized he looked down a muzzle, could see the black tip of a nose.

He crouched out of view of the mirrors until he got between the rear of the pickup and one of the service vans, and suddenly stood tall and visible in the parking lot lights. His words came out as snuffling grunts. "Hi, folks. Looking for me?"

The sudden movement caught the driver's eye in his side mirror. Everybody quickly turned to see him.

He made out one man's face.

A familiar face.

Younger.

Something moved through him, up from his gut into his chest, surged down into his legs. He smelled his grandfather's clove aftershave.

Gio smiled and waved. His hand looked like a bear's paw.

The driver put the pickup in gear and spun the tires pulling out of the parking space, down the drive and onto Ivy Road towards the Tylers' home.

Gio watched the pickup's lights flicker away. Some snow fell out of a tree and splatted his head, wet his nose. He wiped them off with his hand.

His human hand. His human nose.

Tiny, cold water rivulets trickled down the sides of his head.

A raven cawed and took flight above him.

Thursday, 31 January 1974

Ed Thompson nudged his brother. "Harry, wake up. Come on, Harry, wake up. We have to get going."

Harry shrugged Ed away.

Ed remembered Harry finding that cave their first night free. Ed remembered Dave warning them about caves in winter. "Bears don't hibernate like everybody says. They can wake up and when they do, they'll be hungry."

But Harry found the cave and nothing Ed said mattered. Harry was tired and that was that.

They went into its darkness and fell asleep. Ed woke up to a bear cub mewling at him. A second cub pawed Harry. He swatted it away and it barked. A moment later the sow raised a sleepy head and growled at them. Her eyes fixed on Ed. Not fully awake, she swatted him with her paw. Blood flowed down his scalp, wetting the already soaked clothes he stole from Mason's drawers.

Ed pulled away from the sow and her cubs, grabbed Harry's hand, pulled.

They ran until they couldn't. Ed remembered Dave's woodlore and built a snow cave beside an old oak where the snow formed a heavy crust. They huddled together for warmth and woke up shaking. Ed, his head throbbing with every step, kept them walking towards the sun until they found this camp, closed for the winter, and broke in.

"The bear's coming, Harry."

Harry sat up on the bed. The blankets Ed wrapped around him stayed in place. His eyes danced over the cabin walls, door, ceiling. The windows were boarded and no light came in. "Where's the bear?"

"There's no more food, Harry. We need to find people, someone to help us."

Harry pulled the blankets tighter around him. "No. You can't trust people. We trusted Dave. He let Todd and Mason take us."

"We can't stay here."

"You don't know where we're going."

"If we keep going in one direction long enough we'll come to a river or stream or road. We have to find people to help us."

"You go. I'm staying here."

"There's no food, Harry."

"I don't care."

Ed stared at his brother. "Some big brother you are. You didn't do anything when Mason took me away."

Harry huddled under the blankets. "I'm staying here."

Ed put on layers and layers of whatever clothes he could find. The boots were a woman's but they were smaller and fit better. He put a bottle of aspirin in his pocket and cleaned and dressed his wound the best he could with some alcohol he found. He looked at his brother's lump on the bed one more time, turned, and left.

Harry stayed under the blankets as long as he could. Ed wouldn't come back. He was a rotten brother. He never wanted to do anything and now he wants to do everything.

He got out of the bed and ran to the door, opened it and yelled, "You'll be sorry you left me alone. I'm telling Mom and Dad!"

Nothing.

Tears wet his cheeks and burned his face in the mid-winter cold.

He went back inside, covered himself in the blankets Ed got from the closets and shelves, and wept covered by their darkness.

\\\\\\\\

Gio rolled up his dorm mate's sleeping bag as tightly as he could and shoved it into its sack. The camp stove was next. Should he do the tent now or wait?

After Stephanie and the two men with her in the pickup truck bolted last Friday, he went back to his dorm.

She didn't say she'd be with someone, and the way they took off.

Strange.

And ravens. How come there were so many ravens around all of a sudden.

He hadn't seen ravens since...

His grandfather used to...

His grandfather talked to a raven. With a raven.

No, not a raven. Raven.

One of Gio's dorm mates loved the woods. He often talked about camping. Gio knocked on his door. "Could I borrow your tent?"

"Sure. This late at night?"

"If it's okay."

"You ever been camping?"

"Not really. Not that I remember."

"How long you going for?"

"No idea."

His dorm mate showed him how to set up the tent. "You'll need a sleeping bag. Probably a stove, too." He showed Gio how to use them, how to put together and carry a backpack.

Gio stared at his completed gear and nodded. "Better call Jess, let her know."

He waited for her to answer and played with the phonebooth light. "I won't be around for a while. A few days. I'm not sure how long."

"Where you going?"

"Walk - " Gio stopped. An old word. His grandfather used it sometimes. He hadn't thought of it in a while. Something his grandfather learned in his travels. "Walkabout."

"You're going for a walk?"

"Yeah. Something like that. I didn't want you to worry if you didn't hear from me for a few days."

"You sure you're okay?"

He laughed. "Yeah. Why? What have you heard?"

"I love you."

"I love you, too."

The parking lot behind Ramsey's Admin building ended in a dirt road that wound into acres of woods behind the campus. He adjusted the backpack's straps and headed into the dark.

Just over a week later he packed for his return. "What was this all about, John?"

He wondered after his time out back, of its purpose. His purpose. Nothing much happened. "Raccoons, a skunk who thinks he owns the world, an opossum and a deer." The raccoons foraged and he wondered if they should be hibernating. The skunk wandered through his camp as if Gio was the guest and the skunk the rightful owner. An opossum sat in a tree and watched him for about an hour. A young doe inspected his camp when he came back from a walk. He left crackers and cereal out from that day onward. "And you shared your bounty with The Wild."

He paused.

The Wild?

Another term his grandfather used.

"Yeah, you're such a good boy, Gio."

Once or twice ducks skated across the frozen ponds. He cracked a hole in a shallow to get some water but it was too brackish to drink. Instead he melted snow. His one or two trips back to campus he gathered peanut butter packets, jam and jelly packets, ketchup packets, wrapped crackers, boxes of cereal, tea bags, instant coffee and creamers. He mixed the food stuffs into a gooey porridge, save the ketchup. Those he used to make a thin tomato soup and dipped the crackers in. Instant coffee sickened him. He remembered sitting on his grandfather's knee on their back porch sipping espresso.

He smiled. "The old man use to give me a drop of Sambuca, too."

It was, all in all, uneventful.

Except for that time he almost drowned.

He found an animal's path. The snow trampled flat by lots of tiny feet, an indication the path was well-used. Limbs from low-growing trees and brush formed a twiggy ceiling about a foot up from the snow. That showed the size of the animals using this path: skunk, raccoon, opossum, gray fox. A little to the right was another path made with larger feet and no brush ceiling overhead. That would be where the predators walked: bobcat, coyote, probably bear.

He hadn't seen any bear.

He walked the path slowly and listened for movement. Smaller animals would flee, a larger one might challenge him and he had no weapons.

The two paths converged at a slight dip in the land.

That's where he fell in.

Over his head.

A pool of water, deep, not frozen over.

He wore heavy hiking boots and a thick wool jacket. The boots filled and the jacket sucked up water like thirsty sand.

He let himself sink. There had to be a bottom somewhere.

Well, yes, probably there was, and he wasn't reaching it any time soon.

He reached out. The walls were close. Slimy. Pond scum and water weeds. He couldn't get a grip.

He spread his legs to dig his feet into the sides of the pool.

No good. He kept sliding.

Don't panic.

Wow. Didn't think this was how I was going to die. Didn't see this coming. Jess, I love you.

"No, not yet. You have much to travel before you rest."

Something came up underneath him and drove him to the surface like a whale breaching.

His arms reached up, out, and slammed down on the edge of the pool. His hands clamped twigs, limbs, brush. An oak's branch touched the ground just out of reach.

He gasped for air. "Come on, just a little more."

A raven cawed in the oak's branches overhead. Gio looked up. The raven shook its head, no. The voice. A woman's. "Stretch. Reach."

Gio stretched his arm, flung it in an arc over his head, slammed it down, grabbed the branch, pulled himself out, lay on the edge of the pool, shivering, gasping.

The raven cawed. Gio looked up. It nodded then flew off.

He made it back to his camp, hung his clothes on branches around his site, and used his stove to make a raging fire.

That was midweek. Now?

Now he finished tying things onto the backpack frame and snorted. "Funny I didn't remember that. Pretty goddamn significant, almost losing my life when no one's around to notice."

A raven cawed but he couldn't see it in the trees, nor did it fly overhead.

"Wonder if anybody would've come looking for me."

\\\\\\\\\\

Dave packed nothing. He looked around his apartment once more to make sure it looked like he meant to come back. He paid up for a full day's electricity and gas and put a kettle on the stove on the lowest heat setting it had.

He'd gone out daily and found nothing. Ed would be a challenge to find. Harry, too, if he stayed with his brother. Ed watched everything Dave did. He asked a lot of questions and always wanted Dave to correct him or show him how to do things better. Yeah, he'd be the challenge. He'd know how to hide if he wanted to.

Harry? Harry stayed hidden because he knew nothing. It would be the luck of the amateur if he survived this long. Or he was with somebody else, someone just as sick as Todd and Mason.

Dave shivered with the thought.

But he couldn't find them. Either of them. A few signs but nothing. And between the deep woods snow's surface melting and refreezing daily, no fresh tracks to find them.

Todd said Rene and Sterne muled drugs up 201 for him. Then get off 201. Take Todd's advice. Get to a city. A big city. So he could hide.

But Todd knew people in Portland and Boston. Probably knew people in Hartford and New York, too.

Montreal.

Yeah. He'd be safe in Montreal.

Or maybe Saint John, New Brunswick.

At least he spoke the language in New Brunswick.

No. It would be Montreal. Bigger city. More metropolitan. He could hide. Maybe even take classes somewhere.

How to get there.

Stay off 201, for sure. Stay off 95, too. All the interstates.

Backroads. They'd be snow covered. No logging roads. Town roads through the backcountry. They'd be plowed.

Yeah, they'd be plowed.

And if not, he'd go slow.

Didn't matter. So long as he got away.

Yeah. Get away.

\\\\\\\\\

Gio found a sealed "From the Office of the President" Ramsey College envelope taped to his door. It carried the scent of roses. "Wow. The college president wants to see me? Did he get my grades from the physics exam already?" He inhaled the rose aroma. "Maybe he wants to go on a date?"

The president's secretary escorted Gio into the large, plush, president's office. A vase of roses stood by the windows. The president, whom students referred to as Doc Ock because his tentacles reached everywhere, adjusted his glasses and waved Gio to a seat once the secretary closed the door. Another door at the back of the office was also closed.

Gio smiled.

I wonder what it's like to be so important you can't pee and poop with mortals.

Doc Ock cleared his throat. "I will dispense with formalities. I had a visitor today. He provided information about you."

Gio shrugged. "Okay."

"You have an Uncle Nicholas de Leo?"

"Uncle Nicky? Yes, I have an uncle Nick."

"He's involved in organized crime."

"If he is, this affects you how?"

"You're not surprised?"

"Have you talked with Cathy Lucchese about her uncle?"

"Ms. Lucchese is from a good New York family."

Gio laughed. "Who are supplying an amazing endowment to the college to let her attend. But let's get away from the Italians. How about Ed Lynch? You changed the academic requirements so he wouldn't get suspended failing four out of five courses two terms in a row - "

"Mr. Lynch's affairs are not your concern."

" - after his family provided funds for a new dormitory."

"How did you - "

"Bit of a gift to me, that, considering how poorly I'm doing in my classes. I get to stay in school because the Lynches paid for a dorm. I should send them a thank you card. I'm on work-study and have to do groundswork to pay for my schooling. This time it didn't cost me a cent."

Doc Ock rose from his seat and tore his glasses off his reddened face. *Stretch. Reach.*

Gio stared at the closed door in the back of the office. He walked over and opened it before Ock moved to stop him. A late-middle-aged short, stocky man, his light brown crewcut going to gray and wearing a blue business suit, sat on the toilet wearing earphones and making notes on a pad of paper.

He looked up as if interrupted during a particularly glorifying shit.

Gio cocked his head and frowned for a moment. The man smelt of hospital rooms. He shimmered. Gio saw him on his knees beside a hospital bed holding the hand of a woman recently passed.

The shimmer faded and took the image with it.

Gio held out his hand. "Hi. My name's John Chance. Everybody calls me Gio, though. You are?"

Doc Ock pulled Gio back from the door and slammed it shut. "Get out." He pointed towards the office door. "Get out!"

Ock watched him cross the quad from his office windows. "He's gone now, Mr. Kagan."

The bathroom door opened. "How did he know I was in there?"

"Did you get what you wanted?"

"He dangerous?"

Ock opened his desk's top drawer desk and pointed to a handgun. "He's not more dangerous than that."

Kagan stared at the pistol for a moment and shrugged. "Yeah. Okay. Do you have anybody here on campus who can keep an eye on him?"

Morelli read the note stuck to his locker. Franklin County State Police had something of interest. Seemed to match what he was looking for. A man, early twenties, athletic build, found dead in his car, gone off Rt 27 north of Eustis and into Chain of Ponds a mile north of the viewpoint. Fingerprints indicate he was a David Eugene LaVerne, one time male prostitute in Ogunquit.

"Was it an accident?"

"We thought so at first. Snow squalls, you know? Snowmobilers saw it happen. One of them said they smelled brake fluid when we took the report. One of our techs checked and sure enough, the rear line ruptured just south of the reservoir. That made him check further and he saw the steering reservoir was also jigged. Only a matter of time, he was going down at some point."

"The car's make and model?"

"A '59 beat to shit light blue Dodge Dart. Mean anything to you?"

"Means a wagon I found a few weeks back belongs to some folks. Thanks."

\\\\\\\\\\

Gio held Jess close. He took his eyes off I-295 weaving through Portland long enough to watch the crescent moon rise over Casco Bay while she found a clear-channel station low on the AM band that played rock all night. Focus' *Hocus Pocus* built to one of its many crescendos before the drums and electric guitar brought everything back down. This was the live, whistled version. The high-pitched tone sliced open the silence like a knife in the night.

"You were gone quite a while. What's a walkabout?"

"Something my grandfather told me about. It's from Australia. Some Indian tribes call it a Visionquest. Ever hear of that?"

She pulled free of him, knelt beside him on Bessie's front seat, and nibbled his ear. "No. You were gone quite a while."

"Pretty much you go off by yourself."

She kissed his cheek and neck. "Quite a while."

"What's the *Rebbe* talking about tonight?"

She unbuttoned his shirt and ran her hand over his chest. "Long time."

"You've driven this road before. Where's the next rest area?"

\\\\\\\\\\

Alan Dykstra looked at Gianna Hevalier's smooth, strong thighs. She'd just come out of the shower and had a towel around her long, white hair and another around her thin, boyish torso.

She caught his gaze and smiled. "You want some more, don't you, Daddy? You want a little more?"

"Oh, you know I do."

She climbed on the bed, crawled towards him, pushed his legs apart through the covers, and punched him in the balls. "I'll let you know when you can have some more."

Dykstra curled up and wheezed. "I love it when you do that."

"I know you do, Daddy. I know you do. That's why I treat you like shit. Because you know you are." She got off the bed and let the towel drop from her torso. She leaned over her dresser to apply some lipstick and thrust her ass into the air, checked the mirror to make sure he watched and shook it at him. "When are we moving?"

"Soon."

"How soon? Inquiring minds want to know."

"May. May or June. Once my boys are out of school and on their way to college, that's when we can move."

She picked a flyer up off her bureau and tossed it over to him. "That's the place I want. I marked it, see?"

He spread the flyer. Madre de Dios Estates, Costa Rica. The perfect retirement community for Norte Americanos tired of the cold winter weather. "Yep, that's the one. Making payments every month. It'll be ours by the time we leave, just waiting for us."

She smacked her lips, testing the lipstick's stickiness. "It's in my name, right? So your wife can't take it away from me? Us?" She walked over to the bed again. Dykstra, his hands under the covers, instinctively protected his groin.

She sat down beside him, gently pushed his hands away, and started stroking him. "You wouldn't want that, would you?"

He spread his legs, groaned, and watched her pull down the covers and smear lipstick all the way down his penis.

He closed his eyes and smiled.

I'm reading a book about how a man can rupture a woman's shithole, did you know that, Gianna? Written by a doctor with a German name so he must know what he's talking about.

He opened one eye and watched her mouth glide up and down his penis.

It's about being careful. Knowing what to do and what not. How to make it pleasurable for everybody involved.

He felt himself climbing the slope.

'Course, that means it lets you know what not to do, what could hurt if you do it wrong. Make some serious injuries.

He pulsed. She lifted her head and slapped his penis hard. "No, you've already cum once today. That's enough. You need to learn control, save that for later."

You don't think I have control? I'm patient. And I'm so going to enjoy rupturing you, cunt. Todd's going to get me some stuff. You'll know what I'm doing but won't be able to do a thing about it. Be able to feel everything and won't even be able to scream for help.

You're good for a turn or two, but you think I'm going to leave my family for you? I can always find another one of you. But Macy? I'm going to give up twenty-two years for a blowjob and a grunt and groan or two?

I'm going to split you like a rotted melon, cum up your ass, then leave you with nothing but bloody sheets to remember me by.

His erection died and he smiled.

\\\\\\\\\

Sam and Jess stood in their driveway chatting with people getting into their cars and waving as they left.

"Gio was a big hit with the *Rebbe*, Daughter."

"Yeah. Think you can convince the *Rebbe* to call me Jess? Nobody calls me Jessica anymore."

"Claimed never to have studied Kabbalah but knew the concepts pretty well."

"No, huh?"

"Understood *gematria* immediately."

"Doesn't New Hampshire have a lottery? I wonder if my name is a winning lottery number."

"Jessica, maybe. Jess, no."

"Already tried, huh?"

"Not enough letters in Jess."

"Guess we're not winning any lotteries, then."

"He turned things around on the *Rebbe*, too. Told him how Elohim and *hateva* are equal in number, hence God and Nature are joined. You sure he's not Jewish?"

"He is circumcised."

Sam glared at Jess. She smiled back at him.

He paused. "*Rebbe* made a pretty strong push for the two of you to get together."

"He made a strong push for Gio and *Jessica* to get together."

"A strong push for permanently."

Jess stuck her hands in her jeans' pockets and blushed. "Tell me about it."

"He'll apologize later."

"No need. If it worked."

"You like him? Gio?"

She sighed. "Yes."

"Heavy sigh, Daughter. You two on good terms still?"

"I wish he was more..."

"Jewish? Nobody's perfect."

She laughed.

"May I ask what's the issue? Does he lie? Cheat? Steal? See other women?"

"You know that's the first time you've called me a woman?"

"You think I'm blind, Daughter? Besides, I call you a woman a lot, just not to your face. And I see how he looks at you. He cares for you. Deeply. He's never said so?"

"How come you're so interested in who I'm dating now? You never talked with me like this before. What's going on?"

Sam shuffled his feet. "Before we started tonight, the *Rebbe* asked me who was coming. I showed him the list of people invited. Nothing. I started walking away and turned back. 'Oh, by the way, my daughter and her boyfriend are coming up. Hope that's okay.'" Sam laughed. "You should've seen the fireworks in his eyes. He says, 'Tell me about him.' But I don't know much. Then he has me sit down with him. He tells me an angel came to him, an angel of water in the shape of a woman. She tells him to help the lost one find his way. 'How will I know this lost one?' he asks the angel and she tells him 'He will tell you he is lost.'"

Jess smacked her forehead with her palm. "I fell asleep on the way up and Gio overshot the exit."

Sam nodded. "You two came in, first thing he says is 'Sorry for being late. I got lost.'"

They both turned at the sound of laughter and Bella's barking from inside the house. Sam gave his daughter a hug. "I better get back in there before the *Rebbe* starts teaching him Hebrew."

Saturday, 2 February 1974

Jess leaned over and kissed Gio's forehead. "Morning, Sleepyhead. You going to get up today?"

Gio blinked as she opened the blinds. "What time is it?"

"You can make lunch if you try. Want some music while you get dressed?"

"Sure."

Bella bounded through the door and jumped on the bed. She crawled over Gio's covers to lick his face and thump him with her tail.

"Somebody missed you. Pop took her for her walk. She was terribly disappointed. What time did you and the *Rebbe* call it quits?"

"He said something about the Sabbath being over."

Jess laughed. "Not likely, but I get the idea."

Joni Mitchell's breathy mezzo came over the radio -

Help me, I think I'm falling…in love again…

Jess lay on the bed opposite Bella and pinned Gio under the covers. "Talk about anything interesting? Talk about your favorite enlightened *Bayla*?" She batted her eyes.

"*Bayla*. I remember that word. Let me think."

Jess punched his arm. "Me. Did you talk about me at all?"

"You mean aside from all that talk about the significance of the wedding ceremony?"

She blushed. "You impressed the *Rebbe* with your interpretation of the ceremony. Where'd you come up with that?"

When I get that crazy feeling I know I'm in trouble again…

"You mean the breaking of the glass representing the breaking of the hymen?"

"Guess we won't have to worry about that."

"That symbolism's in a lot of cultures. It goes back…"

"Yeah?"

Gio shook his head, dislodging the memory, letting it surface. "It goes way back. Something my grandfather taught me. About similar practices going across cultures."

"Care to impress me with your knowledge of ancient practices?"

"He told me I have some decisions to make."

…you love your lovin'…But not like you love your freedom.

"I told you that."

"I told him you told me that."

"What did he say when you told him?"

"He said Jews are very wise people."

She laughed. "You going to make decisions?"

"I am. I have."

"Care to enlighten me?"

"Number one, I love you."

"You already told me that."

Help me I think I'm falling in love too fast
It's got me hoping for the future and worrying about the past.

"I'm telling you again. Also, I don't want to lose you."

"How would you lose me?"

He looked into her eyes. "You wanted me to show you what I do?"

"We still talking about ancient practices?"

"We'll stop seeing each other once this is over. You'll say you need time to figure things out. What it'll really be about is you deciding if you want a quiet, secure, Maine life with that guy you dated in high school or the kind of life you'll envision with me."

"What? Bullshit." She pulled back and frowned. "Wait a minute. I never told you about him. How do you know about him? Don't tell me my family said something. They know better than to do that. How did you know about him?"

"You asked me to show you what I do, remember? And we'll stop seeing each other once this is over."

"And I repeat, bullshit!"

He lowered his head and shook it slowly. "Wait and see."

Her eyes narrowed on him and she took a deep breath. "Oh yeah? What happens if you're wrong and we live together happily ever after?"

His head came up. "I want to be wrong."

She kissed him long enough for the bed covers to rise slightly. Bella jumped off the bed, gave a doggy shrug, and left the room.

"So much for losing me. What else did you talk about?"

"That if I have a gift, or a calling, or a purpose, I have to decide to use it or not. Once I decide, no turning back. Make a decision, live with it."

"Well, we are a wise people."

"But if I decide to use it, I will lose you. If I decide not to use it, I'll keep you."

She stared down at him. "But you'll hate yourself every time somebody needs help. Is that it? You can be Superman but I won't let you near a phonebooth? Screw that. I'm not going to be the cause of you having a miserable life. I'll leave you before I let that happen."

Gio cocked his head, raised and eyebrow, and nodded.

Jess covered her mouth with a hand. "Fuck me."

Joe Radwel sat in his office in the Ramsey College maintenance barn watching a tall, skinny kid stand off to the side of the open garage door carrying what looked like an oversized lunchbox. He watched the four row houses Ramsey converted into dorms, specifically the last one nearest the highway.

The kid stayed in the shadow and ducked in further every time a car passed.

"Something you need, son?"

The kid spun, his eyes wide, unaccustomed to the cavernous interior of the barn-like structure, searching for the voice.

"Over here. What's your name, son?"

"Tim Annandale."

Joe lifted a clipboard and scanned the papers on it. "Are you supposed to be here? I don't have you listed."

"Here for what?"

Joe lowered his clipboard. "Well, this is the maintenance barn. Lots of students come here for work-study jobs, maintenance jobs. Had one fellow a while back was a real good mechanic, had a knack with his hands. Even had his own tools. Thought those might be your tools you're carrying around with you there."

"Where?"

"What have you got in your hand, son?"

Annandale looked at the box as if shocked to find it there. "Electronics."

Joe nodded. "Oh. Yeah. Lots of things got electronic ignitions now. Nothing we have, sorry."

"Sorry about what?"

"Sorry I don't have a job for you."

"What makes you think I'm here for a job?"

"What makes you think you can hang around my barn? If you're not here for a job, you're here to cause trouble. Get out."

"I'm Tim Annandale."

Joe nodded, went into his office, came out with a .22. "Tim? Meet Gracie. She usually takes care of critters going after the seed I keep out in one of the sheds. But I'm sure she'll take a bite out of you if you don't get out of here before I count to three."

"You can't - "

Joe took aim. "Two."

Annandale tucked his box under his arm and hurried across to the nearest row house, the one closest to Rt 128.

\\\\\\\\

Gio kneeled in the driveway next to Bella while Jess backed Sam's Chrysler out. His hands rested gently on either side of Bella's head and he stared into her eyes. Every few seconds she licked his face.

Jess rolled down the passenger window. "What are you doing?"

"I'm asking Bella permission to..."

"You're asking Bella's permission? Oh, this has got to be good. Asking her permission to what?"

"To borrow her nose."

"You're going to take her nose? Don't you dare hurt my dog. My father'll kill you if you do anything to our dog. And when he's done, I'll hurt you, too."

He stood and rubbed Bella's head. The shepherd looked from Gio to the car and back.

"You have to stay here, girl. Take care of the house, okay?"

Bella did a dejected doggy walk to the backyard, turned, sat, and watched them leave.

"You're going to borrow her nose?"

"I already have. I think. I don't really remember. Things are coming back to me slowly. I'm not sure."

"You borrow dogs' noses a lot, do you?"

"Hey, you're the one who told me to practice, right? And the *Rebbe* telling me I have to make decisions? Remember that? And let's not forget whoever it was saved me from drowning. She said something about not yet, there's more for me to do, like I'm not supposed to die yet. Something like that."

Jess pulled over to the side of the driveway. "Drowning? You never told me anything about you drowning. When did this happen?"

"When I went walkabout."

She punched him hard.

"Hey, that one really hurt."

"Good, goddammit. Don't you know I love you? Why in the fuck would you try to drown yourself?"

"It's an ancient practice?"

She screamed at him. "Bullshit! What am I supposed to do if you die, Gio? Goddammit." Tears formed tiny streams down her face. She sobbed openly as her face twisted into a theatrical Buskin. She pulled back her fist a second time. "And you said 'she' saved you from drowning. She who? If you were off in the woods with somebody else for fuck's sake tell me. Let me die in peace, can't you?"

He slid across the seat and held her tight, her arms pinned to her sides.

"Let me go, goddammit." She struggled in his grip. "Let me go!"

He focused.

Lower-Center-Relax-Breathe.

He relaxed his grip, wrapped his shimmer around her, kissed her.

His shimmer. Messages to the heart. Memories of warm embraces. Of panting exhaustions. Of walks under moonlight. Of guffawing at stupid jokes. Wrestling on late summer grasses. Of first meetings. Of soft, first urgings. Of things he'd forgotten. Of his grandfather's laughter. His grandmother's kisses. The scent of bees making honey. The feel of things growing under his feet.

All through one, gentle kiss.

He pulled back but kept his arms around her.

She inhaled deeply and dried her eyes as they fluttered open. "You never kissed me like that before."

He sat back. "That was me practicing."

"Promise me you'll do that again?"

"I promise."

She put her hands on the wheel and quivered. "My god, I'm so wet I feel like I pissed myself."

He laughed. "That's because..." He paused and frowned.

"Another memory?"

He nodded slowly as more memories filled him. "That's because we have four bodies. Everybody does. Western culture teaches us to focus on only two: the mind and body. That kiss. It followed the mind-body axis."

"What are the other two?"

He rubbed his face with both hands as if washing it. "I. Don't. Remember. Something to do with alignment. Like when you ask someone something, if you want to be sure of their answer, ask them three times. Something my grandfather told me."

"Want to ask me if I want you to kiss me like that again three times? How 'bout you just kiss me three times and we'll call it even. Ask me if I want you to make love to me like that. Go ahead. I dare you."

He laughed.

She put the car in gear and headed down the driveway. "Well, any time you want to practice finding those other two bodies, you just let me know and I'll be there for you. Use this body to look for the other two. I mean, you just tell me what you want me to do and I'll do it. Anything to help."

He laughed. "Gotcha."

"You just tell me."

"Understood."

"You got something you need me to do - "

"Yes, Jess."

"Point me in a direction."

"I heard you."

"No, I mean, point me in a direction." They stopped at the bottom of the driveway. "Which way do you want to go?"

He laughed so hard he couldn't breathe.

"Got you that time, eh, Skippy?"

He pointed right and kept laughing.

\\\\\\\\\\

Gianna sat on one of her apartment's radiators and watched Dykstra pull out of the building's parking lot. She snickered. "What was it Mae West said? The landlord came to collect the rent and I'm drying out the receipt?"

She grabbed a bottle of Stolichnaya and drew three long swallows before bringing it back down. "You think I don't know what you're up to? Christ, what a dumb fuck." Another long swallow. "Remember who introduced us, Daddy?" Another swallow. "You honestly don't think you're that grand a fuck, do you? And that Costa Rica villa? That's icing on the cake, jackoff."

She got up, drained the bottle, and tossed it in the trash. "Todd better decide what he's going to do with you because I'm a little tired of you joozing me."

She pulled back from the window and noticed a car pull out of the MacDonald's parking lot across the street. The car was there yesterday, too. It pulled in after Dykstra entered her building. She never saw anybody get out or go in. Now it takes off after Dykstra's car goes around the corner down the street.

"I'm not liking this." She picked up the phone. "Yeah, hi. Don't know if it means anything, but I think the Sarge is being tailed. Yeah, no, I can't say for certain. Big blue car. Sedan. I'm four flights up, you think I could read the plates? Well, fuck you, too. I'm doing this for both of us, remember?"

She hung up the phone. "Jackoff."

\\\\\\\\\\

Jess drove through Gardiner out towards the lakes. "Do you know where we're going?"

"Where does that road go?"

"Probably out to Parker Pond."

Jess turned down the road. "Let's get out here. Don't want to get stuck in the snow."

A battered tow truck passed them going in the other direction. Jess pointed. "We could always call a tow."

Gio lifted his head and sniffed the air; once, two, three, four, five times.

"No. Not that one."

They stood side by side in Maine's February cold under a cloudy sky and held hands. Their breaths misted around them.

Jess looked around. "What do we do now?"

"I love you, Jess."

She looked up at him. He scanned the woods, the road - the only break in its snow covered surface a set of fresh tire tracks - and finally the sky. He took a deep breath. His body sagged as he exhaled, frowned, looked down and shook his head, his face wrinkled with sad lines.

"What's wrong?"

"Nothing. Practicing. Not doing it right."

Jess opened the door. "Hey, wanna get back in the car and fuck?"

Gio fell back against the car laughing. "Jesus Christ, girl. Only a guy would say something like that."

"I have two older brothers."

"No, you don't."

"I always wanted say that, though. It's so cliched." She let him catch his breath. "You back with us now?"

"And in your father's car, too. Sheesh."

"And Ramsey College students shouldn't take the lord's name in vain."

He shook his head, took her hand in his, held it behind him, and guided her down the road.

A quarter mile in she held him back. "Hey, Nanook. Let's take a minute, okay?

"Stay in a tire track. Less effort that way."

"Where are we going?"

"No i - " He pulled his hand away from her, dropped to all fours, his nose to the ground, and sniffed.

"Gio?"

He stayed on all fours, bear-like, and trotted off the trail into the woods.

Jess stood with hands on hips. "Pop's not going to like this."

A state police cruiser came up the snow-covered road making a second set of tire tracks as it headed out to the main. Jess stood off to the side and waved. The cruiser stopped and the officer rolled down his window. "Everything okay, miss?"

She pointed. "My boyfriend took off that way."

The officer looked at Gio's tracks in the snow. "He alright?"

"Yeah."

"Have to relieve himself?"

"I think he's looking for something."

"Looking for what?"

She shrugged.

"What's your name, Miss?"

"Jess Rosen. What's yours?"

"Tony Morelli. Who's your boyfriend?"

"John Chance. Everybody calls him Gio, though."

Morelli frowned and cocked his head. "Gio? Gio. Gio Chance?"

"Please don't tell me he's wanted for something."

"Not that I know of. It's a familiar name, though; Gio. Any idea where he's heading?"

She pointed again. "Him go that-a-way, Kimosabe."

Morelli laughed. "Tell you what, let me get out to the road. I'll turn around and back in. If he's not back before I am, we can head down to the water and look for him there."

Jess saluted. "Aye, Captain."

She watched him drive away. He talked into his mike on the way out and came back a few minutes later.

"No sign yet? Hey, you're shivering. Get in." He reached over and opened the door for her. "By the way, I checked. No records on John Chance, Gio Chance, John Gio, nothing. He's clean."

She held her hands over the dashboard heater vents. "My father will be so happy."

They stopped at the water's edge and got out. Jess cupped her hands around her mouth. "Gio."

Nothing.

"Gio!"

Morelli joined in. "John Chance."

Nothing.

Jess rubbed her hands together. "You sure he'd come this way?"

"We're on a peninsula that narrows to this point."

Something moved towards them through the thickest part of the woods.

"Gio?"

"Mr. Chance?"

Nothing. Morelli drew his weapon. He smiled at Jess. "Just in case it's a moose or something. Just to scare it off."

She nodded and stood by the cruiser.

Treetops wavered over a slight rise.

"Gio?"

"Mr. Chance?"

Gio came on the rise, still on all fours, bearwalking, his nose to the ground, his head moving back and forth, his nose routing in the snow.

"Gio?

"Is he on anything?"

"No. He's never on anything." She hurried towards him.

Morelli held her back. "Just in case."

Gio moved quickly, his body like an animal's, its rhythms keeping it low to the ground, hunting. He passed them without a word, his nose still routing.

Twenty feet past them he dug, his hands and arms moving like a dog's forepaws and legs, throwing back the snow.

Morelli traded his revolver for his baton. "You stay here. Anything happens, lock the doors, key the mike, give them my name, tell them we're off the end of Fellows Cove Road. Repeat that back to me."

"Lock the doors. Key the mike. Officer Tony Morelli. Off the end of Fellows Cove Road."

"Good girl. Back in a minute."

Gio remained on all fours and dug. His hands threw clumps of frozen earth behind him.

Morelli got ten feet from him. "Mr. Chance?"

Seven feet. Morelli spoke louder. "John Chance."

Five feet. Gio thrust his face into the shallow hole he'd dug. Morelli struck an exposed stone outcropping with his baton and yelled. "Gio!"

Gio raised his head with a child's sneaker in his mouth. He stood and spit it into his hand. "No need to shout." He held the sneaker out. "This is evidence."

"Of what?"

"Ed and Harry Thompson. Two little boys gone missing back in September." He held the sneaker to his nose and inhaled deeply. "This was Ed Thompson's, I think. Smells like Ed's."

Jess came up beside them. "What the hell was that about?"

"I had to go pee and got lost?"

She punched his arm. He winced, gave the sneaker to Morelli, and rubbed where Jess hit him.

Morelli's eyes went from the sneaker to Jess.

She smiled. "I have two older brothers."

Gio rolled his eyes.

Morelli slid his baton back into its belt loop. "How about you two sit in my cruiser and give me some details about what's going on."

Gio headed to the cruiser without hesitation. "Good idea. I need to rest a bit." He fell asleep as soon as he sat down.

Jess filled Morelli in as much as she could without mentioning Gio's foray into the woods. In the middle of her explanation, Morelli's radio squawked.

"Morelli, go ahead." An anonymous tip, another cabin break in. He replaced his mike when the call ended. "That's the third one this week. That's what brought me down here, in fact. And everything's coming in anonymous." Morelli looked in his rearview and saw Gio watching him.

"You're not Tony Morelli's boy, are you?"

Morelli shifted to look at him directly. "My dad is Tony Morelli. I'm Tony Morelli, Jr."

"Your dad was with the Boston PD? Or Everett? Something like that?"

"Did you know my dad?"

"He and another officer…oh, god. What was his name? Clarkson? Charlie Clarkson, I think."

Morelli clapped his hands. "Uncle Charlie. You knew Uncle Charlie?"

"Long time ago. I was two? Three? Less than five, anyway. They used to come by and ask my grandfather for things."

Morelli slapped the back of his seat. "Gio Fortuna. You're Gio Fortuna. That's right. Fortuna is Chance in English. And Gio? Giovanni, right? John in Italian?"

"Do we know each other?"

"I remember my dad telling me about your grandfather. You, too, now that I have all the pieces."

"That was a long time ago."

"Yeah, and every time my dad told me stories I'd say, 'Right, Pa,' and he'd wag his finger at me and say, 'You don't know, son.' It was my last year of high school and he'd quote Shakespeare at me. There's more things in heaven and earth than are dreamt of in your philosophy? Something like that." He nodded towards the hole Gio dug. "So what was that about?"

Gio sighed and looked out the window to the exposed areas of water. "Her dog, Bella. I borrowed the dog's nose to track a scent because my nose isn't sensitive enough." He turned to Jess. "I need to thank Bella for her help. Can we stop and get her a new taco on the way back?"

She punched his arm.

"Damn, girl. Want to use the other arm and give this one a break?"

Morelli glanced at Jess. "She know?"

Jess battered her eyes. "Oh, I'm just a girl. I don't know anything." She turned to Gio. "Is this where you to tell me you can't find things people have lost and you can't make people feel better and you don't know what people are thinking?"

Morelli clapped his hands and laughed. "Oh, yeah. That's what my old man said. That's exactly the kinds of things my old man told me about you and your grandfather. Jesus Christ, imagine meeting you after all these years."

Gio looked into the sky. "It'll be dark soon. Can we get out of here?"

"One minute." Morelli went into his trunk and got a can of fluorescent orange spray paint. He made a wide circle where Gio dug out the sneaker and came back. "You know I have to report this."

"Can you leave me out of it? You can take all the glory, okay?"

"How do I explain it?"

"Did your dad ever mention my grandfather in any reports?"

Morelli put a hand over his mouth and pulled down as if smoothing a mustache. "For our fathers' sakes, then. My father and your grandfather. But what if I want to talk with you again. How do I reach you?"

Jess gave her parents address. Gio added, "I go to Ramsey College in Mass. You can reach me there."

Morelli left them at Sam Rosen's Chrysler, waved, and drove off.

Gio watched Morelli and exhaled slowly. "Tai He Morn."

"It's coming on night, O' Man O' Mine. Morning's long past."

"Tai He Morn. Tiger-Crane. Officer Morelli's totems. For now. Tiger, quiet strength. Crane, he'll move on once this is done. Or shortly after."

"Coffee. Wouldn't you love a good cup of coffee right about now? Or we can get naked in the backseat and you can keep me warm that way."

"Coffee."

"Phphtt."

They drove off.

Across the pond, hidden by trees and unmoving until he was convinced everyone had gone, Todd Andersen lowered his binoculars. "Dykstra's becoming a problem." He waited another minute, listening. "Okay, let's go."

Behind him, at the end of a road opposite the end of Fellows Cove Road and hidden by more trees, Mason got in his tow truck and did a tight three-point turn. Todd got in and they drove off.

Jess and Gio let her dad's Chrysler warm up for a while. "So you followed Ed's scent? After how many months? Or was this recent? Is that the break-in Tony was talking about?"

"Tony? Already he's 'Tony'?"

"Don't change the subject."

Gio closed his eyes. "Bella's got a good nose."

Sunday, 3 February 1974

Gio lifted Jess's laundry into the backseat. "We need to stop by the Thompsons' on the way back."

"Stephanie won't be there."

"I know. You want to know what I do. So do I. Seems like a good place to start."

"Thought you started yesterday when you kissed me."

"Like that?"

"Oh, very much so. Any time you want to do that again, don't hesitate. Don't even ask. Just go ahead. Don't worry about me, I'll catch up."

He smiled and looked away.

No, Jess. You won't catch up. My path...you could never follow.

She reached up and gently turned his face to her. "You okay, Gio? You looked so sad for a second there."

"I'm fine. But let me prove it to you."

He drew her to him.

Lower-Center-Relax-Breathe.

The world shimmered.

One kiss.

Her knees buckled. He held her up, against him, not straining, his lips always on hers.

One kiss. That spanned eternities in one second.

Because I don't know how many more kisses I'll give you.

And I want you to know I love you.

They separated. He leaned her against Bessie until she steadied on her feet.

She opened her eyes slowly and focused on him. "Hey, don't stop on my account."

"Thanks for helping me practice."

\\\\\\\\\

Harry turned the Cheerios box upside down and banged it on the bedpost.

Nothing.

Empty.

He ran his hands over the blankets feeling for crumbs.

Nothing.

No more wood by the bedroom fireplace, either.

Ed probably took it all when he left.

"Bet you didn't know I hid this box of Cheerios, did you? Huh? Huh? Huh? That's why I didn't tell you about the crackers and chocolate bars, either, 'cause I knew you'd leave me here without any food."

The stench from the cabin's bathroom hung in the rooms like a cold mist. Ed would go outside but Harry wouldn't. He used the toilet and when it didn't flush, he used the sink and finally the bathtub.

Where was Mom? She always said Harry was better than Ed. Even in front of them both. She'd nod when asked. Yes he was! He could make things happen, she said. When Dad and Ed were in the garage, his mother told him only important people could make things happen. She made things happen. Pay attention, Harry. This is how you do it. Some day you'll be important. You'll make things happen. You are somebody important when you can make things happen.

Mom was important. She made things happen. She got the church to do things. She got the Tennis club to do things. She organized the snowmobile rides in winter and the parade floats in summer.

Mom was somebody important.

Harry nodded.

She made things happen.

He pulled the blankets tighter around himself and nodded.

She brought Dave home and made him take care of Harry and Ed.

His eyes slowly widened and the blankets fell loose in his hands.

Mom brought Dave home?

She wanted this to happen?

Little nostrils flared. Pudgy, boyish hands clenched the blankets. His face tightened.

She made Ed leave him alone here with no food and no firewood?

Because...

Because she lied to him!

She? Lied to him?

His eyes narrowed.

\\\\\\\\\

Bill greeted them at the door. "Gio, Jess. Stephanie's not here."

They came in. The grandfather clock ticked. Gio caught the light against the maple case. It turned into wood-tinted rainbows.

"Could you call Pam down, please?"

"She's not feeling well."

"She's at the top of the stairs listening."

Bill pulled back. He frowned, his gaze going from Gio to Jess and back. "Pam? Could you come down here, please?"

Pam passed them on her way to the kitchen. "I have to make myself a cup of coffee. Come in here if you want to talk."

Bill shrugged, shook his head, and waved them into the kitchen.

Pam poured Nescafe into the flowing stream mug and put some water on to boil. She gazed out the back window. "What do you want, Mr. Chance?"

"I want you to - " He stared at the mug. "Where'd you get that?"

"What? This cup? Some crazy Indian lady gave it to me."

Gio took the cup from her hand and held it up to the light. "This is the mug I used before, isn't it?"

"You expect me to remember something from a month ago?"

The flowing stream on the mug moved. "Where'd you get this?

"I just told you. Some Indian lady gave it to me. You don't listen?"

Gio watched the waters flow in the mug's image. They quickened, shifted, lifted, became a woman of water and reached out to him.

Gio shook his head, lifted the mug to his lips as if to take a sip. He frowned, shook his head, held the mug in both hands as if gripping the hilt of a sword, as if preparing to cleave the world asunder.

"What are you doing?"

The water-woman stood in the stream. She spoke to him and he heard water rushing, flowing, moving. "Running Water?"

"Yes, that was her name, I think. What difference does it make?"

I remember, Grandmother. I remember.

Gio kept his hands around the mug, kept his eyes on it, as if drawing life, drawing energy from it. "Do you want me to find your children?"

Bill stepped forward. "Yes. If you think you can, yes."

Pam turned back to the living room. "No. I don't want you near my children."

"I need you to say yes three times. Do you want me to find your children?"

Bill nodded furiously. "Yes."

Pam kept her gaze out to the backyard. "No. You stay away from us. From me. From them."

"You have to both say yes."

"I'll never say yes."

Bill spun his wife to face them. "What is your problem, Woman? Nobody else has done a goddamn thing to find our boys and here's this young man willing to help. What could it hurt? Say yes, goddamn it."

"No."

"Why?"

"Because he's evil. Because he's the devil. Because she's with him."

Jess pulled back. "Wow. Nice, Mrs. Thompson. Want to spray me with blood when I walk out the door?"

"Shut up."

Gio cocked his head at her for a moment, sighed, and straightened back up. "No. I'm not evil. What is it?" His head swayed slightly as if sensing a speed trap on the highway. "You. You? You don't want to face your own evil. If I find them, you have to face...what? You're hiding something, Mrs. Thompson. What are you hiding? You're hiding something from me."

Pam shook herself free of Bill's grip. "Get out! Get out of this house! Get out of here! And take that cup and your Jewish tramp with you."

Bill spun her towards him. "Pam, how dare you?"

"Oh, what do you know, William? You haven't done anything to find our boys, have you?"

"I was the one who got the police involved. You certainly didn't want to, remember?"

"Lotta good they're doing, huh?"

Gio stood still, his eyes on Pam, ignoring their exchange, then, "It has nothing to do with me, except that I might succeed. Why? What makes you think I might succeed and find your...No, not find. What then?"

He rocked back and his eyes opened wide. "Sweet lord, Mrs. Thompson. Creatures in the wild don't sacrifice their young the way you have. Do you think you're medieval royalty? How does it feel to know you're less than the creatures of the field?"

She lifted the steaming kettle from the stove and threw it at him. He knocked it out of the air. It flew across the kitchen and embedded itself in the drywall like a bullet from a highpowered sniper's rifle. Boiling water washed down the wall and steamed on the floor.

Jess whispered, "Steve was right. You are strong."

Pam took a butcher's knife out of a drawer and held it up at them. "Shut up! Shut up and get out."

Gio hurried Jess out the door.

Bill ran out after them. "My god, Mr. Chance, Jess. I am so terribly, terribly sorry. I've never seen her like this. I - "

Gio held up Running Water's mug. "May I keep this?"

Bill looked at the cup and back. "Yeah. Sure. I - "

Gio's nose wrinkled. "Be careful, Mr. Thompson." He nodded back at the house. "Be careful with that one."

"You said you needed to ask me three times. Yes, yes, yes. Is that good enough?"

"You both have to say it. Separately. Three times. Each."

Bill squared his shoulders. "Come back in, please."

Pam stood at the kitchen sink, the butcher's knife in one hand and a steaming, wet dish towel in the other. She held the rim of the sink, shaking.

Bill pointed to the still damp floor. "Be careful Gio, Jess."

Pam lunged at them. "I said get out!"

Gio caught the wrist of Pam's knife hand. He turned slightly and inhaled as he did so. She spun around him as if his breathing was a hurricane. He put a hand on her chest. She flew through the kitchen door and landed on her back in the middle of the living room.

Bill followed, Jess and Gio close behind.

Jess whispered, "Can you teach me how to do that?"

"You breathing deep is already impressive."

"What?"

Bill stood over his wife and held up a finger. "Pam? Oh, my dear wife, Pam? You either say yes or I'll start divorce proceedings and make sure you don't get a cent. I'll sell off everything I have and live in that north country trailer I found you in before you get a dime."

"No!"

"Say it!"

Pam held her hand out to him. "Help me up."

He ignored it. "Say it!"

She screamed at him from the floor. "No."

Bill smiled. He spoke calmly. "Say it three times, Pam."

He turned to Gio. "Does it matter if she means it?"

"I...I don't really know."

"We'll hope for the best then." Bill lifted Pam by her wrists until she stood but he didn't let go. "Say it."

She kicked him in the shins.

He snapped her arms down so sharply her shoulders cracked.

"I'm sorry, my love. I didn't quite hear you. Could you repeat that? For our guests, please?"

"Yes."

"One."

He shook her. "Yes."

"Two."

"One more or we're through."

Pam sank into her settee and sobbed. "Yes, yes, yes."

"Thank you, dearest." Bill let go of Pam and turned to Gio. "Gio, yes yes yes."

Gio nodded. He took Jess's hand and they walked out the door.

Bill hurried out and stopped them before they got in Bessie. "Gio, what did you mean about Pam sacrificing her children?"

"You'll have to ask Pam that."

"Gio, we're talking about my boys, and I don't think Pam's going to be talking to me for quite a while now. How come you can't tell me?"

"I will tell you your story and as much of mine as you care to hear, but I will never tell you someone else's story or tell someone else your story."

"What?"

"Sorry, Mr. Thompson. Those are the rules."

Bill scratched his head. "You can find my boys?"

"I will do my best. No guarantees. It's more likely now."

"Because we said yes?"

"Definitely helps."

Bill waved as they drove away.

Jess turned the radio on and dialed through some stations until she heard Todd Rundgren.

Hello, it's me. I've thought about us for a long, long time…

"Gio, is that 'I won't tell you anything about anybody' thing another one of your grandfather practice things?"

He nodded.

"What can you tell me about me?"

Wednesday, 6 February 1974

A dorm brother knocked on Gio's door. "Woman to see you downstairs, Gio."

Gio rubbed his eyes and closed his book. Things got busy since Rachel quit school. She wasn't even pregnant, just late and frightened. Most of them were just late and frightened. He used an old technique his grandfather taught him: slow your breathing while looking them in the eye. Most people relax without realizing it, their breathing matching yours. Depending on the people involved, you could relax them to the point they fell asleep.

Once relaxed, their own bodies took over and did what needed to be done.

"Yeah, thanks."

If not Ramsey co-eds, friends of Jess's and friends of friends from Iperia, townies, even a few from North Shore Community and Salem State made their way to him. None of them needed more than a smile, a nod, a holding of the hand.

He made his way downstairs. "Hello, may I - Stephanie. Hi. What's up?"

A twisted smile scarred her face and she held her hand out to him. "That's how you do it, isn't it? You touch their hand?"

"What was that all about, couple of Friday nights back?"

"You said you knew my brothers were alive, remember?"

"That was then. What about it?"

"Those were my uncles. They wanted to know how to find them. My mother sent them."

"Your mother wanted help from me? Then how come they took off like the devil himself was on their tail?"

"You scared them."

"I scared guys with a gunrack in their truck?"

"Do you know where my brothers are?"

"Doesn't matter. They separated. Last Thursday?" He closed his eyes for a moment and nodded. "Yeah, last Thursday."

"And you didn't call and tell me?"

"Oh, I don't know. Maybe because I tell you they're alive and you arrive with the cast of *Deliverance* in a pickup who take off when I show up? Maybe because your mother insults Jess? Maybe because she makes it clear she doesn't want me involved? Maybe because I'm just a freaking puckerbutt? I'd use stronger language if we weren't on campus."

Stephanie looked away and pursed her lips. "Yeah, well, sorry about all that."

"And the week after you show up with the Everly Brothers I get called into the principal's office and told my family's in the Mafia. Any idea where that came from?"

"Your family's in the Mafia?"

Gio flopped into a seat and stared at the ceiling. "I give up. I freakin' completely give up. Does anybody think rationally anymore?"

She sat opposite him. "Am I pregnant?"

"I told you you were before, remember?"

"How can you tell? You didn't even look at me. Don't you have to look or something?"

He lowered his head, stared into her eyes, looked back at the ceiling. "Yes, you're pregnant. Better?"

She stared at him. "Is this what you do? Destroy people's hopes? Destroy their...I don't know. Do you have to... Somebody comes to you needing help and you trample all over them? What kind of doctor are you?"

"Okay, I will use foul language. What the fuck makes you think I'm a doctor? What have I done to make anybody think I'm a doctor?"

He shimmered. His tongue flicked over his teeth. His nostrils flared. The color and shape of the room changed. His body shifted in the chair. His voice echoed in his chest. "Unless you mean a *houngan*, a witch doctor? Do you people need me to be a witch doctor? Would that satisfy your needs?"

The shimmer faded. He shook his head.

Where the fuck did that come from?

He blinked. A friend of his grandfather's. From Haiti. His grandfather's friend waved.

Gio raised his hand to wave back, snapped his head, put his hand down.

Stephanie stared wide-eyed at him.

He cleared his throat, tested his voice before speaking. "You ask me to open my eyes then curse me when I see the truth? Did I see something you didn't? Before you saw through a glass darkly, now you see clearly."

She looked down and away. "Don't quote scripture to me."

"As you wish."

"Get rid of it for me."

"I'm going to ask you three times. Don't answer me immediately. Let my question sink in. Take your time. Consider all the outcomes."

"Just ask me your goddamn question."

He shrugged. "Do you want to terminate the pregnancy?"

She laughed. "So technical. Yes."

"Are you sure you want to end this pregnancy?"

She nodded. "Yes."

"Once more, just to be sure; Do you want to abandon this child?"

She hesitated. Her hands went to her belly. She cocked her head to one side and heard the wind stir the trees outside. "Yes."

The room shimmered.

"It's done."

"What do you mean it's done?"

"It's done. You lost the child. It never existed."

"What do you mean it never existed? Then what was all that three times bullshit about?"

"It's about you being sure before you make a decision."

"Was I ever pregnant?"

Gio walked up the stairs. "Yes, and now, no, you never were."

Stephanie stared after him as he closed the door to the dorm rooms.

⸻

Sid Lyndon peeked out to bright Augusta sunshine from behind heavy drapes he installed on all his windows. He cradled his phone between ear and shoulder and nodded occasionally.

"No, nobody knows, nobody suspects."

More nodding.

"You think we're ready to move in March?" He checked an Audubon wall calendar. Different birds for each month. Penguins for February, a raven for March. "It's your call. You tell me when everything's in place and I'll set the trap, you spring it."

Nodding.

"What did you find out about Chance? Really? How come we never heard of him? Okay. Whatever you say."

He hung up, went to his bed, lay down in the darkened room, and checked his watch. Six double-shifts in the past two weeks. The union rep gave him the hairy eyeball the last time he passed through the squad. When not working, he performed surveillance. Hopefully unobvious surveillance. His eyes closed. "You're going to get sloppy if you don't rest, Sid."

He opened the drawer in the little night table beside his bed and took out an unmarked pill bottle, popped the top, and shook out a couple of reddish pills. "Ya ba. Do you know what I could get down on the corner for you? Even up here in hick country?" He checked his watch again. "Fuck it." He swallowed two pills. "Ya ba dabadoo." He lay back and waited for the meth-caffeine mixture to hit his system.

\\\\\\\\\\

Stephanie sat on Jess's bed in her dorm room. "Your man's a prick bastard, Rosen. And before you ask, I'm sorry for the way I acted last time we talked. Sorry about my mother, too. No idea where that came from."

Jess held up a bright blue tube top. "What'd'you think? Yes? No?"

Stephanie fell back on the bed, laughing.

"Yeah, I didn't think so, either."

"He told me I'm not pregnant."

"That's good news, right?"

"But he said it like I was, but not anymore."

"And that's good news, right?"

"He made it sound like I was but never was, at the same time. And he knows things. How can he know the things he knows?"

Jess shrugged.

"How can you be around him? Doesn't he scare you?"

"Sometimes."

"You're still seeing him?"

"Not since we got back Sunday night."

Stephanie stood by Jess's door. "I thought you two played the beast with two backs nightly."

Jess shook her head.

"What happened?"

Jess put on a jacket. "He kissed me."

Stephanie put a hand on her hip, leaned towards Jess, jabbed the air between them with a crooked finger, and spoke with a cracking voice. "We'll have none of that here, young lady! Kissing. My goodness. Who knows where that will lead?"

"You know how you said he knows things he can't know? Imagine being kissed and knowing everything about the person you're kissing.

Everything. The most wonderful things and the stupidest things. Imagine them giving you everything they are in one kiss."

Stephanie's hands smoothed the front of her skirt. "I can't."

"Neither could I. But that's what he did. And it scared me."

"You going to see him again?"

"I have to."

"Oh, god, Rosen. Don't tell me you're pregnant."

Jess's face reddened with laughter. She caught her breath before answering. "No. I really liked that kiss."

\\\\\\\\\

Joe Radwel sat in his office going through his budget books. He had plenty to last him through the term to summer break and he'd get another infusion then.

If he didn't, Doc Ock's extracurricular activities in the seed shed would be on the front page of *The Salem News*, *The Peabody Times*, and if the story was big enough, either *The Globe* or *The Herald* would pick it up.

Right now he focused on his maintenance expenditures and his payroll, the former made up of dated but quality equipment and latter made of reliable work-study students, some amusing, some naive, some both.

His real find was Gio Chance. The kid worked on farms. He knew how to use everything from a dumper, a plow, a backhoe, a loader, down to a hand shovel and rake. He knew what plants to put together for color and aroma and what fertilizers to use when and where. He even helped put in the docks and pier on the Ramsey ponds. First time Gio came in for a job, he stared at the photos on Joe's wall and asked, "May I?"

Joe watched the boy. "Be my guest."

Gio took his time, looked at the detail, at the capturing of the light, at the shading. "These are amazing. Where'd you get them?"

Joe kept evaluating. Nobody ever commented on his photographs. "I took them myself. I do some amateur photography when I can."

Gio shook his head and went from one photograph to the other. Fishing boats leaving Gloucester harbor, the maintenance sheds on the Ramsey campus, a field from who knew where, all black and whites. "Beautiful."

Joe thought this kid would have entered the photographs if he could. Nobody appreciated his artistry. Who was this kid? And what was he doing here?

Joe invited his crew over for beers one night and the kid sipped real gentle, didn't guzzle like the others, took his time.

Joe caught him coming out of the head, stopped him before he went back out to join the others, told him he'd help him get into an Aggie school if he wanted. Get him into a good state school, too, if that was his way.

"No, I've got stuff to do here at Ramsey. But thanks. I appreciate your help."

Joe debated his next line. "Gio, I know you're not doing well here. I hear things. These people are out to get you. Most of them, anyway. Get the fuck away from here before they do some damage to your life."

Gio tipped his bottle in Joe's direction. "I appreciate it, sir, I truly do. I know I won't last here, but there's something I gotta do first."

"What?"

"No idea. I'll find out when it hits me."

He brought his girl by Joe's house once, like Joe was the kid's dad and he wanted his parents' approval before getting serious.

During drinks on the patio, Gio made some silly-ass comment and his girl whammed him in the arm. Gio worked hard not to but Joe saw him wince.

He remembered smiling. That the kind of hit you're talking about, Chance? Seems you've met your match in this one.

The next day, as Gio prepped the vehicles for the day's chores, Joe pulled him aside, handed him two twenties. "Do something nice for that girl, Gio. She's a keeper."

Gio folded the twenties into this pocket. "Thanks. I know. I plan on it."

So what the fuck brought that weasel-dick Annandale into Joe's barn the other day? On a weekend. Did he not know Joe came in routinely on Saturday afternoons to prepare his books for the coming week? God forbid he come in on a Sunday and do work. They'd have him pray with Father Chris for blaspheming the Lord's day.

Imagine if they learned he would rather say a few Hail Marys!

Good Catholic that he was.

He picked up his phone and dialed the work-study office. He had a friend there, one of the few who did more than say hello in passing to him on this campus, and when she answered her phone, he said, "I got a kid came by this weekend looking for work, Tim Annandale. Wouldn't know his way around ground equipment with a cane and a guide dog. What can you tell me about him?"

He heard papers shuffle, a filing cabinet drawer open and close. He listened to his friend's information, thanked her, hung up the phone, leaned back in his chair, and looked out his window to the four row houses across the road. "What does an upcountry bumpkin like that want with those four houses?"

\\\\\\\\\\

Todd put his phone down and watched Mason do dumbbell curls in the bedroom.

Mason smiled and blew him a kiss. "Any luck?"

"Nobody answered."

"What do you want to do?"

"You said you drove past the Thompsons a few times and some old car was in their driveway? Not one of theirs?"

"Sixty-Four Mercury Comet. Looked in mint condition. Should we be concerned?"

"Did you get the plate?"

"Got the owner's name and everything. The joys of being on the state's approved tow service list."

"Feel like a road trip? To the *Giambatta*?"

Mason showered while Todd counted out several thousands in hundred and twenty-dollar bills and added them to the cash already in Caroline's envelope.

"Ready?"

"Ready."

Mason pulled his battered tow truck up around front. Todd got in and slid across the front seat. The cracked naugahyde on the seat caught his jeans and gouged his ass. "We've got to get you a new truck, Mason."

"I like my truck."

"Whatever."

Three hours later Todd opened the gate to a small, slush covered garden patio with a few tables surrounded by a low, black, ornamental fence. A sandwich board sign on the sidewalk read *Osteria Giambatta*. A heavy, dark paneled oak door stood across from the gate's entrance. Some windows showed no lights on inside and, like the door, were barred.

Todd got halfway to the door when it opened and a dark-complexioned man wearing a dark Armani suit, wrap-around sunglasses, and built like a fullback, came out. "We're closed."

"I know I'm not expected. Perhaps if you explained to my friend that I'm opening new territories he'd be willing to see me off schedule?"

Mason came around the corner, saw Todd talking with the man, and leapt over the fence. Two more men, mates to the first in all ways, came out of the building.

Todd held up his hands. "Everybody relax. We're all friends here. I can wait if this isn't a convenient time. I'm here because I need to up my supply and we could have a problem."

The third man said, "What kind of problem? Competition?"

"More an annoyance. An aggravation."

"Wait here."

A moment later a tall, thin, sartorial, elderly gentleman, with thick black hair with snow white flares at the temples and a pencil mustache came out dabbing his mouth with a silk napkin. He brow lifted and he parted his hands.

The third man, standing behind him, said, "Go ahead."

"Thank you for seeing me without notice and off schedule, sir. I do appreciate it." He handed the first man Caroline's envelope. "First, I'm expanding my territory and would like to establish an inroad before summer hits. I believe what I gave this gentleman is a sufficient down payment for a second, early shipment."

The man opened it, ran his thumb over the bills, nodded.

"The second problem is more delicate. Someone might interfere with my business expansion. I'd appreciate your help." He handed the same man the name and address Mason gave him.

The man read the name and address, nodded.

Todd stood, waiting.

The third man said, "Anything else?"

Todd shook his head. "No, I appreciate any - "

The elderly gentleman turned without speaking and went back inside. The first man walked to the gate and opened it. The third man said, "We'll be in touch."

Outside the fence, Mason unzipped himself and pissed on the gate. "Oh, sorry, should've let us in. I could've used the can."

The three men watched Todd and Mason walk away.

Sunday, 10 February 1974

Pam stood shivering in the slush at the end of the receiving line in the church parking lot. She wore sensible heels, dark blue nylons, matching blazer and skirt, and a lighter blue blouse cinched tight at the neck. Everyone else wore boots and coats, gloves and hats.

But oh, no, not Pam. She was going to show them how much she suffered. Fewer and fewer people stopped to talk with her at the end of service over the past weeks. They stopped caring about her two boys. Didn't they know her little darlings could be lost, might be dead, their little bodies frozen stiff at the bottom of a lake, probably fish food or eaten while still alive by a bear or wolf or coyote or bobcat?

Bill came up beside her. "Pam, you don't belong here. These people are here for a wedding."

She ignored him and walked up to a face she recognized. The woman smiled, excused herself, went inside.

Gardiner's skies cleared momentarily. A shaft of sunlight moved across the parking lot, turned before it reached her, went to the other side, warmed other people. She walked towards it. Clouds gathered, the sunlight hurried away.

"C'mon, Pam. Let's go home."

In the car she adjusted her slip. "Your Mr. Chance has been no help, has he."

"At least I tried. I at least asked for help."

"And the police, too. You wanted them involved and nothing."

"What I want is to have our sons back safe."

"But you know nothing."

"And you do?"

"I know more than you, Mr. William Thompson."

Bill turned to his wife. "What are you talking about, Pam? You know something about our sons? And you haven't told me?"

"You're such a stupid fool, William. Such a stupid, stupid fool."

Bill turned back to the road and sighed. "Yeah, we already did this part. You have anything new to add to this conversation?"

"I've done something."

"Oh? What has the queen deigned provident?"

She smoothed her blouse and straightened the sleeves on her blazer. "Papa and my brothers are going to bring them home."

"What do you mean 'bring them home'? Not 'search for them' or 'find them', you said 'bring them home'. Does your father or brothers know where they are?"

"I don't know. They don't tell me everything."

Bill shook his head to let her words sink in. "What do you mean they don't tell you everything? They've had the boys all this time and now you're telling me this?"

"You don't know anything, Bill Thompson."

"You're as full of bullshit as you claim I am. You don't know where they are, either, and you're hoping Backwoods Bill and the Boys can find them, right?"

"My father and brothers will bring them home."

"When did you learn all this?"

"Today. I talked with Papa today."

"Bullshit."

"You don't talk to me like that."

"Harry and Ed are missing how long and now you call your family to come track them? Oh, big moves, Mrs. Thompson. Big moves. Everybody watch out. Pam's on the case. We're all in trouble now."

They entered the house through the porch. Bill entered first, not even holding the door for her.

Pam picked up the big vase on the table and crashed it over Bill's head. He fell and didn't move.

"How about now, Bill? Am I in trouble now?"

She stepped over him and went into the house. Standing in the kitchen, she made a pot of coffee. It perked in the background as she dialed the phone. "Papa? I need your help. Bill's had an accident."

\\\\\\\\\\

Laurie's door closed without her touching it as she entered her room after her last afternoon shift.

Tim stood there. "You humiliated me."

"What are you doing in here? How did you get in here?"

"Why did you do that? What did I ever do to you?"

"You? You don't have the gonads to do anything to me. You couldn't hurt me if you tried, Mr. Annandale."

"I could love you."

"You? Love?" She held her stomach and laughed. "Your love I don't want. You don't know what love is. Your love's an entrapment, a jail. There's no freedom in your love, there's no caring, no giving, only taking. I've seen what your kind of love does. If your love is anything like your love for your brother Christians, I want none of it."

"You'll be sorry you said that."

"I'll scream if you don't get out of here now. How would you like that? A man in my room and it's not even open dorm? With the door closed?"

"I'll tell them you smuggled me in."

She laughed again. "Yeah, I'll bet I did. All five-four of me hid all six-plus feet of you under my skirt, right?" She opened her door, clenched her fists and shook as she spoke. "Now get out!"

He checked the hallway for open doors to other rooms and made a quick dash to the lobby.

Laurie closed her door. A tremor started in her hands, followed by a sense of ice sliding down her back. Her whole body started shaking. She sat on her bed, put a pencil in her mouth, and lay down. She got out "Should've taken my medication earlier" before her mouth foamed and her eyes rolled up in her head.

When her eyes opened it was dark outside. Her clothes were soaked, her muscles ached, and her beautiful hair matted to her head. She took the pencil from her mouth and ran it through an electric sharpener until no tooth marks remained. "*Mi protector*, I need you."

\\\\\\\\\\

Morelli sat in his unmarked Ford in the West Gardiner service plaza. This late at night anybody planning to party was already up north partying. He made a note in the logbook on the seat beside him and prepared to leave his post for the night.

A midnight blue sedan parked next to him. The driver got out and opened Morelli's passenger door. "Morelli."

Morelli stiffened. "Lieutenant Jamison. I - "

"Relax. Thought I'd stop by. Unofficial. See how you're doing."

"Thanks. I - "

"How's your home life? Pulling double shifts and volunteering for surveillance. Good money, rotten marriage."

"My marriage. I - "

"Yeah, I figured that. Think it'll work out?"

Morelli shrugged.

"Yeah, I figured that too. Paperwork came through last week. Her attorney's asking for alimony right off the top, before you even see it."

"Lieutenant, I'm - "

"Don't worry about it. Happens. You got yourself a lawyer yet?"

"I...no, I - "

Jamison pulled a card from his jacket pocket. "Department's lawyer. She doesn't handle divorces but she knows people who do, and I'm suggesting you get one."

"Sir, I - "

Jamison cleared his throat. "I'm suggesting you get one."

"Yes, sir."

Jamison watched late night drivers hurry from their cars to the plaza's restrooms and walk back, a coffee in hand, their look of relief showing in the plaza's overhead lights. "Ever notice long-distance haulers and truckers never hurry like that?"

"No, I - "

"Ever see them open the door to their rig, empty a coffee cup, then get out and do what they have to do?"

"Yes, I - "

"They piss into the cup they just drank from. Slow or stop that rig when you don't have to, you're spending money should go in your pocket. I knew a driver up in Michigan's UP - ever been there?"

Morelli hesitated. "No, sir. I - "

"Beautiful country. Like Aroostook but with fewer people between the towns. Big mother NORAD base up there. Got an antenna dish so big, you get within five-hundred feet of it and it'll cook you alive when it's operating. How 'bout that, huh?"

"Sir, I - "

"So this driver, he didn't want to stop, didn't want to stop, didn't want to stop. Ended up bursting his bladder. Found him and his rig turned over on the side of the road. ME even said, 'Jesus Christ, motherfucker, hang your dick out the window or piss on the floor, but this? Jesus Christ.'"

Morelli watched Jamison survey the parking lot, the only sound the crinkling of their leather jackets in the cold.

Morelli broke the silence. "Sir, I - "

"Yeah, I know. Enough buddy-buddy with some brass pencil-pusher hasn't sat in a cruiser for a decade, right?"

"Lieutenant, I - "

"You know a trick to good police work? You make things happen. That kid's sneaker you found. We can't tie it to anything. Your report indicates it belonged to one of those Thompson kids. We can't make that connection. We haven't shown it to the parents yet. Without more evidence, we don't want to get their hopes up or cause them pain and suffering for no reason." The lieutenant pushed his Stetson up revealing a high, thoughtful brow. "So my question is, how'd you come up with that?"

Morelli swallowed.

"Yeah, that's what I thought. Now, off the record, you and me, how'd you come up with that?"

"I had some help?"

"Morelli, you're a good officer, you get the job done. I saw those books in your locker. Studying for the sergeant's exam. You know the DEA's looking for good people? I know some folks there. That's where you belong, Tony. Maine's too small for someone like you."

"Lieutenant, I - "

"If I let this go through without some explanation, you'll be passed over this year and stuck in accident investigation until you retire."

"I - "

"So what I need to know is, how'm I going to play this?"

"You won't like it."

"Don't prejudice the jury."

"I know a guy who's good at finding things like this."

"Some of your 'Nam buddies? You were a spook, right?"

"Ranger. Selected for GCATTCS training but they closed the program before I got in. But no, nobody I knew in 'Nam."

"I'm listening."

"I didn't actually call him in. He was where I was and we hooked up."

"Sounds like a date."

"He was with his girl walking in the woods around Parker. I was checking on a cabin vandalization. He found the kid's sneaker."

"Just found it?"

"You're not going to like this."

"He's a psychic? A dowser? The spirit of god led him to it? He talks to angels? I'm thirty years in this business, you think I haven't heard of this kind of thing? Christ, we had a dowser tell us where to dig our well. Got the depth and the number of gallons per second spot on. I'm one-quarter Penobscot for chrissake, you think I haven't seen this kind of shit? So what is it?"

"My dad knew his grandfather back in Mass. Boston, Everett, and State PD's called on the old man once in a while to help them. Met him once as a kid. My dad brought over cannoli as a thank you. I was with him. Saw the grandfather and the kid. My dad said they were always together and the old man was teaching him things."

"And you think the kid's got his grandfather's talent?"

Morelli shrugged.

"He's just there and finds the kid's sneaker. How come he's not a suspect?"

"Solid alibi."

"Reliable?"

"His grandfather sure was."

"What was he doing up here?"

"Visiting his girlfriend's family. They're from Gardiner."

"You trust him?"

Morelli nodded.

"Is he coming back?"

"No idea. We left it I could get in touch with him if I wanted."

Jamison pursed his lips. "This Thompson thing. Every lead anybody gets ends in a hole. Gardiner doesn't want it on their books and they're claiming it goes over county lines so they tossed it up to us." He picked up Morelli's logbook and scanned the night's entries. "There's no evidence of anything interstate so we can't toss it up to the FBI. I'm here because unsolved cases don't help anybody's career." He closed the logbook and put it back on the seat. "Nice entries. Clean. I like that. See if your friend wants to come up again. Unofficial. I was never here."

He opened the car door and put a foot out. "But if he finds anything, I'm your first call. Correct?"

"Correct."

Jamison stopped halfway out the car.

"Correct, sir."

Jamison got in his car and left.

Wednesday, 13 February 1974

Todd sipped his tea and looked out the big front window of Windham Donuts. A jelly cruller rested on a paper plate in front of him. A plastic knife went across the top of the plate and a plastic fork speared the side of the cruller. Artificially reddened jelly oozed out between the fork tines like fresh blood from a deep-fried whale. He stood when Caroline pulled into the parking lot.

He pulled out a seat for her. "Coffee? Tea? Water? Soda? I'm afraid the offerings here are slight. Probably far less than you're used to."

She slid an envelope across the Formica tabletop to him. "Nothing, thanks."

He put it in an inside jacket pocket. "Thanks. I appreciate it. Every little bit helps."

She nodded and focused on the traffic going up and down Rt-1A.

"Checking to see if you were followed?"

She laughed.

"He still doesn't know?"

"Don would never look for me here. If his friends saw me here it'd be for the same reason I'm here. Or something similar. And he's too stupid to hire a detective."

"Can't be the same reason you're here. I don't know any of them."

"What do you do with the money I give you?"

"Originally, to buy things I never had before. One of which was a business education. Then I used it to start a business. Now I'm using it to expand my territory."

"What business are you in, again?"

Todd shook his head. "Oh, nothing much. What they call a startup. Import-Export. That kind of thing."

"Anything else?"

"No."

"Not going to count it?"

"I trust you."

She stood up.

"Leaving so soon?"

She sat again. "Is there something else?"

"You never tell me about yourself. Your family. You have two little boys, correct?"

Caroline's eyes narrowed. "What about them?"

"You never bring them with you. It'd be nice to meet them, say hello."

"You stay away from them." She paused, then lied. "They're with their nanny and she knows where I am."

Todd sipped his tea. "Wow. They have a nanny. That's amazing. I never had a nanny. What's her name?"

"Stephanie. Stephanie Thompson."

Todd took a slow sip. "Must be nice to have a nanny. She take good care of them for you?"

She got up and went out the door. "We're done here."

Todd followed her into the parking lot and waved as she got in her car. "Good seeing you again, Mom. Tell my brothers I said hi."

\\\\\\\\\

Gio walked the dark, unlit paths around campus. Few people walked them during the day, fewer this late at night. Couples, if any, and Gio knew which couples required discretion versus intervention.

Even so, it was a no-win situation. Women who refused their escort's advances thanked Gio when he suddenly appeared. They hurried away and their escorts threatened Gio. Couples who wanted their moments wondered if he would somehow use his nightly knowledge against them.

He chuckled. Only a few people wanted to get to know him when he started school here. Unless they wanted to evangelize him.

But their shallow arguments and irrational reasoning didn't interest him. It became clear most didn't understand their own faith; it was rote, repeated often enough it became true without thinking, a "fish don't know they live in water" kind of thing.

Which was a pity because, as a book of wisdom teachings, the bible was a gem. Much of what his grandfather and others taught him was in its pages.

And if you spent time learning the original languages it was written in? Before politics and fear and egos and agendas took over the translations? My god, the teachings! Amazing!

The campus had been neutral to him at first, an invited outsider, someone to test their evangelical skills on.

Not now, though. Battle lines were being drawn and it didn't matter what he did. A zealous momentum was building and he was its focus.

He turned towards the student center. The lounge lights were dimmed but he saw one petite figure - Laurie - wearing a green house-cleaning apron, her hands busy in the pockets placing cans and dust rags just so.

She pushed a vacuum back and forth, its big janitorial canister followed her, rolling every few feet to catch up, its cord an umbilical feeding an unwanted child.

Gio walked up and tapped on the glass.

No response.

He made a fist and banged.

Nothing.

Lower-Center-Relax-Breathe.

Laurie.

Her head shot up and she looked straight at him, startled. A smile came upon recognition. She waved him in and shut the vacuum off.

"You don't need my permission to come in, Gio. The lounge doesn't close until eleven-thirty on weeknights."

"Didn't want you to have to clean things twice."

"Anything I can do for you, *hombre mágico*?"

"Just need a friendly face for a change. For a Christian school, there are more Januses here than in ancient Greece."

"I was going to tell you."

"Tell me what?"

"Tim called somebody about you just before noon. Coogan? Kagan? I was washing the bathroom on his floor and heard him in the phonebooth. He didn't even close the door. Sounded proud when he talked. Almost boastful."

"What did he say?"

"Something about you and some boys, I think. And being pregnant."

"Do I look pregnant?"

She laughed. "Did you get someone pregnant?"

"Et tu, Laurie?"

She shook her head. "Just...curious."

"If I was going to sleep with anybody on this campus, you'd be the first to know."

She blushed.

"How are your classes going?"

"I made Dean's list again. Is that what you mean?"

"You've made Dean's list every semester you've been here, haven't you?"

"So?"

"So how come your work-study is doing janitorial work? How come you're not helping some professor's research? How come you're not getting field assignments? How come you're not getting internships up and down 128?"

She shrugged.

"How come the most work-study I can get is grounds work or hauling trash or being night watchman?"

"I don't - "

"How come we get the jobs nobody else wants? Is it because of our names? The color of our skin?"

"I asked for this job."

Gio pulled back. "You wanted to do janitorial work?"

"I wanted something that let my mind relax. I know I'm not wanted here." She snickered. "Except as somebody's trophy."

"Laurie, I'm so sorry. I - "

"Don't be. This is where I am now, not forever. I'm here because I'm supposed to be. Learn what I can. And not just in classes. This isn't a curse, Gio. It's a blessing."

He shook his head.

She laughed. "Besides, there'll always be a need for good janitors, not always for good sociologists. I'm learning a trade."

The world shimmered. Gio watched her graduate, find a job, marry, have children, then a bright light that was not his shimmer.

He took the vacuum from her hands, pulled her towards him, let his shimmer envelop her like wings, and kissed her.

He let her go and she drew herself back to him. "Don't stop on my account. What brought that on?"

He held her lightly, feeling her pulse, her breathing, smelling her scent change from friend to woman. "You're a good teacher. Thank you." He let her go.

She smoothed out rills in her apron. "Let me know if there's anything else you'd like to learn."

"How to be a better friend. That's enough."

"Keep telling me the truth and I'll be your friend. If I don't have a chance with you, Gio, so be it. But if I ever do..."

"You'll be the first to know."

In plain clothes and dressed for the slopes, Morelli could pass for a typical rich tourist.

Until you saw his car. His winter beater car. Anybody raised in New England - okay, the real New England. The Boston-Worcester-Springfield-Pittsfield line. Basically north of I90 - knows you have two cars: your summer car you put all the insurance on and your winter, beater car you put minimal insurance on because it already looks like it came from a demolition derby.

But nobody selling would sell to somebody driving a winter beater. Winter beaters are a sign the person is smart but penniless. What the Brits call "Posh voice, no cash."

So he'd start his eight hour shift three hours early to beat the dealers and left three hours after they'd left.

Tobey Harding drove up in his hot pink '63 Cadillac De Ville. He frequently told Morelli "Just 'cause it's a beater doesn't mean it has to be ugly."

"Yeah, but those rear wings could be used as outriggers on most cars."

"Jealous?"

Today's meeting, though. Tobes' message mentioned the Ghost Children tourists were talking about.

Harding came in without looking at him, got a cheeseburger and a can of Coke, looked around, and walked up to Morelli's table. "Mind if I join you?"

Morelli sat with his back to a wall, facing the crowd, and looked over the top of the Bangor Daily News. "Help yourself."

His back to the travelers, Harding talked low and only spoke when he took small bites from burger, keeping it close to his mouth.

"So what about it?"

"What are you talking about, Tobey?"

"Oh, come on. You don't read the newspaper? You don't listen to the radio? You don't watch TV?"

Morelli folded the paper in half and put it beside him on the bench seat. "No, I don't believe bullshit stories from out-of-staters who think they can flash a wad of cash and get anything they want."

"What if somebody got pictures?"

"You got pictures?"

"No, I said what if somebody did have pictures?"

"Until you got pictures nobody's moving on this. We already sent two cruisers out and found nothing. Besides, the reports are too far apart to be taken seriously. So far no locals have reported anything, everything's coming in from hopped up tourists, so the brass is dismissing these as pranks."

"You found that kid's sneaker, though."

"Yeah?"

"And remember that wreck we found? The one with no registration tags? Not even on the engine block?"

"Yeah?"

"I'm just saying, it's gotta be something, right?"

"Okay, you find somebody with pictures and I'll make something happen. But nobody's got pictures, right?"

"Christ, Tony. You think everybody has a camera in their pocket with a strobe that can take pictures at night? Something 'right handy they can just pull and shoot away with? C'mon."

"That's what I thought."

"I'm looking, though. I can feel it's something. I'm looking."

"Good. Good."

Tobey wiped his mouth, finished his Coke, and left.

Friday, 15 February 1974

Gio's dorm phone rang ten times. One of his dorm brothers picked it up. "Excuse me, what?" Pause. "Could you say that again, please?" Pause. "What?" followed by "Wait a moment, please."

His dorm brother tapped on his door. "I think it's for you, Gio. It sounds Italian and it sounds like 'Gio's my fortunate favorite' but I know I got the 'Gio' part right."

"Thanks."

"I'll wait in case they want somebody else. You're studying. I'm taking a break."

Gio closed the door on the phonebooth. The inner light came on with an audible click. Gio looked up at the light and opened the door. The light went out with an audible click. Close the door, light on, audible click.

His dorm brother pointed at the light. "You never noticed that before? Been like that for about two weeks now."

Gio put the phone to his ear. "Hello?"

A deep, resonant, clear voice. "*Gio Fortuna, per favore.*"

Gio opened the door. Click. He looked up at the light before nodding to his dorm brother. "Yeah, it's for me." Then into the phone, "Who's calling, please?"

"*Sei tu, Gio?*"

"Uncle Nicky?"

"*Posso offrirti la cena?*"

"It's a little early for dinner, isn't it, Uncle Nicky?"

"*Posso offrirti un pranzo tardivo?*"

"Okay. A late lunch. Sure. When will you be here?"

"*Adesso sono fuori nella mia macchina.*"

Gio hung up the phone and went to the front door. A stretch burgundy Lincoln Town Car, thick-tired and quietly rumbling due to an oversized engine, parked at the curb. Thin plumes of exhaust escaped dual mufflers. A darkened rear window lowered and Gio's Uncle Nick, sartorial as only Italy's finest could sartorize, waved his car phone at his nephew. "Operator says its first time she placed a call from a car to a payphone." He put the phone back up to his face. "Thank you, operator. I have my party now."

Gio smiled and waved. "Give me a minute."

In the car, two men sat opposite Gio and his uncle. One tapped the privacy panel and the limo headed for Rt128 with no sense of motion.

"How you doing, nephew?"

"I'm hungry now. Does that count?"

Nick laughed.

"Am I in trouble, Uncle Nicky?"

"Never. You couldn't get in trouble if you tried."

"Then how come you spoke Italian on the phone?"

"Because nobody at a Ramsey College would speak Italian and I wanted you to know it's important."

"Okay. I'm not in trouble and it's important. What is it?"

"You got a girl?"

"Yes, I got a girl. What is this, Uncle Nicky?"

"We're going to a little place in Gloucester. Lots of good, small places to eat there."

"Uncle Nicky?"

"I said you're not in trouble. You don't trust your family?"

"Implicitly." He nodded at the two men sitting across from him. "And I still want to know what's going on."

The two men stared straight ahead as if Nick and Gio weren't there.

"You know, you were your Grandpa's favorite."

The doors locked automatically.

"You stay calm real good."

"I had a good teacher."

Nick nodded. "I don't want you nervous, so I'll tell you; you have an enemy who wants to be my friend."

"I do?"

"Fellow up in Maine. Doing some business expansion. Wants me to supply him product."

"I don't know anybody doing business in Maine, Uncle Nicky."

"I know. You're a good boy. If you weren't, you'd be working for me." Nick cocked his head towards Gio and smiled. "You want to work for me?"

"Uncle Nick."

"Can't hurt to ask. You never know. By the way, you got a refrigerator back in that house you're staying in?"

"Yeah, why?"

"Just asking. I like to know things. Now this fellow in Maine. You don't know him. Not by name. Yet. He says you're going to cause him trouble. That's going to cause me trouble. So I need a favor from you. You want to do your Uncle Nick a favor?"

"You know what I will do, and you know what I won't do."

Nick shook his head and waved his hands back and forth in front of him as if signalling No Foul in a game. "Nothing like that. You think I'd ask you to do something like that?"

"You said it couldn't hurt to ask. Just making sure."

"You're a clever boy, Gio."

"I had a good teacher."

Nick chuckled. "Yes, you did. Anyway, I need you to back off a bit. I know you got a girl up there." He nodded to one of the two men. The man reached into his coat and came up with a roll of hundred-dollar bills. "You take her out, enjoy yourself, buy her nice things. You still driving that old car?"

"Bessie? Yes. Why?"

Nick nodded a second time. Another roll of hundred-dollar bills came out. "Buy yourself a new car. Buy her one, too. A gift. From your Uncle Nicky for doing him a favor."

"I need to know what exactly I'm doing and who I'm doing it to, don't I?"

Nick sighed. "Yeah, you do. It goes like this." Nick explained.

Gio listened. The world shimmered. Clouds turned into puzzle pieces and made pictures in the sky. "Uncle Nick, if this is who I think it is, you know he kidnapped two little boys? Maybe done more than kidnap them, if you get my meaning. And they're civilians. Not involved in any business at all, not them, not their family."

Nick sat back. He looked out his window and remained silent for several miles up Rt 128. "Gio, I need you to do something else for me, and don't worry, you're not going to hurt anybody or get hurt by anybody. This is something your Grandpa did for me a few times."

Gio pulled back.

"I swear, Gio. On Larry and Annette's and Mary's lives, I swear."

"How are my cousins?"

"I need you to look. No, not look. That's not how your Grandpa said it. He said - "

"*Ascolta.*"

"*Si! Grazie!*"

It was Gio's turn to watch the traffic. They entered the Grant Circle Rotary and he shook his head. "I don't know if I can anymore, Uncle Nicky."

"Just so I know, you won't or you can't? Or you just haven't done it in a long time?"

"Door number 3. It seems everybody wants me to get back into it."

"Not important what everybody else wants. Even me! What do you want?"

"You want to know my first answer, Uncle Nick?"

Nick mugged at him. "Oh, this has got to be serious. I'm Nick now? Not Nicky? *Qual è il problema, Gio?*"

"I don't want to lose my girl."

Nick considered. "She that special?"

Gio nodded.

"You think she won't understand?"

Gio rolled his eyes. "Uncle Nick, I don't understand. How'm I supposed to explain something to her I don't understand myself?"

Nick shrugged. "I can listen. I can give you my shoulder. I can help if you get in trouble. That's all, though. Your Grandpa kept his life - your life! - separate from the rest of the family. He'd help us if we were in trouble but we never got to ask what he did or how he did it." He shrugged a second time.

"What do you need me to do?"

"You say my friend's kidnapped two boys. Okay, I believe you. I don't know that he has, but he and his playmate are scum-sucking bastards so I believe you. That's something they would do."

Nick paused as the limo pulled into a restaurant's parking lot. "But you say these boys' family isn't involved."

Gio held up a finger. "I know their father's not involved. Their mother, I'm not sure about."

Nick nodded. "Ah. Okay. I need to be sure about this. Could you be sure about this? Could you *videre? Ascolta?* Let me know if that's true or not?"

"That's it? Nothing else?"

"I think I know the answer and you make me doubt. I know you don't want to know my business, but I'm really like any other businessman. I provide services and consumables. They are premium quality so I get a good price. Soon as the government figures out how to tax what I do and who to bribe in the church so people can be forgiven for their sins, I'm out of business. I stay in business by knowing as much as I can about everything I touch and everything that touches me. *Capire?*"

Gio nodded.

"So you let me know who's involved and who isn't. That's all I want. Okay by you?" Nick held out his hand.

Gio shook it. "Okay by me."

The moon's last quarter shown, earth shine illuminating the rest, and rested straight ahead in the sky as Gio and Jess drove across the Piscataqua River Bridge from New Hampshire to Maine, inviting them into the mythic.

"Everything okay, Princess? You've been awfully quiet."

"Stephanie told me what happened a couple of weeks back."

"I can already tell this is going to be good."

"Would you help me if I got pregnant?"

"How come we keep covering the same ground all the time?"

"It's important. Would you help me?"

"It's important? You think it's important." He pulled into the breakdown lane, stopped, and put his arms around her.

"What are you doing?"

"This is important. Right now. This. Want to know what else is important? Will it be me or someone else doing this to you in five months? Five years? How about fifty? Whose hand will you hold when your daughters graduate high school? College? Whose bed will you sit beside until the coma passes? Whose face will be the last you see at night and the first in the morning? Those are important questions, Jess. Ask about this moment going forward, something real, now, something in your hands, not something that might never come to pass."

"I didn't know you thought about such things. Do you want that with me?"

"I want you in the worst way. And please don't use that 'standing on our heads in a hammock' line, okay?"

They drove in silence until the other side of York.

Jess tapped on the passenger window. "Is it true? You can tell the future?"

"I can tell the future lots of things. Does it listen, though? That's the important question."

"Stop kidding around. This is important. Can you tell the future?"

"What did she say happened?"

"How come she's afraid of you?"

"Are you afraid of me?"

"Should I be?"

"Jess, have I ever done anything to make you afraid? Have I ever hurt you? Have I ever lied to you?"

"Are you sleeping with Rachel?"

He watched the moon shift position as he headed north towards Portland. "You drink poison and call it wine."

"Are you?"

"When did I join the cast of a soap opera?"

She punched his arm.

"That's the Jess I know and love."

"Answer me, goddammit."

"First, I'm not sleeping with Rachel. Or anybody. Only you."

"How do you know what's going on with Harry and Ed?"

"Because…" Gio watched the moon. "Because I know things. Weren't you the one who told me to practice these things? Remember? That whole 'Go wide' conversation the last time we were up here?"

"What do you know?"

Gio turned the heat up in the car. "Things I shouldn't know. Things about people. Private things."

"I asked you what you knew about me before and you never answered. Care to answer me now? What private things do you know about me?"

"Only what you want me to know about you."

"So people can block you? Stop you from finding things out somehow?"

"More like I can tell when I'm not supposed to know something, when I'm supposed to stop looking, when I'm close to something people don't want me to know, so I stop."

"You stop?"

"Yeah, it's another of my Grandfather's things: Do not go where you are not invited."

"But you stop. People don't stop you. So you could find out anything you want?"

"That's not how it works."

"Okay, how does it work?"

"You ever go shopping?"

"What do you mean, do I ever go shopping? Of course I go shopping. We've gone shopping. Why are you changing the subject?"

"I'm not. You go shopping. You have a list. The things on that list are things you know you want. Probably most of the things on the list are things you've purchased before, right?"

"Where is this going?"

"But let's say a friend wants you to pick something up for them, something you've never seen or heard of before. Say I take you into Boston's North End and ask you to pick me up some wrapped prosciutto - "

"What's prosciutto?"

"Exactly. You can be standing right in front of it but if you don't know what it is, you have no idea what you're looking at. It's like that. I have to have some idea of what I'm looking at in order to know what something is."

"Is that why you study so much? And so many different things? And why you're always asking people questions about things? Even the stupidest, silliest things?"

"Yes."

"So you'll know what you're looking at?"

"You are a brilliant, brilliant woman. You know that?"

"Yeah, I'm an enlightened *Bayla*. And being built like a brick shithouse helps."

Gio shrugged and nodded. "Well, it doesn't hurt. It's how you got my attention."

"You mean when you offered me a ride during that rainstorm? You kept your eyes on mine the entire time. I watched you. You kept your eyes on the road or on my face. How did I get your attention?"

"It was a warm fall day and a sudden downpour. You wore sandals, cutoffs, and white and blue t-shirt with a kind of cloud pattern on it.

You carried a notebook and a text entitled *An Introduction to Human Psychology*. You could have run for cover and didn't."

"You have a good memory. So what?"

"You ran with your notebook and textbook over your head. I stopped beside you and offered you a ride."

"Yeah?"

"You held your notebook and textbook in front of you. But I never took my eyes off yours the entire time, right?"

"Right."

"Then how'd I know the title of your book?"

"You're a shit, you know that?"

"Decided right there and then I wanted to be your t-shirt."

She punched him.

Gio kept his eyes on the traffic in front of them. "There's two people in the front seat of the car about to pass us. A man is driving. He's wearing a sport coat, looks tweedish, could be part of a suit. He doesn't have a tie on, though. The woman's wearing a dress coat, open to show a white frilly-front blouse and some kind of jewelry - a cameo, maybe? - at her neck. There are two kids in the back seat leaning against each other asleep."

"You have amazing peripheral vision."

"And that's how you caught my attention."

She punched his arm again.

"That's the woman I love. By the way, you caught my attention because you were studying psychology. You know I meant because you were studying psychology, right?"

She massaged his arm. "Do you love me, really?"

He glanced at her hand stroking where she punched him. "Lower."

She dropped her voice half an octave. "Do you love me, really?"

He laughed. "Yes. And you're intelligent. And you have an amazing figure. And you make me laugh."

"We've done that one before." She sat back. "So what can you know that I don't care if you know?"

"Easy stuff. Simple stuff. Like when you're going to have your period. When you're lonely. When you've played too much tennis and need a rubdown. Where your body aches after you swim."

"Would you know if I slept with someone else?"

"Do we have to go back there?"

"Would you?"

"You wouldn't. And if you did, I hope you'd tell me. Before."

"But would you know without my telling you?"

He shook his head. "Possibly. You'd smell different to me. You wouldn't smell like my Jess."

"You can smell me?"

"Of course I can smell you. Everyone can smell everyone else. That's why there's a perfume and deodorant industry. I pay attention to what I smell, that's all. And I call it 'smell'. I have no idea what it really is."

"Like using Bella's nose?"

He corrected her. "That was borrowing Bella's nose. Like that. And different."

"You serious about this?"

"Stuff like this is in every culture throughout history. If it wasn't, the *Rebbe* and I wouldn't have talked through the night."

"Would you know if I was going to sleep with someone else?"

"You planning to?"

"You don't trust me?"

"What's going on here, Jess? What happened to my enlightened *Bayla*? Remember you asked me to show you what I can do? Didn't your grandmother ever tell you to be careful what you ask for?"

"My grandmother died in a concentration camp."

"My grandfather told me if people learned what you can do they'll hunt you down and kill you."

"Now you're saying the Holocaust was to get rid of witches? All the Jews knew black magic? Is that what it was?"

He turned away. "What do you want from me, Jess?"

"I want to know if you'll ever hurt me. I want to know if you'll ever lie to me."

"Because you think I would?"

A tear slid down her cheek. "I don't know."

"As long as you have doubt, as long as that is your fear, leave me now. Relationships based on fear are never happy ones."

"Pop really likes you."

"He's a wise, perceptive man."

"But you said we're not going to stay together."

"Self-fulfilling prophecy, it seems."

"I want to stay together."

Shimmer.

"Yes, you do."

"What are you doing?"

"The real question is can you be with someone you won't always understand?"

She leaned into the windshield and looked for the moon.

"Or would you rather have someone whose sanity you're always sure of?"

She put her hands between Gio and the dash lights.

He caught her scent of fear and took his eyes off the road for a moment. "Perhaps someone who doesn't glow in the dark?"

\\\\\\\

Sam and Bella came out of the house to greet them in the driveway. Bella passed Jess and romped around Gio. "How's my girl? How's my special, good girl?"

"How does he do that without treats in his hands?"

Jess shrugged.

Gio lifted her laundry bag out of the rear seat. "I'll take these in."

Sam watched Gio and Bella go in through the garage. He turned to Jess. "What did you two argue about?"

Jess looked up at him.

"Must have been a pretty bad one."

Jess shrugged.

"You found out he's antisemitic? What?"

"He loves me."

Sam watched his daughter. "Yeah, I can see how that might upset things."

"He's different, Pop."

Sam nodded. "Must be. He's the first one you've brought home I give a damn about."

"You really like him?"

"We all do. What happened?"

She shook her head. "I wouldn't know how to begin."

"Because he can see the future? Your future? Because he touches people and heals them? Because he knows where to dig a well? Because he knows things about you you don't know about yourself? Because he's a *mazek*."

"You know?"

"The *Rebbe* said something about it."

"What? When? Why didn't you tell me?"

"The morning after he and Gio marathoned. Early. He woke me and asked me to pray with him. But he didn't want to pray."

"Oh?"

Sam shook his head. "He told me what to prepare for." He lifted Jess's face so their eyes met. "He told me what to prepare you for."

"Prepare me for what?"

"Ben Zev used an old word. He had to explain it to me. I'd only heard it once or twice before. He said Gio's a *mascha'ak*, literally a messenger but more than that. Ben Zev said Gio carries messages between the worlds."

Jess smirked at her father. "Which worlds? Good and evil? This world and the next? Light and Dark?"

"The prophets were *mascha'ak*."

"I thought we were Reformed Jews. Ben Zev is Orthodox, isn't he?"

Sam affected a thick Yiddish accent. "So we don't know a *Tzaddikim* when it comes to us?" He dropped the accent. "He's Hasidic and we listen to everybody." He paused. "He wants you to know what life with

Gio might be like going in. He asked me, 'You think Jessica is ready to be the wife of a prophet?'"

Jess rolled her eyes. "Again with the Jessica."

Sam ignored her. "Better she knows now rather than she ever wants to cut his hair.'"

"Gio's strong, he's not blind."

"I'm just the messenger, Daughter."

"The *mascha'ak*."

"This time, yes."

"Jesus Christ, Pop."

"Ben Zev said you should be honored such a *kluger mentsh* is interested in you."

"This is way too much for me right now. Does the *Rebbe* plan on spending his life with Gio?"

Sam laughed.

"Gio said the *Rebbe* told him he has a lot of decisions to make."

"Funny. Ben Zev said the same thing about you."

Saturday, 16 February 1974

Sam, Gio, and Bella played fetch in the backyard. Bella kept bringing her frisbee back to Gio and Sam kept shaking his head in mock disgust. "How come you never bring your laundry up, Gio? We really don't mind if you bring it home with you."

Gio tossed the frisbee and Bella snatched it out of the air. "Home?"

"Did I say 'home'? I meant 'our home'. Jess's home. Here. Where we live."

Bella dropped her frisbee in front of Gio and waited for him to throw it. "Part of the family now, am I?"

"Depends. It's late in life to be circumcised…"

Jess joined them with a cup of coffee in hand. "I already told you he is, Pop."

Sam whirled. "Oy meyn Got, Daughter! Shame in public you say such a thing!"

She took one of Gio's arms in hers, leaned against him, looked up into his face and batted her eyelashes at him. "Oh, father. He is the man of my dreams. Please say yes when he asks if he may have me." She leaned into him and mock whispered, "Don't you love it when he goes all Yiddish on you?"

Gio laughed. "Am I being set up? 'Cause if I am, I'll need two goats and two good cows. A couple of hens, too. Good layers, if you please."

Sam went back in the house. "I look like Tevye now?"

A raven landed in the backyard, stared at Gio, and flew off to the northeast.

Bella barked and Gio threw her frisbee. "Your father likes me."

The raven flew back, landed, looked at Gio, cawed, and flew off to the northeast.

"Very much so. So does my mom, my brother, my sisters. The *Rebbe*."

"I'm not Jewish."

The raven returned a third time. It landed, stared at Gio, and stamped a claw.

Who are you? What do you want from me?

The raven cawed and flew to the northeast but didn't return.

"Doesn't matter."

"Ben Zev is your *Rebbe*?"

"One of many. More a family friend."

"None of you really know me."

"I know you."

"You just like the way I kiss."

"They trust me."

"I love you."

"You should kiss me again, just so I can be sure."

A Maine State Police cruiser pulled up the driveway. Bella sat at their feet between them and the cruiser. It parked next to Bessie and Tony Morelli got out.

"Am I interrupting anything?"

Jess threw her hands up and went inside.

"Uh. Sorry."

"How'd you know I was here?"

"You passed me on 295 North. The mint condition green '64 Mercury Comet caught my attention. You don't see many of those around these parts. I called in the plate and there you were."

"Should've waved."

"Couldn't. I was off duty, heading home in an unmarked car, undercover." Morelli explained Posh-voice-No-cash to Gio.

Gio listened. "So you could flush them out if you flashed some cash?"

"Pretty much."

Gio got his jacket out of the car and pulled out the two bankrolls Uncle Nicky gave him. "These help?"

"Jesus Christ. Where'd you get these?"

"You don't want to know."

"From your uncle?"

"You know about Uncle Nicky?"

"You didn't notice this patch on my sleeve with the Maine State Police logo?"

"Use it as you see fit."

"How'm I going to explain this in my report?"

"I already asked you to keep me out of it."

"That's why I stopped by. Want to talk to my lieutenant?"

"That's keeping me out of it?"

"It turns out we got two different forces at work. Serious drugs are coming up from the south, weed and the like are coming down from the north."

"How can you grow pot up here in winter?"

"Greenhouses. Hidden under blueberry bushes growing on terraces. Right now they're each working to be the majority supplier so they're not getting along. Sooner or later someone with good business sense will move in, unite them, or side with one and destroy the other."

Gio snorted at Morelli's mentioning "good business sense."

You better not be playing me, Uncle Nicky.

He dismissed the thought. *Mia Familia* was many things and among the many was a high sense of honor. Plus getting Gio involved when he clearly said 'No' was against all the rules.

But that did explain why Uncle Nick wanted to be sure of his information.

So long as you keep me out of it, Uncle.

"If I can get a promise to keep your name out of it, will you talk to him?"

"I've already been set up once today."

"Huh?"

"Nothing. Jess and I are getting serious."

"Lucky you. She's a smart, beautiful woman. You have a problem with that?"

"Having a smart, beautiful woman get serious with me? No. But if I'm truly my grandfather's son, what kind of man am I to commit a woman to a life like that?"

Morelli stared at him. "Son? You said you're your grandfather's son. You mean grandson, right? And it's her decision to make, not yours. All you can do is give her the best information possible to work with. The rest is up to her. Besides, did somebody have to counsel your grandmother before she married your granddad? They were from the old country, she must have known what he was about. Or had a good idea, anyway." He scratched Bella behind the ears. "Unless the real problem is you're afraid of getting serious, or afraid you'll lose her, she'll decide no, she's not up for this. Is that it?"

"Aren't you the caring big brother."

"You're an idiot, Gio. She's smart and look at her face when she's around you. She loves you. You know how seldom that happens in life? Really happens? Jesus Christ, Gio, if she were fifteen years older I'd be after her."

Gio stared at Bella and nodded.

"You're scared? Of love? Of commitment? Do you honest to god think the next one'll be better? Than her? And I've seen her in action. She can hit. You think she's going to let you get away with any shit?"

"Okay, alright."

"Gio, tell her everything. Tell her you're afraid. Tell her what you're afraid of. Talk. God dammit, talk. Tell her how you feel. Tell her if you're unsure and what you're unsure about."

"You don't know - "

"What can slip from your hands when you're not paying attention? I sure'n fuck do. Tell her the truth, Gio. Let her decide. She may need time. Be patient. You don't let the good ones get away."

Gio raised his voice. "Okay. Alright. Enough."

"Sorry."

Bella barked at the wind and Gio focused on her. "How's my girl? How's my good Bella?"

"We cool, Gio?"

"Sounds like you're talking from experience."

"I am unfortunately."

"Set it up with your lieutenant. I'll do what I can. By the way, what's in that direction?" Gio pointed the direction the raven flew.

"That direction? I-95 North. Augusta, Waterville, eventually Bangor and the eastern half of the state. Why?"

"Why is it important?"

"Depends what we're talking about. To me? Because probably seventy-five, eighty percent of what comes into the state in winter ends up in the ski towns. Waterville's a ski town. Lots of areas have Waterville as their hub."

"I have to go there. Waterville, I think. This weekend, sometime."

Morelli handed Gio his card. "You call me before you head up there, okay?"

"Why?"

He put his arm around Gio and hugged. "Because I never had a little brother and I don't want to lose the one I got."

The sun glinted off a passing tow truck's dome lights. "Who's truck is that?"

"I missed it. Trouble?"

"No idea. Somebody's tow truck."

"Probably somebody can't start their car, somebody blew a tire." Morelli opened the door to his cruiser. "You call me before you go, okay?"

Gio played with Bella while Morelli drove off. Sam came around the side of the house. "Bella. Come."

Bella sat on Gio's boots.

"How do you get her to do that?"

"I'm good with animals?"

"Gio, my family likes you. I know we haven't spent much time together and I want you to know we like you."

"Thank you, sir."

"Cut the 'sir' crap. Did I see you hand that patrolman money?"

"If you were looking when I did it, yes, I'm sure you did."

Sam scratched Bella's head. "Are you in any trouble?"

"No, sir. Sam. Mr. Rosen. No."

"Is my daughter going to safe with you?"

"She is my greatest concern."

"That's nice and it doesn't answer my question. Is Jess going to be safe around you?"

Gio cleared his throat. Bella got up and circled the two men. "If I thought something I did, was doing, or will do would harm or hurt her in any way, neither she nor you nor your family would ever see me again."

"Good answer. Just so you'll know, Jess can take of herself if she has to. I'd rather she never has to."

"You teach her to hit like that?"

"Yeah, she packs a wallop. Got her brother crying more than once."

"I'm sure."

Sam put his arm around Gio's shoulder and guided him towards the house. "Now that's out of the way, what are your intentions for my daughter?"

\\\\\\\

Gio, Jess, and Bella pulled into the Thompsons' driveway and parked beside Bill's F150 in front of the garage. Pam hurried out dressed as if spring cleaning. "What do you want here?"

"Hello, Mrs. Thompson. You okay?"

Pam put a hand over her chest. "Why wouldn't I be?"

"You're panting and sweating. Do you need some help moving something?"

"I told you before we don't need your help."

Gio nodded. "I understand. I don't want to bother you. May we come in, though? Just to share what I've learned. You can do what you want with it and I'll be gone."

Pam's eyes narrowed. Her nostrils flared as if beating with her heart. "Okay. But you keep that dog out of my house."

Jess let Bella sniff around and followed Gio inside.

He glanced out the back kitchen window to the edge of the Thompsons' backyard. Two men huddled around a piece of equipment at the treeline at the far end of the yard, a gas can and oil can on the ground beside them. A pair of binoculars stood by the sink. Gio lifted them and focused on the men. "Mr. Thompson's not around?"

A moment later the equipment fired up. One of the men pulled a fallen branch out of the forest's edge and fed it to the machine. It ground the branch and wood chips flew everywhere.

Gio put the binoculars down. "Nice woodchipper." The chipper quieted and the two men high-fived each other.

"Bill left a few days ago on business. I don't know when he'll be back."

Jess looked out the front kitchen window to the head of the driveway. Bella pawed the asphalt by the garage doors, sniffed, pawed again. "Isn't that his pickup?"

"He flew. I drove him to the airport. I left his truck outside so I could clean out the garage." Pam followed Jess's gaze. "What's your dog doing?"

"Sniffing your garage door. Probably picked up a coyote or bear scent. Is that a problem?"

The two men started walking back to the house. Gio shimmered. An image dropped out of the sky onto the two men. Stephanie sat between them.

Stephanie's uncles? Where's their truck? Where're their rifles?

"She gonna scratch the doors. Put her back in the car."

"Yeah, sorry to trouble you, Mrs. Thompson. We'll leave."

The porch door to the garage opened. Heavy, limping footsteps moved through the porch and opened the kitchen door. Gio's nose crinkled. The man stood half a head taller than Gio and about as broad, with a heavy salt&pepper beard completely covering his face. He swayed a bit, unsteady on his feet, the right leg a few inches shorter than the left due to a crick at the knee forcing the man to walk tip-toe on his right. He held a three-quarters empty bottle of Dewars in his hand that aided his unsteadiness.

His gaze went from Gio to Jess to Pam and back to Gio. "You got a problem, Little Girl?"

"No, Papa."

He held the bottle out to Gio. "Want some?"

"No thanks. I'm driving." Gio glanced out the kitchen window. Stephanie's uncles were halfway to the house.

The man laughed, deep and resonant.

"These are Stephanie's friends, Papa. They're leaving."

Gio took Jess's arm, steered her past the swaying man and out to Bessie. "Bella, in."

Bella licked Gio's face from the backseat, then Jess's. Jess scratched the shepherd's muzzle. "Who the hell was Jeremiah Johnson?"

Gio backed all the way to the road. "Pam's father, I believe. Did you see the two men in the backyard?"

"What two men?"

"I didn't think so."

"Yeah, well, Jeremiah was drunk."

"Never let good Scotch go to waste."

"What's he doing here besides drinking?"

"You didn't notice what he was wearing under his jacket?"

Jess shook her head.

"You didn't notice his boots?"

"No, why?"

"Bella did." Gio reached in back and scratched the dog's head. "Good girl, Bella. Good girl."

"So what did you and Bella see?"

"He wore a butcher's apron. There were bloodstains on his boots. Bella smelled blood."

\\\\\\\\\

Lyndon and Towne drove past the Thompson home as Gio, Jess, and Bella got in Bessie. "Isn't that Chance? With his girlfriend? What was her name?"

Towne shrugged.

"Don't you take notes?"

"My partner takes notes."

"I'm your partner."

"Ten-four that."

Lyndon pulled out a pocket notebook and flipped through it while he drove.

Towne watched Lyndon flip pages. "What language that in?"

"English."

Towne pointed. "Don't look like English. Looks like, what's that called? Arab? You an arab? Lyndon don't sound like an arab name."

Lyndon closed his notebook and put it back inside his jacket's inner pocket. "It's shorthand. Ever seen shorthand?"

"You don't want me to see your notes?"

"I don't have time to explain them to you."

"Because they're not in shorthand?"

"You said they didn't look like they're written in English. You've never seen shorthand? You never talked up somebody's secretary?"

"You learned that arab writing talking up some secretary you knew?"

"I know some shorthand. Picked it up when I was on the force in Montana."

"I thought you were from Minnesota."

Towne reached across Lyndon's jacket. "Let me see your notebook, see if I can read it."

Lyndon knocked his hand away. "I'm using it now for a side gig I'm doing."

"We're not supposed to do any unapproved side jobs. Sarge know about this?"

"Nobody knows about this. I want to keep it that way. I'm doing some PI work, security work, in my off hours, okay? Sometimes it overlaps with the job."

"How much you make doing this private PI security shit?"

"Not much."

"You need a partner?"

"No."

"You know you can get fired for doing unapproved side jobs?"

"That's why I want it kept quiet."

"That's why you need a partner."

Lyndon gritted his teeth.

Towne sat back and pulled the front flap of his winter-gear hat down over her eyes. "Ten-four that."

\\\\\\\\

Guy Rigaux watched Gio back out as Meville and Xavier came through the porch to the kitchen. He wiped his mouth and beard with the hand holding the bottle.

Pam pushed him back on to the porch and had him stand on a large plastic sheet she used for replanting. "Papa! You're shaking! You cold? Take your clothes off. I'll get you a towel and run you a bath."

Guy kept his eyes on Gio and pointed with the bottle. "Boys, you know that man?"

Meville picked up the binoculars. "It's him, Xav. Look." He handed the glasses to his brother. Xav looked and nodded. Meville took them back and looked again. "He's the man Stephanie told us about."

Pam took the bottle from Guy's hand. "Papa, what's going on?"

"Your man had good tools. How come he never built nothing?"

Xavier nodded at the retreating car. "You know him, Papa?"

"I knew the boy. Long time ago. If that's him. He came up with his old man. Remember we run traps on Indian land?"

"That's him?"

"That's the son. Or grandson, maybe."

Meville sat in a chair. "He going to fuck us up again, Papa?"

"He and that squaw girl he was with."

"They turned that bear on you, Papa."

Xavier nodded. "Came out of nowhere, that one did. Couldn't even get our rifles up. Seemed it knew what rifles were, too. Went right for them first off, broke them clean in half."

"And left me with half a leg."

Pam watched her father. "You want that bath?"

"Got more to do. Meville? Xavier? He's ready. Good thing you dragged him out here, Pam. He stayed frozen. Easier to handle."

"You took too long getting here. Somebody could've asked questions. That Chance fellow asked questions."

Guy Rigaux coughed, spit on the plastic around him, and nodded. "He like his old man, he gonna be trouble. You think he scare easy?"

"Yes. No. Maybe. I don't know."

"He like his old man, he not scare easy."

"He's always with that girl was with him. I know her and her people. I know where they live. You take care of it, Papa?"

Guy smiled at his sons. "What you say, boys? She be fun, huh?"

Meville and Xavier laughed. Back in the garage, they filled a wheelbarrow with Bill's remains and wheeled it out to the woodchipper.

\\\\\\\

Gio helped set the Rosens' kitchen table for dinner. Built like a long picnic table surrounded by short bench seats, Sam caught Gio staring at it his first night there. "We feel it promotes more of an equality-family atmosphere than 'father at the head of the table, mother opposite' - "

Jess filled water glasses. "Or worse, off to his side."

Gio looked around. "I can't imagine any male fool enough to put a Rosen woman off to the side."

Sam laughed. "Oh, he's good. He's really, really good, Daughter."

"However, makes it difficult to pull out a chair for you, my dear."

"Makes it easier to sit right beside you, my love."

Gio clasped his hands to his chest. "I am loved." He sat where Jess pointed. Bella came up on his other side and nuzzled his free hand.

Sam pointed to her dog bed against the wall. "Bella, go."

Bella sulked away.

Gio watched her go. She turned her head and looked at him for a moment then continued to her bed.

"Anybody mind if I sit with Bella?"

Sam, Rachel, Jess, the entire Rosen household looked at him.

"Did I say something wrong?"

Sam turned to Jess. "Is he like this with all animals or just my dog?"

"Animals, yes. People, not so much."

"Smart man." He faced Gio. "She gets no scraps from the table, understood?"

"Of course not."

"Of course not she doesn't get scraps or of course not you don't understand?"

"Of course not."

Sam shook his head. "Let's go back to that 'Sir' thing, okay?" He tapped the tabletop. "Bella, come."

Bella trotted over and sat next to Gio.

"My dog and my daughter. What's next?"

This night, Bella rested her head on Gio's lap until he pushed back from the table. "Delicious, Mrs. Rosen."

Jess's mom glared at him.

"Ma'am?"

More hairy eyeball.

"Rachel. I mean Rachel."

She nodded.

A raven landed on the Rosens' back porch railing. It stared in through the kitchen window. Bella walked to the back door and looked back at Gio.

"How far is it to Waterville from here?"

Sam followed Gio's gaze. "Half hour by either 201 or 95. What's up in Waterville this time of night?"

"Thought it might be a nice drive."

"This time of night?"

"I want to spend some time with Jess alone?"

Sam pursed his lips and nodded. "Hey, I have an idea. Jess, why don't you show Gio our cabin? There's been some break-ins reported. Why don't you two make sure it hasn't been burgled?"

Jess took the cabin keys off the hook. "Good idea, Pop."

Gio didn't rise from his chair. "I'd rather you stay here, Jess." He rubbed Bella's back. "You, too, girl."

Bella whined.

Sam called back as he went upstairs. "Gio, you know how to use a gun?"

"No, sir."

Drawers opened and closed. He came down polishing a .38 police special. "Well, Jess does."

"Sir, I - "

"And she's going with you."

"Forgive me for asking, sir, but why?"

Sam looked at the 38 in his hand and handed it to Jess. "Because the *Rebbe* said to make sure you survived this. I have no idea what 'this' is, but the last time a *Rebbe* warned us about something we ignored him and I lost half my family to the camps. Now I err on the side of caution."

"Sir, I - "

"Don't make me hurt you, Gio."

Gio sat back. "What?"

"Well, for starters, I'll make you eat kosher. If that doesn't work, I won't let you play with my dog. I can be mean when I have to be, son."

Gio laughed. He turned to Jess. "I see where you got your sense of humor."

"And I'll take away Jess's sense of humor."

"Okay, fine. Jess can come."

"With the gun."

Gio nodded.

They drove 201 to Waterville. Gio put his arm around Jess, felt the shoulder holster, pulled his arm away. "You folks do a lot of shooting up here?"

Jess snuggled beside him. "You don't use a handgun to hunt game."

"And I scare you? What the hell are you doing with a handgun?"

"My parents are Jews who lost family in WWII and who are raising their children in one of the most non-Jewish states in the nation. We're liberal, we're not stupid."

"You ever had to use that?"

"Nope."

"You know how to use it?"

She pulled it out too fast for him to follow. "It's a drop holster." She held the .38 in front of her in a two-hand grip and aimed through the windshield at nothing in particular. "I'm certified. Got a card in my wallet says, 'Watch out! Angry Jew-girl with a gun!'"

"But you've shot targets, not people."

She pulled away from him. "Jesus, Gio, I'm not a lunatic."

"Guns are cruel and indelicate things."

"They're supposed to be. You don't use a gun to perform surgery, you use it to stop someone."

"There's a difference between shooting a target and shooting a person."

"You think I don't know that? Besides, just showing you have a gun is enough."

Gio shook his head. "Just showing a gun is an invitation for the other person to use a gun. And you've never had to return fire. You've never dealt with someone who means to hurt you, maybe kill you?"

"What are you talking about? We're going to my family's camp in Maine, not Viet Nam."

"Just asking."

"Well don't, okay?"

"Okay if I put my arm around you?"

"Why wouldn't it be?"

"I wouldn't want to...you know..."

"The safety's on. Worried you'll fire it?"

"No, worried I'll piss off an already angry Jew-girl with a gun."

"With everything we've done you think I'm going to tell you to keep your hands off me now? Would you like me to take it off?"

"Where'd you find one that fit?"

"I'm taking it off."

"Just the shirt. Put the holster back on. I want to take a picture."

She punched his arm. "Sick."

A tow truck fell in several cars behind them.

Jess tuned in a Portland station. Five Man Electrical Band's *Signs* came through the speaker. Gio's eyes fixed on a hitchhiker. She followed his gaze. "What the fuck?"

The hitchhiker wore a faded, dark blue pinstripe suit, spats, a carnival huckster's white boater with a red on black band and held a cane in its hand.

"How come we can't see his face?"

Gio's eyes danced from the hitchhiker to the road and back. "Wait for it."

The hitchhiker performed a perfect pirouette.

"He has his clothes on backwards."

"No, it doesn't. Not for what he is."

Facing them, the hitchhiker wore clown makeup; white face, darkened eyes, exaggerated red lips and a bulbous green nose. it pointed to a highway sign with its cane: Waterville - 2 miles.

They passed the hitchhiker. It pirouetted in their wake.

"What do you mean, it?"

"Look behind us."

Jess turned in her seat. "He's gone."

"No, it isn't." Gio pointed ahead of them. A raven flew ahead of the car. "It's contrary and sacred clown, both not quite and more than."

"I'm going to talk Jewish to you. See if you can make sense of it." She turned back to Gio. "The *Rebbe* said that about you: not quite and more than."

"It's a truth-sayer. All cultures have them. My grandfather told me about them. Him and - " Gio snapped his fingers. "Running Water. Ha."

"Ha what?"

"It's a sign. A sign of what, I don't remember, but I remember that much."

Five Man Electrical Band sang

Sign said you got to have a membership card to get inside. UGH!"

Jess emphasized the *UGH!* as Five Man Electrical Band sang it. "I'm never going to have you to myself anymore, am I?"

"We're alone now."

"When we get there, to the cabin, could you make love to me the way you kissed me before?"

He pulled her close.

"It felt like being held by soft lightning and kissed by quiet thunder."

"Poetic."

"Just once. If I'm going to lose you, I want that as my memory."

Sunday, 17 February 1974

The bed covers moved slightly and the cold cabin air nipped Jess's shoulders. Not fully awake, she rolled towards Gio and reached for him. Her hand gathered sheets still warm from where he lay.

Her eyes opened slowly to the darkness. A deeper shadow, Gio, sat up in bed. He folded his arms across his chest and moved his head slowly. She reached for him. "Care to do that again?"

He answered, his voice no louder than rustling sheets. "Listen."

"To what?"

"Somebody's outside."

"Probably raccoons coming out of hibernation."

"Raccoons don't hibernate."

"Bear then."

"Not moving like a bear."

"Come back under the covers. I can put the holster back on and we can play Bad Goy-Boy and Angry Jew-Girl."

Gio looked at their clothes scattered on the floor. "You left it in Bessie."

Footsteps stopped by the porch's front door. The handle turned slowly until the lock caught. The footsteps went along the cabin porch to the side door. That handle creaked then stopped.

"You locked all the doors?"

"You think a bear's going to open a door?"

"You think a bear knows how to turn a doorknob?"

Jess quietly opened a drawer and pulled out a flashlight. "You think it's the same folks breaking into cabins all around the lakes?"

Gio shook his head but kept his ears focused on the footsteps walking around the cabin. They moved from wooden porch to crackling snow and back. A light flashed on the bedroom window from outside. A hand pushed against the glass and fell back, its imprint clear through the curtains. The light moved on.

"He's not coming for the cabin, he's coming for us."

Gio lowered his head, closed his eyes.

Lower-Center-Relax-Breathe.

Footsteps by the front door again. The handle creaked again then stopped. The doorframe creaked as someone put their weight against the door.

Jess whispered, "What are you doing?"

"Calling for backup."

The footsteps went around the cabin one more time. Hands touched windows, not attempting to be quiet.

Jess held the flashlight like a club. "I could run to the car, get the gun."

Gio didn't answer.

The cabin shimmered.

The front door window shattered. The door flew open.

Footsteps moved through the living room towards them.

The bedroom door creaked.

Bright lights broke up the night. Engines roared through the woods. Pickups, two-tons, plows, all with their engines racing, surrounded the cabin and quieted to idle. High beam headlights illuminated the cabin's exterior and surrounding land. Blinding light came through the windows, through the curtains, through the broken front door and lit the cabin in harsh daylight.

The footsteps ran out the side door. A truck engine roared. Wheels slipped on frozen earth. The engine raced through the gears, its sound grew dimmer, audible stars fading in the morning light.

Jess relaxed her grip on the flashlight. "What the hell was that?"

Gio got out of bed. He grabbed a heavy wool blanket, white with a red, blue, yellow, and black ban running its length, and wrapped it around himself as he went outside.

Tow truck lights raced down the cabin path to the main road.

Gio turned to the surrounding headlights and put his hand over his eyes. "Hello?"

One by one the lights flooding the cabin went out. One set remained and flicked to low .... A tall man, dark skinned with long, black hair and a hook nose, walked up to him.

"Who are you?"

The man pointed up into the trees. A raven cawed and danced back and forth on some branches.

"Thank you."

The man looked at Gio's blanket. Gio took it off and held it out to him. The man took it and rubbed it against his cheek. A moment later he and his truck were gone. Gio never noticed the others leave.

The raven flew into the night.

\\\\\\\\

Gio waited for Jess beside Bessie. He stroked the car's hood as if comforting a friend. "He slashed her tires."

Jess walked around the car. "There's a gas station about a mile down the road. We can call AAA from there. We have a family membership."

"He slashed her tires."

"Gio, we can get new tires." She retrieved her holster and gun from the floor under the dash.

He walked down the cabin's pathway to the road. Jess put on the holster and gun under her jacket as she trotted after him. "Hey, thanks for waiting."

Gio walked with his eyes to the ground, an old man walking through a field looking for ruts and rills ready to trip him.

She took his hand. "Your hand's cold. I can't remember you ever being cold. We've been naked in the back of your car on the beach in winter and you're a furnace. What's going on?"

"Thinking."

"About what?"

"Nothing."

"Jesus Christ but you're a rotten liar. Are you upset because some asshole slashed your tires?"

He looked up at her, lifted her hand to his lips and kissed it. "Have you ever cherished anything? Cherished it to the point it became a part of you, an extension of you?" He rubbed her hand against his cheek.

"We talking about your car or something else?"

"Doesn't it bother you that somebody broke into the cabin last night? Definitely looking for us. Whoever it was slashed Bessie's tires so we couldn't get away. Somebody looking for a quick boost would've turned back as soon as they saw a car in the driveway. They came looking for us and they meant to harm us."

"The world is full of assholes. And I know you won't let anything happen to me."

Gio threw his arms wide and shook his head at the gathering clouds. "Oh, well, if you're so sure of that then who am I to worry."

"You wouldn't protect me?"

"I've had this conversation with your father."

"You must have said yes or you wouldn't be here with me."

"And he gave you a gun."

"You he trusts but you talk to police, his trained guard dog obeys you and not him, you freaked out Ben Zev, ... "

"But not you? You said I scare you sometimes. Do I still scare you?"

"I'm handling it."

He pulled her to him. "God, I love you." He put his arms around her, felt the gun in the holster, and pulled away.

"Does my knowing how to use a gun bother you?"

He kept walking.

"You don't mind I can hit but you don't like I can shoot a gun?"

He faced her again. "Honestly? You punching me is sexy because you don't punch anybody else. And I know you could punch a fuck of a lot harder if you wanted to. So it's a turn on."

"Turn you on more if I punch you harder?"

He rolled his eyes and sighed. "And you wearing nothing but a bra, panties, and a gun in that holster? That's a major dick throbber."

"I could do that now if you promise to keep me warm."

They turned onto the main road.

"But it also frightens me. You're a strong woman - "

"Thank you."

" - and I wonder if you'll find me weak in comparison."

"I don't know whether to hold you to my breast and comfort you or slap you upside your head for being such a typical male jerk."

"Do I get a vote?"

"No, not until we resolve this."

A Maine State Police cruiser approached them. It turned on its blues and stopped on the shoulder in front of them.

Jess punched Gio's arm then smiled at Tony Morelli as he stepped out of his cruiser. "Officer Morelli, what perfect timing you have."

"Did I interrupt something?"

"Again. You interrupted something again. But what the hell. I'm getting used to it."

"Tony, what are you doing up here?"

"I went to the Rosens' looking for you." He nodded at Jess. "Your dad told me where you were."

"Everything okay at the Rosens'?"

Morelli dismissed Gio's concern with a quick wave of his hand. "Yeah, they're fine. Where's your car?"

"She's back there. Tires are slashed. We're going for help."

Morelli opened the door to his cruiser and lifted out the mike. "I need one of our flatbeds to..." He looked at Jess. She pointed to a sign nailed to a tree by the side of the road. "There's a sign with

Romeo-Oscar-Sierra..." he finished phonetic coding the sign and gave directions. He looked at Gio "What size tires she take?" Gio told him. "Catch that? Bring a set of four, nice and shiny new ones, and get that car to Sam Rosen's on River Road in Gardiner."

Gio snapped his fingers. "Should have asked for a tune-up. She coughs sometimes taking off."

Morelli lifted his eyebrows at him, the mike still in his hand.

Gio shook his head. "No, it's okay. Thanks. I was kidding."

Dispatch signed off.

"Ten-four that."

Gio stared at him.

Morelli smiled and shook his head as if unaware of a joke. "What?"

"Ten-four that?"

"You've never heard that before?"

Gio blinked, nodded. "Yes...I...heart it. Before."

Jess wove her arm around Gio's and pulled him into her. "He gets like this sometimes. I've decided it's endearing."

"Jamison wants to see you."

Jess clapped her hands and stood on tiptoe. "Ooh. A police station. Can I come, too? Do I get to be in a lineup? Ask him if we can use his handcuffs, Gio, please?"

Gio opened the rear passenger door for her. "You're going home."

She sat down and pouted. "You're no fun."

\\\\\\\\

Joe and Cody Flying Bear checked their trap lines. Joe stopped short and rested a hand on his young son's shoulder. "What do you see?"

Cody looked around him, to the sky, the bare elm, birch, and oak, the snow-covered northern pines. He listened to the soft wind blowing a hint of thaw and Spring up from the Atlantic. His eyes lowered. He followed the trap lines. He pointed to depressions in the snow.

"Good job, Cody. Good job. Now tell me what they are."

Cody moved towards them and Joe held his son back. "From here. Get too close and if there's danger, it's too late."

Cody nodded. He studied the path the depressions made, their width, their spread, determined movement, direction. "Not an animal. A child? Someone my size?"

"Good tracking, Code. Good tracking."

They approached the depressions slowly, together.

Joe's eyes went wide.

Footprints.

Not bootprints, not shoeprints. Footprints.

Joe pointed.

Cody picked up a green fiber and handed it to Joe.

Joe shook his head and pointed at the fiber. "Smell it. Sniff it. Hold it between your thumb and middle finger. Is it rough? Smooth? It'll be cold but is it brittle? Wet? From sweat or melt? Is it dry? Spit on it. See if it changes color. But don't put it in your mouth. You've got a lot to learn. Learn slowly and the learning lasts."

He watched Cody practicing his woodcraft. His eyes wandered the trail of the footprints.

"Coming out of the deep woods but not on any path or animal track, Pa?"

The prints went from tree to tree, standing under leafless elm and birch, staying away from the heavy limbs of sheltering pines.

"They don't know the woods, Pa."

Joe called out, "Hello?"

No response.

Joe sniffed the air. Too cold. Nothing carried. Nothing recent. "Those prints aren't more than five, six hours old. C'mon." He started a light jog through the woods, slow enough for Cody to keep up.

The footprints wandered, no specific direction.

"They're lost, Pa."

They stopped at a pool of dark yellow snow and sniffed.

"It's a boy, Pa. He's sick."

Joe nodded. Dehydration and hypothermia. Not a good mix.

Cody pointed. The edge of a forest green blanket stuck out from a tree fifty yards away. They ran.

Joe held Cody back. "Jesus Christ." A naked boy, close to Cody's age, curled into a stiff ball and wrapped in the blanket to ward off the cold. He checked for a pulse. Weak, fluttering. Joe raised the boy's eyelids. Only whites. "This blanket's soaked." He lifted the boy, placed him on top of the snow and rubbed the boy's torso roughly. "Open his mouth, Cody. Be gentle. Slow. He's frozen. Cup your hands over his mouth and breathe for him. Long, slow, breaths."

The boy's body remained stiff. Joe opened his thick parka and held the boy against him, not putting his arms in his sleeves, cradling the boy. "Zip me up, Cody."

\\\\\\\\\

Gio sat in Morelli's front passenger seat watching the scenery as Morelli drove to the Augusta barracks. Jess sat in back and she and Tony jabbered about the area; local events, did they know anybody in common, favorite restaurants, and such.

Gio half listened.

What if Annandale and the rest of the Christian Vigilantes are right? What if I'm in league with the Devil and don't even know it?

Jess and Morelli shared a laugh.

An intelligent, witty, beautiful woman he loved who made him laugh.

A friend dimly remembered from childhood who treated him with respect, didn't necessarily believe but also didn't laugh, a big brother who could counsel and guide him.

The *Rebbe* told him life is full of trades, exchanges, sacrifices.

He remembered more and more of his grandfather's teachings. Things long buried. His grandfather made them a game.

Why am I afraid?

Jess's voice roused him. "Hey, you passed all the Augusta exits."

Morelli nodded. "Right. I'm taking you home. My little brother here wants you kept safe, and I'm not going to piss him off so you're going home."

"Gio?"

"I'd rather you be home, Jess. I don't know what's going to happen. I don't want you caught in anything..." he cleared his throat. "...I can't get you out of."

She folded her arms on the top of the front seat and rested her head on them, facing Gio. "God, I wish you were back here so I could kiss the living shit out of you. I love it when you get all macho on me."

They drove up the Rosens' driveway and Sam and Bella came out to meet them. Gio and Jess got out. Morelli waved at Sam and turned his cruiser around.

"Daughter? Are you okay? Gio?"

"Yes, sir. She is."

"Jess?"

"I'm fine, Pop. Really."

"Why are you here in a state police car and not Gio's Mercury?"

Morelli rolled down his window. "Gio's helping an investigation, Mr. Rosen. I swear everything's fine. Nobody's in trouble and nobody's going to get in trouble."

A white van drove up the driveway. Four burly men dressed in chef's whites got out. The driver rolled down his window. "Excuse me, folks. I'm looking for the Rosen house. You folks the Rosens?"

Sam pulled Jess close. "What can I do for you?"

One of the men opened the van's rear and side doors. Smells of various Italian delicacies wafted out. The driver waved at racks of food. "Present from Nicholas de Leo. He said if you folks were going to be family, you should get used to the cooking."

Morelli's nose twitched. "My god, I haven't smelled things like that since before I went to 'Nam."

Gio watched the caterers. "How did my uncle know I was here?"

The driver shrugged. *"Ha detto che un suo amico ti sta guardando e voleva che tu sapessi che anche lui ti sta guardando. Questo è tutto quello che so."*

Gio nodded. Morelli cocked his head. "What did he say?"

Gio glanced at the gold-plated nametag pinned over the driver's breast pocket. "It's a gift." He nodded at the driver. "Like Riggerio said."

Riggerio smiled and bowed slightly.

Gio returned the smile. "*Riggerio, di 'a mio zio che sono in debito con lui. Una volta.*"

Riggerio nodded. "Your Italian's pretty good. Your uncle wasn't sure you'd remember any."

"I'm remembering as I go."

Sam ran a hand over his head. "Where are we going to put all this food?"

A second van came up the driveway. Riggerio pointed. "That'll be a chest freezer. You can put it anywhere. Outside even, so long as you got power to it. But you wouldn't want to freeze this stuff. Ruins the taste."

Morelli got out of his cruiser. "I can take some back to the barracks. You folks'll be able to commit murder without fear when they see this spread." He leaned into Gio. "Lotta words to say it's a gift, Brother."

Gio leaned into him. "Now you know Italian?"

\\\\\\\\

Lieutenant Jamison looked at the officers in the mess. "Who the hell turned my station into a goddamn Italian kitchen?"

Officers laughed and filled each others' paper plates with ravioli, ziti, pesce, calamari, bisteak, cannoli, neopolitans, eclairs, ...

Jamison shook his head. "I see one bottle of wine and you're all released."

Somebody handed him a plate full of Italian pastries.

"Morelli! In my office. Now."

Morelli and Gio stood before Jamison's desk, heads bowed, hands clasped behind them, two schoolboys in the principal's office.

"Whose idea is this?"

Morelli pointed at Gio. "It was his idea."

Gio's head snapped up at Morelli. "You liar!"

Jamison laughed. "You two should play hooky together. You might be more convincing." He put the plate of pastries down on his desk. "Gio, right?"

Gio nodded.

"You drink coffee?"

"Yes, thank you."

"Tony, could you get us some coffees? Take your time and close the door on your way out."

When the door closed, Jamison looked at the cannoli, bruttiboni, gianduiotto, panforte wedges, and other delicacies. "What's good?"

"You like almonds?"

"Almonds are okay."

Gio pointed at the bruttiboni. "You'll like those."

Jamison took a bite. "Wow. These are good. But if I ate this stuff everyday my wife'd be taking out my pants every other day." He took another bite. "Tony says you know things."

"I'd rather not get involved."

"You feed twenty men and don't want to get involved? That ship's sailed, son."

Gio shuffled and held his hands behind him.

"There's a chair behind you against the wall. Pull it up. Take a seat. I can keep you out of the papers. I can keep you out of the reports if you do nothing to help us. But if you help us, I've got to give a name. Doesn't have to be yours, but I have to use a name. This is a what? Cannoli?"

Gio nodded.

Jamison took a bite. "Christ you people know how to eat." He licked sweetened ricotta off his fingers. "So, Mr. Cannoli, I'd like your help. But if you do help us and it turns out your help is good, people will want to know your real name and how to get in touch with you again. And again and again. Understand?"

Gio looked away, nodded.

"Your real name doesn't have to be used, Vince. You don't mind if I call you Vince, do you, Mr. Cannoli?"

Gio cocked his head at him.

"In fact, Vince, there's policy against it. We'll do everything we can to keep you a secret. But you got to know, the better your information is, the more we're going to want your help when things get stuck."

"I don't know what I do exactly. I don't know how to control it."

Jamison pointed. "What's this?"

"Angel wing."

"Supposed to be this sticky?"

"Honey."

"Maybe it's time to learn how to control it, how to use it the way you want. Maybe somebody wants you to learn what you can do and we're the whetstone going to give you a fine edge. Ever consider that?"

A knock on the door.

"Come."

Morelli came in with three coffees. He put them on Jamison's desk and pulled creamers, sugars, and stirrers from his pockets.

"Vincent here is going to help us. Aren't you Mr. Cannoli?"

Morelli looked from Jamison to Gio. "Who?"

"Your friend here. Vincent Cannoli. What would you like for a nickname, Vincent?" Jamison licked his fingers. "Cream-filling? No, way too awkward. How about 'Honey'? Yeah, I like that. Vincent 'Honey' Cannoli. I can make that work."

Tony looked at Gio. "You going to help us, whoever you are?"

"Isn't somebody supposed to say 'Who was that masked man?' when I leave the room?"

Jamison pointed at his plate. "What's this?"

"Slice of panettone. A sweetened, holiday bread."

Jamison broke off a piece. "How come you're not five-hundred pounds, kid?" He chewed the bread and rolled his eyes. "Before you decide, o' masked man, let me up the ante for you and your faithful sidekick Tonto here. Tony, remember I mentioned the DEA to you? Well, I made some calls and pulled in some favors. Turns out there's an agent working undercover right under our noses. When he reports in next, his AOC will tell him to talk to you."

"Did you get a name?"

"Not yet, except it's a guy because his AOC kept saying 'he' and 'him' and 'his'. He doesn't want his man compromised, so when his agent is ready, he'll call me and I'll call you."

Morelli nodded.

Jamison pushed his plate away. "Now, Gio Vincent Masked Man Honey Cannoli Chance, you feel like you want to help us?

Tony looked at Gio, his eyebrows up and hopeful. "This could be good for both of us, Little Brother."

Gio lowered his head to his hands, rubbed his forehead, and stared into his palms. "I make no promises on accuracy or anything I can do, period. Understood?"

Jamison nodded. "I can live with that. You can live with that, Morelli?"

"I can live with that."

Thursday, 21 February 1974

Tobey danced in front of Morelli like a spider building a web. "Tobes! What canary did you eat?"

Tobey held a manila folder by its sides in front of him. He held it out and pulled it back, held it out and pulled it back. "Who's your friend? Huh? Who's your best buddy?"

"Tobey!"

"I got what you asked for. I bet you don't even remember what you asked for, do you?"

"I asked for Jimmy Olsen to dance in front of me?"

"Ha ha ha." He opened the folder and pulled out a grainy picture of a winter landscape. "What do you see?"

"Looks like a bad tourist photograph taken from the middle of a lake looking back at the shore."

"Lord, you gave them eyes but they still can't see."

"What am I supposed to see?"

"Look closer."

"You got a fuzzy picture of a thin guy on a lake shore somewhere?"

"I got a picture of the Ghost-Child. Remember that? Everybody thought it was a hoax? Some wild story ski bums made up and it never went anywhere? You asked me to get you proof so you could investigate, I got your proof."

"Where'd you take this?"

"Sheepscot Pond."

"There's never been a Ghost-Child report at Sheepscot."

"That's because this kid's good."

"Kid?"

"The image you're looking at is through a shit telephoto. Folks have unregulated ice shanties out there. Friend of mine's big into tech and has a shanty out there he uses to get away from his wife. Last time he went he said it looked like somebody been there and made themselves at home. He made a camera that tracks by sound. This is what he got."

"One grainy photo of a skinny guy on a lake shore?"

"He got five before his equipment belly-upped. That one's the best."

"This could be another hoax, Tobey. For all I know this is somebody practicing to be a Down East Bigfoot."

"I'm going to investigate."

"You know where to find me."

\\\\\\\\\\

Merlin Choate and Gio sat facing each other in Gio's dorm room. Gio sat at his desk. He watched a bright, emerald green serpent with body-length, yellow flashings and red spots evenly spaced inside the flashings coil around Merlin, its face level with Merlin's face and staring at him.

Merlin took Gio's roommate's desk chair and turned it to face him. Gio closed his textbook and capped his marker. "Go ahead."

The serpent's tongue flicked out and snatched words before Merlin spoke them. "I don't know where to begin."

"If you really want to make an apple pie from scratch, you must first create the universe."

Merlin stared at him.

"Say whatever you have to say. Just get it out. Don't filter it. Don't worry about offending me. My skin's pretty thick."

"I don't get you."

"Didn't know I needed to be got."

"You're not making this easy."

"What am I making difficult?"

"I came here to apologize to you."

"Okay, that's a place to start. What are you apologizing to me for?"

"I'm ashamed of this."

"Then apologize to yourself first, me second."

"Doesn't it bother you what people say about you?"

"What do they say?"

"Is it true you can stop pregnancies?"

"Are we talking about the girls who come to me thinking they're pregnant?"

"You mean they don't know?"

"What they know is they're late, they've missed their period. Because they're young and don't know any better they assume A equals B, which makes them tense and nervous, plus Ramsey girls assume they're pregnant as a punishment for their sins. Tell me that's a healthy reason to bring a child into the world and I'll stop helping them this minute. Otherwise I'll do what I can for them. But what most of them really want is to be forgiven for some supposed sin. They can't forgive themselves and they can't talk to anybody about it because every time they do they're treated like dirt, their belief they've sinned is reinforced on overdrive, and they're told to pray. They're not helped or comforted. You going to share with the world you think you're pregnant when you know all you're going to get is condemnation and ostracism? Hey, sign me up for that!"

"So they're not pregnant?"

"They're nervous and afraid. Did you eat yet today?"

"No, I haven't been hungry. Why?"

"You haven't been hungry because you're nervous and afraid. Of me. Who did nothing to you. Now consider this: you're afraid of something outside of yourself and it's stopping you from eating and drinking, something your body needs to do to survive. Imagine you're a girl who's afraid of her own body. Relax and you'll be hungry again. Help them relax and they'll have their periods."

"People say you can read their thoughts. Can you read minds?"

"I can read moods and attitudes by watching how people act. Ever hear of body language? It's as simple as that."

"You're strong."

"I worked on farms back home and do groundskeeping here. Physical labor tends to do that."

"You're saying there's a reasonable explanation for everything you do?"

"There's a reasonable explanation for anything anybody does. The trick is to look for that reasonable explanation, to be willing to find it. Do that and you're a lot closer to understanding the person. But looking for reasonable explanations takes time and training and most people would rather form opinions out of their own fears than work to remove their ignorance. You don't judge people for the choices they make when you don't know the options they had to choose from. Don't even judge them then. You're a Bible major, right? Doesn't the Bible have something about 'Judge not lest ye be judged'?"

"Matthew 7:1. How come you never told anybody this?"

"How come I have to tell Christians what's in the Bible? In case nobody's noticed, I mind my own business until people ask me to make something my business."

"This isn't going how I imagined it would."

"Good for you! Congratulations! Learn to appreciate what you meet. That way you accept things as they are, not make them into what you need them to be. That would be the angels unawares thing."

"Hebrews 13:2. You know the Bible pretty good for someone who claims he's not a Christian."

"Never said I wasn't, never said I was. People made an assumption because I wasn't doing what they were doing or what they needed me to do. What people don't understand, they fear."

"So are you a Christian?"

"Now you're asking if you shall know someone by their faith alone or if their works demonstrate their faith."

A chrysalis formed around Merlin. The emerald snake tightened its coils around it. "Can you just answer my question?"

"You came to me to apologize about something you're ashamed of. Have you apologized to yourself yet?"

Merlin pulled back and sat up straighter. The chrysalis cracked slightly. "Huh?"

"That's another part of the Bible. Forgive so you can be forgiven? Something like that? Funny that people don't start the forgiveness with themselves. Somewhere along the way they learned to forgive others but keep beating themselves up. Do that often enough and you begin to think everybody else is better than you. They deserve forgiveness but you don't. That sound like a plan to you?"

Gio watched the realization work its way through the snake's coils into the chrysalis. More cracks. The serpent tightened its coils. "I never thought of that. Thank you."

"What did you want to apologize about?"

The demon's head from Gio's car appeared on Merlin's shoulders. Gio blinked and it disappeared. "Is this about that...I don't know the proper name for it...sculpture? Bust? That artwork somebody left in my car a while back?"

"Yes. I want to apologize for that. And taking that picture of you in the cafeteria."

"Not for the yearbook, huh? Fine. Apology accepted. All's forgiven. You don't have to be nervous and anxious anymore. Easy, wasn't it?"

"That's it? Apology accepted and all's forgiven?"

"Isn't that how it works? You apologize, I accept and forgive. Am I missing something? Did I forget a part?"

"Aren't you angry at me?"

Gio clapped his hands. "Oh, you want me to be angry at you. I'm sorry. I didn't know that was required. Do you want me to punish you? Would that make it better?" He reached out and took one of Merlin's hands in his and gently slapped it. "Bad Merlin. Bad, bad. Feel better now?"

"I didn't come here to be made fun of."

"What did you come here for?"

"To ask your forgiveness."

"And you got it. Next?"

"You are not making this easy."

"No, you're not making this easy. You haven't forgiven yourself first. Now we're talking Cain not being able to find remorse, forgiveness. Except the only person putting a mark on you is you, not me and not god. He's all about forgiveness, right? And we're supposed to be like him, right? So allow me the opportunity to exercise my spirituality and forgive you."

Gio watched the serpent twist around Merlin's head, contorting his face and stretching his neck. "My head is spinning."

"What you wanted is for me to be angry at you. That way you can get all defensive to protect yourself from my anger. You can then turn that defensiveness into righteousness. You apologized, I should forgive, but instead I'm upset, therefore you were right in doing what you did because I'm not a good, forgiving person, i.e., not a Christian. Correct?"

"I think I'm going to be sick."

Gio pushed his wastebasket over to him. "How did you come up with it? The head. The face, fangs and all?"

Merlin took off his glasses. His eyes looked larger and his pupils became pinpoints. "Took a picture of myself in a mirror. They called me Moonface in high school because of my acne."

Gio's face burned. His body followed. His skin blistered. Pustules erupted on his face, chest, back, and arms. Fluid seeped down his skin like a thick, sticky sweat. Within moments the pustules receded, his skin healed, glowed.

He held his head and shook it slightly. "Wow. First time that's ever happened." He looked up. Merlin's eyes were wide on him. Gio smiled. "Ah. Okay. Now I get it."

Merlin pushed back from him, the serpent's coils crushing him. "Get what?"

Gio pointed at the mirror on his closet door. "Take a look?"

Merlin touched his face. He opened his shirt and looked at his chest. He rolled up his sleeves and ran his hands over his arms. The serpent fell from the chrysalis. "How? How did you...?"

"A gift. Of forgiveness. Pass it on. To others. And thanks."

\\\\\\\\\\\\\\

Tim Annandale sat in his dorm's phonebooth, his right leg crossed over his left at the knee, a notepad and pen in his lap, his left foot firmly on the floor supporting them all. His right foot tapped against the phonebooth's door, tap-tap tap tap-tap tap, again and again while he waited for the call to go through. He'd been on hold for five minutes and he was running out of quarters. He'd either have to bum some quarters from his dorm mates or not do his laundry this week.

Tap-tap tap tap-tap tap.

The voice came on the line. "Kagan."

"Agent Kagan. Tim Annandale. You asked me to keep you informed about John Chance. Are you ready?"

"What do you have this time?

Annandale talked for five minutes; Gio's courses, classwork, times he ate his meals, what he liked to eat, how he pampered his car, how he kept his room, comments from dorm mates, gossipy professors, classmates, admin, house father, other students in general.

"That's not much. He sounds like any other college student I've known."

Annandale looked around the phonebooth. "He talks to Friendly Angels."

"Means nothing in a court of law unless he claims they told him to hurt someone and he did."

Annandale held the phone against his ear with his shoulder and made a note: Must hurt someone. "How do you want them hurt?"

Silence.

"What are you after, Mr. Annandale?"

"You mean physically? Hurt them physically?"

"Physically, financially, something where person A can demonstrate person B caused them harm intentionally."

"So stealing is okay?"

"Okay? What the hell are you going on about? Did Chance do something or not?"

"He's dating a Jew."

Silence.

"Agent Kagan?"

"I'm here. Who someone dates is irrelevant. Unless person A harms them in some way or causes them to participate in or perpetrate a crime. And for the FBI to be involved, it's got to cross state lines."

"He goes to Maine a lot."

"Where in Maine?"

"I don't know. He goes somewhere with his *Zonah*." Annandale made another note: Hurt the *Zonah*?

"*Zonah*?"

"His jewish harlot."

Silence.

"Agent Kagan?"

"Are you saying he's involved in prostitution?"

"No, but he is seeing a Jew. I'm sure they're sleeping together."

"How come you're so sure who he shares his bed with?"

"Because that's the way he is. He's not like us. He's not one of us."

"One of us?"

"Yes. You know. One of us. Christian."

"Right. Is Chance involved in criminal activity?"

"I can find out. I know who might know."

"Call me when you have something I can work with. Understand?"

Annandale' palms sweat. Another note: The FBI's giving me the go-ahead on this!!!

"Understand, Mr. Annandale?"

"Oh, yes. Yes, I do. Thank you, Agent Kagan. Thank you very much." Annandale made notes.

"Anything else?"

"Am I going to get paid for this?"

〰〰〰

The new moon filled the night with stars. Gio and Jess walked Singing Beach holding hands. He carried a huge picnic basket in his free hand and draped a thick blanket over their shoulders. She huddled against him to block the winds coming off the water. "Do you know why they call it Singing Beach?"

Gio sang out, "No-o-o-oo. But I'll be-e-et you o' wonderful you are going to te-e-ell me-e-e-e."

"Funny. Because the sand squeaks when you walk on it."

"Don't all beaches do that?"

Jess shrugged. "Evidently not."

"Maybe they're all saying 'Ooh! Ouch! Stop! Get off! You're hurting me!' and nobody's listening?"

She huddled closer. "We've been a little off our game since our last trip home."

"We have?"

"How come we don't make love anymore?"

Gio spread the blanket down in front of them and put the picnic basket on it. They sat and pulled the blanket around them like a two-person tent without the stakes. He took a small transistor radio out of the basket, tuned it to a late-night Blues station and they listened to Esther Phillips sing *Double Crossing Blues*.

Jess sat tight against him. "You going to answer my question?"

"Your father intimidates me?"

"Bullshit."

"Your brother might beat me up?"

"Bullshit."

"I worry I'm not manly enough for you?"

"Oh double bullshit."

"Because I'm afraid of you."

"Because I know how to use a gun?"

"I talked with the guy who made that demon's head I found in the car today."

"You're switching the subject."

"He wanted to get to know me, learn why people are afraid of me."

"I'm not afraid of you."

"You know how to use a gun."

"aHA! I knew the gun was involved." She pulled the blanket up around them.

"He apologized for making that thing. He wanted me to forgive him. I did, but he hasn't forgiven himself."

"You sure he's not Jewish?"

"So I gave him a gift. Of forgiveness."

"What did you do?"

"I...I think I cured his acne. He had it pretty bad. They called him Moonface in high school. That must have sucked."

She pulled back. "How did you cure his acne?"

"It seems I took it from him. I gave myself his acne."

"Okay, I'm a little afraid of you now."

"I suppose I should have asked."

"If he wanted to get rid of his acne?"

"I don't really know."

"You going to grow breasts when our daughters go through puberty?"

"If I can grow breasts I'll never leave the house."

She sighed and cuddled against him. "So we're going to have daughters. Good. Daughters I can handle. Sons, I don't know."

"Jess."

"Didn't sneak it past you, huh?"

"You wanted me to respond?"

"I want you to nod and make babies with me."

"We're off our game because I'm afraid of you."

"The gun again?"

"I'm afraid of losing you."

"Because of the gun? Fuck it, Gio, I'll throw the goddamn thing away."

"No, I'm glad you know how to use a gun. It's taken me a while, but yeah, I'm glad you know how to use a gun."

"Jesus Christ, Gio. Has my interest in you changed since you learned I knew how to use a gun? I've had a permit since I was sixteen. Did I want you more before you knew? Do I want you less now? I'm the one talking about making babies or didn't you notice?"

"I noticed. Making love is important to you?"

"The only time I feel like I really have you, all of you, is when you're inside me."

"That's only a small part of me."

"You're the first guy I've known to admit his penis is small."

He laughed. "Thanks."

"The rest of the time I don't know if I have even half your attention. You always seem to be in two places at once."

Esther Phillips crooned

"Don't my kisses satisfy you anymore?"

"You're the one who said we're not going to last. I'm going to do everything I can to make sure we do."

"Plan on repeatedly seducing me, do you?"

She knocked him back on the blanket and unzipped him. "Every chance I get."

He pulled her back up.

"Amazing how it shrivels in the cold, isn't it?"

"Don't you want to know about what that guy at the cabin and I talked about?"

"You really weren't listening to me just now, were you?"

"Didn't you want me to remember things my grandfather taught me?"

"Now you listen? That you heard but not I want you inside me? That you don't hear?"

"Do you think I'm that much of a *schmuck* I wouldn't want to roll with an enlightened *zaftig Bayla*?"

"You know I get all goosebumpy when you go Yiddish on me?"

"Your father offered me chickens. Remember that?"

"So why don't you roll me when you get the chance?"

Gio tucked the blanket under them. Jess looked at stars rising from the water on the horizon. "Okay. You win. Show me. Enlighten your *Bayla*. Just don't grow breasts. A lot I can handle. You with breasts, probably not."

\\\\\\\\

Gio felt a tapping on his arm under the blanket. Jess quietly snored cuddled against him.

Tap tap tap. Tap tap tap.

Jess slept on his other side, curled to get his warmth.

Tap tap tap. Tap tap tap.

He opened an eye. A raven stood beside him and tapped his arm. He whispered, "Can I help you?"

The raven hopped towards the water, turned, and watched him. "Caw."

"Shhh."

The raven hopped back, tapped his arm, hopped away. "Caw."

He extricated himself as gently as possible. Jess continued to snore. He tucked the blanket around her.

Borrow.

Gio shook his head and looked around. "Who said that?"

The raven paraded back and forth between Gio and the ocean as if guarding the Tomb of the Unknown Soldier.

Borrow.

Relax-Lower-Center-Breathe.

Gio felt himself change. The raven took wing. Gio looked down as he flew over the ocean.

Lyndon sat in his one chair by his one table and hung up the phone. The baritone on the other end gave him the go ahead. It was time. Dykstra made his Bangor forays like clockwork.

He pulled back a drape from the window just enough to peer out onto Augusta proper. Spring melt made the streets down below a river of slush. The morning sun lit the tops of the buildings. Lyndon watched the sunlight wash the buildings from the top down as the sun rose. He watched the sunlight do similar things in the Blue Ridge Mountains back home when he was a kid, when his dad and grandpa would take him hunting. The family had a cabin way up in the hills and they'd wake up early to watch the sun warm the valleys.

"Not the same."

He pulled back the drapes full and the sun warmed him through the window. He put his feet up on the windowsill and leaned back.

It was going to be a good day.

\\\\\\\\\

Gio half listened to Jess affect a Viet Namese accent on the phone. "Me love you long time, Mistah Soldjah. You like me love you long time?"

He opened the phonebooth door. Light on and click. He closed it. Click and light off.

Not the same.

"Gio?"

"Just a second, Princess."

He unscrewed the bulb and closed the door to the rhythm of his slowing breaths. Crickly crickly cli-i-ick.

"You okay?"

"There's an intersection between the worlds of light and darkness."

She laughed. "Is that the new movie at the Cabot?"

His hand climbed the inside wall of the phonebooth like a spider, its feet testing for good purchase, for safety.

A twisted wire. By the door's light switch.

Lower-Center-Relax-Breathe.

Taste along the line.

The spider followed the lines to a microphone tucked behind the top of the molding.

Gio's fingers touched the microphone gently, the spider testing its footing.

A familiar taste. A bitter taste. An unwanted, hateful taste.

The spider followed the microphone line to a low power, Edmunds science kit transmitter hidden in the back of what used to be the closet's top shelf, now used for phonebooks and the like.

Follow the energies. Smell what they tell you.

He gazed into a full-length mirror. Not his reflection. Too thin, too tall. Wrong color hair. Naked, not enough muscularity on the chest, arms, or legs. No pelt. Jess always kidded him about his pelt. A small, tinny speaker in a box echoed Gio and Jess's conversation.

Gio gazed into the mirror.

Come on. Look up. Show me who you are.

The reflection masturbated, eyes on its owner's penis, its left hand stroking feverishly, a handful of tissues in its right.

The right hand came in front. Tissues engulfed the penis' pulsing head. The face looked up.

He's wearing a mask. A photograph blown up into a mask.

Gio stared at the reflection.

"He's wearing a mask of me."

Jess said, "Who's wearing a mask of you?"

"Sorry, Princess. Just another minute. I promise."

The eyes fluttered behind the mask. The wrong color eyes. Not Gio's eyes.

The hand with the tissues came up, lifted the mask off the face.

Annandale's face. He smeared his semen on the mask's face.

Gio's eyes widened and he shook his head.

And people think I'm fucked up?

He made sure the microphone was back in place and screwed the lightbulb into its socket.

"Gio? You there, Gio?"

"Sure am, Princess. Sorry, didn't mean to concern you."

"Mom and Pop invited you up again this weekend. Want to go?"

"Me but not you, huh? Wow, your folks are progressive. You sure they won't mind?"

"Ha ha ha funny man. You could have a career on the borscht belt if you wanted. Can I tell Pop we'll be up?"

"It's Spring break in a couple of weeks and I have midterms coming up before then. Do you think your folks could tolerate me for a full week?"

"I get to have you all totally and completely to myself for a whole week?"

Silence.

"No, huh?"

\\\\\\\\

Stephanie handed Caroline a matching sock. "You don't seem surprised."

"That Don's fucking you? No, not at all. He's never been any good at cleaning himself off when he's done. You were hoping to shock me?"

"Frankly, yes."

Caroline picked up one of DJ's underpants between index and thumb as if picking up a particularly ugly, dead, insect. "I found one of my bras with...stains...on it."

"He told me he'd wash them."

Caroline folded DJ's underpants and matched two socks. "Them? There was more than one? I must've missed those."

"Sorry, Caroline. Donnie said - "

"Don't believe everything people tell you. But don't worry. We're okay?"

"We're okay?"

"Yes." Caroline placed folded laundry in the basket. "Shortly after Robbie and DJ were born, Don told me I was too stretched out to be of any use to him. I suspect it had more to do with some...tastes...he had I was unwilling to accommodate. Since then, I've played the loving, idiot wife, and bided my time."

Stephanie cradled the laundry basket on her hip. "Bided your time for what?"

"For me to have a reason to clean him out. Humiliate him." Caroline's voice remained calm. She held a hand in front of her and checked her manicure. "Leave him weak and wounded and with no one to turn to."

Stephanie made sure the basket was between her and Caroline. "What about me? Do you have plans for me?"

Caroline laughed. "Oh, you young, precious thing. Don't worry. No plans. Nothing. You're innocent. More or less. Stupid for getting involved with him, but I've been stupid, too. Can I hate you for being as foolish as I was at your age? You've got a lifetime of mistakes ahead of you. Learn from them. Besides, you got a nice car out of it. Sell that and buy yourself something reasonable. You'll have enough left over to enjoy yourself for a while."

Stephanie shifted the basket and looked around for clothes they'd missed.

Caroline flicked off the light. "That's all. We're done here."

\\\\\\\\\

Gianna cradled the phone by her ear as she applied black toenail polish. "You know I want you, Daddy." She stretched out her leg and evaluated her toenails, then held her foot and applied more polish to her big toe. "You know I like it like that, Daddy. Oh, yes. You now I like that." She breathed heavily into the phone. "Oh, Daddy, I'm going to cum. You're going to make me cum." She stretched out her leg, held it against the other, and compared the paint jobs while shaking a cigarette out from a pack on the table beside her. "Oh, Daddy, thank you. Oh, god, I'm so wet. You always get me so wet." She lit the cigarette. "Good for you was it? Good, I'm glad. You made the payment on the Costa Rica villa? Tomorrow? You'll have the money tomorrow? When are you getting off work?" She took a deep breath and blew smoke rings while she listened on the phone. "Okay, sounds good, Daddy. I'll be here, my legs spread wide and waiting. See you then, love you, bye."

She hung up the phone. "Fucking asshole." She picked up the phone and dialed another number. "Yeah, hi. He'll be here tomorrow night. Can you make it?"

\\\\\\\\\

Tobey stood under a red light in his darkroom developing pictures he hoped would reveal the Sheepscot Pond Ghost-Child. More than one ice-fisher said their shack'd been rustled, now he had several days of shots made with his tech friend's gizmo camera but this time with a quality telephoto lens on the camera.

Thirty-six shots over seven days, most of them either out of focus or near-focus, none of them decisive. Could be vandals, could be high school kids looking for beer, could be somebody without a license scoffing, could be somebody setting up squatting when no one's looking.

He held two negatives up to the light. Each had the kid looking almost square into the camera as if he knew it was there.

Could he hear the shutter?

Not at that distance. Better than five-hundred feet from shack to shore?

And whoever they were, they were good. Didn't take the same path twice, wouldn't leave a recognizable trail now that the Spring melt was on.

Tobey put the negatives down.

The Spring melt.

People would be taking their shanties down by the end of March.

The ice would be thinning.

How good was this kid's woodcraft? Would he know the shanties would be increasingly unsafe? Especially if their stoves got fired up?

Tobey remembered being a kid, making friends with some raccoons in his backyard. He saw one from his back porch window one day. The same raccoon came by every day, same time.

Tobey talked to it, got it used to his voice. Once it didn't shy from his voice, once it stayed and watched him, he opened the door and let it see him. A few weeks later he could throw it food: cookies, peanuts, that kind of thing. A little more time and he could walk up to it and it'd take food from his hand.

He opened his darkroom door and called up to his wife. "Hey, Martha, we got any old blankets we don't need, crackers, peanut butter, jams and jellies? You were in the Campfire Girls, what did you learn about survival packs?"

He held up the negatives again.

"Come on, little raccoon. Let's see if you'll talk to me."

\\\\\\\\

Kagan's phone rang. The oncologist spoke quietly, decisively. Kagan spent yesterday afternoon and evening with his wife. They talked. Sure, she tired, but she took naps and woke up and they continued talking like nothing happened.

Kagan swallowed. "How long?"

Not long.

"Is she in pain?"

Not likely and they monitored her closely.

"Will she know if I'm there?"

Maybe yes, maybe no. She comes and goes.

"Okay. Thank you. Please keep me posted. You can leave messages for me here."

\\\\\\\\

Joe Flying Bear sat in his kitchen with the elders. Most had cups of strong coffee in front of them. Two held Coke cans. Their voices were soft and low, like the lights from the lanterns hung on the walls. Thin drapes covered the windows barely holding back the night. Joe looked at a pan of water on his woodstove. The water steamed without boiling, keeping the stove's heat from drying out the three room house.

One elder sipped his coffee and nodded to Joe's room. "Good you brought him back, Joe. He'd be dead otherwise." The others nodded, grunted assent.

Joe looked around the table. "What are we going to do with him? I mean, he's white. We can't keep him here. I can't keep him here. I got just enough for me and Cody."

"You found him. He's your responsibility. We won't know anything about him until he wakes up and that might not be for a while. You want to bring in the police? Have them come on our land? We can get one of the women to help you if you want. You want that?"

"Don't you think somebody's looking for him?"

A middle-aged woman wearing a shopkeeper's apron opened the door. She stamped her boots on the step outside and banged them against the doorjamb to knock off the remaining snow. "Cold out there."

The elders grunted. Joe watched her and said nothing.

She came forward to the table. The two Coke drinkers got up and made a space for her. She shook her head and continued standing. "Definitely somebody's looking for him. Lots of people. Him and someone else. We have to make sure he gets with his people. Now the wrong people are closer. Keep him here, where he's safe."

"But here, in my house?"

"You found him on our land? Keep him on our land until he doesn't have to be on our land any longer. Keep him here, in your house."

Joe Flying Bear looked from Running Water to his room where the boy slept. "Yes, Grandmother. Understood."

\\\\\\\\\\

Gio woke hearing a tap-tap-tapping on his dorm room window. He leaned over his bunk.

His roommate snored peacefully below. Sometimes his roommate's girlfriend threw pebbles at the window when she wanted to talk. Gio would get the lovers together without involving anybody else.

But the pebbles she threw struck the window in a random pattern, like someone knocking over a set of tiny cymbals. This wasn't random pebble tossings.

Tap-tap-tap. Tap-tap-tap.

His roommate rolled over.

Gio pulled back the curtain.

A raven balanced on the windowsill and stared at him.

"Did you bug Poe every night?"

The moon offered a bright first quarter. The raven stood out clearly as moonlight glistened off its feathers.

"I was only kidding about Edgar Allen Poe. You know that, right?"

His roommate rolled over and mumbled in his sleep.

Tap-tap-tap. Tap-tap-tap.

"Time to practice, huh?"

Tap.

Tap.

The raven and Gio looked each other in the eye.

Tap.

Gio held up a finger, put on some sweats, and went outside.

He stood under the first quarter moon and shivered in his dorm's backyard. Steam rose from his nostrils and his teeth chattered. The raven perched on the tree across the yard and watched him.

Caw.

Simple things. But do it intentionally. Whatever it is, do it because you want something done.

Caw.

And no matter what anybody else says, believe you got it or some part of it done.

Caw.

When you know you do it, make notes on everything. Recreate the experience and you'll recreate the event. When you know you don't do it, even better. Now you know you need to do something else.

The raven flew down in front of him and paced back and forth.

Caw.

Lower-Center-Relax-Breathe.

Caw.

What do you see?

The raven grew. At about half his height, its shape changed. Its black feathers grew transparent, glistened in the moonlight. Its shape became fluid, water, then like a woman's.

Lower-Center-Relax-Breathe.

Running Water took his hand.

We don't have much time. Hurry.

Saturday, 2 March 1974

Morelli sat in his treestand with his night goggles and scanned the Kennebec. He checked his watch.

Right on time, the Rogue River dories with their small putt-a-putt outboards powered upstream. The lead boat flicked its UV light at the bed sheet in the trees just up from the shoreline, the last boat broke off and headed for it.

Morelli counted twenty drop points yesterday but missed who set them up.

The blue light flicked again and the second boat broke off.

A raven perched on the limb beside him and pecked at his service pack. He brushed it away. It returned and pecked pecked pecked, pecked pecked pecked.

What the fuck. He had what he needed. He climbed down. The raven hopped from limb to limb and followed him down. A twig cracked some twenty feet to his right.

"Shit, can you move quiet?"

"Did you mark the tree where the stand was?"

Fuck!

Morelli sat at the base of the tree, on the far side from the voices. The raven flew through the limbs unbothered by the dark.

Morelli counted three sets of steps, all male: one heavy on his feet and out of breath, the other two heavy but in shape, not breathing hard.

Two voices but three men.

The raven flew through the limbs across their advance.

"What was that?"

I know that voice.

"Just a damn bird. Shut up."

Morelli sat unmoving, all his SERE training on full.

"Over there. That's the tree."

The raven flew back through the limbs and perched on the lower limbs.

Caw.

The out of breath voice rasped, "What's that damn bird doing?"

I know that voice. That's Dykstra's voice.

Three men approached the tree.

The raven spread its wings and danced back and forth on the perch. CAW CAW CAW. CAW CAW CAW.

One of the stronger voices. "Come on. Probably has a nest in the tree. Probably in that tree stand. She's making that much noise for us, she'd be raising hell if anybody were up there now."

Dykstra again. "What about the car?"

The other strong voice. "I slashed the tires. They're not getting far."

Slashed the tires? Is that the guy who did Gio's car?

The first strong voice. "Any idea who it is, Sarge?"

Dykstra rasped, "No idea."

Sarge? One of them's calling Dykstra 'Sarge'? One of them's on the job?

The second voice. "You have your gun? Go back and wait by their car. Whoever shows up, kill them."

The two strong voices separated. Dykstra got about ten paces back into the woods and sat down to catch his breath.

Morelli's training got him back up to the road double-time, double-quiet.

Yep, all four tires slashed. His car wasn't going anywhere.

He passed some homes about a mile up the road when he came in. He crossed the far side of the road into the trees. Obscured from view, he followed the road and reached the houses in six minutes flat.

\\\\\\\\

Joe Radwel pulled his pickup into the maintenance barn. Two students, a thin, frail youth, more boy than man, and a young woman with long black hair and a recognizable figure, faced the row house closest to the highway, their heads bowed, and their hands clasped. They didn't move when he pulled in. "You two okay?"

The boy looked up. "Are we in your way, sir?"

"No, you're fine. Can I help you?"

The woman looked up. "We're praying for a friend. Is that okay?"

"You want to come inside and do it where it's warm? I was going to change the oil on my pickup. You won't be bothering me."

They came in. The boy looked around. "Are you in charge of the grounds crew?"

"That what it says on my paycheck. Something I can do for you?"

"Can I get a job here?"

"You got work-study?"

"I don't know. A friend recommended I get a job doing grounds work."

"Who's your friend?"

"John Chance."

"Gio? Gio said you should talk to me about a job?"

The boy blushed. "Not exactly. He said grounds work would help me."

Joe looked the boy over then looked at the woman. "Did you want a job, too?"

She shook her head. "I'm on the housecleaning crew, thanks."

Joe nodded towards the row house. "If you're looking for Gio, that's his dorm. His car's not here, though. Usually parks it here. Easier to get to and less people to concern themselves with his comings and goings. You two concerned about his comings and goings?"

The young woman stood by an electric heater. "We're praying for Gio."

"He in trouble?"

"Some students are trying to get him kicked out of school."

Joe nodded. "Not you two, though?"

They shook their heads.

"Why do people want him kicked out of school?"

"Because he's different."

"Yeah, that he is. Well, pray away. Let me know if there's anything else I can do for you."

"Would you like to pray with us?"

Joe smiled. "I work here and I do my best to play by the rules, but I'm Irish Catholic. Sometimes I think we talk to different gods."

They chuckled.

"What are your names?"

"Merlin Choate."

"Laurie Sánchez."

"Gio in a lot of trouble?"

They shrugged. Laurie looked over to Gio's dorm.

"You worried about him?"

They nodded.

"Gio can take care of himself, I'm sure of that. But if you think somebody's out to hurt him, doesn't matter who, you should let him know. I mean, praying's all well and good, but if you know somebody's going to hurt him and you don't do anything about it, how well you going to sleep at night once he's hurt?"

They shuffled their feet. Merlin cleared his throat. "I'm not much of a fighter."

Joe's eyes opened wide. "You think somebody's going to physically go after Gio?"

Laurie looked back to the campus. "The spirit of Salem is alive and well at Ramsey College."

"Listen you two, if you won't tell Gio, tell me." He went into his office and came back with two business cards and handed one to each. "That's my home number on the back. You call me anytime, you hear?"

"You're Gio's friend, too?"

"Long time ago my father's orchards were dying. We couldn't figure out why. This old man comes by with his grandson and a big, round woman. Used to buy peaches from us to sell off the back of his truck. They walk into my dad's orchards and this woman gets sick. I mean sick. She comes in all full of life and ten minutes later she's thin as a rail and puking her guts out. We're going to call an ambulance and the old man waves us off. He holds her up. Five minutes more and she's standing on her own. More than that, the trees are sprouting green."

Merlin and Laurie stared at him.

"God's truth. The old man, the woman, and the boy walk back to his truck. My father's running after them. 'What can I do? What can I do?'"

The old man pats his grandson's head. "Watch out for my boy." Then he looks straight at me and nods. "He'll need your help someday."

Laurie shuddered.

"Well, that old man was Gio's grandfather. Gio's never let on if he remembers me. I doubt he would. He was a toddler at the time. But his grandfather and that woman saved my dad's farm. So am I his friend? Yeah, I guess you could say so."

Merl frowned. "How did you know Gio would come to Ramsey and get a job on the grounds crew?"

"I didn't. Truth is, I damn near forgot it myself. But as soon as he walked in, I knew who he was. Funny how things work out, isn't it?"

Laurie looked back at Gio's dorm. "So you'll help him if he needs it? He can trust you?"

Joe chuckled. He glanced out to the seed sheds and back. "Oh, I'll pull a few strings if I have to."

\\\\\\\

Lyndon sat low in his car, away from streetlights and in an alley down the street from the rear officers' only entrance to the Gardiner' Police Department. He clocked out at the end of his shift, exactly 11pm, without writing up his reports. At his car he opened the trunk, got out a Maine State Police uniform, and changed from his civvies into it as quickly as he could. Back in the car, he kept his window down just enough so his breath wouldn't fog up the windows. Every time the officers' entrance opened, he sat forward. Every time it wasn't Dykstra, he sat back.

He pulled his plaid trapper hat's ear flaps down. "Maybe he used the main entrance?" He considered. "Nah. He doesn't even use that to go to that sub shop he frequents."

The door opened and Lyndon keyed his ignition. Dykstra hurried to his '73 Torino. He pulled out of the police station parking lot and headed for the highway. Lyndon gave him a thirty-second start and followed.

Half-way to Bangor, Lyndon put a Deitz revolving light on the roof of his car and accelerated to get within five-hundred feet of Dykstra. He hit the light and flashed his highbeams.

Dykstra pulled over, rolled down his window, and reached for something as Lyndon approached, one hand on his holster, the other holding a large, heavy, six-cell flashlight which could serve as a club when the need arose.

Lyndon hesitated. "Put your hands where I can see them, please."

"I'm on the job out of Gardiner." Dykstra held his ID out for Lyndon to see.

Lyndon came up and shone the light right in his eyes. "No, you're not."

Dykstra shaded his eyes with his ID. "Lyndon? What's this bullshit?"

Lyndon cut his light. "You're a busy man, Sarge. I've been watching you for a while. You've been a naughty boy, spending all that money on that little honey you keep up north."

"What?"

"Oh, come on, Sarge. I don't mind you getting some relaxation from time to time. But you been greedy, keeping all that extra cash for yourself."

"What cash?"

"Oh, tell me you don't know Todd Andersen, Sarge. Nobody keeps two homes the way you do without something coming in on the side. I been watching."

"You got nothing."

Lyndon quoted an address.

"Big deal, an address. You looked in a phone book."

Lyndon reached into his jacket and pulled out pictures of Dykstra coming and going, two with a boyishly thin woman holding on to him with one hand and a bottle of Stolichnaya in the other. "Want to see a beautiful frontage shot of your villa in Costa Rica?"

Dykstra's nostrils flared and his lips tightened. "What do you want?"

"Half. And I want to meet Andersen when you collect. Want to make sure I'm getting my fair share."

"Hey, wait a - "

"Now, Sarge, this lack of cooperation isn't going to help you reach retirement."

Dykstra pulled himself into his winter police jacket like a tortoise pulling itself into its shell. "Yeah, alright."

"When can we expect the first payment?"

"I get paid the last day of the month. April first's my next take."

"Ahh, Sarge. You're lying again." Lyndon broke the rear driver window with his flashlight.

"Alright, alright."

"You get paid every two weeks. You make a deposit in Bangor, give some to your little honey - "

"I said alright."

"So your next payment is...?"

"Friday the fifteenth."

Lyndon patted Dykstra's face. "Good Sarge. That'a boy. Good little doggie."

Dykstra receded in the darkness of his Torino, his face a dashboard green mask of tightening rage.

"Anything else?"

Lyndon shook his head. "No, we're good. Don't fuck me over now, Sarge. It's not nice fucking over your business partner."

"Can I go now?"

Lyndon tapped the roof twice and stepped back. Dykstra rolled up his window and pulled away. Lyndon watched Dykstra's taillights disappear over a hill. "That was too easy."

Towne opened his eyes at the touch of Gianna stroking his cock. He reached for her and discovered his wrists and ankles were tied to the bedposts. She straddled him, reached behind herself and brought up a ten-gallon cowboy hat. She put it on as she straddled him, began a gentle back-and-forth rocking, and smiled down at him. "You sleep too soundly."

He couldn't answer. She ball-gagged his mouth with duct tape.

"Who's following Dykstra?"

He shook the bedposts struggling and felt himself preparing to cum. Gianna stopped moving until his throbbing stopped.

"Who's following Dykstra?" She began rocking again.

He shrugged and shook his head.

She swaggered her hips to the rhythm of her words.

"Who's...

"...following..."

"...Dykstra?"

He began throbbing again. She stopped moving. "I can keep this up all day if I have to."

He groaned.

"Almost sounded like you said, 'Aww, come on,' there. Is that what you said?"

He made the same sound.

She swung her hips in a circle on his erection. "Who's..."

"...following..."

"...Dykstra?"

Beads of sweat broke out on Towne's forehead. She pinched his nose shut. "This makes it interesting, doesn't it?" She hurried her motions. "Do you know there's an actual name for not being able to breathe when you cum? Asphyxiophilia. Amazing what you can learn walking through the stacks of your local library, isn't it?"

Towne's face turned red, then blue.

Gianna moved faster and faster.

Towne's eyes fluttered.

She got off him as he began ejaculating, ripped the tape off his mouth, pulled the ball-gag out, and watched his semen fly in long arcs over the bed. "I guess what they say is true. Men do cum stronger when they're dying."

Towne's ejaculations weakened as his cock grew flaccid.

Gianna slapped Towne's face until his eyes cleared and focused. "You should call that thing Vesuvius, Harry."

"God that was good."

"So who's following Dykstra?"

"I think you're imagining things. I didn't see anybody here and I waited all night, an hour before he came to an hour after he left. Nobody."

"Nobody? Really?"

"Nobody."

She tilted the cowboy hat back. "I don't know, Harry. I think you're lying to me." She picked up the ball-gag and roll of duct tape.

"Hey, wait a - "

She shoved the ball-gag in and taped his mouth shut despite his struggles. "Guess we're going to have to start all over again until you tell me." She reached down and grabbed his cock.

\\\\\\\\

Uncle Nick took Jess's hand in his and kissed it gently. "It is my pleasure to meet you, Ms. Rosen."

"Hi, Uncle Nick. Jess's fine."

An elderly man in a business suit save the jacket and with an apron tied around his ample waist brought tiny coffee cups on a tray. He stood quietly at the side until Nick, almost imperceptibly, nodded. The man put the cups down. "Ever had real espresso, my dear?"

Jess smiled up at Gio. "So gracious. Is he checking out my boobs, too, without my realizing it?"

Nick clapped his hands together and bent over laughing. "I can see why you love her, Gio."

Jess looked around the Osteria Giambatta. "I'll bet I can get real Italian food here."

Nick leaned forward. "Are you hungry, Ms. Rosen? Would you like something to eat?"

Jess held up her hands. "No, no. I was just thinking."

"Because if there's something you'd like, anything at all."

Jess laughed. "What do you have kosher?"

Nick turned towards the kitchen and called out in flawless Yiddish. "*Rbi, zent ir heynt?*"

Jess looked across the table to Gio. "Oh, he's good. Can I marry him if you're not available?"

A man with a prayer shawl under his apron and a black, broad-brimmed hat opened the kitchen door.

Nick smiled at Jess. "I invited a friend just in case."

"I love your Uncle Nick, Gio. I just want you to know that."

Nick shook his head and the man turned back into the kitchen. Nick sipped his espresso. "Jess, I asked Gio to bring you here because things are accelerating back in your hometown, things Gio is not a part of. I want you to know that. Although not a part of these events, Gio may be impacted by them, and because of your relationship to him, I worry they may spill over to you and your family."

Jess, espresso cup at her lips, slowly lowered it to the table. "What are you saying, Mr. De Leo."

Nick smiled. "Please. Uncle Nick or Nicky, as you wish. Please do not hear my words as a threat to you or your family. I want you to know Gio is under my protection and again, by extension, so are you and yours."

"So what are you telling me?"

Nick considered. "Gio tells me you know how to use a gun. Correct?"

"NRA certified."

Gio chuckled. "Angry Jew-girl with a gun."

Nick smiled and nodded. Two men, both over six feet, thick through the chest and arms, clean shaven and with curly black hair, diamond pinky rings and gold cufflinks, wearing dark blue business suits, came forward. "I would like you to take a good look at these gentlemen. They work for me. You may notice them from time to time." He looked at the two men and his face took a serious turn. "But only if they're not doing their jobs as they should. Understood?"

The two men nodded and left.

"Are you offering me protection, Mr. De Leo? Are you telling me I and my family'll have bodyguards?"

"Nicky, please. Don't think of them as bodyguards, or protection. Think of them as..." He hesitated. "As..."

Gio cleared his throat. "Friendly angels?"

Nick looked at him. "Friendly angels?"

Gio shook his head. "Nothing, Uncle Nicky. Inside joke."

Nick chuckled. "Do you accept my friendly angels, as Gio calls them, Jess?"

"One condition."

Nick sat back slightly and glanced at Gio. "And that would be?"

Jess smiled at Gio. "Can you tell them to arrange it for Gio and me to be alone so we can make love more often?"

Gio blushed and hid his face in his hands. "My god, Jess."

Nick gently tapped his nephew's shoulder. "Oh, I really do like this one, Gio. You keep this one - "

Jess nodded vigorously. "You listen to your Uncle Nick, Gio. He's a very wise man. I can tell. I'm Jewish and we can spot very wise men a mile away. So you listen to your Uncle Nick, okay?"

" - and let me cater the wedding." He smiled at Jess. "And I promise everything will be kosher."

Gio shook his head. "I'm being set up. I can tell. Everywhere I go, I'm being set up."

"Jess, please excuse me while I talk to my nephew in Italian for a moment." He turned to Gio. "*Mi hai fatto il favore che ti avevo chiesto?*" Were you able to do the favor I asked?

"*Avevi ragione. I ragazzi sono ostaggi.*" You were correct. The boys are hostages.

One of Uncle Nick's limos drove them back to Iperia. Two of Uncle Nick's heavymen sat across from them in the passenger compartment, their eyes fixed and straight ahead, their hands relaxedly clasped in their laps, their bodies unmoving except for the gentle lifting of their chests as they breathed.

Jess cleared her throat. "You guys worked for Gio's Uncle Nick long?"

No response.

"They won't answer you, Jess. They're not supposed to, unless there's a problem."

"That last thing you talked about with your Uncle Nicky, in Italian?"

"Yes?"

"You weren't talking about my boobs, were you?"

The man across from them on the left gently coughed and lifted his hand to cover a smile.

\\\\\\\\\\

Tim Annandale stood with arms folded by the window in Herder Hall's third floor rec room. The room filled and he kept looking out on to the quad, actively paying no attention as students gathered.

The shuffling of feet and moving of furniture quieted. Some people cleared their throats. Tim pulled away from the window and inventoried his disciples.

Laurie Sánchez stood in the back, her eyes intently upon him.

"You're not welcome here, Ms. Sánchez."

"Oh? It's open dorm, isn't it? And this is the rec room, isn't it? I have every right to be here. Unless some of you want to physically remove me. That'll be amusing."

Eyes went nervously from Tim to Laurie and back.

Tim shrugged. "As some of you know, John Chance has a history with organized crime."

People inhaled sharply, held their breath.

Laurie's eyes opened wide. "Organized crime? You mean the Mafia?"

"I'm not at liberty to say."

She laughed. "You don't know, Tim. Do you? You're guessing because you hate him and want him gone. Isn't that right?"

Tim smiled at the nervous faces. "And I've shared with some of you my confidential exchanges with the Boston office of the FBI."

"Bull!"

Annandale shook his head. "I appreciate how difficult this must be for you, Laurie."

"It's difficult for me to believe." She looked around the room. "How many of you are taking part in this witch hunt?"

More nervous gazes around the room.

Annandale held his hands up. "People, we all know John Chance is a good talker." He stared at Laurie. "Look what he done to some of our friends."

Laurie laughed. "Yeah, and by his words you shall know him, right, Tim?"

Tim smiled at the people gathered. "Exactly so."

"So why don't you tell people about you calling and asking to be paid for informing on Gio?" She walked in front of Annandale and stood with her hands on her hips. "Anybody here ever hear of anything like that? Somebody wanting to be paid to inform on somebody?"

People stared at Tim. His face reddened. He looked over everyone's heads. "I have no idea what she's talking about."

"Liar!"

He reached out for her. "Laurie, I'm so sorry you've fallen into his trap, fallen for his ways."

"Keep your hands off me, you filth, you liar. You sicken me." She backed away and faced the gathering. "What is it with you people? You're afraid of him? Because he's different? Because he speaks his mind and heart rather than what he's supposed to say to fit in? Maybe he doesn't care about fitting in so much as he cares about being true to who he is. Ever think of that?"

Tim looked at the anxious faces and shook his head, shrugging and holding up his hands. "You see what he's done, people. I told you, he's a good talker."

"Damn right he is. If he were here now these people would know the truth."

Annandale shrugged again. "She curses, friends. You heard it from her own lips. And you've all seen her talking with him, walking along the campus pathways, late at night, sometimes under a full moon."

Laurie screamed and shook. She left the rec room and hurried to her dorm room, locking the door once there.

Tim shook his head as she left. "I ask you, what more evidence do you need?"

\\\\\\\\\

Dykstra leaned against the counter in Vagabond Village Subs and watched the counterman load toppings onto his *Special*. The counterman put one pass from each tray on the sub, placed a sheet of wax paper on the counter, and started wrapping.

"Hey. That's not how I like it."

The counterman unwrapped the sub and went back to the trays of hot peppers, onions, tomatoes, and other toppings, adding a second scoop of each.

Dykstra heard the little bell over the door dingle but kept his eyes on the counterman and his sub.

"My god, the smell in this place. It's so...so...plebeian."

Dykstra turned around. "We got a problem, Andersen."

Todd took his felt, burgundy hat off and held it over his face like a mask, only his eyes showing over the brim. He walked up to the counter, eyed the menu, and shuddered. "Have you ever had real Italian food, Allen?"

The counterman turned around. "Hey."

Todd held up his hands. "Oh, no offense. I'm sure every backwoods, north country gourmand knows of this establishment. Do you have real flush toilets or do your patrons have to drop their drawers out back when the need arises?" he waved his hat in front of his nose to waft away the scent of the toppings.

The counterman turned back and finished wrapping up Dykstra's sub.

Andersen donned his hat, lit a clove cigarette, and blew the smoke over the counter. "What did you want to see me about, Allen?"

"Like I said, we got a problem."

"What problem do you have that you're asking my help for?"

The counterman handed Dykstra his sub. Dykstra waved at the rear door with his sub. "Go do something out back for five, ten minutes."

"I got to - "

"What you got to do is what you're told." Dykstra's hand went to his gun.

The counterman hurried out.

"Ah, delicate as always, Allen. Now explain why I'm here in a place which needs significant fumigation, please."

"Somebody knows about us. A lot about us. More than they should be able to know. More than they could learn by being on the job."

"Are you talking state?"

Dykstra shook his head.

"Federal?"

Dykstra shrugged.

"I know thinking's not your strong point, Allen, and I'll need more to go on. Let's start with this: Do you think this person is in or out of law enforcement?"

"I don't know. But their information is good and they have enough of it to be a threat."

"Good and lots of information doesn't tell me anything. Does our troublemaker have a name?"

"Sid Lyndon. A police officer. Works out of Gardiner PD."

Andersen spread his hands. "Ah, there you go. You've been stupid. Lyndon either saw something on your desk, overheard you on the phone, something like that. What are *you* going to do about it?"

"Me? I was hoping your boy could deal with it."

"That will cost you."

"One month, one third."

Todd considered. "Yeah, well...for a friend. Okay. When would you like this done?"

"Before our next payment. You can deduct it from my take."

"Oh, that will require some work, something to be done that soon. I'll reserve two-thirds as security."

"Jesus Christ, Andersen."

"Oh, no. Not Jesus Christ. Please. Never confuse me with him. We may look alike but that's as far as it goes. I'm not even Jewish. Want me to undress and prove it?"

"You sick fuck."

"Ah, you want me, I can tell. At least I know how to lie down and take it like a man."

Dykstra held his sub up like a shield. "Are we done?"

Andersen stepped aside. "Of course."

Dykstra hurried past and headed towards the police station.

Andersen watched him stomp through the last of the winter's snow. "Oh, Allen. Your little Bangor honey's more man than I am, m'lad, and you don't even know it." He leaned over the counter and cupped a hand to his mouth. "It's okay, you can come back now."

He left a hundred-dollar bill on the counter.

"Poor fellow deserves a good tip, working in a place like this."

Thursday, 7 March 1974

Morelli saw Tobey as he pulled into the barracks' parking lot. Tobey spotted him and came over so quickly he practically hopped. Morelli had to wave him out of the way so he could get a parking spot. "You got to pee, Tobes? You know they'll let you in if you have to pee."

"Yeah, ha ha, funny man." He pulled a manila folder out of his jacket. "I got what you wanted." He singsonged. "Who's your friend? Who's your friend? Huh? Huh? Huh? Got what you wanted. Got what you wanted."

"Your wife put up with you when you're like this?"

Tobey tucked the folder under an arm. "Hey, I can take this inside, Tony. You don't want this, I can find somebody who does."

Morelli lifted a duty bag out of the backseat. "Christ, we're touchy today. Okay. What'd'you have?"

Tobey laid four black&white photographs on the hood of Morelli's car. "It's the Sheepscot Pond Ghost-Child. We put a good telephoto on the camera and fixed it on one spot, then I had my wife put together survival packs - you know, canned foods, quick energy stuff, warm clothing, matches, fatwoods - and left one each day on the camera's hot spot."

"Christ, Tobey, it's a kid."

"I told you. It's the Ghost-Child."

"Poor bastard must've been frozen near death. What's the blotch on his face and neck?"

"No idea. Blood? Mud?"

"Nobody's come forward about him? Nobody's looking for him?"

"Wait for it. I've saved the best for last." Tobey pulled out two more photos. Grainy closeups. Tree trunks in the near background gave a good approximation of size.

"You know when the kid shows up? We can get a rescue team together. Get family services involved."

Tobey took one more photo out of his folder. "TADA!"

The kid looked square into the camera.

Morelli shaded it from the morning glare. "Holy fucking shit."

"Good, huh?"

"Come with me."

Morelli moved through the barracks quickly, Tobey in tow. He grunted hellos to his fellow officers and stopped at a set of filing cabinets in the main patrol room. He opened a drawer, flipped the hanging folders until he hit "T," thumbed thumbed thumbed until he hit "Thompson," pulled out the folder and put it on the coffee-stained table opposite the filing cabinets.

"Give me that picture again, Tobes?"

Morelli put Tobey's square on face shot side-by-side with the last picture of Ed Thompson Bill took.

Tobey stood beside Morelli and repeated Morelli's earlier revelation. "Holy fucking shit."

\\\\\\\\

Caroline sat at their usual table in the Windham Donut Shop and watched Todd run his tongue over the tip of his cream-filled cruller. She looked away in disgust.

"Oh, come now, Mother. You've never had one this big in your mouth before? You don't know what you're missing."

She pushed a thick envelope across the table to him. "I can only make one more payment after today."

He wiped his fingers on a paper napkin, lifted the envelope, and placed it in his inside jacket pocket. "Oh? And thank you, by the way."

"The well's run dry."

"Oh, I doubt it's run that dry. Certainly - "

"No, I've tapped out everything. You want to see my bankbook? We're already two months behind on our mortgage."

Todd stared out the window at Caroline's blood-red Mercedes 450 SEL. "I'm sure we could get at least another half payment for that. Want me to take it off your hands and manage the sale?"

"No, thank you."

"You're sure? Because it'd be no bother. I'd get my standard commission on top of next month's payment minus forfeiture and handling fees, of course."

Caroline sneered. "Of course."

"Do you have the title with you? I won't be able to sell that properly without the title."

"Forget it. The car's mine."

Todd's eyebrows lifted. "Oh? Do I sense some domestic unbliss? Something wrong on the homefront, Mother?"

Caroline looked out the window. "Nothing to concern you."

"Now, now, Mother, everything that concerns you concerns me. What are favorite sons for?"

Caroline brought her eyes back to Todd. He stared directly into her eyes, his cruller on his paper plate, his brow furrowed, his head cocked slightly to the side, his hand gently circumferencing his styrofoam cup of tea.

She snorted. "There may be one more thing you can help me with. Do that for me and the car is yours, period."

His brow furrowed further.

"But then we're done. Completely, totally, irrevocably done. Understood?"

His hand gently turned his cup. He nodded slowly with each turn. "Of course, Mother. Of course."

She nodded and left.

Todd delicately nibbled the tip of his cruller as he watched his mother get in her car. Even inside the shop with the clatter of cups and saucers and patrons' conversations, the resounding thunk of the Mercedes door closing stood out.

"Ah, quality. You just can't beat it."

He waved as she left the parking lot.

He held his cruller in front of him, raised the paper plate to his lips, and spit out the little he'd chewed. "Yes, quality." He plonked the cruller in his almost full tea cup. Tea spilled over the sides and ran along the table. He moved some napkins onto the spill, took out a roll of bills, ripped off a fifty, and put it on the table. "Nobody should have to rely on a place like this for their bread and butter."

He went outside. Mason's battered tow truck flashed its amber dome light in the IGA parking lot across the street. Todd waved. The truck crossed Route 1A and he got in.

"You got her money?"

Todd pulled the envelope out of his inner jacket pocket and tossed it on the top of the dashboard.

"Where to next?"

"Take me to the Giambatta."

Once there, Todd pointed to a parking lot down the street. Tall buildings on either side sheltered the lot from the early March sun which did its best to melt away dirt and soot covered snow. "Park there and stay in the truck, please. This is an unscheduled visit. I'd rather focus on business than have to deal with a pissing contest."

"Hey."

Todd stood beside the tow truck's open door and stared at Mason, his face blank.

"Yeah, fine."

Inside, Todd sat across from Nick flanked by heavymen. Nick sat at an angle to the table, his right leg crossed over his left, the *Boston Globe* spread-eagled in his lap, and his right arm resting on the table next to an espresso cup and saucer. He lifted the cup once to sip gently and kept reading the paper.

Todd looked around and realized no one was going to offer him an espresso.

The heavyman closest to Nick stared down at Todd like Jove readying thunderbolts. "Go ahead."

"I'm afraid I'll be short of cash in a few weeks and would like to arrange for a loan."

Nick sipped his espresso and continued reading the paper.

The heavyman said, "How much?"

"Ten thousand."

Nick turned a page.

"When?"

"Sometime between the fifteenth and twenty-fourth."

Nick turned a page. "*Non è quando Gio e la sua ragazza sono in vacanza?*" Isn't that when Gio and his girl are on vacation?

The heavyman reached into his sportcoat and pulled out a Day-Timer. He nodded.

Nick continued reading the paper.

The heavyman asked, "What do you need the money for?"

"I'd like to negotiate a truce with my competition. A mutual expansion of territories. You'd benefit by having easy access to the north country, French Canada, and the Maritimes for your product."

Nick turned a page.

"Have you looked into the other problem I mentioned, the one at Ramsey College?"

The heavyman nodded. "Yes."

Nick sipped his espresso.

Todd waited. "And?"

Nick folded the paper and placed it on the table beside his empty cup and saucer, adjusted his sportcoat, and walked away.

Todd looked around. His face reddened and he stood.

The phalanx of guards formed a wall between him and Nick's exit.

The first heavyman made a note in his Day-Timer. "Someone will contact you regarding your funding. The usual terms will apply. Acceptable?"

Todd nodded.

The heavyman pointed. "The door's that way."

Todd opened the door to see Mason pissing on a newly placed box of crocus, daffodil, and tulips. He stepped out and the door closed quietly behind him. "Jesus Christ, Mason. Holy Jesus Christ."

"What?"

Todd hurried to the parking lot. Mason zipped himself up as he came up behind.

Nick peered out the Giambatta's main window as Todd and Mason walked away. "*Riggerio, manda altri due uomini nel nord a prendersi cura di mio nipote e della sua amata.*" Riggerio, send two more men up north to look after my nephew and his beloved.

Riggerio nodded and went into the kitchen. The others stood quietly, their eyes forward, their hands clasped gently in front of them.

\\\\\\\\

Jess cuddled up beside Gio between thick wool blankets on the quiet sands of Singing Beach. "We could get a room if you like. I don't mind paying."

Gio didn't respond.

"Not that I'm cold. You're like a furnace." She put a hand on his chest. "You've always been like a furnace. I remember the first time we slept together wondering if you were sick."

Nothing.

"Are you listening to me?"

She lifted up on one elbow. "Gio?"

He wasn't breathing.

Gio?"

She put a hand over his chest. You could sometimes hear his heart beating in a quiet room. His chest would visibly rise and fall like an island forming and receding in the sea. Now she couldn't feel his heart at all.

She threw the top blanket back, straddled him, and started CPR. "One-Two-Three-Four-Five." She pinched his nose, put her mouth over his, and slowly exhaled. "One-Two-Three-Four-Five." Pinched nose, mouth over his, slow exhale. She repeated the exercise for some thirty seconds when she noticed he was frowning and looking at her.

"Gio. Oh, thank god."

"That is the strangest foreplay I've ever encountered. Want to switch positions and I'll massage your chest for a while?"

She punched his arm. "Don't make fun of me, goddamn it. I thought you were dying. Jesus Christ, Gio, what the fuck's going on? Don't you know I love you? Don't pull that shit on me."

"I'm sorry. I didn't mean to concern you." He reached for her. She pulled away and he sat up. "You love me. I know you've said it. I care that you've said it. It means a lot that you've said it."

"Don't you love me?"

"Yes. More than I ever have before. More every time I look at you. More every time I'm near you. More every time I breathe the air you breathe. I would give my life for you."

"You would?"

"I will. I already have."

"Huh?"

He looked at the position of the constellations, the full moon's placement in the heavens. "Lum's is still open. Hungry?"

She began folding their blankets. "We're not through with this. I want to know what happened to you. I don't want you dying on me. Even if it's for just a minute."

They headed south on Rt 128 to Danvers. She scooched up next to him. "This I like. This is good. You and me going places. This is a good thing."

He smiled.

Where I'm going, you can not follow.

She reached forward and turned the heater up full.

"You okay?"

"I just felt a chill. Strange. Maybe I'm getting a cold."

"No, you're not."

"So what happened on the beach?"

"Remember you and just about everybody else is telling me to practice?"

"That was you practicing?"

He nodded.

"You practicing how to die? Because we're not having any of that. You're staying alive. I've got plans for you and me and they don't involve either of us dying for a long, long time. Understand, Mr. Chance?"

"Fortuna."

"Huh?"

"My real name's Giovanni Fortuna. I should go back to using my real name."

"Is Bessie's heater working?"

He checked his gauges. "I'm about ready to take my jacket off."

"Now you're talking."

He laughed. America's *Muskrat Love* came over the radio.

And they whirled and they twirled and they tangoed
Singin' and jingin' the jango
Floatin' like the heavens above
It looks like muskrat love...

Jess tucked herself into him and they sat against each other, her hand on his lap and his right arm around her, as they headed down the highway. "What did you mean when you said, "I did. I already have.""

He checked his mirrors and switched lanes. "What we think of as this life, this universe, this...totality...is one of several. Everything we do, every decision we make, changes our path. There's either a way we should have gone and didn't, or a way we shouldn't go and did."

"Before you go on, do remember I'm an occupational therapy major, okay?"

"You decided to date me the day I picked you up in the rain. Remember?"

"How did you know that? I made you wait two weeks before I went out with you. I made you work for it, mister."

He smiled.

"I came by every night."

"Yeah, Sprite and peanuts. Every night. A can for you and a can for me and we shared the peanuts."

"You made me leave after we finished the peanuts."

"You figured that out, huh?"

"Why do you think I ate them one at a time after the first few nights?"

"I wondered."

"You wanted to make sure I put in the effort."

"Yes."

"That I wasn't after you for - "

"Exactly."

"That I was worth it."

"Yeah.

"That I was - "

"I get the idea. Next, please?"

"Have you ever wondered what would've happened if you said no when I asked if you'd like to go for a walk on the beach with me?"

She shook her head and shrugged. "Uh, no?"

"Want to find out?"

"Huh?"

He pulled off the highway at Rt 62 and turned right. Half a mile later he pulled into the Danversport Yacht Club.

"What is it with you and water?"

"Ever hear of Elementals?"

"You mean like oxygen, hydrogen, helium?"

"More like Earth, Air, Fire, Water, Ice, Metal, ..."

"No."

"Don't worry about it." He parked facing the harbor. "Put your head on my chest."

She smiled.

"No funny stuff."

She pouted.

"You want to understand this stuff or not?"

"Oh, alright." She rested her head on his chest.

"Hear my heartbeat?"

"Of course." She closed her eyes and sighed.

"Listen to my heartbeat. Let your mind wander." He slowed his pulse. His voice lowered, became quieter. "My pulse will slow. Just listen. Keep your eyes closed. It'll be like you're going for a ride."

He kept slowing himself until his bodies prepared to separate, a technique his grandfather gave him long ago, now remembered. He felt her relax as well, felt her body prepare to sleep.

He kept her awake enough to be aware, asleep enough to accept the experience, as if aware something is a dream.

She saw herself sitting at her dorm's front desk. It was her turn to let her dorm mates know when someone came calling. Gio'd come in each night just to talk with her. Some nights they played cards. Some nights he brought in a small 13" portable B&W he had and they watched fuzzy shows out of Boston. Tonight he asked her to go for a walk with him. She thought about it, decided no. "Maybe another night?" She shrugged. "I don't think so. Sorry. You're a nice guy and all, but, no." He smiled, thanked her for her honesty, shook her hand, left. She never saw him again. She transferred out of Iperia at the end of that term. Went to the University of Southern Maine. Studied hard, got good grades, came home for the holidays in her junior year and an old high school friend was using a backhoe in the Rosens' backyard. They caught up on things. He asked her out. Married. They had two sons, two daughters.

The dream ended.

A voice, low, resonant, quietly somnambulous, gently shaking with its words. "Want to see what happens if you never accepted my offer for a ride?"

She mumbled something and snuggled against Gio's chest.

The guy in the car drove on. The rain turned into a genuine downpour. She got soaked, wanted him to turn around, come back. He didn't. She got back to her dorm, changed, later went to dinner.

Learned of a mixer at Salem State. Went with some friends. A tall guy with a brilliant smile offered her a drink. It was sweet with a strange after taste. She woke up in his room, naked, not knowing how she got there. He was nowhere to be found. She pulled a bed sheet around herself and opened the door. This wasn't a dorm. She had no idea what this place was. She came back into the room and pulled back the drapes. It was morning. The ocean was a few streets away. She pulled more sheets around herself and walked, barefoot, to the ocean's edge. She stood there for hours as the waters rose, as the tide came in, not aware of where she was or what happened. She heard car doors slam. Someone said, "Are you okay, miss?" She didn't respond. Two men in police uniforms approached her, stood in front of her, the water up to their belts. "Miss! One of the neighbors up the street is concerned about you. Miss?" She stared at them. "Huh?" They called an ambulance. A counselor met her at the hospital. She began to remember.

Her hand clasped Gio's heavy plaid wool shirt. She whimpered.

The low voice again, gently shaking her. "Forget."

She opened her eyes, sat up, yawned. "Wow, what a dream."

Gio's eyes opened and his chest expanded with his breath. He frowned at her. "Which one?"

"Which one what?"

"Which dream?"

She laughed. "I only had one. About going back home. A guy I knew in high school. Barely. Funny."

"Never doubt that I love you. Realize that not all realities are this one. In more than one of them, I give my life for you."

She cuddled against him and sighed.

"You okay?"

"I am so hot for you right now."

Sunday, 10 March 1974

Gio stood under heavy storm clouds in his dorm's backyard. The clouds moved quickly, rushing through the skies, separating and re-forming, separating and reforming. Shapes, hideous and wonderful, creatures from myth and imagination, rolled through the skies, told him things, shared their knowledge with him.

He fell to his knees, one hand reached to stop his fall, slipped through the slush-covered earth. He came forward, his other hand reached for his eyes, wiped tears away.

"I can't. There are too many of you. I can't."

Something came up under him, lifted him. The clouds stopped roiling, pulled apart. A waning gibbous moon shone through.

He rode a whale's back. The whale kept him above the slush covered sea of grass, kept him above the waves of fear, of exhaustion, gave him a moment's rest, let him breathe. A slap of its fluke and they swam through the hole in the clouds. The whale sang, "There is a darkness coming."

Gio looked at the moon through clearing eyes, counted the days. "New Moon in two Saturdays. That's when the darkness will be complete. When Spring Break is over. When I'm in Gardiner, with Jess."

The whale returned him to the earth, melted into it, breached then dove into its crust.

Raven perched on a limb in front of him.

Gio stood, nodded. "Okay. Continue."

\\\\\\\\

Ed couldn't get any supplies. There were too many people in the woods. It wasn't safe. They shouted. "Ed! Ed! It's okay, you can come out now. Ed! Ed!"

Ed?

He was Ed.

He was Ed?

Where is Harry?

Who's Harry?

He went to a shanty on the far side of the pond. Nothing except a gun and a box of bullets. He took them. The aching in his head came and went with his movements. He headed southwest. Something said southwest. A big bird, yes. A big black bird came into the tree over his shelter. It told him to go home.

"Home?"

Caw Caw.

Caw Caw Caw.

He pointed. "That way?"

Caw Caw Caw.

Caw Caw Caw.

He set off two days ago, traveled at night, hid during the day.

The moon guided him.

These woods. I know these woods. I know that mountain. That's my mountain?

He looked around him. Animal signs. Trail signs. Big animals. Bear. Coyote. Wolf? They'd be hungry.

Shelter up in the trees. Back from the edge of the wood.

The moon touched the top of the mountain and illuminated the Thompsons' backyard to their house.

"I know that house."

He wanted to go forward.

His head ached.

The raven, the big black bird, perched above him.

Caw Caw Caw.

"It's not safe?"

Caw Caw Caw.

"It's not safe. Stay here tonight."

He climbed twenty feet up a pine and sheltered for the night.

\\\\\\\

Jamison stopped Morelli on his way to the showers. "Three days, twenty men, and nothing?"

Tony shook his head. "I'd rather not call this off, Lieutenant."

"I have to justify resources and from your reports whoever it is - "

"It's Ed Thompson, sir."

" - isn't taking the bait anymore. Anybody suggested this Ghost-Child moved on?"

"You saw Tobey's pictures, sir. It's Ed Thompson."

"Then where's his brother?"

"Sick? Dead? Wounded? Injured?"

"And what? A seven-eight-nine year old kid is outsmarting a team of experienced trackers and woodsmen while taking care of his wounded, dead, sick, or injured older brother? That's some kid, don't you think?"

Morelli shrugged.

"What about Joe Flying Bear? He could find shit in a sandstorm, that one. What does he say?"

"We left word for him with his grandmother. He doesn't have his own phone."

"You been checking with her? She got word to him?"

Morelli held up his hands. "She says she'll let him know when it's time."

"We got anybody else could do this?"

They met each other's eyes and spoke simultaneously. "Gio."

\\\\\\\

The sun peeked over the Thompson home. Meville and Xavier walked through the wood. Meville pointed. "Bear shit."

Xavier nodded. "Yeah, bear." He nodded towards another pile. "Coyote."

"Yeah."

"Come on. We're done. We got to tell Papa there's nothing left of brother-in-law Bill except bear and coyote shit."

Xavier knelt under Ed's tree. "What's that?"

Meville looked over his shoulder. "Bobcat."

"Looks awful big for bobcat."

"Bobcat."

"You think Bill put himself back together and took a shit in the woods? You think he's the pope?"

"There's magic in the woods. You know that. You remember that old man and his squaw? And now his kid's come up to haunt us."

"Christ you are your old man's son. It's 'cat shit. Come on. We've got work to do."

Caw Caw.

Xavier ducked. "See? Raven. I told you. Magic. Raven."

Raven perched above them, in an elm away from Ed.

Caw. Caw.

Meville formed a snowball and threw it.

The raven lifted from the branch and dove for him.

"Jesus Christ."

"You see? Raven! I tell you! Magic."

"Give me a gun and I'll show you magic. Come on, I said. She's probably hanging around for scraps and wants us out of her hunting ground." Meville pushed his brother towards the house. "Go."

"I'm telling Papa."

\\\\\\\

"Neil Jamison on the phone for you, Gio. Sounds long distance."

"Get a number and tell him I'll call him back in ten minutes, thanks."

Gio grabbed the phone number and his jacket and ran across campus to the Student Center.

Jamison answered on the first ring. "Catch you at a bad time, Mr. Chance?"

"What can I do for you, Lieutenant?"

"I'd like to formally request your help."

"Formally?"

"Put you on the payroll, give you a title."

"Sorry, that's not how it works."

"Yeah, Morelli said you'd have trouble with that. What can I do to make it worth your while?"

"Nothing. You don't have to do anything to make it worth my while."

"Are you saying you're out? You don't want to help us?"

"No, I'm saying I'm doing it for my own reasons."

"Mind if I ask what they are?"

"Just about everybody I run into seems to be telling me I should do this, or practice whatever it is I do, something like that. Even you told me that. Remember?"

"How accurate will your information be?"

"It'll be accurate but I don't know if anything I learn will make sense."

"Accurate nonsense. That doesn't sound too helpful, Mr. Chance."

"That's why I don't want to be on a payroll. Adds performance pressure."

"You don't work well under pressure?"

"I don't work well, period. People are asking me to do stuff I vaguely remember my grandfather talking about when I was a kid. I'm telling you not to expect much. I'm not going to give you information unless I think it's good, accurate, and useful."

"How 'bout you tell us what you find out and we'll decide how good, accurate, and useful it is?"

"You wouldn't understand it. No offense."

"Oh, I don't know, Mr. Chance. We got some pretty smart people here."

"Lieutenant, it doesn't work that way and if I'm going to do this, it's going to be on my terms."

"Okay, let me see if I've got this straight. You might discover something like 'the tiger walks in the spring' but have no idea what it means or how that applies to our situation so you won't share it?"

"Poetic, and yes."

"Are you willing to compromise? Let us know if the tiger's walking somewhere and that's it. Don't worry about telling us what it means? Let us figure it out if we can?"

Silence.

"Of course, if you do know what it means, you'll share that, too, right?"

Silence.

"Mr. Chance? Gio?"

"You called me, Lieutenant, and I'm happy to bow out."

"Morelli overheard a couple of greengrocers while he was undercover at the Gardiner Service Plaza."

"I can just tell I don't want to hear this."

"They made a reference to the Massachusetts Spook Boy spending time with the Gardiner Jews. I don't know about you, but that sounds like you and your girlfriend's family. You tell me, is that something I should be concerned about? Or you? Or the Rosens? I'm asking, is the tiger walking through the woods or in the spring or whatever the fuck I said?"

Gio closed his eyes.

Lower-Center-Relax-Breathe.

Look through Raven's eyes. From above. High. See it all. Through time.

"Mr. Chance?"

"Nothing's going to happen for a while yet."

"And you know this how?"

"I plan on coming up this weekend and staying a week. I'll explain what I can then. Okay?"

"But you're sure nothing's going to happen between now and then?"

"Nothing's going to happen because they're waiting for me to come up."

"They who?"

Gio inhaled. The scent of gunpowder.

"I don't know who, only that firearms are involved. One, anyway."

"Firearms? What are you talking? Handguns? Rifles?"

"The Tiger walks in the Spring."

Gio heard a pencil tapping on Jamison's side of the conversation. "Anything else, Mr. Chance?"

Gio watched a sika deer rush into pines. At the side of a road. Gunshots.

What?

"Mr. Chance?"

"No, nothing right now."

"But you'll call if you learn more about the tigers? Or anything else?"

"Yes, sir, I will."

"Thanks, Mr. Chance."

"See you in about a week, Lieutenant."

\\\\\\\

Tim Annandale sat in Doc Ock's office, his long legs tucked under his straight-backed chair, his church suit still in place, his tie strangling him through his collar, his face pulsing red.

"I thought you were going to deal with this problem for us, Mr. Annandale."

"Sir, I - "

"He's still on campus, isn't he?"

"Sir, I - "

"Using this campus as a base for his heathen operations, I understand."

"Dr. Ock - "

"I introduced you to that FBI agent, didn't I?"

"Sir, - "

"And Chance is still whoring with that Jewish girl from Iperia, too. Isn't that right, Mr. Annandale?"

Tim erupted. "Sir, if you'd just let me speak."

Doc Ock glared at him. "Don't ever use that tone of voice with me, Mr. Annandale. You're not invulnerable here. You think you live so pure a life we don't know things about you?"

Tim's eyes opened wide. He bowed his head and stared at the rug patterns.

Doc Ock paced back and forth behind his massive oak desk, his body righteously straight and tall, his shoulders back, his hands clenched behind his back. Daylight glared off his glasses as he paced left, light from his banker's desk lamp as he paced right, his footsteps silent on the thick-pile rug. "Spring Break starts in less than a week, Mr. Annandale. I'm giving you that much time to remove that plague from our shores." He spun and faced Annandale. "Do you understand me, Mr. Annandale?"

Tim nodded.

"I can't hear you, Mr. Annandale."

"Yes, Sir. I understand."

\\\\\\\\

Jess watched Gio stand at the edge of the ocean. His body rocked back and forth with the waves but he never lost balance. He moved his hands in front of him, almost in circles as if shaping wheels in front of himself; his arms out straight, shoulder height, his hands clasped, pulled down, pulled in, came up by his chest, his hands opened as they rose, palms out, push forward, again and again and again. His breathing matched his movements. A few minutes in she noticed his motions, his breathing, and the waves synchronized. For a moment it seemed he became part of the ocean, or controlled the waves, or the waves controlled him.

"Stop it!"

His hands came down, his eyes opened. Waves crashed against the shore in confusion.

His head turned to her mechanically. "Yes?"

"Stop it. Just stop it. I don't know what you're doing and stop it."

"I'm practicing."

"I don't care. Make love to me."

"I always make love to you."

"I mean fuck me. Come on, fuck me."

"No."

She came over and punched him. His body splashed as if it were water. Something plopped out in the sea. "You're water. You're Jesus Christ Fucking water!"

"Jess."

She reached out for him. Human arms held her. She sobbed into his chest. "I'm losing you. Goddammit, I'm losing you and I don't even know what it is I'm losing you to."

"You told me to practice. Everyone's told me to practice. The *Rebbe* told me to make a decision. I did. Do what my Grandfather taught. Isn't that what everybody's telling me to do?"

"I meant make a decision for me."

"I love you."

She clutched him, a child seeking comfort. "Tell me that you'll always love me. Tell me that I'll never have to be afraid or alone."

He sighed. "Yes. I will always love you." And in fifty years I will write a story about you. About my memory of you. About how much joy you brought me and how much you taught me. That's how much I love you.

"And?"

He looked, to be sure. "And you'll never have to be afraid. Or alone."

He rocked her in his arms as the ocean's waves wrapped her in sleep.

A figure rose from the water out beyond where the waves broke against the beach. The ocean swelled over it as it approached, its shape made of water and distinct from it. "You must tell her."

Gio held Jess against him. "Go away."

The figure became a woman whose shape flowed with the waves. "You must tell her."

"I said go away."

The woman stayed of water, her beauty that of the deep sea. Moonlight shone through her. She waited.

Gio sighed. "I know. I will. But now, please go away."

The shape slowly sank beneath the waves. A woman's face spread across the water. Her eyes winked in the moonlight. She was gone.

Gio rocked Jess in his arms. She slept.

Lower-Center-Relax-Breathe.

The hair lifted on his arms.

The world shimmered.

A doorway formed.

Part of him separated, stepped through.

Jess sat at her desk in her dormroom, a textbook open, a highlighter in her hand.

"Hello, Princess."

She looked up. "Gio? How did you get in here? I must be dreaming."

"Yes, you are."

"What are you doing here? I thought I heard you talking to someone a moment ago. Was I dreaming that, too?"

He walked over to her, gently lifted her from her chair. "Would you like to dance?"

She looked at the cramp quarters of her dorm room. "Here? Now?"

"I can think of no better place." The sides of her room fell away. They were alone on a dance floor. He wore a tux, she wore a full length, low-cut, form-fitting gown. The moon shown down as a spotlight on them.

"I don't know how to dance."

"I do."

"Can you teach me?"

He shook his head. "No, Princess. I can dance with you. I can hold you and have you move with me. But it's not in you to learn this dance."

A stage appeared. Paul McCartney and Wings waved and lifted their instruments.

Baby, I'm amazed at the way you love me all the time,
And maybe I'm afraid of the way I love you.

Maybe I'm amazed at the way you pulled me out of time,
You hung me on the line.
Maybe I'm amazed at the way I really need you.

Baby, I'm a man, maybe I'm a lonely man
Who's in the middle of something
That he doesn't really understand.

Gio and Jess glided across the dance floor.

"You're awful light on your feet for such a big man, Gio."

"Jess, my Princess, my Beloved, you who are everything in the world to me, understand you and I cannot be."

"What are you talking about, Gio? We dance so beautifully together."

"You want an unspecial husband, someone who works hard and whose efforts you can understand."

They lifted into the sky, into the heavens. Roberta Flack took the piano far below them.

Strumming my pain with his fingers
Singing my life with his words
Killing me softly with his song
Killing me softly with his song
Telling my whole life with his words
Killing me softly with his song

They climbed higher, beyond the sounds of the stage, beyond the sounds of the earth.

I heard he sang a good song,

I heard he had a style
And so I came to see him,
To listen for a while
And there he was this young boy,
A stranger to my eyes…

The music changed again and they spun to a waltz of celestial harmonies. "And as much as I love you, I would not burden you with a partner you could not understand, one who walked between worlds as easily as you walk between rooms in a house. Because the Universe is my house. Choosing not to walk it is to deny who I am, what I'm supposed to be, what I'm meant to do for myself and others." They neared the sun. The waltz became improv swing to Bruce Channel's *Hey Baby*.

Hey
Hey, baby
I wanna know
If you'll be my girl.

Their clothes shifted to retro-pop classic. He wore red suspenders over a cream fitted shirt with red pleated pants, cream stockings and red on cream fairways. She wore a teal and pink striped paradise dress, high-waisted and emphasizing her bust, with matching pink on teal balboas. "If you were to decide, would you want me knowing the me you have is not the me I'm meant to be?"

When I saw you walkin' down the street
I said that's the kind of gal I'd like to meet
She's so pretty, Lord, she's fine
I'm gonna make her mine all mine…

"But I love you."

"I love you, too. That's why I can let you go. If I didn't care, I wouldn't care about your happiness. And I cannot burden you with me."

"But we can dance!"

"Look down."

The earth receded from them, continuing its path around the sun. She clutched Gio's arms, wrapped her legs around his.

"Hello, Princess."

They were back in her dorm room. She frowned, looked up from her textbook, noticed the highlighter in her hand, put it down. "Gio. Hi. Wow, did I have a weird dream."

He smiled. "You still are." He turned into water, a mist, and evaporated as she watched.

Thursday, 14 March 1974

Kagan listened quietly, his only sounds a grunt in response to the chief oncologist's words.

"Do you understand, Mr. Kagan?"

"Unh."

All the other agents in the office quieted. Several grabbed their coffee cups and left. The others took cigarette packs out of their pockets and mumbled something about going for a walk around the building.

"We've put her in a coma to manage her pain."

"Unh."

"We're monitoring her closely, and you must prepare yourself."

"Unh."

"We suggest you contact your rabbi and your synagogue."

"Unh."

"If she comes out of coma..."

"Go on."

"Well, it's not likely she'll come out of coma. But if she does, it won't be for long. I don't know what to tell you. We could set up a cot. You could stay beside her..."

"Unh."

"Let us know your wishes. The sooner the better."

"Is she in pain?"

"It's difficult to say. I wouldn't think so due to the medication."

"Can you do that...what's it called? Euthanasia?"

"That's illegal, Mr. Kagan."

"Unh."

Kagan heard the doctor's beeper go off.

"I have to go Mr. Kagan. Let us know what you decide, okay?"

"Unh."

Kagan sat alone, his eyes focused on nothing, his hands in his lap, the ventilation system's whirring the only sounds in his world.

Another agent's phone rang. Kagan jumped. He stared at the phone, at the white button blinking on its base. The blinking and the ringing weren't synchronized. He'd never noticed that before and today it fascinated him.

"Unh."

His boss stood in the doorway and cleared his throat. Kagan didn't respond, his mind locked on the blinking, ringing phone on the other agent's desk.

"Mark?"

Blink blink ri-i-ing. Blink blink ri-i-ing.

One of the other agent's came, coffee cup in hand.

Mark's boss pointed at the ringing phone. "Get that." The agent hurried over. The boss stood in Kagan's line of sight. "Mark!"

Kagan looked up. "Yes?"

"I'm ordering you to take time off. As much as you need. Understand?"

Kagan nodded slowly. "Unh."

"Tell me you're going to take some time off, Mark. More than a day. A week. Understood?"

Kagan slowly gathered papers and put them in folders. He opened drawers and placed the folders into files.

"Mark, when was the last time you slept?"

"Unh. I don't know. Yesterday?"

His boss turned to the other agent. "Can you get Mark home? Get him in his house."

Kagan's fog lifted. "I can find my way home."

"I'll post a goddamn guard at your house if I have to, Mark."

Kagan waved him away. "I'm fine. I'll take the rest of this week and next off. Okay?"

His boss nodded. "Good."

\\\\\\\

Stephanie played hide-and-seek with the twins. She was it and the great challenge was not finding them. She'd see little butts sticking out from behind furniture, towels walking like Hallowe'en ghosts, hear chuckles when she said, "Where are those bad little boys, hiding on me like this? Oh, wait 'till I find those two little imps!"

Caroline walked into the living room in dress slacks, creme ruffled shirt and blood-red blazer with her best jewelry on. She pointed to a small slippered foot protruding from behind a sofa.

Stephanie pounced. "Gotcha!"

Squeals of laughter as the twins raced around her into another room.

"Stephanie, could I ask you a favor? I need a package delivered to a friend back in your hometown. Any chance you could drive it up there for me? You could make a day of it. Get out and have some fun. Maybe see your folks and some old friends while you're up there."

"Sure. What about the boys?"

Stephanie shook her head. "Not a concern. When could you make the trip?"

"Tomorrow works."

"Perfect. I'll let them know you're coming. Where's an easy place to meet you?"

"Tell them the Gardiner Service Plaza at two. Everybody knows where that is." Stephanie arched her back forward, curled her hands into claws, and rose on tip-toe, Nosferatu stalking her victims. "Ooh, where are those children? Yum yum yum yum yum." She followed the sounds of their laughter through the house.

\\\\\\\\

Gio and Jess drove back from an afternoon matinee of *Billy Jack* at the Cabot in Beverly, up along the coastal scenes and country homes lining Rt. 127, away from Iperia and Ramsey to Singing Beach in Manchester-by-the-Sea.

"We never come here in the daytime."

"I practice at night."

"Is that why I never see you anymore?"

"I'm here now."

She leaned against the passenger door and turned to face him. "Hey, thanks for sparing me some of your time."

"You think I don't want to see you anymore?"

"You used to come by every night. You were clockwork. Don't you want me anymore?"

Pilot's *Magic* came over the radio:

> *Oh, ho, ho*
> *It's magic you know*
> *Never believe, it's not so*
> *It's magic, you know*
> *Never believe, it's not so*

He took her hand. "Don't you know how much I want you? How my blood boils thinking of you? You are my comfort and my solace."

She snapped her hand back and looked out to the ocean. "You sound like a Simon and Garfunkel song."

"Jess - "

"What do you spend your nights doing exactly? What is it you're practicing?"

> *I love my sunny day*
> *Dream of far away*
> *Dreaming on my pillow in the morning*
> *Never been awake*

Never seen a day break
Leaning on my pillow in the morning light

He sat back. The hairs on his arms lifted slightly. "Remember the *Rebbe* wanted me to make a decision? You said if my grandfather had me practice then start doing what he taught me? Remember saying that? Morelli wants me to help him catch bad guys because he thinks my grandfather helped his father catch bad guys. Morelli told his boss and now he wants me to help him catch bad guys. Everybody - "

She interrupted. "Did he? Did your grandfather catch bad guys?"

He shook his head and gazed at the ocean. "I don't know. I was a kid. I don't remember."

She faced him again and crossed her arms over her chest. "I don't believe you don't remember. You may not remember it all and I'll bet you remember something."

He slouched until his head rested against the seat and closed his eyes. "Yes. I remember." The air in the car started silently crackling, subatomic lightning creating infinitesimal flashes, micro auroras in the afternoon light.

"What do you remember?"

"I remember my grandfather telling me don't ever let people know what you can do. If they know what you can do they'll hunt you down and kill you."

"Wow. Not too melodramatic. So you're psychic. Intuitive. So you know things. Hey, Maine's starting a lottery this year. Let me know if you can pick the winners."

"It doesn't work that way."

"Then it's not too useful, is it?"

"You don't use it for things like that. There are rules - "

"Again with the rules."

Steely Dan's "Do it Again" came over the radio:

You go back, Jack, do it again
Wheel turnin' 'round and 'round

You go back, Jack, do it again

"Have you ever heard "Power corrupts. Absolute power corrupts absolutely"? That's why there are rules. So we'll know when we break them. If this stuff was easy everybody would do it and there'd be chaos. But it takes work, practice. Lots of practice. It's like being a concert pianist. It's not what you do anymore, it's what you are. You're not a pianist anymore, you're the music you play at the piano. The rules are so we won't abuse what we can do, do it wrongly or for the wrong reasons."

When you know she's no high climber
Then you find your only friend
In a room with your two timer
And you're sure you're near the end
Then you love a little wild one
And she brings you only sorrow
All the time you know she's smilin'
You'll be on your knees tomorrow

"Who decides what are the wrong reasons? You and the rest of Woo-Woo Incorporated? How do you get into the club? Can I join?"
"Sure you can. Practice."
"But I don't know what to do."
"Welcome to the club."

You go back, Jack, do it again
Wheel turnin' 'round and 'round
You go back, Jack, do it again

"Oh Jesus Fucking Christ. You and these goddamn rules you never talk about, but you know there are rules and you won't violate them. Rules like what? You can only do things at night? You're a vampire? Or is it only from nine-to-five? This is your job?"

"What do you want from me, Jess?"

"I want proof. I want evidence. I want to know you're not sleeping with somebody else. You said some woman pushed you out of the water that time, remember? Who is she and what's she doing jumping in a pond with you?"

"You want proof. Evidence."

She opened her window a crack and unzipped her jacket. "Yeah, that'd be nice. Something to let me know you're not keeping me in the wings until you know you've got something better."

"You think I'm bullshitting you."

"It's happened before, somebody I cared about keeping me on the hook until he found something better."

He inhaled. Air came in Jess's window and ruffled her hair. "I cannot conceive of anyone better. When you've tasted ambrosia do you think you can be satisfied with vanilla? Once I've tasted your kisses could I be happy with anyone else's?"

She reached out and pulled back. "No. Don't make nice to me. I'm not falling for that again. Heartbreak once in a person's life is enough. You tell me you're practicing and that's why I don't see you anymore? Great. Make me believe you. Show me what you practice. Read my palm. Drink some tea and tell me what the leaves show you. Tell me about the tall, dark stranger who'll sweep me off my feet and take me away."

His eyes opened. His irises receded until only centers of black in a sea of white remained. "You want me to show you what I can do?"

She folded her arms over her chest again. "Yes."

"You are sure that's what you want?"

"Yes. How many times you going to ask me? Stephanie said you asked her three times. What is this, magic? You going to wave your hands and utter a spell?"

"Once more, so we're both sure; you want me to show you what I can do, correct?"

"Oh, Jesus Fucking Christ. Yes, yes, yes. Okay? Yes, yes, yes. Go ahead, Genie. Come out of the bottle."

He relaxed into the seat. The springs creaked as if a great weight fell upon them. "Because you asked..."

The storms in Bessie's passenger compartment grew into inaudible whispers.

Jess looked around. "What's that sound?"

The world folded around her, exposed her, opened layers of her thoughts, colored her body according to its needs, revealed her fears and joys, hopes and dreams.

The arteries on Gio's neck swelled.

"What are you doing?"

A uterine cyst dissolved. "You had a cyst. It's gone."

"How did you know about that?"

"I didn't. I knew you couldn't get pregnant by me. That was why. You're on the pill just to be sure, just in case, but you could never get pregnant by anybody, not and carry it to term. Now you can. Better stay on the pill, my darling."

She clutched her chest. "That's...what..."

"You had a heart murmur. An aberration in the muscle wall. I've heard it, never knew what it was. It's gone. You'll live a long life now. No worries about having children or going to the dentist."

"What?"

"You have a weak vein in your left leg. You can't run because of it. It's why you didn't run out of the rain when I first met you."

Her leg shot out and kicked Bessie's floorboard.

"It's gone. You can run, jump, hike, do anything you want. No worries about your leg falling asleep." He sighed. "Or falling off. Needing surgery."

He sat up and turned to her. The colors floating around her body gathered into maelstroms in her mind. His eyes became blackholes swallowing her thoughts.

She stared at him, thinking the words but her mouth unable to speak. *How did you know those things? I didn't tell you those things. Who told you those things?*

His face became blank, neutral, expressionless. His head cocked slightly to the side but his eyes remained on her. "No, you didn't. Nobody did."

His head lifted and cocked to the other side.

Her eyes widened, she pulled back against the passenger door.

He quoted her thoughts to her. "He got a hold of my medical records at Iperia."

He paused. His face saddened.

"FUCK FUCK FUCK FUCK FUCK! My god, this is real. FUCK FUCK FUCK FUCK FUCK! This can't be real. I'm dreaming. I'm hallucinating. What's he doing to me?"

He paused again.

"OH MY GOD HE'S IN MY HEAD!"

She blocked her ears with her hands.

He reached out but like a blind man, groping. She pulled back, away, fearful of the leper in her presence.

He repeated her thoughts, waiting a beat between each utterance until the thought fully formed. "He's for real. This is for real."

Beat.

"I can win the lottery."

Beat

"I'll never be sick again."

Beat.

"I don't trust him."

Beat.

"Can I never have a private thought?"

Beat.

"Even when I'm not with him will he know what I'm thinking?"

Beat.

"Is he going to be jealous if I see a cute guy and think he'd be fun to bang and think I don't love him?"

Beat.

"What's going to happen if other people find out?"

And then beatless as her thoughts raced faster than he could say the words. "Is he never going to be mine because everybody's going to be coming to him to do things? Is he going to be obligated to help them out?" "We can live the life of Riley." "He can heal me." "He can prevent any kind of disease." "He fixed the murmur. He fixed the cyst. What else can he do?"

And then as a stream because fear broke through her like a river breaking through a dam. "If we have kids...Oh my god who'll they be like? Me? Him? Combination? What if the kid is...can't do what Gio does. Will Gio love him? Or her? I don't want him knowing my every thought. What if I don't want him to know something? How do I stop him from knowing my thoughts?"

She gripped the door handle. "Stop it."

"What if something changes in the relationship?

"What will he do if he doesn't love me anymore?

"How much control does he have of what he can do?

"Can he do things by accident? Unintentionally?

"He could hurt me. Without realizing it."

She screamed. "Stop it!"

"Can he control governments? Money? People? Anybody?"

She slapped him. Her hand passed through his face as if it were vapor. Little swirls of mist followed her fingers back to her own face, settled there. She felt his lips on her lips, neck, breasts.

She opened her door and scrambled on to the ground. She crawled five, six paces and stood, ready to run.

He stood before her, his hand out, ready to help her up. "You asked."

She curled into a ball and whimpered, lost.

Friday, 15 March 1974

Dykstra met Lyndon before start of shift at the Vagabond Village Sub Shop. He slid a thick, white, size 10 envelope across the table to him. "That's your cut."

Lyndon pulled back the flap and ran his thumb over the enclosed bills. He stopped randomly and checked the denominations, held the envelope to his nose and inhaled deeply. "Ahh. Smells about right."

He sealed it and tucked it in an inside jacket pocket.

Dykstra pushed back from the table. Lyndon tapped the tabletop and shook his head.

"What? That's what we agreed on."

"How do I know that?"

"What do you mean?"

"It's a nice catch, sure, but how do I know I got my cut? Maybe you decided 50/50 didn't work for you. Maybe you decided 60/40. Or even 70/30."

"Quit busting my balls. You got your money."

"I want to see you get it. Gotta know how much you take so I'll know how much I should take."

Dykstra shook his head. "Ain't gonna happen."

"Make it happen."

"Or what?"

"Oh, you never know. All sorts of things happen to people up here on these back woods Maine roads. I'll take this and call it even. But next payment, I want to be there when things go down, want to take part, have a seat at the table."

Dykstra looked at Lyndon. He put his hands flat on the table and pushed as he stood.

"Easy, Sarge. You don't look too steady on your feet."

Dykstra grunted. His lips pulled back into a silent snarl. He shook his head and left.

\\\\\\\\\\

Caroline shivered in the phone booth outside Windham Donut. "C'mon c'mon c'mon."

"Hello?"

"I'm sending you this month's blood money. Our nanny's bringing it up. I asked her where would be convenient to meet you. She said the Gardiner Service Plaza would be best. Do you know it?"

Hesitancy. "That's not what we agreed to."

"The nanny. I don't want her coming back."

More hesitancy. "Okay."

"Understand?"

"What are you asking me to do?"

"I don't care what you do. Just make sure her, her car, and anything else never makes it back. Make them lost. Get rid of them. How else do you want me to say it?"

"Blunt and direct is best. No confusion that way. Do you want me to kill her?"

"Yes."

"Say it, Ma. You'll feel better if you do."

"Yes, I want you to kill her." Caroline shook with more than the cold. She clenched the receiver tight against her ear with both hands, their knuckles almost pushing through her skin. "Dead. I want her dead. Do you understand? Dead, dead, dead."

Calmness. "Any particular way? Car accident? Torch the car, everything in it, and while she's still inside? Knife her? Slit her throat? How about a gunshot? Belly wounds hurt like hell and kill you, I hear."

"I don't care."

"But she'll have my money? All of it?"

"Yes."

"So something after. On her way home, perhaps."

"I don't care. Just make sure her, her car, and everything in it never makes it back. Understood?"

"Of course. Anything for you, Mother. Happy to be of service."

Caroline stared at the phone hanging on the receiver. "Do I care you fuck him? No." Her face turned into a snarl. "But not in my bed, in my clothes." She inhaled deeply and exhaled as if spitting venom. "You Down East slut."

\\\\\\\\

Lyndon drove to the Gardiner Service Plaza and parked in front of the phone booths. A bushy-bearded man, dark skinned and wearing heavy clothing, nodded and spoke in one of the booths. A beat pickup with a tarp over the back idled beside it.

Lyndon waited until the man and pickup left. He entered the second booth, closed the door, and dialed a number.

"Hi, Ma. How's Dad?"

"Just a minute, Son. I'll put him on the phone."

A moment later. "Go ahead."

"I got the first payment. I'll put in the Portland Savings strongbox at the end of my shift today."

"It'll be safe until then?"

"I'll keep it on me until I can get to Portland."

The baritone grunted. "Call me when it's in the vault so we can begin processing."

"Understood."

\\\\\\\

Kagan opened his eyes, blinked, and smacked his lips, the sound slightly louder than the talking heads on his television. He looked around his living room. The shades were drawn. The talking heads sat at a desk with a clock on the wall behind them. He squinted.

"Nine?" He didn't know this show. Must be a morning show. "Nine AM?"

His left hand loosely held a bottle of bourbon by the neck. A styrofoam cup lilted in his right, its contents dribbling down his thigh. He sat in his shorts and t-shirt in his living room and worked hard at drinking himself to death.

The phone rang. No blinking lights, though. Must be for him. He blinked and sat up. "Yeah."

His boss' voice came through the receiver. "Kagan, we've had a development. You still have time off, I don't want you to come in. This is a courtesy call, understood?"

Kagan shook his head violently to clear it. "Give me a second to get a pen and paper."

He went into the kitchen and put on a pot of water to boil. His next stop was the bathroom. He kneeled in front of the toilet, stuck his finger down his throat, and cleared his belly. Several retches later, his face red, his abdomen weak from convulsions, he made it back to the kitchen, scooped out two heaping tablespoons of Sanka and made a cup of bitter coffee. Halfway to the living room he turned back to the kitchen, got a pencil and notepad, and returned to his living room. "Okay, go ahead."

"Jesus Christ, Kagan. Did you drive to Kmart?"

"Sorry, had to piss."

"This came in on your wiretap. Your CI plans to drop somebody. You want details or you want me to patch it through to you?"

"He naming names?"

"Not full. All we know is Stephanie somebody."

"How long ago was the call made?"

"Forty-odd minutes ago according to the tap log. Inbound to your man."

"When will he do this?"

"That's not on the call. Sometime today."

"How many other voices?"

"One. A woman's. He calls her Ma, Mom, Mother. He's an orphan, though. Isn't that what you said? She's sending him money so she's not likely part of the supply chain, right?"

Kagan nodded. "It's my CI in Windham. We followed him hoping he'd lead us to de Leo and he took us to Windham instead. A woman. We did a deep background to find the connection. She's his mother. Some janitor at a posh Swiss boarding school she attended. We got a yearbook and were able to isolate the likely candidate: a guy with a thick, dark mustache, wavy hair, and wiry frame, purportedly from Sabrosa, Portugal. Her parents had him fired, her transferred, and sent my boy to a New England orphanage before she even had a chance to see him."

"How'd he track her down?"

"He's clever and persistent."

"Dangerous combination."

"We can't do a backtrace to get the caller number?"

"It'll take a while and it's doubtful."

Kagan considered. Was Todd talking to Caroline? Kagan knew Caroline and her husband employed a nannie for their twin boys. Was that Stephanie? And if so, why would Caroline want Stephanie murdered?

\\\\\\\\\\

Caroline unlocked the Suisse Chalet's suite room door. She sat on the king-size bed and smoothed the coverlet, pulled down the blanket and fluffed the pillows, went to the bathroom, checked her makeup, came back, took a 5x7 framed picture of Donnie from her purse, set in on the dresser facing the bed, went back and sat on the bed.

Someone knocked on the door. "Come in."

A tall, thin, middle-aged man with graying hair and dark brown pencil mustache came in.

"You're...Bob?"

"Hi Caroline. Don't know if you remember meeting me at the church picnic Labor Day weekend."

Bob saw Donnie's picture on the dresser. "Donnie not joining us? He still at the banking convention in Philly?"

"Didn't you do that great imitation of Donnie talking business on the phone?"

Bob laughed. "You want me to talk like Donnie now?"

She smiled and unbuttoned her blouse. "Do you want to start or wait for the others?"

"Ted and Charlie pulled in behind me - "

Caroline closed her eyes and moaned. "That sounds delightful."

Bob smiled. "Bill's at the liquor store. Gary's going to be a little late." He put a hand in his pocket and massaged himself.

Caroline caught his movement and smiled as his pants bulged.

They turned at a knock on the door. Ted and Charlie entered.

Everybody exchanged greetings.

Charlie put an accountant's briefcase down, opened it, and placed ropes, handcuffs, ben-wa balls, and other sex toys on the bureau opposite the bed.

Another knock came on the door. Caroline stiffened. Bob held up a hand. "Don't worry. Just some new guys wanted to watch. No problem with some folks watching, is there?"

Caroline breathed slowly and relaxed. "No."

Two late middle-aged men walked in. Bob introduced them. "Everybody, this is Spencer, this is Chris."

Spencer was middle-age heavy but walked as if he'd once been strong, a college football player who didn't keep it up once he got an office job. Chris was lean and Caroline saw his pants bulge as he walked in.

She slowly licked her ruby red lips. "Boys, I can't wait. Let's get started."

Lyndon and Towne drove their squad past the Thompson home. Lyndon, driving, nodded at a battered pickup at the head of the driveway. "Who's that? That's not Chance's car is it?"

Towne shrugged.

Lyndon's eyes went from the road to the pickup and back. "You've been awfully quiet lately, Harry. Everything okay with you?"

Towne sat back and pulled his hat down over his eyes. "You put in for time off?"

"Family business. Just a week."

They turned onto Graham Road.

"You leaving tonight? After shift?"

"Got to catch a late flight home. Out of Boston."

"Home is where again? Virginia somewhere?"

Lyndon caught himself. "Montana."

"Chance said you were from Virginia."

"No idea where he got that."

"Said you weren't what you seem, too."

"For a guy who doesn't keep notes, you got a good memory."

A mile in, Towne sat up. "Pull over. I got to piss."

"You can't wait until we get to the service plaza?"

"What do you care? You'll be gone soon enough, right? You want me to piss the seat?"

Lyndon pulled off to a wide shoulder that sloped into heavy trees. Towne got out. He unzipped himself before he hit the tree line but kept walking through the snow until he was hidden in the woods.

Lyndon checked his watch.

A car slowed approaching from behind. He turned on his dome lights and waved the car past.

Towne didn't appear. Lyndon checked his watch again.

"Jesus Christ, Towne. You got a bladder or a bucket?"

Gun shots.

Lyndon got out of the cruiser and raced through the trees following Towne's prints. "Towne? Towne?"

He held his weapon at the ready.

The prints stopped at the base of a tree. A foot ahead of them was a yellow pool of melted snow.

"Hey, Sid?"

Lyndon looked up.

Towne put two bullets in his head. He jumped down from his perch, reached into Lyndon's inside jacket pocket, and took out the envelope full of hundreds.

"Ten-four, that, huh, Sid?"

\\\\\\\\

Tobey Harding visited his tech friend who, after a few drinks, invited him into his basement with "I got something you'll get a kick out of."

Tobey's eyes bulged when he reached the bottom of the stairs. "You could open a Radio Shack with all the shit you have down here."

The two of them sat at the friend's workbench. The friend pointed at a metal box with the top off. Tobey sipped his bourbon. "You took your ham radio apart?"

"No, I put this together over the past week. I call it The Snooper. It listens to police calls, military, aircraft, CB; if somebody's talking, my Snooper'll pick it up."

"Show me."

The friend couldn't wait. Lights blipped back and forth. A meter's needle wanged across its scale once or twice.

Tobey downed his drink. "Yeah, cute. I'm going to get some more - "

The Snooper's scratchy speaker squawked. "Do you have any cars on Graham Road? Somebody called in about gunshots close to the road about a mile south of the Dairy Queen sign, said they saw a Gardiner cruiser there. We don't have any reports."

A lone response, almost too garbled to understand. "Car 7. We'll check it out on the way home."

"Report if it's anything."

"Ten-four that."

Tony raised his eyebrows and nodded. "Nice." He took out a note-pad and wrote "Graham Road, mile south, Dairy Queen sign."

His friend glanced up. "Hey, you're not going to get me in trouble, are you?"

Tobey laughed, showed the note to his friend. "You think anybody's going to be able to read that?"

"Christ, what is that? Chinese? Greek? Chicken scratchings? You should've been a doctor with penmanship like that."

He put the notepad back in his pocket and patted his friend on the back. "Never know when something might come in handy." He said his goodbyes and left.

\\\\\\\\\\

Caroline came up her drive and parked by the front door, past the garages. She took off her coat and scarf, hung them in the front hall closet and went into the kitchen.

There was a note on the table.

> Decided to leave early. Have the boys with me. Figured they could use a day out. Back before dark. - S

Caroline's legs gave out. She collapsed onto the table and scattered the lazy susan in its center. Salt and pepper shakers crashed to the floor. Cloth napkins in festive spring prints in colorful holders rolled to the table's edge, hesitated, then followed the salt and pepper shakers. A central pitcher of water fell to its side and soaked the tabletop. Heavy crystal water glasses clashed together like football players after a dropped ball.

She picked up the kitchen phone, dialed Todd's number.

No answer.

She dialed again.

No answer.

One more time. She watched the kitchen clock, something to fascinate the boys, a cat with a clock face, its tail swishing back and forth ticking off seconds, its eyes going back and forth as the second swept around its face.

The eyes looked at her. It's your fault.

The eyes looked away. All this to get back at Donnie.

The eyes looked at her. You've killed your boys.

The eyes looked away. You should be ashamed of yourself.

The eyes looked at her. You tramp. You slut.

The eyes looked away. What you did with those men.

The eyes looked at her. Happy now?

She grabbed a knife from the butchers' block. What's that movie she and Donnie and their friends saw? *MASH*? The theme song? *Suicide is painless*?

She imagined Donnie coming home. Blood covering her blouse and pants? Her eyes vacant? Lifeless? Her body sprawled on the floor in a pool of her own blood?

She laughed. He'd probably jerk off on her corpse.

She grabbed her purse, coat, and scarf.

Gardiner Service Plaza. That should be easy to find.

Her Mercedes spewed gravel leaving the driveway.

\\\\\\\\\\

Stephanie walked out of the Gardiner Service Plaza with a child on each hand, each child held a small ice cream cone in their free hand. They all giggled.

She slowed when she saw a tow truck parked beside her Monte Carlo and the 'Carlo's hood popped. A man in overalls leaned over the engine.

Another man came up beside her and looked at the Monte Carlo, tow truck, and serviceman. "Somebody broke down, huh?"

"I don't think so. That's my car."

The man took a felt, burgundy hat from his head and bowed formally. "You must be Stephanie. I believe you have something for me." He nodded at the twins. "And who are these little darlings?"

\\\\\\\\

Gio heard the phone ring in the dorm's phone booth. A moment later and a dormmate tapped on his door. "Call for you, Gio."

He closed the phone booth door and chuckled as the click matched the light.

"How did I get back to my dorm yesterday?"

"Hi, Jess."

"I know I'm not supposed to call you at this number but I figured what the fuck, you probably know what I'm going to say anyway."

"No, I don't."

"Are we still going to my folks this week?"

"Do you still want to be with me?"

"You don't know? You knew everything about me yesterday and today you don't know? Is distance an issue? Is that it? You have to be around people to do your woo-woo?"

"What happened yesterday is between you and me and only happened because you asked me yesterday. Today is a new day. Do you still want to see me?"

"Is this more of that rules thing? There really are rules to this?"

"Lots of them."

"You make it sound like the *Aseret ha'Dibrot.* Is one of the rules don't hurt your girlfriend?"

"Most of them."

"Can we talk?"

"You feel safe being alone in a car with me for two-plus hours?"

"Pick me up at the usual time?"

"Yes, ma'am."

Silence.

"Jess?"

"Yes?"

"I love you."

Silence, then "See you at the usual time."

\\\\\\\

Caroline formed and reformed her plan driving up I-95. Todd would laugh, want to bargain.

Bargain for her boys. She didn't give a shit about Stephanie, that little harlot would get whatever she deserved, but her two boys, her little angels, they made life tolerable. DJ had problems, sure, but that was all Donnie's doing. And it didn't matter. DJ could get help. Robbie was a gem.

Right across the Maine border she saw the exit for the Kittery Traffic Circle. How she managed to avoid state troopers to this point amazed her. Seventy-five, eighty, sometimes ninety miles an hour and nothing.

But now she wanted to think, to prepare, to make sure she got the upper hand.

A large blue sign with a huge bullseye greeted her on the Circle. Kittery Trading Post.

The older man behind the counter nodded as she walked up and looked at the rifles, shotguns, handguns, and ammunition. "What can I do for you, young lady?" He had a grandfatherly smile.

"Could you recommend a gun to me?"

"What are you hunting?"

"Wolf?"

"Here in Maine?"

"Coyote?"

He nodded, looked at the ammunition in the glass case, looked at some weapons. "How much this coyote weigh, you think?"

"About one-thirty-five one-fifty."

"Big coyote."

She nodded.

He looked at her coat, her scarf, her purse. "You'll not want this coyote getting up, will you? I mean, one shot, you want him dead?"

She stared at him.

"Him, ma'am. Coyote that big's going to be male. Probably a cheating male."

She cocked her head.

"Or a male done something he shouldn't have? Made off with something important to you?"

She nodded.

"You'll want something with lots of stopping power, accurate, doesn't require lots of thinking. Lift, pull, shoot? One shot, dead and done, right?" He leaned across the counter slightly, looked right and left and surveyed other shoppers near and far, lowered his voice to barely a whisper. "I understand, Miss." He exhaled slowly, looked down and to the side briefly. "That's how my daughter wanted it."

Her eyes opened wide. She pulled back slightly.

He continued at a whisper. "With her coyote."

She nodded, her eyes narrowed.

"I'll tell you like I told her when she told me about her coyote. You got to do this in the woods, off the roads. Let the scavengers take care of the body. And once it's done, you go away. Don't look back, don't touch the bod…coyote. Understand?"

She swallowed, nodded.

"Ever seen that Italian movie, *The Godfather*?"

Nod.

"Remember that young soldier fella? He had to go into a restaurant and get rid of the coyotes shot his father? You remember that?"

"Yes."

"You got to be like that. You drop the gun and leave. You got gloves?"

She pulled a pair from her purse.

"You put those on now. You never touch anything with your bare hands. Understand?

She nodded.

"You ever fired a gun before?"

She shook her head.

He took two handguns and two boxes of shells from under the counter and nodded towards a door at the end of the gunracks. "Come with me. We have a firing range out back. First we'll get you used to holding a weapon, then we'll see which one suits you, then we'll make sure you hit what you're aiming for and nothing else. Sound good?"

Caroline smiled, nodded, and followed him.

\\\\\\\\

Gio and Jess drove up I-95. They crossed the Mass-NH border listening to Joni Mitchell's *Court and Spark*. Jess looked at the glow of the radio as Mitchell's soprano filled the car.

> *When something strange happened*
> *Glory train passed through him…*
> *She snickered. "Well, ain't that fitting."*
>
> *It seemed like he read my mind*
> *He saw me mistrusting him*
> *And still acting kind*
> *He saw how I worried sometimes*
> *I worry sometimes…*

"You said you wanted to talk. You've been awfully quiet so far."

"Noticed that, did you?"

"You don't punch me anymore. I miss that."

She wound up and hit him so hard he swerved into the next lane.

"Jesus, Jess." He got back in his lane and rubbed his arm. Cars honked their horns and accelerated past him.

"Oh, so I can hurt you, huh?"

"You can hurt me with a look."

"Tell me more about this."

> *And you could complete me, I'd complete you*

"You said there are rules. What are the rules?"

"The big ones are don't go where you're not invited, don't do what you're not asked to do. There are lots of others, but those two stand out. They're kind of the basis for all the rest."

"Who made the rules?"

"I have no idea. My grandfather shared them with me as things came up, to deal with things as they happened."

"What happens if you break the rules."

"You don't do that."

"But can you?"

"I have no idea."

"Try."

"No."

"Come on. Just a little one."

"No, because that's one of the rules. You break one once, you bend one once, and that's it, it's over."

"What's over."

He shook his head. "Do you really care what the rules are? Isn't it enough to know I won't violate them?"

"How will I know if you've violated them if I don't know what they are?"

But I couldn't let go of L.A.
City of the fallen angels.

"How about we do it this way: you ask me questions and I'll answer them if I can. Okay?"

"'Kay. Did you know everything I ever thought when we were together?"

"No."

"Why not?"

"Because you didn't give me permission. That's the - "

"Don't go where you're not invited?"

"Yes."

"Am I...are we always going to be on the lam if the government finds out about you? Morelli and his boss already know. Are you safe? Are we safe?"

"Where'd that one come from?"

"aHA! You're not in my head right now, are you?"

"Of course not."

"Or are you lying to me. How can I trust you? Yesterday...I woke up in my dorm feeling violated. It's like you raped me without even touching me."

"I asked you three times before I did anything. Remember?"

"Is that another rule? Ask three times?"

"Yes."

"But how do I know you really asked me? Can you put thoughts in people's heads?"

"Never tried."

"But could you?"

"I have no idea."

"Give it a try. Do it now. To me. Come on. Make me think or do something I wouldn't normally do."

The tone in his voice spoke finality. "No."

"All those other things you did - giving people periods, knowing what someone's thinking about, where the radar traps are, all of that stuff - you've always had good explanations. You made this one relax, you read their body language, you watched oncoming traffic. How much was what you said and how much was you doing..." She rolled her eyes up in her head and shook violently.

"I really look like that?"

She punched him again.

"That's the woman I love. Want to pull over and have sex?"

She sat back. "No. Not until I'm sure it's me wanting you and not you wanting to get your rocks off and making me want you cause I'm handy."

He sighed and shook his head.

They crossed the Piscataqua River Bridge and he caught her staring at him.

"What am I thinking now?"

"Huh?"

She reached into the backseat, pulled up her laundry bag, and covered her face. "Can you hear this? Huh?"

She put the bag back in the backseat. "How about this? Can you hear this?"

"We playing peekaboo now?"

"When are all the good sales happening?"

"What?"

"Did Geena steal my necklace?"

"Who?"

"If you can really do these things we're going to be so good at pub trivia."

He sighed. "Well, at least that tells me we're going to go out again."

They went through the York tolls. She sat up and her face hardened. "Did you know this was going to happen? That we'd have this discussion?"

"I knew if we're going to stay together we'd have it at some point."

"If you knew this was going to happen, then how does it end up? If you're so smart, if you know what's going to happen..."

"I knew this was going to happen because it's right up there with 'do you want kids?' and 'how many?' It's right up there with will we raise them gentile or Jewish? It's right up there with diabetes runs in my family. Or cancer. Or all the men die in their early thirties. It's something you share if you want someone to be in your life. Did I need special power to know we'd have this discussion at some point in time? No, all I needed to know was I want you in my life and I want to be honest with you. All I need to know is I love you and I want you to know what you're getting yourself into. Part of my decision was whether I was willing to risk losing the only thing that's had meaning in my life. If that meant telling you the truth and risk losing you or lying to you the rest of my life, I'll take the risk. That's how important you are to me. Those are my rules, not my grandfather's, mine."

She sat back.

"Now you have to decide. I've opened myself to you. Now you know all about me. You have to make the decision. I've told you who I am, now you have to decide." CSN sang *Guinnevere*

Guinnevere drew pentagrams like yours, m'lady,
like yours
Late at night when she thought no one
was watching at all.
On the wall.
She shall be free.

Bessie's heater kept them warm, nothing else. The air didn't crackle, Gio's eyes remained fixed on the road.

Saturday, 16 March 1974

Kagan peeked through the curtains of his room facing the Gardiner Service Plaza. The Bluebird Motel wasn't the classiest of places but it was exactly where he needed it to be. Not able to reach Andersen and not officially on duty, he checked in across the street from the one place he knew Andersen operated out of.

And no Andersen.

He checked his watch.

He'd call Janey's doctors in a few minutes and see if he should rush back.

More cars coming and going.

No Anders - What the...?

Caroline Tyler? Walking as casual as can be?

From here? From The Bluebird?

Holy Jesus Christ.

What's she doing up here?

Holy Jesus Christ.

How's she mixed up in this?

Holy Jesus Christ.

Did she plan on doing Stephanie Thompson on her own?

Holy Jesus Christ.

Kagan ran his hand over his hair.

Holy Jesus Christ.

\\\\\\\

Morelli walked through the Gardiner Service Plaza towards his usual seat and noticed the smartly dressed, mid-30s woman who came in midafternoon yesterday, sat around for a bit, then left. Her clothes, the same she wore yesterday, were rumpled, her makeup disheveled, and she sat by the window where she sat yesterday. He got two coffees with creams and sugars on the side and walked up to her. "Mind if I sit down?"

She looked around at the empty tables. "Plenty of empty chairs."

"You looked like you could use some coffee." He shrugged and held it out. "I got you a cup."

"I'm not looking for a date."

"Didn't say you were, not my intention, and okay, I'm completely mistaken. I recognized you from yesterday. Thought maybe something was..." He let it hang. She kept looking through the parking lot. He pointed to his usual seat. "I'm sitting right back there if you want to talk. Enjoy the coffee." He put it down and continued to his usual seat by the wall where he could watch all the comings and goings in the plaza.

He found his gaze stopping on her every five, ten minutes. At first, she didn't touch the coffee. The next time he looked, her long fingers encircled the cup and spun it every few seconds, a kind of tick-tick-tick-quarter-turn-of-the-cup, tick-tick-tick-quarter-turn-of-the-cup.

When he looked again the top was off, one sugar and one cream lay opened on the table in front of the cup, and the wooden stirrer came out of the top like the lone reed in a very small pond.

A commotion in the parking lot caught his eye. Nothing. Frat boys rough housing.

The woman walked up to him. "You said you saw me here yesterday?"

"Yes, Ma'am, I did."

"You spend a lot of time here?"

How do I answer? She doesn't look like a seller. A buyer? "Yeah, kind of. I come here to hitch rides up and down I-95."

She snickered. "No, you don't. You're too old to hitchhike and your clothes are too upscale for someone who needs to bum rides. Unless you're house-rich and cash-poor, or vice-versa, can't afford a car."

He winked. "You caught me."

"May I?"

He nodded and she sat facing him, her back to the clutter of people. "I'm looking for someone. Maybe you've seen them?"

"How's your coffee? Need a warmup?"

\\\\\\\\\\\

Tobey saw a gray 1965 Ford Falcon parked on the side of Graham Road about a mile south of the Dairy Queen sign. A hundred yards further up, a dirt road led to a closed camp. Maybe he could get some shots of a break-in? Had the Ghost-Child been on the move? Something clicked. He took out his notepad, flipped some pages.

He slowed as he neared the Falcon.

A man came out of the woods, dark complexion, beefy, and dressed for the outdoors like a Mainer would be: wool-lined red cap with ear flaps, heavy, mid-calf Bean boots, green wool pants and red-on-black flannel shirt. He held a double-headed axe in his left, his grip high on the neck, woodsman style. He carried a dark green industrial plastic garbage bag under his right arm. Whatever was inside was bulky, heavy, because the man tipped towards his left to compensate as he walked.

The man stopped. He looked at Tobey's car, at his license plate, then at Tobey. The man's eyes locked on Tobey's. Two jets of steam rose from the man's nose as he exhaled.

Tobey kept up his speed, drove past, didn't look at the man, kept his eyes straight ahead. He checked his rearview. The man still held the axe and garbage bag but now stood in the middle of the road, his eyes on Tobey's car.

The man pushed his cap up with the axe head. He watched until Tobey lost sight of him on a turn.

Jess and Gio drove through the center of Gardiner on the way to the Augusta State Police barracks. Gio came to an intersection, put on his left directional, and went straight through.

Jess pointed. "You had it right, Gio. That's the way to the highway."

A block further they came to another intersection. Gio put on his right directional.

"Gio, you could have gone left there and doubled back."

"Not..." He wagged his head as if sensing a speed trap. "...yet."

"What are we looking for?"

A laundromat. He slowed.

A taxi dispatcher's office.

He put on his directional and entered a parking lot down the street from the Gardiner PD.

"Vagabond Village Subs? You hungry?"

Gio hurried in. Jess followed. Some high school kids played pinball in the corner. Two others shared a can of Pepsi in a booth.

Sergeant Dykstra stood at the counter. "Come on. You know how I like it. Extra extra hots."

The man behind the counter nodded. "You got it." He shoveled hot pepper toppings on an already enormous grinder.

Gio walked up and stood beside Dykstra. He inhaled deeply, turned towards Dykstra and inhaled again.

"You got a problem, kid?"

"Oh, no, no. It smells incredible. What is it?"

"You from around here?"

Gio thumbed over his shoulder to Jess standing by the door. "Up visiting my girlfriend's folks for the week."

The man behind the counter nodded up to the menu above him. "It's the Special. I make 'em like my papa did in the North End. You know the North End?"

"Of Boston? Sure. My grandfather used to take me there for the *festa.*"

"Eh! *Pisan!*"

Dykstra put a five-dollar bill on the counter. "Come on, come on."

The man behind the counter finished and wrapped the sub tight, put it in a bag, and handed it over the counter. "Here you go."

Gio smiled. "Enjoy."

Dykstra shook his head and walked out. He gave Jess's chest a long look as he passed.

Gio turned back to the counterman. "Friendly sort."

"Allen Dykstra, aka The Sarge. You steer clear of that one, you hear? What can I get you?"

"Thanks." Gio waved Jess up to the counter. "What'll you have, Good-Looking?"

\\\\\\\\\

Jamison, dressed in jeans, t-shirt, blue cotton Baracuta jacket and matching cap, pulled into the Gardiner Service Plaza and parked between a beat pickup loaded with vegetable baskets and an equally beat tow truck. He walked in, ordered a coffee, saw Morelli talking to a woman and took the next table over.

Morelli smiled and nodded as the woman spoke. He looked over to Jamison as Jamison took a seat and smiled and nodded as one would to another tourist making a rest stop. The woman sipped her coffee and smiled at Morelli as he spoke.

Jamison held his coffee up and looked out the main windows as traffic came and went. He turned an ear towards Morelli and the woman. The background noise was just the other side of too much for him to pick out the conversation but he'd studied body language and she was flirting for sure.

But so was Morelli.

Jesus Christ, Morelli. Score on your own time, okay?

He emptied his coffee and got up to get another. A moment later Morelli followed. They stood in line at the counter, Jamison in front, Morelli right behind him.

Morelli looked around, saw they were the last in line and the other lines were far enough away what they said didn't matter. "Lieutenant, something's come up."

"I can see that."

"That's Caroline Tyler. Her kids and their nanny are missing."

"We're getting lots of that today. How long they been missing?"

"Going over twenty-four hours now."

"And she hasn't reported it in yet?"

"The nanny is Stephanie Thompson, sister to the missing Thompson boys."

Jamison took his cap off and ran his hand over his graying crewcut. "This is getting better by the minute."

"She thinks they've been taken by Todd Andersen."

They got to the counter. Jamison offered his cup to the counter girl and nodded for Morelli to come forward. "Refill, please. And whatever my friend's having." The girl smiled, took their cups, left, and he faced Morelli. "Todd Andersen? Drug kingpin Todd Andersen? Does she have anything we can go on?"

"She's his mother."

"Christ, what a web. You couldn't make this stuff up. Does it get any better?"

"Andersen's under FBI surveillance. He's had the Thompson boys all along."

"And they did nothing?"

"Evidently he's protected."

"No wonder the man's teflon. Who the fuck else is stepping all over my state?" The girl returned with their cups full, creamers, sugar packets and plastic stirrers, all on a tray. He handed her a five. "Keep it."

They walked back to their tables slowly. "I heard from my guy at the DEA. He's got problems and wants to toss it into our lap."

Morelli looked up and stopped.

"His man hasn't reported in and was supposed to last night. Sid Lyndon. Working undercover as a Gardiner patrolman. Don't recognize the name, but if he's doing his job I shouldn't, right? You know him?"

Morelli glanced around.

"And your friend Gio's coming by this afternoon. Said he's going to help."

Morelli focused out the main windows into the parking lot. He ran to the door, outside, scanned the cars.

Jamison put the tray down on a table and followed him.

Morelli's nostrils flared. "She's gone. Goddammit to hell, she's gone."

\\\\\\\\

Joe Radwel watched Merl Choate get in one of Ramsey's service vans. He adjusted the seat, adjusted the rearview, adjusted the side mirror, rolled down the passenger window and adjusted that mirror, looked at the dashboard, adjusted himself in the seat, and repeated the entire process a second time. He looked up and saw Joe watching him. Merl smiled, turned the van over, put it in drive, and crawled out of the parking lot.

Joe'd spent most of the morning teaching Merl simple maintenance procedures on the college's and grounds' crew vehicles. The kid was a hard worker but as sharp as a sack of wet mice. He changed Joe's truck's oil, alright. He changed it with transmission fluid.

Joe thought the poor kid was going to burst into tears when he yelled "Stop!"

God was that kid sorry.

"It's okay. It's all part of the learning."

Joe steered their conversation to Gio and the kid was a goldmine of information.

The mine ran dry about 11:35. Joe showed Merl how to close a hood without catching your fingers and asked, "You know how to drive a standard?"

Merl looked around the equipment. "What's a standard?"

Joe nodded. "Do you know how to drive? A car?"

Merl nodded enthusiastically. "Yes, sir. I do."

"You hungry?"

"I'm happy to work longer."

Joe looked at his equipment lining the barn. "No, you've done enough..." Joe caught himself. He almost said 'damage'. "...for the day. So you hungry?"

"I can get lunch in the cafeteria, sir."

"Yeah, but I can't. You like burgers? The kind with real meat in them? Handmade?"

More enthusiastic nodding.

Joe handed him a tenner and the keys to one of the service cars. "You know where the Burger King is in Beverly?"

"Yes, sir."

"Good. Don't go there. A quarter mile up 1A North from it is Rusty's. It's got a red roof and a door. Go there. I'll call it in and you tell 'em Joe Radwel sent you. Now, how many burgers you want? And fries? And what you drinking?" Joe wrote down Merl's order. "Take your time. You may have to wait."

He waved as Merl drove off; accelerate a little, foot on the brake, accelerate a little, foot on the brake. "Kid'd be a danger in a fuel crisis."

Back inside he called Rusty, gave him the order, and added, "Call me if he's not there in fifteen minutes, okay? Probably wrapped himself around a tree."

He came back in, grabbed a clean towel from the lave, went into his office and looked through the windows. Satisfied no one was around, he unlocked the bottom drawer of his filing cabinet and used the clean towel to take out a folder, which he opened. It was full of photographs. The one on top was his last seed shed. Its small window showed the light on inside. He thumbed through the photographs and smirked. "Yeah, Doc, you're an educated idiot."

\\\\\\\

Gio drove as Jess sipped a can of Coke. "Which way is it to the Thompsons'?"

"Aren't we going to the State Police barracks?"

"Eventually." He waited at an intersection for directions.

She pointed. "That way, Kimosabe."

He turned around and headed back to her house. "Can I have all the directions?"

"Where are we going?"

"I'm taking you home. I don't want you with me when I go there."

"I don't think you're Pam's type. And Bill might object in any case."

"Bill's not there."

"Aren't you supposed to say 'Bill's not here, man.'?"

"I don't know who's there, only that I'm supposed to go there. I don't want you there if there's trouble."

"Can't you woo-woo and find out?"

"Right now all I'm wooing is that I'm supposed to go there."

"I'm going, too."

"Jess."

She mimicked his tone. "Gio."

"By god you can be frustrating at times."

"You need some tension relief, sailor?"

"From last night to this morning you decided you want me in your life?"

"From last night to this morning I decided I'll see how it goes. Can't see how it goes unless I understand more. Can't understand more unless I spend more time with you." She stared at a passing field. "Men are investments. You got to know he's worth it and the only way to do that is to spend time with him."

"You get that out of one of your Occ Therapy books?"

"No, my mom. She said it once about my pop. They did everything but live together when they were seeing each other. That's how she knew he was the one."

"Smart woman."

"Runs in the family. Now it's your decision. You want me in your life? You got to take me with you."

"Do you have any idea how sexy intelligence is?"

"Big brain on top of big boobs, that's me. Your balls must be aching."

"Do you want to get your gun?"

She patted her side. "Already have it. I'm wearing it just where you like it. Want to see?"

"You can draw it from there?"

"Want to frisk me and find out?"

"How do I get to the Thompsons' from here?"

Five minutes later they pulled into the Thompsons' driveway. Out of the car, Gio reached for Jess's hand. "Stay close."

"Doesn't look like anybody's home."

Gio's head wagged and his nostrils flared. "Dead? Dead. Bill's dead."

"Should we call the police?"

He closed his eyes, shook his head. "Dead a while now. Not why I'm here." He rose up on his toes and walked to the back of the house, his moves slow, quiet, a wolf stalking prey.

Jess whispered without realizing it. "Everything okay?"

He turned to look at her, his eyes open wide, unblinking, his nose twitching. He touched a finger to his lips and continued into the expansive backyard, his steps directed and cautious.

At the tree line the wind shifted. Jess's nose wrinkled. "What is that smell?"

"Predators."

She reached for her gun.

He shook his head. "No need." A few steps into the tree line he nodded and touched the ground. "Bill's dead."

"Where's the body."

"You're standing on it."

She jumped back without letting go of his hand.

He waved around them with his free hand. "His body is all around here. Remember I mentioned two men? They cut him up. Something like that, anyway. That's what's drawn the predators. They'll come back later, maybe. Guess whatever happened happened over several nights, not all at once."

"They killed him then cut him up here?"

"No, he was killed in the house and cut up there. Remember Bella acted funny the last time we were here? That's why."

"Is this what you came here to find out? Can we go now?"

Gio walked to a pine. Put his hand on the tree. "Ed's been here."

"Ed Thompson? Here? How come he didn't go to his house?"

Gio looked up, past the Thompsons' house to the road beyond. He tightened his grip on Jess's hand. "We have to leave."

"Slow down. Where're we going now?"

"No idea. Only that we can't be here. Soon."

They walked quickly to Bessie. Gio backed all the way to the road without turning around. On the road he checked his rearview. "Shit." He tromped it.

Bessie stalled.

"Come on, girl, not now." Gio kept his eyes on his rearview as he turned the key.

Bessie cranked but didn't turn over. "Christ. Now? You got to do this now?"

Jess turned around. "Isn't that Jeremiah Johnson's truck?"

A puff of exhaust erupted from the back of the truck as it accelerated towards them.

"Now would be a good time to woo-woo, Gio."

The world shimmered. Bessie turned over. They drove away.

\\\\\\\\

Guy Rigaux watched Gio's Mercury pull away. "What engine he got in that thing?"

He pulled into the Thompsons' driveway, used his key to unlock the garage, and parked his truck inside. He sold Bill's F150 for cash to a Quebec City cousin who was joyriding it in the Gaspe.

He checked his watch against the big grandfather clock, went back into the kitchen and stood by the phone. A minute later it rang. *"Oui."*

He listened, got himself a glass of water, listened.

"They give us Stephanie and two others?" Pause. "Little ones?" Pause. "Who they belong to?" Pause. "His mother?" Pause. "He let his brothers go?" Pause. "She got money?" Pause. "Okay, do the deal. You got anything else? No? Then listen."

He pulled out a kitchen chair and sat.

"That boy his grandpapa hurt us? Yeah him. He back and up to no good. I don't know if anybody with him, I just see his car. Uh-huh. You know where his girl lives? Good. You take care of that for papa, *oui*?"

He nodded.

"*Bien. Oui. Tres bien.* You stay here at your sister's house. I be gone for a week, make sure we got *Ville de Québec et Montréal* alright. You take care of things here. Have this done when I get back, okay? *Bien.* Bye."

\\\\\\\\

Gio and Jess cuddled next to each other on the drive up to the Augusta barracks. Three Dog Night's *Liar* came over the radio. "Tell me about the rules."

> *I won't ever leave*
> *If you want me to stay*
> *Nothing you could do*
> *That could turn me away...*

Gio tensed momentarily. "What rules?" His voice became authorial, a lecturer in an intro level course. "In baseball, there are many rules. Each team gets nine players - "

She pinched his leg. "That's not what I mean. Come on. I want this to work out. I want to understand what I'm getting myself into."

"You're right. I'm sorry. What exactly are you asking?"

"There are rules. Why do you have rules? Right now all I know is you can't go here or there and you can't do this or that unless you're asked, which seems pretty goddamn stupid if you ask me. You could help a lot more people if it wasn't for those rules, couldn't you?"

Hanging on anyway
Believing the things you say
Being the fool…

"You're talking about my grandfather's rules? They're not just his, although I don't know where he got them. I remember him reciting them to me once. I didn't understand them all but I kept imagining Charlton Heston in *The Ten Commandments*. You know, that finger of fire scorching the words into stone?"

"You think you're Charlton Heston?"

"Better that than Moses, don't you think?"

"I'm serious, Gio. What am I getting myself into with you? You walk into a field, touch a tree and know what's happened half a million years ago? You know somebody's coming for you, us, and to get the hell out of Dodge? How does it work? What are the rules?"

You've taken my life
So take my soul
That's what you said
And I believed it all…

"Maybe not so much rules as boundaries. Ways to do things. How to be careful. Jews have rules about being kosher, right?"

"When it's convenient, yes."

"Aren't there some Jews who obey the rules no matter what?"

"Yes, but they wear funny hats and have rotten haircuts."

"Like the *Rebbe*?"

"He's an exception. He can be Jewish and not Jewish."

He glanced over at her and frowned.

"What? What did I say?"

Gio nodded and spoke slowly, more to himself than to her. "No, he can't. He's always Jewish inside. Passing. My grandfather talked about it. It's called Passing."

"Passing what?"

"My aunt Connie. Growing up, she had dark skin like mine and tight, curly hair like a negro's. That and a broad, Sicilian nose. People called her nigger and made fun of her. She had trouble finding a job because people said she was a light skinned negro *passing* as a white."

"People are assholes."

"Eventually she learned how to use makeup and had her hair straightened. Then she could get jobs where she wanted."

"What's this got to do with the *Rebbe*?"

"My aunt knew who she was inside. It didn't matter what other people said to her. The *Rebbe* can shave his beard, get rid of those wanky sideburns, dress like straight people - "

"Watch it."

"You know what I mean. He could do those things and people wouldn't know he's Jewish unless he stood up and shouted it at them. He wouldn't have to change a thing and people who'd never seen a Jew wouldn't have a clue what he was."

"What's your point?"

"The *Rebbe* can be in both worlds but he has to give something up to be completely in one or the other. On the outside. Inside he's always a Jew."

"The best people are."

"That's what the rules are about. That's what they're for. So we'll know how to dress, what to eat, where to go. To be safe."

I want to be with you
Long as you want me to
But don't move away...

"You said 'we'. You're the only person I know who can do this. Where are the others? If we stay together do I have to go live in some *Twilight Zone* town? Wait a second. Would I even be welcome?"

> *If I ever leave*
> *Would you want me to stay?*

Gio nodded. "Everybody likes to be with their own kind."

Sunday, 17 March 1974

Tim Annandale sat naked in his dorm room heating a can of SpaghettiOs on a hotplate. He told his parents he'd be spending Spring Break on campus and they sent a care package of goodies, all the things he loved when he was home. SpaghettiOs using graham crackers as a spoon was a favorite. They sent him five cans and a box of grahams and he knew he was loved. A sandwich size plastic bag held a mix of instant coffee, creamer, and sugar substitute put together by his mother. She'd taped instructions on the outside: One teaspoonful per cup. That's all you need. Love, Mom.

His dad included five dollars, six cans of Cheez Whiz, and a box of saltines.

His dad loved him, too.

The snack shop was open during break but only certain hours. The cafe was closed until Sunday when students returned. Several foreign students - Laurie Sánchez among them - had their meals at professors' homes.

Nobody invited Tim into their homes.

He shoveled SpaghettiOs into his mouth, letting the sauce drool down his chin, not stopping when the can was empty, looking at the remaining cans, feeling the hunger inside, wanting more, feeling empty.

He looked around his room. No posters. No plants. No TV. No stereo. No radio. No music. A bed neatly made, brown blanket covering white sheet and pillowcase. White shirts and black pants neatly hung. The only color a box of tissues, the labels on the cans of food his parents sent him, and the spines of neatly stacked books.

Gio's room was full of color. Driftwood collected on the beach became a bookcase. Black and white studies of old European buildings hung on walls. Brightly colored framed excerpts of stories. Movie posters.

And music. Phil Keaggy. Billy Joel. Steely Dan. Joni Mitchell.

And more and more people went to Gio for help.

It had to stop.

It had to stop!

Ramsey had a small fleet of service vans available to students.

He grabbed a fistful of tissues and put on his Gio mask without cleaning up.

\\\\\\\\\\

Joe Flying Bear sat beside the child lying in his bed. People came and went, helping him, relieving him, giving him time to see to his own. His hand rested on the hand-carved headboard, felt its grain through the smooth finish. Each day he spent time with his son, Cody, letting the boy know Cody was his son, his first concern, and this strange white boy lying in his father's bed was a guest and should be treated as such. Sometimes he'd see Cody sitting next to the boy talking to him about school, about their community, about the animals caught in the traps, about tracking and hunting.

Joe once asked Grandmother Running Water why she chose him as her apprentice. She laughed. "We chose each other."

She taught him which herbs helped the boy heal. Still, it was a long process. "Is it right to use the boy this way? As part of my training?"

"We use what we are given."

She taught the old ways. The very old ways. They didn't always make sense. They rarely made sense.

But they always got things done, always achieved their results.

Someone pecked at his door. "Could you see who it is, Cody?"

Running Water flew in, perched on the bed's footboard.

Caw.

Joe tucked the covers around the boy. He looked back and Running Water sat on the edge of the bed, smoothing the blankets. "You have a Brother, both older and younger. He will need help. From both of us."

"What can I do?"

"Lower. Center. Relax. Breathe."

\\\\\\\\

Ben Zev sat in his Brookline, Mass, apartment rocking slightly in a straight-backed chair in his study. Books in different languages covered his desk, each opened and with separate legal notepads resting on them, a pen resting on each notepad. Each notepad had lines of neat, precise Hebrew script which read like gibberish. Spools of hair-thin wires, a different metal each, as pure as pure could make them, their ends coming together on his workbench, under a magnifier, under a lamp the color of the sun.

His fingers tied knots in a thick string, a holy macrame, an intricate braid forming a binding, every few twists of the wires he'd check one of his notepads, check the knots, check the wires, check his notepads, and continue.

He chuckled and shook his head. He wrote in Hebrew but the language wasn't. On purpose. Lest any learn of his studies. In the wrong hands...

The water woman came to him weeks ago, after he met Gio, and told Ben to prepare. She looked at his notes and made corrections.

How did she know?

His code was indecipherable.

Evidently not.

"I need you to make a binding."

"To what purpose?"

"For Jess. To learn."

"Jess Rosen? You know Jess Rosen?

But she was gone. Vanished. Had she ever been there? He'd been working non-stop. Eaten little. Slept less. Was she a dream?

"For Jess? To learn?"

He studied after she left. He'd been a mathematician earlier in his life. Before the War. He'd studied with the greats: Hilbert, Minkowski, Hurwitz, others. He'd danced the tightrope between intuitionism and formalism. Physicists, too: Bohr, Planck, Thomson, Bragg. Quantum and Relativity could not co-exist, they all told him. He proved they did.

And showed no one.

If The Bomb was terrible, what he discovered was more terrible still.

Knots. Special knots of specific metals. To bind energies. To hold quantum states. Or release them.

Tie them correctly, you could bind worlds. Or open them. Knots like pathways to quantum realms.

His books. The Old Ones knew.

The knots of the Rosary? The knots of the *Tallit*? The Buddhist Endless Knot? How many generations knew before the knowledge got bastardized into religion?

How many worlds are there?

"Shhh."

He looked up. A finger touching lips without a face.

He chuckled and nodded. Nodded and chuckled.

Soon his studies would be done.

\\\\\\\\\

Gio kept his eyes on the highway as Jess put a hand on his thigh. "Why are we going to Bangor?"

"To borrow Bella's nose again."

"I swear I'm going to talk to you in Hebrew to see if you can understand what I'm saying."

"Most Hebrew sounds like someone clearing their throat to me."

"What did you and Tony and Neil talk about yesterday while I sat in the officers' mess?"

"Yeah, I'm sorry about that. He thinks the fewer people involved the better. You're a civilian, according to him. And you're on a first name basis with them now?"

"Doesn't he know I'm the love of your life? Your own private enlightened *Bayla*? He's never heard of Nick and Nora Charles?"

"Nick and Nora who?"

"Do they know what you can do? All of it?"

"I don't know all of it."

"I don't know all of it, either. That's why I won't let you out of my sight."

Gio checked his mirrors and rapidly braked into the breakdown lane. He pulled her to him and kissed her. Cars honked as they passed. A gray Ford Falcon slowed and got a door-width away before picking up speed and moving on. A tractor-trailer blew its airhorn in a *rump… rump…rump..rump..rump rumprumprumprumprump* pattern until it was beyond hearing.

The air in Bessie's passenger compartment crackled. Gio relaxed his grip on her.

Jess's head rocked back. She blinked her eyes open. Her head came forward and took deep breaths, her face flushed. "Don't stop on my account."

"That's a down payment. A deposit."

"You want to open an account? When's the rest due? 'Cause I'm ready to collect. I swear I'm ready to collect."

He pulled back onto the highway. "You weren't waiting too long in the officers' mess? Half hour, maybe?"

"Yeah. Don't worry. I made a lot of friends. They had no problem calling me Jess. Bet if I brought my Happy Hooker outfit I could've made a few dollars."

"Don't talk like that, Jess. I don't want you to ever talk like that. I don't want anyone to ever think of you like that."

"I noticed you watching Tony watch my ass when I walked in. Don't worry, Gio. He's a friend. Nothing more, nothing else."

He kept his eyes on the road.

"Wait a second. Gio Fortune-cookies is jealous? You've never been jealous before. What's going on? Why so protective all of a sudden?"

He took his eyes from the road and looked into hers. "Because this story, this part of my life, is coming to a close, and once the final chapter is written you'll be gone, out of my life forever, and all I'll have is a memory. I don't want that."

"I am so hot for you right now."

"Remember you wanted me to make love to you the way I kissed you that time? You told Stephanie it was like all of me was in that kiss?"

"How do you know about that? Did Stephanie tell you? She's such a snitch."

"Do you have the keys to your family's Waterville cabin?"

"I know how to get in."

\\\\\\\\\\

Mason glanced down at Robbie Tyler. Robbie sat next to Mason on a tattered couch in front of a color TV in Mason and Todd's living room. A big bowl of sticky, buttered popcorn rested between them. "You like football, kid?"

"Yes."

"You got good manners, kid."

"Thank you."

"Where's your brother?"

"Potties."

Mason focused on the game. A quarterback fake failed miserably. "You guys can't play for shit."

Robbie chuckled.

"You never heard swear words before, kid?"

"Bad words." Robbie chuckled again.

"You can say them here, if you want. It's okay."

"Thank you."

"Your brother always piss the bed like that? I mean, every night?"

"Yes."

"Tell him to stop it or I'll put a clothespin on his dick."

"What dick?"

Two plays later Mason heard the sound of tiny footsteps in the kitchen. "That you, DJ?"

No response.

A chair dragged across the floor. Drawers opened and closed.

Mason kept his eyes on the game. "What you doing, DJ?"

Metal on metal clinked. Mason turned.

DJ faced him on the other side of the couch. He held a butcher's knife in each hand.

Mason rose and leapt over the couch in one smooth motion. "You little son-of-a-bitch."

DJ dropped the knives and ran.

Robbie kept watching the game. Every time the whistle blew, his tiny hand grabbed some popcorn and he dropped kernels into his mouth.

\\\\\\\\

Caroline entered her room at The Bluebird. She asked for and got an upper room facing the front so she could watch cars come and go across the street but parked around back in case Todd spotted her car. She didn't see too many blood red Mercedes 450SELs driving up. The cars she did see gave her the impression there weren't too many Mercedes anythings up here. Not with in-state plates, anyway.

She spent much of Saturday trying to understand Morelli. He listened and only asked the occasional question. He looked into her eyes, the parking lot, at his coffee, sometimes the other people sitting at tables, going to the restrooms, ordering food, but mostly into her eyes.

She snapped her head back to reality.

You did a sixer three days ago, Caroline. Don't get ideas.

And you told him too much. He could put two and two together. Maybe.

She cleaned up, checked her pistol the way that kind, old gentleman taught her, put it in her purse, and looked up the Thompsons' address in her room's phonebook. In the lobby she purchased a Waterville-Augusta-Gardiner street map.

If Stephanie was alive, she'd be there. Right? And if Stephanie was alive, she'd have her boys with her. Right?

The house looked deserted when she pulled in the driveway. She knocked and got no answer. She tried the door, discovered it unlocked, and let herself in.

"Hello?"

She walked through the living room and checked her watch against the big grandfather clock. "That was Bill's pride and joy. He forgot to wind it?"

She walked through the porch and into the garage. "Hello? Bill? Pam? It's Caroline Tyler. Anybody home?"

Back in the house. Upstairs. The beds were unmade, the rooms unkempt.

She came downstairs as a silver Marquis Brougham pulled in behind her and blocked the driveway. She opened the front door and waved as Pam got out of the car.

"Pam! It's me, Caroline Tyler. The door was open so I let myself in. Hope that's alright."

Pam stood by her car, its door open and one foot still inside the passenger compartment. "This your car?"

"The Mercedes? Yes. Yes, it is."

"Why are you here?"

Caroline put a hand over her chest. "Oh, I'm sorry for intruding. I'm looking for Stephanie. Is she here?"

"Stephanie's not in Windham with you?"

"No, she left a few days ago with my boys. I...We haven't seen or heard from her since. I called but never got an answer, so I came up myself."

Pam looked around her yard. "Where Donnie?"

"It's a Monday, dear. He's working today."

"When did Stephie come here?"

"Friday, late morning, early afternoon. You haven't seen her?"

Pam drummed her fingers on the Brougham's roof. "No. She had your boys?"

"Yes. Do you know where they could be?"

"No, but I know who might. You heading back home tonight?"

"No, I have a room in town."

Pam's eyes narrowed. "You plan on staying a while?"

Caroline frowned back. "Well, certainly. Until I find my boys, of course."

Pam's face lit as if thrown with a switch. "That's good. Good, good, good. Tell me where you're staying. I'll make some calls. It might take a while." She checked her watch. "I'll give you a call mid-afternoon with whatever I find out. Then how about dinner?"

"I'm at the Bluebird across from the Gardiner Service Plaza." Caroline shook her head as if to clear it. "Did you say dinner?"

"Hey, a girl's got to eat, right?"

"Will Bill be joining us?"

"Who? Bill? Oh, Bill. Bill's away on business. He won't be joining us."

"Could you move your car? I'd rather not walk back to my motel."

Pam looked at the Mercedes as if shocked to see it there. "Oh, my yes. Of course, of course, of course." She moved the Brougham.

Caroline got in her Mercedes and drove off.

\\\\\\\\\

Gianna looked through the peephole in her door, saw Towne and opened it quickly. "Shit, what are you doing here?"

"Gio Chance is back."

"That supposed to mean something to me? Don't you know Dykstra's not gone home yet? He's out getting takeout. Holy Jesus Christ, Harry."

"Don't worry about him. He's nothing." He pulled her close. "He is nothing, right?"

She kneed him in the balls. He fell back against the doorjamb and gasped for breath. "You think I treat everybody that way?"

Towne spoke through deep breaths. "I don't like you fucking him."

"I don't like me fucking him, either. But he's got money, you don't, and I - " she caught herself. "We need it. Costa Rica, remember?"

"I got money now."

She unzipped him and reached into his pants. "Oh? How much?"

"Half of Dykstra's take."

"Each month?"

"I can swing that."

She grabbed his balls. "Don't feel much swinging right now, Harry."

He groaned. "I said I can swing it. But Chance is going to fuck up everything. He knows too much."

"Does he know about us? Or Dykstra and me?"

"I saw him with his girl driving up here. They pulled over on the side of the highway. I got a good look at them. IDed them proper. Why else would they be coming up this way? She lives with her folks in Gardiner. Anything going on at Orono tonight? Something they'd be interested in?"

She checked the paper. "They ID you?"

"Didn't give them the chance."

"Nothing going on tonight. Is he really a threat?"

"I don't like him. What should I do?"

"Todd gave you the go-ahead on Lyndon, right? Is Chance going to be a threat to Todd? Show some initiative. Take care of that problem before it gets any bigger."

"I don't know..."

She squeezed his balls until his eyes bulged. "Oh, sure you do. You got a problem getting bigger, Harry. You want me to take care of that for you, don't you?"

He rasped. "Yes, please."

"You said his girl lives in Gardiner with her folks? You'd be upset if anything happened to me, wouldn't you, Harry? Somebody told you to back off or they'd end me, you'd back off, wouldn't you? You wouldn't want to risk the love of your life, would you?" She tugged up on his scrotum.

Sweat rimmed his brow. He whispered, "No."

She checked her watch and gave one final tug. He ejaculated into his pants. "Well, there you go. Bet you feel better now, don't you? Now take off. Dykstra'll be back any minute. He goes to the same Chinese place every time. I know exactly how long he takes. Always gets the same eye-crossing hot food, too." She wiped her hand on the inside of his zipper. "What'd'you come up here for, anyway?"

He went into her bathroom and washed himself off. "Just that."

\\\\\\\

Tim Annandale got to the York, Maine, tollbooths and the van he drove began bucking and backfiring. "Lord? Didn't You want me to do this? Or is this a sign. I'm supposed to do something here? Thank You, Lord, for letting me know what I must do."

He got off the interstate in Wells to get gas and explained his situation to the attendant pumping his gas.

"Sounds like water in the fuel line. A can of drygas'll fix it. Might as well fill up while you're at it, give everything a chance to mix."

"Could you take care of that, please?"

The station attendant nodded. "Drygas is a buck-sixty-nine a can." He looked at the van. "Probably take twenty gallons minimum. Ten'll get you that and I'll check your oil while I'm filling your tank."

Annandale watched the attendant place the nozzle in the tank.

"I don't have any money, but I promise I'll pay for it later."

The attendant pulled the nozzle out of the tank. "Boss?"

The proprietor nodded as he listened to Annandale then laughed. "It's supposed to be Tuesday for a hamburger today."

Tim frowned. "What? I don't understand."

"Did he pay for his gas yet?"

The attendant shook his head.

"You gonna pay for your gas?"

Tim pulled out his wallet and opened the billfold.

The attendant shook his head. "That won't cover the gas, Boss."

Tim pulled a card from his wallet, handed it to the proprietor, and smiled.

"What's this?"

"It's my bank card."

The proprietor read it. "Yeah, so? It says you can cash checks at Windham Trust."

"It means I'm good for the money."

The attendant snickered. The proprietor laughed. He handed the card back. "No, it means you can cash checks at a bank I've never heard of two states away. I don't know how much you have in your account or if you even have an account. You could've made that card up, for chrissakes."

"I said I'm good for the money."

"Call the police."

"No, wait a minute." Tim took off his wristwatch and handed it to him.

"Timex? I can get two of these at Kmart for less than filling up your tank." He looked at the Ramsey College logo on the side of the van, took a pen and notepad from his shirt pocket and wrote down the college's phone number and the van's plate number. A decal above the rear bumper read "42." He wrote that down, too.

"Call them up. See if this van's stolen."

"No, no. Please don't do that."

"You going to pay for the gas?"

"I don't have anything else."

"What's that around your neck?"

"It's a cross. The Cross of Jesus." He pulled it out. Was this man a Christian? Would he help one of God's Chosen?

Annandale held it out to him. "See? The inscription's in Greek. The word is 'fish,' but the letters stand for 'Jesus Christ, Son of God, Savior'." He smiled. "It was a secret signal among ancient Christians so they'd know they were among their own."

"This silver?"

"Oh, yes. Pure."

The proprietor weighed it in his palm. "Heavy."

"Yes, Sir." Tim almost wanted to do that...what was it? Something he saw on PBS one night by accident? Wink, wink. Nudge, Nudge? "It's the best."

"I'll bet it is. It's mine now. That and your watch. Now get out of here before I change my mind."

Tim stared at him, at the inscribed silver cross in the man's hand, at the man's face. The man looked up from the cross in his palm to Tim's whitening face.

He called over his shoulder, "Make that call."

A voice came out of the service station. "Making it now, Boss."

Tim got back in the van and drove off.

How could they? Didn't they know how important this was? How important his mission was? How important he was?

He looked at himself in the rearview once he was back on the interstate. His face grew stern and his nostrils flared. "The Lord will not test us beyond what we can endure. If I must be a martyr for Christ, so be it."

Ramsey Student Services Van #42 began bucking again. He got into the breakdown lane, crawled to the Kennebec rest area, pulled into a parking space away from traffic, and wrapped himself in emergency blankets in the back of the van.

He settled in for the night.

\\\\\\\\

Donnie picked his luggage off the carousel, looked around terminal B's arrivals area, and recognized the limo driver from his several business and non-business trips. He'd even invited the driver to join him at the Parker in Boston before taking him home.

In lieu of a tip, of course.

"We got a problem, Mr. Tyler."

"What's that?"

"Your AmEx. The office couldn't post to your AmEx. You're a good customer and all so I'll still take you home, but you'll have to fix this tonight or tomorrow."

"I'll fix it now." He went to the bank of phones, punched in a number. "Yeah, hi, this is Donald Tyler. I have a platinum card and my driver tells me he can't post a charge to it." He listened, gave the card number.

"Sorry, Mr. Tyler, we couldn't extend any more credit to that account. It's grossly over limit as it is."

Donnie laughed. "Let's make sure you got the number correctly." He repeated the number. They asked for date of birth and social security number.

"That account's currently seventy-thousand dollars overdrawn, Mr. Tyler."

"There's some kind of mistake."

"Of course. But this is our emergency number and you'll have to call our main number. That office opens at 9:00AM on the east coast. Would you like their number?"

Donnie hung up. The driver leaned against a wall sipping a can of Mountain Dew. Donnie signaled him to wait. He called the Visa number. The card was cancelled for nonpayment. MasterCard ditto. Diners Club. Signature. Nobody except Caroline knew about the Signature card.

Ditto, ditto, ditto, ditto, ditto.

He reached into his wallet, pulled back a hidden flap, pulled out two fifty dollar bills, and called the driver over. "This get me home?"

The driver swung wide in the driveway and parked by the front door.

"I don't have anything left for a tip."

"You can catch me next time."

The driver popped the trunk and let Donnie get his own bags out. He dropped them inside the front door. "Caroline?"

No answer.

"Caroline? Stephanie?"

He yelled their names so loudly he coughed when he finished.

Somebody would have told him to be quiet by now, the boys would be asleep.

The house was dark. Caroline's coat and scarf were missing from the coat rack.

"Caroline? Stephanie? Boys?"

He went into the kitchen. A butcher's knife lay on the counter. He saw the note on the counter, read it, and looked at the cat clock's tail gently swishing off the seconds.

Tomorrow. He'd take care of this tomorrow.

Monday, 18 March 1974

Donnie boarded the train at the Hamilton/Windham rail stop. Whatever was going on, he'd let his secretary take care of it. He was a VP at State Street, goddammit. This shit didn't happen to him.

Entering State Street's main lobby, the guard behind the security desk watched him walk to the elevator. Donnie nodded. "Hi, Jimmy."

The guard looked down at papers on his desk.

The elevator doors opened and two guards stood there. Bramhall, the Old Man, stood between them. "We need to talk, Donald."

They guided him past his office. There were boxes on his desk. His secretary glanced up and away as he passed. "What's going on here?"

One of the guards opened Bramhall's door. The Old Man entered first. Donnie, his accountant's briefcase weighing him down like flooding ballast in a storm, entered second. The two guards entered third.

Donnie put his briefcase down and pulled out a chair.

"That won't be necessary. You won't be here that long."

"What's this about?"

"Do you know your mortgage is overdue?"

"What?"

"And are you aware your second mortgage is also greatly in arrears."

"Second mortgage?"

"Not even an attempt to pay the interest fees. You're a Senior VP, for Christ's sake. You should know nothing comes to light so long as the interest fees are paid."

"I don't know what you're talking about."

"We checked your financial status once we received notification of a lien on your salary. Do you know your credit cards are maxed out, some even borrowed against to their limit?"

Donnie paled. Sweat trickled down his neck and forehead. "What are you talking about?"

"So I made some inquiries of my own. Do you know your house has been under surveillance?"

"Surveillance? By who?"

"We could turn a blind eye as long as you did your job, did it well, and didn't bring anything down on the office, but this." Bramhall opened his desk drawer, pulled out a dictation cassette tape and tossed it at Donnie. "This gets out and there'll be no holding back the scandal. Our credibility will be shaken if not lost. It'll take years to get it back."

Donnie fumbled, the cassette bounced in and out of his hands like a basketball at the sideline. "What the hell is this?"

"Some sex party orgy you planned. Or held. Your voice is on the cassette."

"What?"

"Get out. Get out and don't even enter the lobby ever again. Get out and don't mention this institution's name, ever. And don't look for any jobs in the financial industry."

"Jesus Christ, Mr. Bramhall."

"You'll be lucky if you can get a job stacking shelves at a north country IGA by the time this is done." The Old Man signaled the guards and shook his head. "Why couldn't you keep it in your pants, goddammit. Or at least make sure nobody had a microphone up your ass."

The guards stood on either side of Donnie. He reached for his briefcase and Bramhall shook his head. One guard lifted the briefcase and handed it to Bramhall. "We'll send it to you once we've made sure there's nothing pointing to us in it. It'll be in the same box as the personal belongings from your office. Contact me directly with your new address - your home'll be locked and secured as soon as the sheriff gets the paperwork. Now leave. I don't want you tainting anybody else in this office. Understood?"

Donnie shook his head, his eyes wide, his body shivering in his three-piece suit and Brooks Brothers overcoat and scarf.

The guards shuffled him out.

\\\\\\\\\\

Gio heard the shower stop and Jess toweling off. He sat up in bed. A moment later she came out of the bathroom wearing nothing but a long towel. She smiled at him and let the towel fall to the floor.

"You like-a one more time, Mr. Sailor Man? I do you nice one more time." She leaned back against the doorjamb, her hands behind her, one leg tauntingly draped over the other as her hips swayed slightly from side to side.

"I've never met anyone as beautiful as you."

She strode over to the bed. "Well, I'm just going to have to fuck you now."

"How about on the way back from Bangor? We can get breakfast, I can do my thing, we can be back by early afternoon."

She went back to the bathroom door, picked up the towel and wrapped it around herself. "I'd rather go home. Is that alright?"

"You mean now? No breakfast? No Bangor? No bang...or...?"

She sat on the edge of the bed. "I have something planned for later this morning."

"Is it important?"

"I asked my folks to make me a doctor's appointment before we came up."

He reached out. "What's wrong?"

She didn't face him. "Nothing's wrong. I - "

He snorted. "You want to find out if you still have a heart murmur, still have a cyst, still have the problem in your leg."

"Yes. Is that so horrible?"

He shook his head. "No. I'm proud of you. Your intelligence is what makes you so beautiful to me."

She looked up at him and smiled. "Yeah, but giving head helps, right?"

"One of the many things I love about you."

"It doesn't bother you, really? You don't think it means I don't believe you?"

"Do you not believe me?"

"You're not concerned I want to know if what you say you did you did?"

He shook his head. "Good for you. It's good to be sure. The real question is, is this going to convince you?"

"You're the one who said you're a good guesser."

He shrugged.

She stood and stared at herself in the bedroom mirror. "You're not concerned? You're not afraid?" She stared at his reflection as he rose from the bed.

"Why should I be?"

"Because what if you're full of horseshit and you can't do any of those things you say you can do?"

He went into the bathroom and turned the shower on. His voice came through the steam.

"No, Jess. You're missing the point. You're not concerned I can't or didn't. If I can't or didn't, I'm insane, a lunatic, a megalomaniac and you're done with me. You'll pity me, worry about me, probably even hope I get the help I need." The air crackled, shimmered. The steam pulled itself into clouds floating on gentle breezes. "No, your real concern is I did do those things. Then your decision becomes real, necessary. Then your decision comes down to 'where does it end?'"

She stood in the bathroom doorway. The clouds descended, wrapped themselves around her, Venus rising from the mists. "Stop it!"

He turned off the water. The world stopped shimmering. The air stopped crackling. The clouds dissolved away from her. He pulled back the curtain. "You're shaking."

"Take me home."

He dried his head and a tear slid down his cheek. "You don't think I'm afraid, too?"

"Of what? What can you be afraid of?"

"As I said yesterday. Losing you. I love you. I don't want to lose you. And these conversations indicate I will."

She turned away and walked into the bedroom. The towel fell at the bathroom door. "Then stop it. Stop what you're doing. You've done enough. No more practicing. Take me home. Now. To Gardiner. Now. Today. Okay?"

He came out with a towel around his waist, grabbed his clothes, and went back into the bathroom to dress.

"As you wish."

\\\\\\\\\\

Dykstra ruffled papers on his desk. He made a show of arranging and rearranging them, dropping a few and loudly grunting when he bent down to pick them up. He tapped his pencil loudly and cleared his throat a few times.

Towne entered the squad room holding a cup of coffee. He looked around. A janitor emptied wastepaper baskets. Three officers chatted next to a slightly open window, coffee cups and cigarettes in their hands. Occasionally they waved little clouds of smoke out the window as they puffed.

Towne took a sip of his coffee and laughed. "Wow, this is bad. Who made the coffee this morning?"

The three officers at the window turned and nodded. Two went back to their cigarettes. One held up his cup, looked at it, and made a mock look of shock. The janitor went on to the next wastepaper basket.

Dykstra spoke as if Towne stood across a large auditorium and not ten feet away. "Yeah, it's shit. I think we got a new supplier."

Towne answered in the same too loud voice. "Sure is bad."

"You saw Lyndon off?"

"Ten-four that. He wanted to get an early start, had to drive down to Boston to catch his plane home. I drove him straight to his apartment at the end of shift, came back and clocked us both out. Wrote up the reports for both of us." He stood in front of Dykstra's desk and waited for him to look up.

Towne's voice changed to barely more than a whisper. "I do okay, Sarge?"

Dykstra nodded and responded in his own whisper. "You did okay."

\\\\\\\\\\

Bella bounded around the house as Gio parked by the Rosens' garage. Jess got out and before she could close her door Bella jumped in and sat on the front seat.

Sam came around the house, saw the situation, and scratched his head. "How does he get her to do that?"

Jess went into the house without answering.

Gio got out. "Here, girl."

Bella jumped and sat beside him. Sam walked over with his hands in his pockets. "You two have a good night?"

"We spent the night in Waterville. Hope that's okay."

Sam shrugged. "Everything okay between you two?"

Gio shrugged. "She's got some decisions to make. Based on how it goes today."

"Oh?"

"The doctor's appointment."

Sam nodded. "You know anything about that?"

"Do I know she's going or do I know why she's going?"

"You obviously know she's going. I don't know why she's going or why she called and asked us to make the appointment for her." He scratched Bella's head and turned to face Gio. "Anything you want to tell me?"

"She wants to know if she'll ever be able to have children."

"You two talking about having children?"

Gio shook his head. "Only that she wants to know if she'll be able to have children. Or run and play with them. Or live a long, full life."

"You two making plans? Things getting serious? Should I be finding a glass you two can break?"

Gio leaned over and fluffed the fur on Bella's sides. "You need to ask her. It's her decision to make. I made mine."

"Give her time. She doesn't like to make mistakes. She just wants to be sure."

Gio nodded. "I know."

\\\\\\\\\

Joe Radwel watched Merl and Laurie stand in front of Ramsey's row houses and wait for the Ivy Road traffic to pass. Merl asked to work through Spring Break and, with most of the students and staff gone, Joe welcomed both the conversation and the help doing routine maintenance on the college vehicles and equipment. Laurie he recognized from her previous visit. He wondered if he was seeing another Gio&Jess moment but their body language said no. Merl guided Laurie to Joe's office and their hushed voices gave Joe a smile. They were planning something. His job was to listen.

Merl tapped his office door. "You got a minute, Joe?"

"Merl, you don't have to clock in for another half-hour. What're you doing here this early?"

Merl stepped aside and let Laurie through. "You remember Laurie?"

Joe rose from behind his desk and offered his hand. "Sán...Sánchez?"

Laurie smiled. "Yes, sir."

"What can I do for you, Ms. Sánchez?"

"Merl said you could use office help. I'm on work-study doing janitorial and tired of getting my hands dirty."

Joe shrugged. "Well, Ms. Sánchez, this is maintenance. Grounds crew. You may work in the office and your hands are still going to get dirty."

"Dirt from the earth I don't mind. And I helped my brothers work on their cars back home. I don't mind that kind of dirt, either. I'm tired of cleaning up people's bathroom accidents, though."

Joe nodded. "Where's home?"

"Nicaragua."

"Long way to go home for a week on break. You want to handle the office? Answer the phone? That kind of thing?"

Merl interrupted. "Tell him."

"Tell me what?"

"She doesn't want to work on the main campus anymore."

Joe frowned. "What happened on campus?"

Merl nudged her.

"I was cleaning Doc Ock's office. He came in to pick up some work and stopped when he saw me vacuuming. I shut it off and pulled it out of the way. He said to his secretary, 'Who's the little brown one?' He meant me."

Joe nodded. "Some people are assholes."

Merl burst out laughing.

Joe pointed his finger at Merl. "None of that, Mr. Choate. They'll know you've been working with me if you laugh at things like that."

Merl laughed harder.

Joe stood over his desk. "Laurie - can I call you Laurie? - what I need most is someone to organize my files. I got inventories out of control, companies sending me samples and wanting follow-ups, maintenance forms I'm behind filling in. You think you can do that?"

"Where do I start?"

He handed her a clipboard. "That's today's maintenance log. Tell this young man here which vehicles are due for maintenance, what kind, and see that he gets it done. Got it?"

She crossed her arms over her chest, held the clipboard there, and gave Merl a stern look. "You're my little puppy now."

Merl shook his head. "I've created a monster."

\\\\\\\\\

Gio left without saying goodbye to Jess. He knelt in front of Bella and held her giant head in his hands. "Bella, my good girl, stay with Jess. Understand? Protect Jess."

The big shepherd turned and trotted in the backyard. She woofed. He heard the deck doors open to the kitchen and Bella enter the house. A tear slid down his cheek.

He parked in downtown Bangor, got out, and sniffed.

Nothing.

How did Grandpa do this?

Lower-Center-Relax-Breathe.

The hair on his arms lifted, the air around him crackled.

Borrow.

The tip of his nose darkened and elongated slightly.

He walked unsure of his destination. Every few steps he stopped and sniffed one-two-three-four times until he caught a familiar scent. "Gotcha."

He stood in front of a Chinese restaurant. "In Bangor?"

The door opened and a thin, young man dressed in black slacks, white shirt, with a clean white apron tied around his waist, smiled at him. "We open for lunch in about five minutes. You can come in if you'd like. Maybe have some tea while you're waiting?"

Gio stared at the man's Asian features. "Forgive me, but you don't have classical Chinese features."

The man's brows lifted. "You know a lot of Chinese?"

"You look more Mongol than Chinese."

"Who are you?"

Gio offered his hand. "I'm sorry. That was rude. My name's Gio. Fortuna. I'm looking for someone."

"You've got a good eye. Your parents missionaries or something? Who you looking for?"

"My grandpa had friends from everywhere. A round-eye, fifty-five, sixty maybe. Five-seven, five-eight. Heavy. Close cropped red hair, more than a crew cut but not bald, on the belligerent side, - "

"You mean The Sarge?"

"You know him?"

"Worst tipper on the planet. You'd think we owe him for ordering our food. What'd'you want with him?"

Gio's nostrils flared and he inhaled. "He was here...yesterday?"

The man pulled back slightly. "What's this about?"

"He may be in trouble."

"Food poisoning? Not from us if it's food poisoning. We run a clean kitchen, deliveries daily. Is it food poisoning?"

Gio shook his head. "Not food poisoning. Thanks. I'll find him."

"He your friend?"

"Not my friend."

"In that case, you want some lunch? If he was your friend I'd tell you 'Oops! My mistake, we won't open for another ten hours'. But you're not, so you want to come in? Best Mongolian food outside of Mongolia."

Gio frowned at him.

"My parents escaped the Communist takeover. My dad had connections at UMO. I was born here. My mom opened this restaurant. You think anybody in Maine's going to know the difference between Mongolian and Chinese? I wouldn't know if it wasn't for my parents."

Gio shook his hand. "Maybe later. I've got to track him down."

The man smiled. "Not find him, track him down?"

"Sorry, my mistake."

The man shook his head. "My parents told me about people like you. Don't worry. Your secret's safe here."

Gio cocked his head. "Huh?"

"Powder your nose. Or wipe it off when you're done. Or whatever it is your kind does.'

Gio's hand covered his nose.

The man chuckled. "And come on back if you're hungry."

Gio followed Dykstra's scent, more recognizable each step. Down a block he stopped and laughed. "Vagabond Village SubShop. Extra-extra hots. Thank god you're a peculiar eater. You're leaving a trail like a snail."

An apartment building loomed in front of him. A raven flew to a window grating. The window was closed, the blinds drawn.

The raven perched, looked down at him, pecked at the window through the grating, looked down at him, pecked again.

A young woman pulled back the blinds, opened the window, thrust her hand out.

The raven's wings opened but it didn't leave its perch.

Borrow.

Caw!

The raven stared at the woman. She thrust her hand through the grating. The raven pecked it, opened a wound, a lightning-like mark on the back of her hand.

Gio saw her hand, saw the mark, saw her face, heard her voice. "Fucking bird. Go. Ouch! Goddammit. Fucking bird!"

The raven fluttered off the grating. The woman reached into her apartment, held a can of beer, threw it at the raven. It hit the grating and bounced back into her face, darkening an eye. "Jesus Fucking Christ!"

The raven looked down at Gio. Gio nodded. The raven flew away.

\\\\\\\\

Donnie woke to the phone ringing on his nightstand. "What?"

Bob chuckled on the other end of the line. "Donnie, your Caroline is amazing!"

Donnie's knuckles whitened on the phone. "Oh?"

"Christ, Don! She didn't need any coaching or training at all. We all thought you'd been teaching her. My god, a cock in each hand, one in her mouth, one in her ass, and one in her cunt? She even licked her own shit off our dicks when we were coming up for round two. And that ice cube thing? I thought my balls were going to explode. Either you taught her or she's been doing a lot of reading. How come you never brought her around before, Donnie? Shame on you, keeping all that to yourself, making us think it was your nanny who was the fun one."

Donnie's nostrils flared. He coughed and swallowed a few times before answering. "Yeah, yeah, that was me, my idea. I wanted to give you boys a surprise."

"You sure did that, Donnie. See you at the Suisse as usual? And bring Caroline, okay?"

Donnie heard some heavy trucks climbing his driveway and carried the phone to the bedroom window. "Yeah, maybe. Don't want you boys to get spoiled. I got to go now, bye."

He hung up without waiting for a response.

The sheriff's car pulled in behind the moving vans.

"What now?" He'd gone to bed when he got home with only his liquor cabinet to comfort him and it'd done a good job of it. His tongue felt glued to the roof of his mouth and his eyes had crusted over. He didn't remember getting undressed or washing up. Evidently he did get undressed. Mostly. His pants were off but not his shirt and tie, and his underwear, the bedsheets, and his hand were sticky with dried semen. His dick had friction sores on it and dried blood covered his left palm.

He heard a car door close. A moment later somebody pounded on his front door.

He put on a bathrobe and his slippers without cleaning himself off or changing his clothes. Opening the door, he saw the moving vans, four mid-twenties men and one older guy with a cheap cigar hanging out of his mouth, a clipboard in his hands, all dressed in coveralls, and the sheriff's car parked in his front drive.

The sheriff, a tallish, middle-aged man graying at the temples and clean shaven, blocked his view. "Mr. Donald Tyler?"

"What's this about?"

The sheriff handed him a piece of paper. "Formal notice of foreclosure and eviction." He called over his shoulders. "Go ahead, boys. It's all yours."

The sheriff came inside and stood in the open doorway, blocking Donnie from stopping anybody. The four younger men came in and oohed and ahhed at the furnishings. One of them sat on a loveseat in the front hallway and ran his hands over the upholstery. "Wow, this ain't cheap shit, huh?"

The older man flipped pages on his clipboard. "Yeah, take that. Mike, help him."

The sheriff nailed a notice to the front door. He turned to see Donnie's reactions as he drove the nail home. "You have forty-eight hours to vacate the property, Mr. Tyler." Finished hammering, he faced him. "Are we going to have a problem with this?"

Donnie shook his head, his face white. He leaned over and retched on the front hall rug. The older man looked at it. "You're going to have to clean that up, Mr. Taylor."

Donnie mumbled, "Tyler."

"Yeah, fine, Tyler. You're still going to have to clean that up before we take it."

What did Stephanie's note say? She took the boys with her? Give them a day out?

They hadn't taken his car yet.

"And I'll bet that bitch of a wife of mine is with her."

The sheriff and older man studied the latter's clipboard. The sheriff looked up. "What'd you say, Mr. Tyler?"

Donnie ignored him.

His rifle was in his study's closet.

Nobody did this to Donald Tyler.

Nobody.

\\\\\\\

Merl wiped grease from his hands and poked his head in the office. "What's next, Laurie?"

She scanned down the work list. "Van 42 needs servicing."

Joe looked up from an equipment brochure. "Oh, yeah. Dodgy fuel pump. It came in last week and I haven't gotten to it yet. It's marked for local use only until we get that fixed."

Merl came back a few minutes later. "Where'd you park 42?"

Joe got up and motioned Merl to follow. "Should be in the lot with the other service vans, near the Snack Shop."

They came back half an hour later. Joe walked straight into his office and moved papers across his desk.

Laurie watched. "Help you find something?"

"You already organized my desk?"

"Did I do something wrong?"

"Where are the weekend's vehicle logs?"

She pointed to a two-tier tray on his desk. The top tier had "In" written on it, the bottom had "Out."

"When did that get there?" He looked through the In pile and pulled out the logs. "Ah, sweet mother of crap." He moved more papers on his desk. "Where'd you put my readers?"

She pointed at his pen cup. He put on his readers, moved the log in and out of focus, and handed it to her. "I see 42's out but I can't read who took it or where they're heading."

She took the log and went pale. "Tim Annandale took it. To Maine."

"Sweet mother of crap."

\\\\\\\\

Gio headed back to Bessie. "I'm going to need a scorecard to keep track of all the players involved in this." He stopped a block from where he parked her. Someone sat in the front passenger's seat. "And who's this?"

He walked up and tapped on the passenger's window.

No reaction.

He bent over for a better look.

A middle-aged woman, short but strong and solid. Long black hair, braided. Dressed like a shopkeeper, with an apron and its pocket full of pencils and pens. She looked up at him.

A raven's face, the nose and mouth a beak, its dark eyes staring up at him. Her gaze returned forward and she pointed.

He got in and drove as the woman indicated. An older, dark-skinned man with a beaded jacket, jeans, and hiking boots stood underneath a tribal marker on a post. He looked at them closely as they passed, saw the raven-woman, unclipped a walkie-talkie from his belt and spoke into it.

A mile further in a younger man, similarly dressed, stood in the road and motioned them to a parking spot in front of a smallish cabin.

Gio parked. A woman, dressed like the raven-woman in Bessie, opened the cabin door, smiled, came over, and opened Bessie's passenger door. "Thank you."

The raven-woman stood and walked into the other, the raven-woman's body merging with the other's as if superimposing two photographs.

Gio quivered with a moment of frisson. "Grandmother Running Water." He walked up and embraced her. "Good to meet you finally. In the flesh." He cocked his head. "This is you in the flesh, isn't it?"

She returned his embrace. When they parted, she took his hand as if guiding a child. "Do I feel like flesh?"

"Yes, Ma'am."

She smiled. "This isn't the first time we met. I knew your Grandfather. He helped us once, long ago. Many times. Once when you were just a child. Just out of diapers."

"Okay, this is getting embarrassing."

They entered the cabin. "Someone needs you. Someone here. We've done all we can." She led him into a smaller room, a bedroom. A boy lay on the bed wrapped in a blanket, his face dripped sweat, his body shivered as if caught in an arctic chill.

Beside him a tall, thin man, dark-skinned, clear-eyed, thick black hair flowing freely down his shoulders, chest, and back, his brow moist with sweat, shimmered, his features moving like fluid between two worlds, one moment a man, the other a man-shaped bird. He looked at Running Water. "I can't hold him much longer."

Running Water motioned Gio towards the boy. "Now, today. You must decide."

The world shimmered beside Gio. He stood on a precipice. Raven stood beside him. "Either fly or crawl on your belly the rest of your life."

Gio stared at Raven.

"What does that book you read tell you? No greater love than to give your life for another?"

Gio stood in the small bedroom. His body began shaking, quivering. He sweat until his clothes dripped as if he stood in heavy rain. He fell to the floor. He convulsed, choked, gasped.

Flying Bear reached out to him. Running Water held his hand back. "No. He must do this on his own or not at all."

Gio rolled onto his side. His tongue lolled, his eyes rolled up in his head. His head rattled on the floor with his shaking.

On the bed, Harry opened his eyes.

Gio's bowels and bladder released.

Harry looked around. He frowned, saw Flying Bear and Running Water, opened his mouth. Flying Bear put a finger to Harry's lips. "You're okay. You're with friends. Don't talk. You've been sick for a while." He lifted a glass of water and helped Harry raise his head. "Here. Drink."

Gio's eyes fluttered. His convulsions grew less. He lay still on the floor for a moment then rolled onto his side, sat up and felt things squish in his pants. "Anybody have some clothes I can borrow?"

Flying Bear crouched beside him. "Hello, Brother."

Gio nodded. "How you doing?" He put his hands on the floor on either side of himself, got a foot off the floor and dropped back down.

Flying Bear offered a hand. "Want some help?"

"All I can get."

Harry fell into a restful sleep. Flying Bear, Running Water, and Gio went into the cabin's kitchen. Flying Bear gave him a glass of water and a fresh pile of clothes in a basin. "There's a pump out back, before the outhouse. Take the basin and wash yourself off. The clothes should fit."

"Anybody want to tell me what happened?"

"You gave your life so another could live."

Gio waved his glass towards the bedroom. "The boy?"

Running Water shook her head. "Yourself."

Mason hit his yellow dome lights and pulled in front of the van in the breakdown lane. He backed up until his tow arm hung over the top of the van.

A tall skinny kid opened the driver door and jumped out, all smiles and his hand thrust forward wanting to shake. "Gosh, thanks. I thought I'd have to walk."

Mason noted the Massachusetts plates on the car and glanced at the decal on the side. Ramsey College.

He knew that name. He'd never been but he knew that name. Todd mentioned it once or twice. When he talked to that old Wop. Isn't that where Chance went to school?

Yeah, that's it, that's right.

So what is Chance's school buddy doing up here in Maine?

Is Chance up here?

Oh, Todd's going to love this.

Mason smiled. "What's the problem, friend?"

Jess fidgeted in Dr. Clement's Augusta General waiting room. Clement opened her office door. "Jess?"

Inside, Dr. Clement motioned Jess to a seat. She had an x-ray on her desk and some scribbled notes. "Okay, Jess. What happened?"

"What do you mean?"

"Your folks call up, you need an appointment ASAP, nobody knows why, you ask me to check for three specific things: two we've known about since you were a toddler and the other since you entered your teens. Now nothing? And you ask me what do I mean?"

A tear slid down Jess's cheek.

Dr. Clement sat forward. "This is good news, Jess. You get that, right? I don't know how we could've repeatedly misdiagnosed these things for years, but we did. I say we did, and I won't be sure until we get final results from the lab. But based on what I have here?" She waved at the material on her desk. "You're good to go."

"I can have kids?"

"Nothing stopping you now except finding the right fella, I guess. Before it might've been tricky, and again, I want to see the full workup to be sure."

"I can run and jump and play?"

"Go get yourself a pair of Keds."

"No more shortness of breath? No more wondering what the pains are in my chest?"

"Aside from heartache?" Dr. Clement shook her head.

"When will you know for sure?"

Clement watched Jess's face. "What's going on, Jess? You're not usually like this. When did you get so serious? You're usually telling me jokes while I'm examining you."

"Just got a lot on my mind."

Clement considered. She glanced at her notes and the x-ray then back at Jess. "You seeing somebody?"

"Yeah."

"You worried he's...?"

"No, nothing like that."

"Cause depending when you became active, nothing might show up yet."

Jess shook her head.

"And you were specific what you wanted me to check. I didn't really check for anything like that."

"No, it's nothing like that. Anything else?"

"I'll put a rush on things. You're on break, right? Staying at your parents' house? I'll call as soon as I know anything. Tomorrow. Okay?"

Jess shook her head and stood up. "No. Don't bother. It won't change anything. I'm healed."

She walked out. Dr. Clement stood in her office doorway. "Jess? Jess?"

The duty sergeant stopped talking with some officers in the MSP waiting area and hurried to open the doors for Gio, a heavily blanketed Harry Thompson in his arms.

"Get Jamison."

They guided Gio to a bunkroom and he placed Harry on a bottom bunk bed. "I didn't know where a hospital was. He'll need help."

"We got it."

Jamison came in and assessed the situation quickly. "Which one is he?"

Gio acknowledged Jamison with a nod. "Harry."

"Where's he been?"

"Can we go to your office?"

Inside, Jamison closed the door. "You're not going to tell me where he's been, are you?"

"Nope."

"I saw the blankets you had him in. You didn't get them at Sears."

"Correct."

"Okay, let's come at this from a different direction. Is he alright?"

"As far as I can figure." Gio hesitated. "A full workup couldn't hurt, though. I'd like one, too, if that's doable."

Jamison stared at him. "You okay?"

Gio collapsed into a chair by the wall. "A little tired."

A distant ambulance siren grew louder in the background.

Gio's head gently rocked back against the wall.

"Gio?"

His hands fell down to his sides.

"Chance?"

He fell forward, rolled onto his side, and started shaking.

Jamison opened his door and yelled down the corridor, "Get that boy secured and tell them we have another one in here. Move it!"

Riggerio booked a suite at the Bluebird a month ago and a second, side-by-side suite with a connecting door a few weeks later, all at Mr. de Leo's request. He made sure he got them on the Bluebird's third floor for the view and with kitchenettes so the men stationed there could cook real food, some of which they shared when other Bluebird occupants asked what the amazing smells were.

Riggerio explained they were wealthy Italian businessmen touring the States and people loved hearing them speak. Two of the men were marvelous tenors and occasionally sang, often drawing applause from the nearer rooms. Whenever others were around, Riggerio's men dressed in L.L. Bean hunting gear. When alone, they cleaned and polished their weaponry.

The men drew cards to determine which one drove into Gardiner once a day to call Gio's Uncle Nick. They kept notes to make sure the caller went to a different phone booth every day. They went at different times each day and drove a different car each day.

Today, Riggerio would make the call. The Bluebird got busy the past few days and Riggerio wanted to keep Mr. de Leo apprised. A smartly dressed woman driving a blood-red Mercedes 450SEL took a room, somebody who had to be an FBI or similar government agent took a room, somebody so out of place he had to be some kind of undercover local cop, probably a statey - kept showing up at the Gardiner Service Plaza across the street and spending the day there, and earlier today Gio slipped the two-team tail they put on him.

Riggerio didn't like coincidences and was concerned. He wanted to share his concern.

He got to the center of Gardiner and glanced at his notebook. Today's call would be from Vagabond Village Subshop. He found it and smiled at the little "Public Phone Inside" sign.

He opened the door and scanned the room. Some kids eating pizza, some kids in a corner making goo-goo eyes at each other, and a fat, old, policeman at the counter.

The counterman looked up as the little bell above the door announced Riggerio's entrance. "With you in a minute."

Riggerio smiled. "Take your time."

The fat, old policeman turned and evaluated Riggerio.

Riggerio waved. "Hi."

The fat, old policeman grunted and turned back to the counterman.

Riggerio flipped through the jukebox offerings until the fat, old policeman left. The counterman smiled. "What can I get you?"

Riggerio leaned over the counter and whispered, "You got change for a fifty?"

"You're kidding, right?"

"How about you give me two dollars worth of quarters, I give you a fifty and you keep it. In case I ever come back and need quarters again."

The counterman hit "No Sale" on his register and handed Riggerio a fistful of quarters. He pocketed the fifty.

Riggerio smiled. "Thanks."

\\\\\\\\\

Mason stood in one of the Gardiner Service Plaza's phone booths with the door open as a chill March wind scoured the last of the winter snow. "Yeah, hi, Todd. You'll never guess who I picked up while I was trolling the interstate for breakdowns." He laughed. "Not even close and you're going to love this."

Tim Annandale watched him from the tow truck's passenger seat, his window down and his left arm cradling his right, its forearm either broken or badly bruised.

Mason kept his eyes on him. He spoke into the phone and nodded.

Annandale reached for the handle and Mason put his hand over the mouthpiece. "You sit right there, dumbfuck, or I'll break your other arm."

He went back to his phone conversation.

Annandale leaned back into the tattered naugahyde seat. He closed his eyes, his head back against the rear window, and whispered a prayer for Jesus to come rescue him. He whispered his remorse for everything he'd ever done. He searched his memory for things he might have done. He wanted a can of SpaghettiOs and some graham crackers so he'd know everything was alright and mom and dad would take care of him.

He opened his eyes and nothing'd changed.

\\\\\\\

Kagan cradled the phone against his shoulder and listened to Janey's doctor. A beat tow truck pulled into the Gardiner Service Plaza across the street. Kagan raised his binoculars and looked. "Holy fucking shit."

The doctor paused.

"Oh, sorry, Doc. I'm working. You sure you have my number here? Okay, good. You'll let me know? I can be back in three hours, maybe two if I have to. Yeah, okay, good."

He waited for the doctor to hang up, wanting to hear good news, hoping for a breakthrough, a change, something to let him know it was all a mistake, Janey was fine, they could retire to Florida or Arizona and live out their lives in warm, sunny peace.

But a dial tone was all that remained.

He gazed through his binoculars. The tow's lift kept a Ramsey College #42 a foot off the ground. "What the hell is a Ramsey College van doing up here?" The driver got out and made a call.

Kagan trained his binoculars on the passenger.

"Holy Jesus Christ."

\\\\\\\

Morelli gave up looking for Caroline. When not surveilling the Gardiner Service Plaza, he silently cursed himself for not getting her full name or number or make and model of her car.

You're one hell of a cop, Morelli. Your father would be proud.

A beat tow truck pulled into the lot with a van on its hitch and parked by the phone booths. Morelli recognized it. He'd never seen it working but it'd come by more than once and the driver'd take a couple of cases of produce from the greengrocers who sold out of the back of their truck.

Wonder why it stopped here rather than going on to a garage somewhere? Calling AAA, maybe?

The van's decal flashed in a sudden blast of sunlight.

Morelli sat up.

That's a Ramsey College van.

They're on break now, aren't they?

Maybe the college choir's going on tour?

He sipped cold coffee.

The van itself was empty.

The tow truck driver got out and entered a phone booth but didn't close the door. His face was all smiles and happy on the phone, and turned nasty and scowling when he spoke to someone in the truck's cab.

A heavy-set, middle-aged man wearing a dark blue sport coat came out of the Bluebird across the street, his eyes on the tow truck and van. He cut a wide arc as he approached so he came up out of the driver's view.

The man reached behind him, his hand lifted his sport coat tail and into his belt.

Gun!

\\\\\\\\\

Riggerio pulled into the Bluebird lot and paused before parking out back.

That's that idiot's tow truck, the guy who's got no respect for flowers and beauty.

That's a Ramsey College van on his hitch. That's Gio's school. Gio called for reinforcements? From those clowns?

He scanned the Gardiner Service Plaza.

The FBI? And a lone agent? Sneaking up on the idiot? That's not standard procedure. What the fuck's going on?

The FBI agent made it halfway to the tow and van when someone hurried out of the plaza building proper.

Oh, jumping Jesus Christ, the undercover statey's coming out, too?

Mr. de Leo didn't give me instructions regarding any of Gio's friends except for his girl.

Riggerio kept his eyes across the street.

Time to improvise.

His Lincoln jumped forward.

The seat's headrest caught his head but he knew it'd be sore for the next couple of days.

He looked into his rearview. A thirties-something woman not dressed for Maine weather got out of a blood-red Mercedes 450SEL and hurried over. "Oh, I'm so sorry. I'm so sorry. I just pulled in. I don't know where my mind was. I didn't even see you there. Oh, I'm so sorry. Are you alright?"

He got out. "I'm fine, ma'am. I'm fine. You okay?"

Somebody fired a rifle across the street.

He knocked her to the ground.

A gun fell out of her purse.

Tuesday, 19 March 1974

Gio blinked his eyes open. He lay on a bed stiffer and higher than he liked. The air had a hospital tang to it. Calming, green painted walls surrounded him. He faced a window with the drapes drawn. His gaze steadied. A bedstand, slightly softer green than the walls, had a phone, a book, *Abnormal Psychology*, a can of Sprite and an unopened vending machine bag of Planters peanuts on top.

He heard Jess' voice. She and another woman - late thirties, thin, doctor's smock, "Emily Clement, MD" on the nametag - stood beside his bed and whispered.

He smiled at them. "Hi."

Jess didn't smile back. She nudged the other woman. "Can I hit him?"

"I'd rather you didn't."

The room's door opened. Morelli walked in. "He awake now?"

Jess pinned Gio under the blanket, a hand on either side of his shoulders and her weight bearing down. She leaned down until her breasts flattened against him, her face inches above his. "Don't. Ever. Do. That. Again."

"I love you."

Dr. Clement cleared her throat. "Now may not be the time - "

Jess glanced down at Gio's crotch. "You ever want to use that with me in the future, don't ever pull this bullshit again."

Gio frowned and shook his head slightly. "Excuse me, you are?"

She smiled and leaned over, not as close as before. "I'm wearing my holster. Right where you like it. Remember me now?"

Morelli came forward. "Is he okay to talk?"

Dr. Clement rolled her eyes. "Jess, can I ask him a few questions before you two - "

Morelli interrupted. "And then it's my turn."

Clement sat on the edge of Gio's bed. "I'm Dr. Clement, Mr. Chance, Jess's family GP. You're in Augusta General. My office is here, so when Lieutenant Jamison contacted the Rosens they asked me to get involved. With me so far?"

Gio nodded.

"Good. What's the last thing you remember?"

"I brought Harry Thompson to the Augusta Barracks. How is he?"

"Fine as far as I know. You'd never know he'd been kidnapped, stuck in a cellar, escaped, lost his brother, survived in the woods for god knows how many days. He's got some crazy idea he talked with a raven."

"Kids these days, huh?"

"Last I knew he was eating ice cream and his mother was visiting."

Gio sat up. "But not his father, Bill, right?"

Morelli moved closer. "No sign of him. Nobody's seen him in over a month. Pam says he's away on business. We have a BOLO out on his pickup. It's gone, too."

Gio gazed at the ceiling. "It's in Quebec City. Wait a minute. A man's taking stuff out of the back and putting in a bright red car's trunk. Looks like he's moving vegetable crates."

Morelli made notes.

Dr. Clement's eyes went from Gio to Morelli and back. She frowned. "Anything else, Gio?"

"He's at a place...looks like a castle from where I am. High on a hill overlooking a... river. There's a park almost diagonal to the castle. The park has a gazebo or something like it in the center. There's a huge field down the road from the castle."

Dr. Clement cocked her head slightly. "The Frontenac?"

Gio shrugged. "Don't see a sign."

Morelli continued making notes. "The car got Maine plates?"

"Tony, I just woke up. Give me a chance, huh?"

Jess noticed Dr. Clement's wide-eyes. "Boys and their games, right? I've decided it makes them adorable."

Gio bobbed his head as if something got in his light of sight. "No, those are Mass plates."

Morelli leaned forward and Gio held up his hand. "Don't ask. I can't read them yet. The guy's putting suitcases in the car's trunk. He's leaving." He pulled back, his eyes widened. "No, wrong." He cocked his head, shook it, blinked, stared at something no one else could see. "Jess, do you have Stephanie's number handy? Can you call her?"

Jess dialed the phone. The room was quiet.

"It's out of service. Probably line maintenance. Let me try the Tylers." Silence. Jess frowned. She hung up the phone. "That's out of service, too."

"Tony, Stephanie's leaving, not the guy. She's getting in the car." He sniffed, wrinkled his nose as if encountering a sour smell. "She gave her uncles the Tyler twins to get a ransom out of Donald Tyler?"

"You asking me or telling me?"

Gio closed his eyes, squinted. His nose ran and he sneezed. "To get back at Donald. Donnie." He turned to Jess. "It was his child she carried." Back to Morelli. "Telling you."

"Can you find them?"

"I'm in a goddamn hospital bed, Tony!"

Morelli picked up the phone. "Okay. Alright. I'm on it."

Clement took a small penlight from her pocket. "Look at me, please, Mr. Chance."

She shined the light in his eyes, on and off his pupils. "Follow my finger, please."

"You're concerned I'm hallucinating?"

"There were no indications of drugs in your system when you came in. You were on an electrolyte mixture due to exhaustion and dehydration. Do you do drugs, Mr. Chance?"

Gio looked at Jess.

She batted her eyes at him. "My man is so special."

Clement looked from one to the other and took a step back. "I'm ordering up a full tox screen."

Jess put a hand on Clement's arm. "The physical I asked for? Gio did those things to me. That's why Morelli's not questioning what he says."

Dr. Clement blinked.

The phone rang and Morelli picked it up. "I'll be there in ten." He looked at the people in the room. "Gotta go. Gio, you'll be at the Rosens'?"

Gio nodded. "You want to check Jess for drugs and hallucinogens, too, Dr. Clement? And Morelli? You should check him, too, right?"

\\\\\\\\\

Clement insisted on a full workup and Gio consented. After she pronounced him sound and whole - but the rest of the world shaky - he got dressed.

The world shimmered around him. Jess gathered her book, notebook, pen, marker, dropped them in a cloth bag, and watched. "Jamison wanted you under guard. I offered my services." She opened her jacket so he could see her gun.

"Did he want you to get me all frothy?"

"No, I wanted that."

He laced up his hiking boots. "You're going to want sex less now."

"Why do you say that?"

"Because you realize you're not going to die tomorrow. You don't have to worry about rupturing a vein or your heart giving out. You don't have to live every moment as if it's your last."

She snickered. "You sound like a zen greeting card."

"Tell me I'm wrong."

"Shut up. I'll do you right here right now if you'd like. Will that prove to you I'm still interested in sex?"

He came over and kissed her gently on the lips.

She shivered. "Please tell me you'll never stop doing that."

"I promise."

\\\\\\\\\\

Gio and Jess drove back from Augusta to Gardiner with Bessie's radio on loud and Jess tight against his side. She mimicked Aerosmith's Steve Tyler as he sang *Dream On*.

> *Half my life's in books' written pages*
> *Lived and learned from fools and from sages*
> *You know it's true*
> *All the things come back to you*
>
> *Sing with me, sing for the year*
> *Sing for the laughter and sing for the tear*
> *Sing with me, if it's just for today*
> *Maybe tomorrow the good Lord will take you away…*

Her hand rested on his thigh, as always, and he rested a hand on hers, their fingers gently intertwined instead of their usual rough rubbing and finger wrestling, each playing to get on top. Gio lowered the volume just as Tyler began screeching *Dream on…Dream on…Dream on…*

Jess punched him. "Party pooper."

He lifted her hand to his lips and kissed her fingers individually.

"You said I was the one who did those things when you mentioned your physical to Dr. Clement. How did it go?"

"You don't know?"

"Not until you tell me, no."

"How come you can know what's going on two hundred miles away but not what happened during my physical?"

"Rules."

She shook her head. "I still don't get that. There are rules. You can't go here and you can't do that. What kinds of rules are they? Are these rules your kryptonite? Why do you have them? Couldn't you help a lot more people if it wasn't for these rules?"

"Do you know what door locks are for?"

"Why do you always change the subject when we talk about this? Can you just give me an answer? Do you want to hear the sound of one hand bitchslapping your face?"

He sighed. "I love that you like the rough stuff."

She rested on her knees beside him in the front seat so her breasts were level with his face.

He turned and smiled at them. "Hello, boys? Miss me?"

She sat back down. "Yeah, okay, you're sound and healthy, like she said. Now, you were going to tell me about door locks?"

"Can't take a few minutes and say hi to my friends?"

"Door locks."

"Door locks aren't to keep people out. Door locks are to let only certain people in."

"So are these rules your door locks? Is that what you're saying?"

"The door locks are so I'll know when I'm going out and when I'm coming in."

"And what about me? How big is this door? Am I out or am I in?

"You know the saying 'In my father's house there are many rooms'?"

"Who cares about your father's house. Right now I want to know about your house. Is there room for me in your house? In your life? You're doing more and more stuff every day and I don't like it. I don't know where it goes or how it ends. Answer me directly if you can: Is there room for me in your life, yes or no?"

"The original language is closer to 'In my father's house there are many mansions', but people don't understand the original meaning. In the big 'U' universe there are many worlds. They are all available if you want to find them, to go looking. The question isn't if there's room for you in my life, it's do you want a world-walker in yours?"

She punched him and he winced. "How 'bout that, Gio? Is there room for a strong woman in your home or mansion or worlds?" She punched him again.

He pulled into the breakdown lane and she slid across the seat away from him. "No, no you don't. Don't even think of starting that. I'm not even sure I want you goddamn near me until I get a straight answer from you. Is the past twenty-four hours the way it's going to be all the time? You disappear and when you come back you need hospitalization? Oh, that's some fucking life I'm signing up for, isn't it?"

He kept his hands on the wheel. The air crackled. "This is what the *Rebbe* talked about. You have to make a decision, too."

She crossed her arms over her chest and stared out her window.

"He's coming to see you, you know."

She rested her head against the window. Tears washed her face. She bit her lip to stop them and control her voice. "Who?"

"The *Rebbe*. Ben Zev. He'll be at your house soon."

\\\\\\\\

Bella jumped on the couch by the living room's picture window. She watched Gio drive off with Morelli and whined. Sam scratched his dog's back. "Does she remember she's not supposed to be on the furniture?"

Jess stood watching Gio leave and shrugged.

"She never listens to me when he's around."

"She never listened to you before, Pop. You thought she did. She humored you."

Sam pointed at the floor. "Bella, down."

Bella curled up on the couch, rested her head on her paws, looked up at him, and wagged her tail.

Sam folded his arms across his chest and stood as tall as he could. "Bella. Down."

The big shepherd wagged her tail harder. She adjusted herself on the couch and gave belly, her tail increasing its back and forth momentum.

"Bella, I pay the mortgage here. I feed you. That wonderful dog bed you have in the kitchen? Who do you think got that for you? It wasn't Gio Chance - "

Jess interrupted. "Fortuna."

"Huh?"

"His real last name is Fortuna. He americanized it to avoid prejudice."

Bella sat up on the couch and barked as another car came up the driveway.

"You expecting company, Pop?"

Sam opened the front door, one hand unnecessarily on Bella's collar. She barked a greeting before the driver emerged. Sam spread his arms. "*Rebbe*! What are you doing back here?"

Jess stood beside Sam in the doorway, saw it was the *Rebbe*, threw her arms up in the air and walked away.

"I need to speak with Jessica. In private. Is she home?"

Jess came back and stood beside her father. "Everything okay, *Rebbe*?"

"You still seeing Gio?"

"Is there a problem?"

"Come. I have something for you." He brushed past Sam and the dog. "Where can we talk? In private."

Sam pointed at the basement door. "How about downstairs? Comfortable, quiet, and I'll make sure nobody bothers you."

The *Rebbe* opened the door and entered into the basement's darkness. Jess mouthed to Sam, "What's this about?"

Sam shook his head and shrugged.

Jess hesitated at the top of the stairs and looked back at Sam. He shrugged a second time. She turned on the basement lights, closed the door, and followed.

\\\\\\\\

Gio followed Morelli into the Augusta barracks' basement. They stopped at a desk manned by an officer with an empty holster. The officer nodded at Morelli and handed him a clipboard. "Empty your pockets, Gio."

"Am I in trouble?"

"No, a friend of yours is. He asked to see you."

"I have friends here?"

Morelli checked off boxes on the clipboard's top sheet and shook his head. "Says he came up here to see you."

Gio heard voices, familiar. He emptied his pockets. The officer behind the desk put them in a tray and handed Morelli a chit with the same number as the tray. "Go ahead."

Morelli led him down a hall to the last holding cell, towards the voices. Halfway there Gio stopped. "Tim Annandale?"

"You do know him?"

Gio saw the man from Doc Ock's bathroom outside the cell. "Hello! We meet again. Were we ever properly introduced? I'm Gio Fortuna. You are?"

Morelli stood beside the two. "Gio, this is FBI SAC Mark Kagan."

Kagan looked at Annandale. "Probably ex-FBI by now."

Annandale came forward, one arm in a sling. His free arm reached through the bars for Gio. "John! Gio! Tell them I'm okay. Tell them I'm alright. Tell them to let me out of here."

Gio's looked at Annandale then at Kagan. "You told him to wiretap me?"

Kagan shook his head. "No. I told him to keep an eye on you. Because of your uncle. He's expanding his operations into Maine. I knew you made several trips up here and - "

Gio turned to Morelli. "Can we arrest someone for lying?"

Morelli faced Kagan. "Mark Kagan, you have lied to an investigating officer - "

Kagan blanched. "He's working for you?"

"Jamison swore him in a few weeks ago."

Gio snorted.

Kagan turned to Annandale. "You are one stupid fuck." He faced Gio and Morelli. "Where can we talk. Jamison's your lieutenant? You'll want him in on this, I think."

They walked back down the hall.

Annandale screamed, "Wait! Where are you going? Are you going to call Ramsey? You can't tell anyone there about this! Don't call Ramsey! Don't tell my parents!"

Kagan kept walking. "Any chance he'll commit suicide in there?"

Gio chuckled. "We can but hope."

The air shimmered. Gio stopped and Kagan bumped into him. "Sorry, I - "

Gio stepped around Kagan and walked back to Annandale's cell.

Morelli came up beside him. "Gio, what it is? What's going on?"

The air inside Annandale's cell sparked. Gio reached through the bars. "Give me your arm."

Like a whipped dog, his eyes wide and fearful yet wanting his master's loving touch, Annandale slowly offered Gio his injured arm.

Gio grabbed it. Something crackled. Annandale jumped as if hit by lightning. The sling caught fire and burned away without consuming him.

"Your arm's fine now. That ends it between us. Understand?"

Annandale slowly moved his arm in an arc, stretched it, pulled it in, stretched it again.

Gio continued on his way, Morelli in step beside him. "Wish we had a few dozen of you back in 'Nam."

Kagan stared wide-eyed and unmoving as they passed him. He followed, slowly, like a man rising from quicksand, and soon got in step behind them.

Annandale shook his cell bars. "Let me out of here! Let me out!"

\\\\\\\\\

Ben Zev sat on a paisley patterned couch in the Rosens' basement playroom. Recessed lights glowed from overhead paneling, the playroom's rear-facing basement windows not yet catching afternoon sun. Steve's motorcycle took up the center of the room and pushed a gaming coffee table, a checker/chess board and cribbage board carved into its top, to the side. Here and there cigarette burns added strange color to the finished wood. The far wall had a cold and darkened fireplace, beside it some logs and kindling.

Jess walked in and sat in a matching lounger opposite him. "You wanted to see me, *Rebbe*?"

He reached into his coat, pulled out a bizarre macrame, and unfolded it slowly as if unfolding sacred scrolls. "Do you know what this is, Daughter?"

She shook her head. "A *tallit*?"

He nodded at her quickness. "No, but it is a prayer." He offered it to her.

She held it in her hands. "Feels...electrical?" She turned it over a few times and ran her hands along its edges. "Is there a battery somewhere?"

"It is an energy, yes, electrical, no. It has a battery, yes." He opened his arms wide and lifted his head, his eyes focused on emptiness. "The universe is its battery. It draws power from everything that breathes."

"What's it for?"

"It's for you. A *dekl*, a *keytl*, a *yokh*."

"A cover? A shackle? A yoke?"

"A control. To make your life happy. A good one. A prayer to answer your prayers."

She dropped in on the table and shook her hands to be free of it. "Cover what? Shackle what? And Yoke? *Rebbe*, with all due respect, I wasn't raised to be bound or controlled."

"You don't understand, Daughter. It is not to shackle and yoke you, it is for you to use on him, to bind your golem."

"What golem?"

"Before he acts, when he transforms..." Ben Zev looked away. His accent grew thick, heavy, slowed his words.

"Are you okay, *Rebbe*?"

Ben Zev turned his gaze directly on Jess. "He breathes."

"Do you mean Gio? Are we talking about Gio, *Rebbe*?"

He grabbed her arms tightly. "He breathes before he can do any-thing. It's in his breath, Holy Breath."

"*Rebbe*, let go. You're hurting me."

"He is a golem. Or can be made one. There are four things he must do before he can act. Breath is the last. To connect to the Divine. I can teach you the prayer."

His grip dug into Jess's arms. She moved her forearms in a small circle inside and around his, something Gio taught her, and her arms fell free.

He continued without stopping, his voice now like a child's play-ground sing-song. "If prayer is pure and untainted, surely that Holy Breath…"

Jess slapped his face. "Stop it!"

His eyes blurred, then focused first on her then on the *dekl*, and frowned. A moment later he nodded slowly. "This may be enough."

He lifted it from the table. "I will show you." He took some rags resting on Steve's cycle, bunched them in the fireplace, folded the *dekl* into a small, neat square and placed it gently on top. The rags burst into flame.

But not the *dekl*. Ben Zev removed it with some fireplace tongs. The fire died out, the rags smoldered, but nothing more.

"Think of it as a governor. Depending how much surface it touches, is how much energy is restrains. Open it in full…" He held it up, raised his eyebrows, shrugged.

"What am I supposed to do with it?"

"The next time you lie with him, when he rests, place it on his chest. You must do it. Only someone he loves can do it. It will yoke him. When he needs to do something, you fold it so he only has as much power as is needed. When he comes back to you, unfold it when he sleeps."

"Won't he know?"

Ben Zev shook his head. "No. He will only think his power is dimin-ished. He won't know why, and knowing he is weakened, he will not do things that might take him from you."

He held it out to her. She sat back, pulled away.

He leaned forward, his hand thrust forward. "Consider, Daughter. We would not have fled Germany if we controlled one such as he."

"What?"

"We could've stopped Hitler. We could've saved Kennedy. Lincoln. We could have stopped Stalin, Napoleon, Ceasar. The Mayans were brilliant mathematicians, way ahead of any others, and all their science is lost. We could've stopped the Conquistadors. Israel would have been a nation, we'd be the ones on the moon!"

Sunlight came through the rear windows. It caught the binding in its light, the metal threads sent rainbows in patterns of bright and dark on the *Rebbe*'s hands, clothes, face.

Jess looked at her family's longtime friend. The binding bent the sunlight and he looked as if seen through a funhouse mirror.

"Take it."

She stood up.

"Take it!"

"No."

"What?"

"I can't."

"But you can control him!"

"No one has the right to control another. If I do, just once, I've become everything our people have hated throughout history."

"No, you don't - "

"Gio says there are others like him. What do we do? Create one of these for every one of them? Can you make this into a fencing? A railing? Then we can herd them into showers and gas them if they don't do what we want?"

"I did this for you!"

She stood up, arms at her sides, hands balled tightly into fists. "No, you did it for yourself. For fear." She turned and shook her head. "Gio loves me. You want me to trap his love, to betray his trust. So you can be safe." She stepped back from the lounger and looked away. Away from the *Rebbe*, from the binding, from herself. "We lived in fear long enough, haven't we? Does that give us the right to control our destiny by denying others control of theirs?"

"Take it. The *Mascha'ak* woman, the angel, she told me to make this for you, for a learning." He rose and towered over her, his outstretched hand shook with the *dekl*'s energy. "Take it!"

\\\\\\\\\

Kagan sat in an interrogation room. He glanced at the two-way mirror, then Gio, then the two-way mirror, then back at Gio. Across from him sat Morelli and Jamison. Gio leaned against the wall opposite the mirror. He faced Morelli and Jamison.

"Anybody on the other side of that mirror?"

Jamison shook his head.

Kagan kept his eyes on Gio. He nodded then held his head in his hands. "I'd like this to be off the record."

Jamison folded his arms across his chest. "Let's hear what you have to say first, then we can decide if it's on or off the record."

Kagan put his hands down. "In that case, I want a lawyer and my phone call."

Gio pushed himself off the wall. "She hasn't changed. You don't need to make that phone call."

Jamison and Morelli looked up at him. Both said, "What?"

Kagan nodded to the mirror. Gio glanced at it then nodded towards Jamison. "He told you the truth. Nobody's back there."

"Have you pressed charges on our boy for Jesus downstairs?"

Jamison placed his hands on the table in front of him. "I'm going to call your office. You're out of Boston?"

Gio shook his head. "No need, Lieutenant. Mr. Kagan's on his own up here."

Jamison cocked his head at Gio. "You know this how?"

Gio shrugged.

Kagan sat back in the chair. "Shall I begin, or do I make my phone call?"

Jamison looked aside for a minute then nodded. "I don't know who you are and you were never here. Okay?"

Kagan started. "Routine surveillance of Nicholas de Leo's North End coffee shop revealed a Todd Andersen making repeated visits starting in January of last year. It quickly became obvious Andersen was petitioning de Leo for product with the offer of expanding de Leo's territory."

Kagan looked up at Gio. "Did you know any of this?"

"I know nothing about my uncle's business."

"de Leo sent a team to determine Andersen's legitimacy. As long as Andersen dealt his own product, the FBI considered it a state problem."

Jamison interrupted, "That no one told us about."

Kagan shrugged. "We would've."

Morelli snorted. Jamison said, "Right."

"de Leo's men reported Andersen was a safe bet and they sent up some test shipments. Interstate trafficking meant we could get involved. I approached Andersen and asked him to be my CI."

Jamison interrupted again. "What did Andersen get?"

"Stupid. He got stupid."

"Go on."

"Shipments coming up from down south caught the attention of traffickers working out of the Montreal-Sherbrooke-Quebec City tri-angle. They were getting their herbals out of greenhouses in northern Maine."

Morelli nodded. "The Rigauxs."

"A turf war was brewing. Andersen had immunity from prosecution while working as an informant and he took initiative."

Gio laughed and shook his head. "He arranged the kidnapping of Ed and Harry Thompson."

Jamison looked from Kagan to Gio. "Why?"

Kagan raised his eyebrows at Gio.

Gio rested back against the wall. "Because Pam, their mother, is the daughter of Guy Rigaux. He wanted a bargaining chip."

Jamison turned cold eyes on Kagan. "You knew he had Ed and Harry Thompson?"

"And we knew he'd never hurt them. They were too valuable, he knew we were watching him, he knew immunity only goes so far, and I talked to the boys every day to check on their welfare via phone. I told them they were working for the government and were junior G-men. They got a kick out of it."

Gio snickered.

"Things proceeded smoothly. As far as we could tell the Thompson boys were well treated. What we didn't know was how the drugs were getting here."

Morelli snorted. "River boats."

Kagan looked at him.

"They brought product up the Kennebec on low bottom boats specifically designed to transport camping supplies to river outposts."

Kagan slapped the table. "And Nick de Leo runs a fishing fleet out of Gloucester. How far out to sea can these river boats go?"

"Far enough, I'm sure."

"That brings us to the middle of January of this year. That's when things went south big time."

Gio sat on the edge of the table. "Because you didn't count on Mason Rangell?"

Jamison looked up. "Who's Mason Rangell?"

Morelli pulled out his notebook. "Tow truck driver, gets callouts for Gardiner PD and the highway department when there's accidents."

Kagan focused on Gio. "You know an awful lot for someone who doesn't know anything."

"Good guesser."

Morelli chuckled.

Kagan continued. "Rangell wasn't the only problem."

Jamison leaned forward. "There was another problem?"

Gio got off the table, walked to the two-way mirror, and looked into the darkness. "Me."

\\\\\\\

Doc Ock's private line rang in his office. He smiled. Senators, governors, congressman, financiers used this line. People who could donate one hundred thousand without batting an eye got this number. He always smiled when it rang. Another addition to Ramsey, another building, another department, another endowment, another gold-plated plaque on the outside of a building and on it in large capital letters

THE somebody BUILDING
THANKS TO THE GRACIOUS GENEROSITY OF
somebody
BLAH BLAH BLAH

and somewhere well underneath in much smaller script "...and to the glory of Jesus Christ, Our Lord."

They'd forgotten to put that on a plaque once. Nobody noticed until that no-good lout Gio Chance said something in convocation when they asked the student body if anyone knew someone willing to contribute to a new dorm. Ock stood on the podium and mentioned the donor would be honored with a plaque.

Chance stood and said, "How about we put Jesus' name on the plaque and leave the donors' names off. Isn't that what the Bible says we should do?"

Ock's face flushed. "You do not understand how these things work."

Chance laughed. In front of everyone, he laughed. Close to one thousand students in the gymnasium for convocation and he laughed and Ock heard nervous chuckles from others echo off the walls and bounce off the bleachers and shuffle through the chairs.

"Oh, I know how things work. I'm not sure everyone else does, but I do. Don't I, Doc?"

That miserable insubordinate little fu -

Doc Ock caught himself. He straightened his tie. He inhaled deeply. He cleared his throat. He tested his voice - "Hello. Hello."

He picked up the phone. Before he said a word he heard a click followed by his voice among other male voices alternately being cheered on and cheering others on. A woman's voice said "Who's next? Who's next? Come on, boys, you can't all be done. You think that's enough? You, with the collar on, you haven't been up my ass yet. What's the holdup? You're Spencer, right? Give me that cock again, I'll get it hard for you."

Ock paled. His voice shook. "What?"

He heard another click followed by "Spencer, this is Bramhall. State Street won't be able to support Ramsey anymore. We're withdrawing all funding as of today. Further, we're releasing any bonds or notes you personally or Ramsey have with us. Any funds due will be deposited to their originating accounts."

Ock paled. The phone slid through the sweat on his palm. He squeaked out, "Hello?"

"And never contact me or this institution again."

The phone went dead.

Doc Ock stared at it. He hung it up and stared at it.

His eyes watered.

Those bastards promised...

\\\\\\\\\

Gio stared into the void a moment longer before turning to the others in the interrogation room. "First, Rangell is Andersen's boyfriend, lover, paramour, whatever the term is, and Andersen can't control him."

Jamison frowned. "Control him from what?"

"Rangell's a pederast."

Kagan stared at Gio. "How the fuck do you know that?"

"I didn't know it. Harry did."

Jamison held up a hand. "You never said how you found the Thompson boy and this pederasty is news to me. I'm calling a halt for half an hour. Nobody leaves the building. Understood?"

Gio opened the door. "Who's got responsibility for Annandale?"

Morelli, Jamison, and Kagan exchanged looks. Kagan raised his hand. "Yeah, okay, he's mine. I'm paying to have his van repaired, anyway. Can we release him and send him on his way?"

Jamison looked at Morelli. "Is he a material witness?"

"Rangell says Annandale tried to help secure the tow hitch and his arm got caught in the wench. Doc says it's a bad bruise, bone level. Must have whacked him with a tire iron. But nothing permanent. Annandale says Rangell beat him, but there's only one bruise and it's not defensive." He looked at Gio. "Is the bruise still there?"

Gio shook his head. "No."

Morelli shrugged. "Besides, they were nowhere near the shooter."

Gio held the door. "Yeah, I almost forgot about that. Tell me about the shooter?"

Morelli flipped pages. "He's your Donald Tyler, Windham, Mass, let go yesterday from a posh position with State Street in Boston."

Gio snorted. "Stephanie nannied for him. With benefits, if you know what I mean." He nodded at Morelli. "I mentioned it at the hospital, remember?"

Morelli looked through his notes and grunted affirmation.

Jamison threw his folder down on the table. "Jesus Christ, is there anybody who's not getting laid in this story?"

Morelli held up his hand. "If we're taking numbers..."

"Out! All of you, out!"

Gio walked downstairs to the holding cells. The officer nodded. "Jamison called, said I could let you into the dungeon. The screamer a friend of yours?"

"Annandale? I know him. Wouldn't call him a friend."

Gio stood outside Annandale's cell and watched him curled up on his cot. He cleared his throat.

Annandale, his face to the wall, didn't look up. "Go away."

"As you wish."

Annandale rolled over, saw Gio, and leapt off the cot. He made it to the bars in two strides and held them in tight, white-knuckled fists.

"Gio. Thank God it's you. You have to get me out of here. Tell them who I am."

"Why?"

"Why what?"

"Why do I have to get you out of here? How did you become my responsibility?"

"Why, because we're brothers, John. Gio. We both go to Ramsey. We're in classes together. We - "

"Classes you worked to get me thrown out of. A school you still work to get me thrown out of. Kagan said he asked you to keep track of me, not bug the dorm's phone, not threaten my roommate and friends, not stand guard in my dorm lounge so nobody would come visit me. All that is yours. You own that."

"I only wanted what was best for Ramsey. Don't you see that?"

"Who decided that was best? You?"

Annandale eyes darted back and forth. "No, John. Gio. I wouldn't do that."

"Then who?"

Annandale looked at the floor and mumbled. "Ock."

"Really? And you fought for me all the way, right?"

Annandale' head came up. He looked Gio in the eye. "Of course. That's right. I fought for you. Me. Tim Annandale. I was always on your side."

Gio chuckled. The chuckle worked into a laugh. He laughed so hard he held onto the cell cross bar to support himself.

Annandale joined him, but his laughter wasn't as rich, as deep, as Gio's.

Gio stepped back, shook his head and walked away. "You're a good teacher, Tim. Thank you for this lesson."

Annandale reached through the bars and his hands clenched nothing but air. "You going to leave me here? Gio? John? You can't do that! I'm your friend. You need me, goddammit!"

"Yes. A very good teacher."

Gio looked at Annandale and saw a snake unable to shed its skin, strangling in its own decaying flesh, wrap itself around him.

Gio stopped at the officer on his way out. "Unless somebody else wants him for something, you can release him whenever you want. I'd appreciate him getting a ride to wherever his van is. I understand Agent Kagan is having it repaired."

Wednesday, 20 March 1974

Todd held Mason's truck keys in his hand. "We're not going to have a repeat of the Thompsons, are we?"

Mason cocked his head. "Are you kidding? These two are toddlers. What kind of sick fuck do you think I am?"

"I just want to be sure. They're going to be safe with you? I'm not going to come home and find them gone and you with your dick in your hands?"

"Todd, my god, you are a sick fuck."

"Okay, just making sure."

Mason turned on the television to morning cartoons. "Go on, go ahead. We'll be taking our afternoon naps by the time you get back. Go."

Todd called his mother's number repeatedly for the past two days and got nothing but not-in-service messages. This was not acceptable. He had her boys and now either she or her husband, Donald, were going to pay. The Thompsons boys were a bargaining chip and that paid off big time. His half-brothers were a different matter entirely. He'd show his mom and her husband what brotherly love was all about.

Let Donald Tyler refuse him a loan now!

Ha!

Bella wagged her tail as Jess opened the door to Gio's room. Bella gently woofed and Gio opened his eyes.

"You got home late last night."

"Can I still call this home?"

Jess sat on the edge of Gio's bed and scratched Bella's head. She spoke quietly, not quite a whisper, as if she drew the words from her heart, unfiltered by her mind. "The *Rebbe* was here. He came to see me."

Gio sat up and reached for her hand. She pulled it away.

"He wanted me to make a decision. Regarding you."

"Regarding me. Not us?"

"Were the Mayans mathematicians, Gio?"

He shook his head, not understanding. "I'm sorry, what?"

"The Mayans. Were they great mathematicians and we lost their knowledge?"

He leaned back against the headboard. "Yes. They were. And some, yes."

"You said you learned from your grandfather. Who taught him?"

"He had many teachers. He talked about them often. He introduced me to some. Why?"

"So there are a lot of people who can do this?"

"There are some and I have no idea how many. Where are you going with this?"

"Could you have stopped Hitler?"

"Jess, I - "

She looked up at him, her voice no longer a whisper. "Could you?"

"It doesn't work that way."

"What doesn't work that way? The rules? The goddamn rules? Has nobody ever broken the rules?"

He reached for her again. She pulled back from him. Her face reddened.

"How far back do your people go? Could you have kept the Jews out of Egypt? Could you have - "

The room shimmered.

Jess jumped off the bed. Bella stayed and lay on Gio's legs, still under the blanket. Creatures of all shapes and sizes, beings from all eternities, swam in a blue-green-gold aura around him. "Is this what you wanted to see? If someone saved the Mayans we'd all be speaking Quiche right now. Would that be okay? If Hitler didn't happen then the Allies wouldn't have moved into Europe and the Soviets would have run it over. France, Greece, Spain, all of them would be Soviet satellites. Should we have sided with Chaka Zulu over the British? Your skin would be a different color if we had. Should we have kept Japan closed to the west? Should the Q'ins have lost to the Hans?"

She wanted to leave but couldn't. The door remained open but she stood transfixed. Horror and beauty filled the room and Gio was its center.

"Who decides? Because you're asking me to decide which future is best of all possible futures, and that's making me a Hitler but the worst kind, the one nobody ever sees, the one nobody ever knows about or recognizes."

The room stilled. Bella snored peacefully beside Gio's blanketed form. Whatever had been there was gone.

"You are not so selfish, Jess. I could not love you if you were. But you knew you could've died at any time, your heart could've ruptured, the veins in your leg clotted. You could've died hiking, making love, during childbirth. Was it fair letting me fall in love with you knowing that? Knowing the most important thing in my life could've been taken away at any second and not giving me the chance to choose if I wanted that risk in my life?"

"I was afraid."

"Because I would choose you. Even if I only had you for a moment. It would have been enough."

"I'm so sorry."

"And now you'll not have to worry about those things ever again. No matter what becomes of us, what becomes of me, whether there's room for me in your life or not, you're free of those concerns, you don't have to be worried. Whether it's me or another man, you can live your life without fear you'll suddenly die."

Jess took the *dekl* from a back pocket and unfolded it. "Do you know what this is?"

He smiled at her and a tear stained his cheek. "Do you know what it is?"

"The *Rebbe* made it for me."

"Did he tell you why?"

"Some angel visited him. She told him it was a learning for me."

"What did you learn?"

She held it out to him. "You take it. I don't want it. I don't want anyone's love that way."

He lifted it from her hand and held it open on his palm. It burst into flames. Above it, caught in fire, small planets revolved around small suns, nebulae came into being and collapsed. The flames died, the *dekl* gone.

"The only rules that can bind us are those we take on ourselves."

She watched the ashes swirl off his palm and disappear. She kept her eyes there, waiting for the winds to rise again, and spoke the question as a statement. "And I will never understand your rules, will I." She looked and wiped tears from his face. "Or know them. All of them."

"If you can not do, you will not know. I'm sorry, Jess, my love, and no."

"I think you should leave now."

\\\\\\\\\\

Robbie Tyler lifted the phone from the coffee table between the couch and TV and dialed 0. A few rings later a kind lady answered. "Hello, how may I help you?"

"I want mommy."

The woman hesitated. "Is your mommy with you?"

"Mason's hurt. I want mommy."

"Is Mason your daddy? Your brother?"

"DJ hurt Mason. Mason's not moving."

"What's your name?"

"Robbie Tyler."

"Do you know where you live, Robbie?"

"With mommy and daddy and DJ and Step'nie."

"Is Step'nie with you?"

"No."

"Are you hurt?"

"DJ's sick. DJ hurt Mason."

She kept him talking for ten minutes, time enough to trace the call and alert the police. She kept him talking until she heard sirens on his end of the line.

She heard a door open then a man's voice. "Hello, son. Are you Robbie Tyler?"

Robbie nodded. "I'm hungry."

"May I have the phone, Robbie?"

Tony Morelli directed his backup to search the house. He took the phone from Robbie's little hands. "We have it operator. Thank you."

Robbie's clothes were blood stained. Morelli did a quick inspection and found no wounds. He kept his eyes on Robbie as more officers arrived. "Find some towels. Look in the kitchen and bathroom."

A moment later he wrapped Robbie in bathroom towels. Two more officers came in the back door. One took the basement, the other the second floor. Working with the existing officers as a unit, they worked the house room by room. Morelli lifted Robbie in his arms. "Do you know where DJ and Mason are Robbie?"

Before Robbie answered one of the other officers called out "In here. Don't bring the boy in."

Morelli kept Robbie in his arms while he glanced around the doorframe from the hallway.

Mason lay on a fullsize bed, dead. Knife wounds went through his clothes and deep into his body. His throat was stabbed, his face, down one leg and up the other.

DJ sat beside him, a long butcher's knife in each hand, singing the Jack-in-the-Box song. Every time he came to "Pop goes the weasel" he stuck a knife in Mason.

One officer hurried to the bathroom and threw up. The other held out his hand. "Are you DJ? Are you hungry? Want to come get some breakfast? I'll need your knives first. May I have them, please?"

DJ nodded, held out the knives, and raised his arms to be picked up.

The phone rang. The officer holding DJ called to his partner. "Somebody get that?"

The officer came out of the bathroom, wiped his mouth and picked up the phone. "Hello?"

"Hello? Who's this?"

"Who's calling please?"

"I'm sorry, I must have dialed the wrong number."

A moment later the phone rang again. He picked it up but didn't speak. The same voice, male. "Mason?"

"This is the State Police. There's been an accident. Who's calling please."

Todd hung up the phone. He tossed his tea and cruller into the garbage can outside the Windham Donut Shop, got in Mason's truck, and drove south to Rt 128, then 128 south onto I-93 into Boston.

\\\\\\\\

Riggerio lifted his Army-issue two-way and adjusted the signal. "Mario?"

"Still at the high school, boss. Nothing happening."

"Marco?"

"He's still at the barracks, boss. Everybody from yesterday's shooting is here. Some kind of big powwow I think."

"Let me know if he moves or anything happens. Vincenzi?"

"I got three state police cars and two ambulance. They took one body out, looks adult but it was covered, and two little boys, one covered in blood, the other eating a cookie."

"Holy Christ. Anybody see you?"

"Deep cover in the woods, boss. But there's another problem."

"Go ahead."

"A boy came out of the woods and walked up to me not long after I got here. I think he's been here a while. Said his name is Ed Thompson. Said he wants to go home."

"Jesus Christ on a crutch. I've got to call this in. Vincenzi, drop that kid off at a hospital. Make sure nobody sees you. All of you, let me know if anything happens."

\\\\\\\

One of Nick de Leo's men brought a phone to his table at the Osteria Giambatta. "Riggerio, Mr. de Leo. He says it's important."

"Grazie, Coulo." He lifted the receiver. "Go ahead." He listened, sipped his espresso, listened. "Thank you, Riggerio. My nephew's alright, though? Uh-huh. And his girl, she's alright? Good good good. Tell the boys I appreciate all their work. Let them know I appreciate it." He hung up the phone, stared at it, sighed.

The bell over the door jingled. Nick continued to stare at the phone. His fingers tapped the table.

Coulo cleared his throat. "Someone to see you, Mr. de Leo."

Nick looked up. Todd stood there. Nick's fingers continued to tap the table. "*Grazie, Coulo. Questa uscirà dalla porta sul retro, per favore.*"

Coulo nodded. He motioned Todd over. When Todd stood beside Mr. de Leo's, with his back turned to Coulo, Coulo pulled out a billy and whacked him on the back of his head. Todd fell.

Coulo whistled. Another man came out of the kitchen wearing a chef's jacket and hat.

Nick looked at Todd's unmoving body, saw him breathing, pursed his lips. "I would like you two to make a delivery for me. Give me a moment to write a note. And I'll need my valise."

Mark Kagan's motel room phone rang. He didn't want to answer it. Only Janey's doctors had this number. It would be bad news. He didn't want any bad news.

But if it was bad news, it would be over, done with. He could rightly mourn and then rest.

With lots of sleeping pills.

And bourbon. He never really enjoyed bourbon, but this time and for this occasion he'd get a bottle of the best, pour himself a tall one, turn on the TV, sit back, and pop the pills like candy. He might even dip them in chocolate.

Janey loved chocolate before chemo knocked out her taste buds.

"Hello."

"Kagan."

His boss' voice. Not happy. Sharp. Demanding.

"You'll have my resignation on your desk first thing tomorrow morning."

"Jesus Christ, Kagan. For a SAC you leave a trail like a snail. You got a package. I took the liberty of opening it on your behalf."

"A package? Me?"

"If I didn't open it, the son-of-a-bitch would've suffocated. Todd Andersen, trussed up like a Thanksgiving turkey, complete with documentation on his activities throughout Maine and his plans for expansion into New Hampshire and the Maritimes. The RCMP's going to love this. Ever heard of the Rigauxs? Big pot growers up that way? Not to mention other illegals. Gun running. Looks like your prayers got answered. You're going to go out in style."

"I...I..."

"And I'll still take your resignation. First thing. When you're done with your little Maine vacation. Understand?"

"Yes, sir."

Joe Radwel knocked on his office door.

Laurie looked up. "Yes, Joe?"

"Thank god you call me Joe. Think you can get your partner in crime to call me Joe? I'm not a Sir. Not since I left the Marines, anyway."

She smiled.

"I need you to mail something for me. Guaranteed overnight delivery."

Laurie checked the wall clock. "The mail truck hasn't come to the Student Center yet, I can - "

"No, Laurie. I need you to go to..." He looked up, shook his head back and forth a bit. "Burlington. I need you to mail it from Burlington. Or even better, somewhere down on the Cape. Rhode Island would be good. Connecticut, maybe? Hartford? Yeah, that'd work."

"That's going to chew up most of my day, Joe. I won't be able to finish filing these receipts for you."

"You can do that tomorrow." He handed her a key to the bottom, locked drawer of his filing cabinet. "You'll find it in there. And take Merl with you. In case one of you gets tired, the other can take over the driving. I want you both back tonight. I need you to come to my house and show me the receipt, okay?"

"Is everything okay, Joe?"

"Everything's fine, Laurie. I just need this done today. And one more thing; I'm giving you a wrapped package. The addressed envelope's inside. I don't want you looking at the address. I don't want you to know where it goes. Just hand the clerk the package, tell him what's inside is guaranteed overnight delivery, and bring me the receipt. Understood?"

"Yes, sir."

"Oh, don't you start that." He dug into his pocket and pulled out a money clip. "Take #16. It's got a full tank and all the maintenance is up to date." He pulled three twenties from his money clip. "Here's sixty dollars. In case you need to fill up on the way back, and so you can get something to eat on the way down and back, and any tolls." He hollered into the maintenance barn loud enough to be heard out back. "Merlin, get your butt in here and clean yourself up. You're going on a date."

"He is not."

"Yeah, but he'll move quicker and be on his best behavior if he thinks he is."

Thursday, 21 March 1974

Sam sat on a chair next to Gio's cot at the Augusta barracks. Bella lay on the cot and snored, her nose buried in Gio's pillow. Sam stood when Gio came out of the washroom partially dressed and drying his hair in a rough towel. "Can we talk, Gio?"

Bella lifted her head and wagged her tail.

"How'd you know I was here?"

"Morelli called and told me. He figured something happened and wanted me to know so I wouldn't worry."

"How's Jess?"

"She's been in her room crying non-stop since you left yesterday. She won't talk to us. Do you mind telling me what happened?"

"She discovered I'm a gentile."

Sam smiled a little and shook his head. "She knew that and it wouldn't upset her. If you'd rather not talk about it, I understand."

"Not much to talk about. She asked me to leave."

Sam watched Gio finish dressing. "Jess asked you to leave?"

"More like she said, 'I think you should leave now' and, always obedient, I did."

"Did you say something to her? Did you decide you didn't want to be with her?"

"I'm a gentile, Sam, not an idiot."

"Would you be willing to come by? Maybe for just a little while? See if she's changed her mind?"

"Not unless she asks me."

"I'm asking you."

The hair rose on Gio's arms. Bella stared in the direction of Gardiner and growled.

Sam looked down at his dog. "Bella, what's wrong?"

"Yes. I'll come by. Give me an hour to finish things up here, okay? Tell Jess I'm coming. Tell her to stay in the house until I get there."

"As much as I can tell my daughter anything, I'll tell her to stay in the house until you get there. I don't think she's in the mood to go shopping, though. I wouldn't worry."

Gio petted Bella. "Go with him, girl. Take care of her for me."

Bella jumped off the cot and trotted out the door.

\\\\\\\\

Riggerio adjusted his Army-issue two-way's signal. "Mario?"

"Still at the high school, boss. Nothing happening. Vincenzi's here but he's behind the AC stack taking a piss."

"Marco?"

"He's still at the barracks, boss. Her dad came by, stayed about twenty minutes, then left. Our boy's still here, though. His car's still here, anyway."

"Let me know if he moves or anything happens."

\\\\\\\\

Doc Ock's secretary knocked on his office door.

"Come in."

She opened the door wide enough for him to see the young USPS employee in his bright, shiny uniform, his shoes polished spit-shine glossy black, and his hat under his left arm. "This gentleman has a package for you, sir."

Doc Ock waved her away. "Fine. Take it."

"It has to be signed for, sir."

"Then sign for it."

"It's addressed special delivery to you, sir. You have to sign for it."

Doc Ock lowered his pen and closed the folder of documents on his desk. "Oh, very well. Come in."

The young USPS employee came in holding a 9x13 manila envelope in his left hand. Doc Ock smiled at the young man's almost salute. "You just get out of the service, son?"

"Yes, sir."

"Got the GI bill?"

"Yes, sir."

"Want to go to college?"

"Thinking about it, sir. Maybe come Fall."

"You a good Christian lad?"

"Do my best, sir."

"Need me to sign that?"

The young man held out a slip with a USPO stamp on it along with routing numbers and such. Doc Ock picked up his pen and signed with a flourish. "Anything else?"

The young USPO employee handed over the manila envelope. "No, sir."

"You may go now."

"Thank you, sir."

"You decide on a college, come see me first, understood?"

"Yes, sir. Thank you, sir."

The young man halted a salute, turned, and walked out.

"Please close the door on your way out."

Doc Ock flipped the envelope over a few times, checked the cancellation stamp, grabbed a letter opener off his desk and sliced open the top of the envelope.

Pictures fell out. Eight-by-Tens.

A typed sheet of paper came out on top. He read it. "Gio stays or these go public."

The first picture was of the last seed shed out behind the maintenance barn. The bottom left had a date and time stamp.

Doc Ock's hands went cold.

The next picture showed Doc Ock himself, looking to the side as he opened the shed door.

The next showed one of the co-eds, a Rachel somebody, coming out and adjusting her skirt as she walked.

His hands sweat.

The next showed Doc Ock walking towards the shed, his sport coat half off. He looked to be walking quickly, perhaps running.

The next showed another co-ed, he completely forgot her name, adjusting her sweater - my god, did he remember that sweater - as she opened the shed door.

Doc Ock loosened his tie and wiped his brow.

The next picture showed Father Chris opening the shed door and lowering his pants.

He glanced at the next picture and looked away. How did they get that one? They had to be looking in the goddamn window, for chrissakes. Nobody heard the shutter?

He reached into his top desk drawer and took out his latest toy, a Budischowsky TP-70 pistol, checked the magazine, and like Simon and Garfunkel's *Richard Corey*, put a bullet through his head.

\\\\\\\\\

Dykstra drove up to Gianna's without calling ahead of time. Things were getting too hot and it was time to fly. Mason was a witness to a shooting, but that didn't matter because some sick toddler fuck knifed him to death in his sleep. Ed and Harry Thompson show up within days of each other, one at the state police barracks and the other at Kennebunk General, somebody calls long distance for Lyndon and he hasn't had a chance to ask Towne what he did with the body.

Oh, if this isn't a shit storm brewing nothing is.

Definitely time to get out of Dodge.

He drove down the street to his usual parking spot and saw Towne's car there.

What the fuck?

He kept driving and parked around the corner where he could watch Gianna's windows and Towne's car at the same time.

Half an hour later, the light in Gianna's went out followed by her and Towne walking downtown.

She had her hand in Towne's pants pocket. Even at this distance, Dykstra could see Towne's face muscles twitch.

"You fucking slut. You goddamn fucking slut."

He waited until they were out of site, exited his car, and walked through the front door of her apartment building. He checked the names on the mailboxes until he found the only one in a basement apartment. He pounded on the door. A middle-aged man dressed in khaki work clothes opened it.

"You the super?"

The man nodded.

Dykstra flashed his shield. "I have to get in Gianna Avily's apartment. We got a report on a problem. You got a pass key?"

The man fumbled with a keychain.

"Just give me the master. I'll bring it back when I'm done."

The man singled out a key and got it stuck on the chain's release.

Dykstra pulled it out of his hand.

"Hey."

"No time. I'll take the whole goddamn thing. This might take a while. Come up if you need them before I get back." He hurried up the stairs to the elevator, rode it up to Gianna's floor, and let himself in.

\\\\\\\\\

Gio pulled into the Rosens' driveway. His nostrils flared and the air inside Bessie crackled.

A raven flew over Bessie, ahead of the car and up beyond the house into the woods beyond.

It perched on an ash starting to bud.

Gio followed the trunk line down to the forest floor.

Something glinted in the sunlight.

Jess ran out of the house, Bella close behind.

Gio jumped out of Bessie, her door open.

A second glint at the base of the tree.

Gio grabbed Jess, spun her so his back faced the woods and he faced the high school. Three gunshots. Bella yelped. Gio clutched Jess and grunted twice. Gio saw black dots on the high school roof, felt the air whistle overhead four times in rapid succession.

His weight fell into Jess. "Gio? Gio!" Jess screamed as he fell. She covered him with her body and drew her revolver. "Pop, call an ambulance." Sam came outside at the shot. Jess stayed over Gio and screamed at Sam. "Call an ambulance!"

Sam ran back inside.

Jess felt Gio move under her. She rolled him over. "Don't move, Gio. Stay still. Help's coming."

She undid his jacket and pulled back.

He sat up and pushed her aside. "Bella's hurt."

She rested on her knees. "What?"

Gio crawled over to the big shepherd. She wagged her tail and looked up at him from where she lay.

"It's okay, girl. I'm here now."

A wound flowed blood from the dog's side. The hair on Gio's arms rose. The air around him shimmered. He placed a hand over Bella's wound.

Lower-Center-Relax-Breathe.

Heal.

Bella's fur crackled. A bullet fell out of her side. Her wound healed. She wagged her tail and stood up, licked Gio's face.

"Take care of them for me, Bella."

The big shepherd wagged her tail and trotted back into the house.

Morelli's cruiser raced down the street and up the Rosens' driveway with all lights flashing. An ambulance followed.

Jamison came up the driveway and parked behind the ambulance crew. "I heard the call on my way home. Gio, you okay?"

Gio pointed up to the tree line. "The Rigaux brothers are up there. I suspect they're dead. Two bullets each, one in the head, the other in the heart." He stood, took off his jacket and shirt, and unstrapped a bullet-proof vest. "You weren't kidding when you said it'd still hurt."

The hair rose on his arms. He turned and looked back to the woods. "Get down!"

Another shot rang out but it went wild.

The air whistled above him twice again.

He stood and lifted Jess up to him. "And Pam, also dead. Head and heart." He shook his head. "Surprised she had one."

A catering van pulled out from behind the high school and drove away.

Jamison looked up at him from ground level. "You sure?"

"You think I'd let Jess stand otherwise?"

Jamison took the vest and picked up the bullet that fell out of Bella. "'308s. Thank god you got some muscle on you. You might still have some cracked ribs, though." He motioned the ambulance crew to Gio. "What happened?"

Jess punched Gio. "You wore a vest? You wore a goddamn vest? How many times do I have to think you've goddamn died on me? You fucking son-of-a-bitch!"

Jamison answered. "Hey, Jess. That vest saved his life. Maybe yours, too, huh?"

Gio scratched his side roughly were the bullet would have entered if he were Bella. His hand came up covered in blood. He fell to the ground and shook.

Morelli came back from the treeline. "Three dead, two men, one woman. The men are the Rigaux brothers. Clean - " He saw Gio twitching on the ground and ran to him. "Gio?"

Gio smiled as he shook. He looked at the three of them. The ambulance crew put him on a stretcher and prepared him for transport. "Got to learn to synchronize healings." He coughed up blood. "Here we go again." His eyes rolled back in his head and he shook, his body snapping in half and back as if being shaken in a giant hand.

Caroline didn't understand Tony Morelli. He picked her up but he didn't. He offered her his bed and took his couch as if he expected doing so all along. He took her out but he didn't. He asked if she liked Italian because he had some leftovers from a friend's uncle that'd knock her socks off, and they did. She told him a little about her marriage. He listened without intruding and looked into her eyes more than anyone else ever did. She attempted shocking him with a few revelations and he shrugged or nodded or shook his head as appropriate.

"Nothing bothers you, Officer Morelli?"

She preferred to call him "Officer Morelli." To establish distance. Just in case.

"I've been in the MSP for fifteen years now, Caroline. It'd take a bit to bother me."

He was pleasant towards her but didn't pull any punches.

And less than a week ago she did a six-way to get back at her husband whom she abandoned and left penniless because he was the worst scum of the earth. Three days ago he attempted to kill her with a small caliber rifle and didn't count on return fire from the nice Italian gentleman she accidentally rear-ended in the Bluebird parking lot.

She shook her head briefly.

You're up here to find your sons, Caroline. Get a boyfriend later, okay?

"How are my sons?"

"We can go see them if you'd like. Doc says Robbie's good to go. Probably need counseling but healthy enough. Donald Junior..." he paused, evaluated his words before he spoke them. "He's handling the trauma differently."

"I'm not surprised. He was his father's favorite. Donnie always took him for walks through the woods back home. He'd leave Robbie with me all the time. Robbie hated that. I could tell."

\\\\\\\

Dykstra sat in Gianna's armless rocker in the corner of her living room, in the dark, his feet on the floor squarely in front. This was their rocker. He would sit and she would straddle him and start the chair rocking and it was an agonizingly slow in...out...in...out...in...out.

Every time he pushed the rocker faster she reached underneath and crushed his testicles. Sometimes she'd stay on him while he came. Other times she'd hurry off and surround his pulsing cock with her mouth, dig her teeth into its head. He'd stop pulsing and she'd get on him again.

Again and again and again.

He rocked slowly, just the way she liked it, and waited.

And now she was with Towne.

How many years had that dumb fuck been on the force and never passed an exam? Only got the union mandated raises?

And she's fucking him?

Footsteps came down the hall.

He stopped rocking.

Voices outside the door.

A key in the lock.

Light from the hallway blinded him. He held his breath.

Towne pushed her up against the door, lifted her skirt.

The slut wasn't wearing any panties.

She was wearing fucking garters and fishnets.

Fucking garters and fishnets!

The ones he bought her because she said they made her feel sexy.

She laughed, pushed him away. "Let me go pee first." She reached into his pants and jerked. "Hold that thought, okay?"

Towne grunted.

She turned on the light. "Alan, wait - "

He emptied his service revolver into them, firing back and forth, one for him, one for her, one for him, one for her, one for him, one for her.

Doors opened up and down the hallway.

He stepped into the hallway. "Get back in your rooms. Police emergency."

He kicked the bodies into the middle of the living room, reloaded his weapon, and held it up against Gianna's lifeless head.

"Remember what I said about fucking you up the ass?"

He lifted her skirt and unzipped himself.

"Today ain't your day, is it, cunt?"

Blue lights bounced off the building's exterior when he went down the backstairs to the street.

Six police came down the hall on Gianna' floor. Two advanced to Gianna's apartment, the other four vacated the floor.

The two entered Gianna's apartment, cleared it, checked for life signs, found none, called it in.

The four talked with people from the other apartments. Yes, they'd seen the murderer many times. They used to think he was her father but you should have heard the sounds coming out of there.

The maintenance man said he often found takeout containers from The King of Mongolia in that apartment's trash.

A squad car went there, its lights and sirens off, approaching on what officers called "good quiet."

Dykstra sat at the bar, his pants and shirt soaked with blood, a Pina Colada with its fruity little umbrella beside a big plate of Mongolian Beef, extra-extra hot, in front of him.

A youngish Asian man stood behind the bar, his eyes wide, shaking and whisking a wok.

Dykstra smiled at the officers' reflections in the bar mirror as they came inside.

He lifted his revolver.

"Drop your weapon."

He shook his head and turned to face them, his revolver still in his hand.

The Asian man behind the bar wanged the wok against the side of Dykstra's head from behind. Dykstra fell off his barstool and lay flat on the floor.

Gio and Jess stood at the top of her driveway under the night sky. Their breath misted in the driveway flood as they spoke. He reached for her and she held her hand up, motioned him away.

"What would've happened if you weren't wearing a vest?"

"I would have died."

"So you're not invulnerable?"

"You see a big red S on my chest?"

"What did you do to Bella? She was shot, wasn't she?"

Gio nodded. "It's what I do. I am what my grandfather called a Healer. I heal people. Things. Animals."

"Is that what you did to me?"

"What I did to you was an infinity ago. I have no idea what I did or how I did it, only that it happened. Now I'm learning more about myself, my limits."

"Could you heal anyone of anything?"

"I take less time to recover each time I do something. I'm still learning, I suppose. I don't know."

"Can you bring back the dead?"

"I'd rather not try."

"What are your limits?"

He shook his head. "I don't know."

"Do you have a choice? Can you decide not to do something? Can you walk away if you want? Never do this again?"

He watched a sliver of moon sail overhead. Tomorrow it would be dark, a new moon.

"I don't know. I'd rather not find out."

"But you don't have to do this, right? 'Cause I don't want to have you dying on me all the time. I want a husband with a good long life. Who'll give me kids. You said once I couldn't get pregnant by you. Can we have kids now?"

"You will have strong, healthy children."

"I will? You said I will. Not us? We won't have kids together?"

He held out his hand to her. The sliver of moon grew bright. The *dekl* appeared. He offered it to her. "We definitely will if you use this."

"And if I don't?"

"Then we learn as we go if we'll have kids together. One is surety, the other a hope, a desire. Which would you rather, my love, surety or faith?"

She took the *dekl* from his hand.

She blinked and shook her head.

Gio and Bessie were gone.

Her body first shivered in the cold, then she fell to her knees, clutched the *dekl* in her hands, and sobbed until the moon passed overhead.

Friday, 22 March 1974

Gio folded the sheets and blanket Tony and Caroline gave him. "Thanks, guys, but I could've taken the floor."

Tony smiled. "Not a problem."

Caroline leaned into Tony and echoed, "Not a problem."

Robbie opened the door to the other bedroom and came out dragging a blanket and rubbing his eyes. Caroline lifted him up and snuggled him. "How's my great big hero this morning?"

Robbie giggled.

Tony's phone rang. He listened and spoke quietly while Gio and Caroline watched.

He hung up and Caroline asked, "Is it about DJ?"

Tony shook his head. "Jamison said Lyndon's case officer hasn't heard from him in a week and he never showed up for his brief and debrief. He wants to know if you can find him, Gio."

"I'd rather get on the road, if that's okay. Gardiner…is too painful for me right now."

Tony nodded and offered his hand. "Don't be a stranger, okay?"

Gio smiled. "Take care of him, Caroline. He's one of the good ones. Don't let him get away."

She snuggled Robbie. "I won't."

Gio shouldered his pack, went to the door, opened it and stopped. "DJ'll be fine, by the way."

"Thank you."

Gio drove back to Ramsey alone and followed the coast road rather than the highway. His hand involuntarily reached for where Jess always sat, close beside him, and ached to play the finger games they'd always played when they drove together. "There are some pains even I can't heal from, Jess."

He pulled into the main Ramsey parking lot surprisingly hungry, left his pack in Bessie, and walked to the cafeteria.

Laurie and Merl sat by themselves at the table Gio normally chose, by the floor to ceiling windows facing the back pond. They waved him over.

"Awfully quiet in here."

Laurie toyed with a blueberry muffin on her tray. "Doc Ock committed suicide."

Gio snorted. "I hope he didn't do it on my account. I'm leaving after today."

Laurie put her hand on his arm. "Why?"

"Because it's time. I've learned everything I can learn here. For now. Maybe later there'll be more. But not now."

"Please don't go."

"May I kiss you one more time before I go?"

Her eyes opened wide. "Please."

He pulled her close. His lips touched hers. Her eyes fluttered, her body went weak. He held her against him in their chairs. His body tingled. He felt his nerves grow hot, catch fire, followed them into her, moved through her body, felt the weaknesses, saw the lesion.

He held her and breathed.

His body took on her disease, cured it, gave her health to replace it. And pulled back.

Her face flushed. She put a hand on her chest and took a deep, slow breath. "You sure you don't want to go for two?"

He stood, chuckled, and kissed her on the top of her head. "I'd love to, and I'm sure. One was enough."

Merl worked hard to not look at them.

"Merl, care to help me pack up my room?"

A note with his name on it waited on his door. He opened it, nodded, folded it, and put it in his pocket. "Let's get started."

Merl picked up a box of books and headed towards Bessie. Gio walked beside him with a box of books and a box of clothes.

"You really leaving, Gio?"

"Uh-huh."

"Do you know the Serenity Prayer?"

"God, grant me the serenity to accept the things I cannot change, the courage to change the things I can, and wisdom to know the difference?"

"I've come up with a new version. A modification based on the past few months. Lord, give me the courage to recognize there are some dang stupid people in the world, the smarts to avoid them whenever possible, and the intelligence not to become one of them."

Gio laughed.

"Some people still think you're the anti-Christ."

"Then they should pray for me."

"I do. Me and some others."

"Thank you."

"You did something to Laurie, didn't you? When you kissed her?"

"Did I?"

"I don't think you're the anti-Christ, Gio. I'm not sure if you're human, but I don't think you're a demon or possessed or anything like that. I did once. Not now. I've seen too much."

They walked to Bessie with the last of Gio's boxes.

Merl put his box on Bessie's roof. "Can I ask you a question?"

"You just did."

Merl snorted.

"Go ahead."

"Can you be happy being you, doing whatever it is you do? You laugh a lot, but over the past few months it seems you've smiled less and less."

Gio took the last box and put it in Bessie's backseat. He closed the door and offered Merl his hand. "Do angels mourn their place in heaven?"

Gio headed towards Boston, to the Beth Israel, and walked up to Janey Kagan's room.

Mark was on his knees beside her, his face on her lap, her covers wet with his tears, and slept.

Gio looked at the monitors, the drips, the skull cap, the prayer shawls, the Bible, and walked quietly to the opposite side of her.

He placed one hand on her chest, another on her hairless scalp, closed his eyes, and breathed.

She opened her eyes and saw an angel standing beside her. The angel said, "He misses you."

"I know."

"There's nothing I can do. Not now. Maybe later, when I'm stronger. When I've learned more."

"That's okay."

"I can give you one more day with him. To play cards. To watch TV. Like you used to."

"That's enough."

"Tell him you love him, that you'll wait for him. Tell him I'm sorry. That's the best I can do."

"I will. I promise. He'll understand."

The angel faded. Mark raised his head. Janey smiled down at him. "I love you, Mr. Mark, my little Love Bunny. Get a deck of cards. Let's see if you can still beat me at two-handed solitaire."

Wednesday, 3 August 1974

Gio drove into the Maine woods as far as Bessie could take him. He got out and stood in the mugginess of the northern shade. "I'm here, Grandmother."

A raven flew to an elm facing him and landed on a bough.

Caw.

"I'm here."

The raven flew down and landed behind the tree. Running Water walked around the other side. "You have journeyed far."

"I have a question."

"Questions are better than answers. Answers stop your journey, questions guide them."

"Was all of this just to get me to practice in earnest? The only reason I went to Ramsey and met Jess to fulfill the Universe's purpose for me? And now that I'm doing what the Universe wants, get her out of the way, it doesn't need her anymore, it's time for her and me to move on to other worlds, other realities? Did she or I have any choice in all this?"

"The question of free will versus predestination is in your philosophies."

"Right, and there are more things in heaven and earth than are dreamt of in your philosophy. This time I want an answer."

She stared at him. Her face darkened and extended, her eyes became the dark void of Raven's eyes.

He looked away. "Sorry, sorry."

Her human features returned. "You can only make a decision to not do something once you know you can do it. Now your decision will have meaning. I have done what your grandfather asked of me."

"Not sure if I should say thank you or not."

"Turn your back, walk away, and the Universe will find another to take your place."

"Thank you for letting me know it's my choice."

"And?"

"And I'm here. My decision's made."

She nodded. "We may study more later, after you've learned from others." She handed him a raven's feather. "In case you need me."

"Thank you."

"One more thing." She waved her hand. The air shimmered under the arc it made. In the shimmer stood Ramsey College, its well-groomed lawns, sculptured walkways, utilitarian buildings, universally well-mannered and attentive students. "They seek to know but not to understand."

"Rituals without knowing the ceremonies?"

She nodded and pointed to one building inside the snow globe of her energies. "This building. You study great minds there."

"What are called hard sciences - physics, chemistry, engineering, things like that - yes."

"They talk about things being in two places at once, things appearing and disappearing, things moving without motion, but never apply it to themselves."

"That would be physics, primarily."

She shrugged and the snow globe shimmered into nothingness. "Apply it to yourself."

"Huh?"

"Be in two places at once."

"Yes, I remember - "

"But you don't understand the obvious because it is obvious. Or perhaps you do not have the training to make it apply."

Gio shook his head. "I'm sorry, Grandmother. I don't understand. Stupid Two-Legger. White-eye. *Wasicu.*"

"Leave the Lakotah for those who wish it." She reached out, her hand at waist height, grabbed something he couldn't see and turned.

A door opened. He heard a crackling, a sparking. A light came on over their heads.

"The phonebooth. In my dorm."

"If you are a spark, be the spark that ignites other people's fires. Teach them how to learn."

He nodded. "I will."

"And also be in both worlds. Yours and theirs. Be a light that burns brightly in both."

His laughter shook the woods. "Levels upon levels upon levels."

Her laughter joined his. "Now you're learning."

Their laughter grew into silence.

"Time for me to leave, Grandmother."

"Yes." She turned and started back around the tree, hesitated, and turned back. "Tell me, Gio. Did you find what you were searching for?"

He snorted. "Myself. Yes."

\\\\\\\\

Jess parked Sam's Chrysler in front of the Osteria Giambatta. She walked up to the front door. A burly man came out. "Sorry, we're closed."

Riggerio came out and took her hand. "She's okay. Mr. de Leo's guest."

The first man nodded and held the door for them.

Riggerio sat her at Nick's table. "Can I get you anything?"

She shook her head.

"Mr. de Leo'll be with you in a minute."

Less than a minute later Nicholas de Leo, dressed as always and not affected by the August heat, came up beside her. "Jess, I'm so - "

She looked up at him.

He pulled out a chair, sat, and pulled his handkerchief from his breast pocket. "Jess, you've been crying. Are you all right, my girl?"

"Do you know where Gio is, Uncle Nick?"

He sat back and shook his head. "Sorry, Daughter. I don't."

"Are you telling me the truth, Uncle Nick?"

He smiled. "Yes, I'm afraid I am."

"Do you know how to get word to him? Can you tell him it's a full moon tonight and I'll be at Singing Beach, like we used to?"

"Jess, I don't know how to get in touch with him."

"Would you tell me if you could?"

"Jess, Gio is lost to both of us. I haven't seen him in months. If he's like his grandfather, he's off learning who he is."

"I made a bad mistake, Uncle Nick. I need him to know I made a bad mistake."

"He knows. I'm sure he knows."

"I love him, Uncle Nick. What am I supposed to do?"

"His kind are not meant to be with us, Daughter. We will never understand because we don't have his gifts. Do you see? He can't be around us, not for any length of time. We are painful to him. Being around people like us kills him for all he must restrain to be what people can be comfortable with, will not fear."

He held her while she cried.

Wednesday, 19 November 1975

Gio stood outside Jess's dorm at the University of Southern Maine. His body filled with the scent of her, the memories of her, her laughing, pressing herself against him, finger wrestling in Bessie, watching the moon over Singing Beach, the way she emphasized "Ugh!" whenever she heard Five Man Electrical Band's *Signs*. He closed his eyes and listened to her, her room. She played Edgar Winter's *They Only Come Out at Night* album, one of his favorites. He stood and listened to *Autumn*.

> *Autumn, the wind blows colder than summer*
> *Autumn, my love's gone with another*
> *I can't demand anything of myself now*
> *So I guess I'll stay here in New England*
> *For autumn*

His body became a mist, rose in the night, came in through her window. She slept, her head resting on her arms, her arms covering an open textbook, *Psychological Stressors in the Workplace*, a marker held loosely in her left hand, a pen in the other. At the top of her desk he saw the card he gave her lifetimes ago: Romantic Enters the World. Beside it a can of Sprite and a bag of peanuts.

The mist became a Gio-shaped cloud. It hovered, watched her, descended. It shaped hands. They reached out, solidified, became flesh.

Gio's flesh.

He brushed her hair back and stroked her forehead. He remembered how she chuckled when he kissed her there, kissed her neck, nibbled her ears and told her, "I love you."

He leaned down. His lips became flesh. He kissed the nape of her neck.

> *Did you ever lose something*
> *That you thought you knew?*
> *Did you ever lose someone*
> *Who was close to you?*
> *Well I lost my lover*

He whispered with a voice of warm winds and gentle waters. "I look down the years and still see you smile, although now it's into another's face. And I know you are happy and well, and that is enough."

He kissed her again, above her ear, and whispered, "I love you, Jess. Goodbye."

She sighed.

"I give you a gift. A bolus. Should you ever need. Truly need. I will know."

His lips hovered over by her ear again. He kissed her one more time, pulled away, and whispered, "Forget."

Her eyes fluttered open. She raised her head.

Strange card. And Sprite and peanuts? Her roommate must have sat at her desk again.

The mist was gone.

Appendix: Principles

What follows is a living document. Things are added. To date (45+ years), nothing's been deleted. Some comes from things my Grandfather taught me, some from life, some from my own studies, journeys, and what have you. A friend, learning much came from my Grandfather, nodded and congratulated me for keeping my Grandpa's teaching alive. "We've lost the elements of honoring the elders," she said.

Someone once asked me if I've lived up to the Principles myself.

"Hell no. That's why I write them down. So they can be a guide to me, so I'll know when I am not following them."

Like so much in my life, they are for me. If others benefit from them, wonderful (and it seems many do). But first and foremost, they are for me.

You may not like them all. You may only be comfortable with one or two.

Good start. Work to integrate them all. Find that difficult? As noted above, if they were easy for me to follow I wouldn't write them down.

I will offer you can't pick and choose. Or at least it seems most people can't. I haven't met anyone who's done so successfully, known many who have tried and failed.

One fellow studied them for a while and told me he couldn't find any contradictions in them. They seem internally consistent.

Reassuring, that.
"Does that mean you'll follow them?"
"No way. I've got a life to live."
And so it goes.

1. Do unto others as if they were you.

In other words, cut out the middle man. Treat others the way you treat yourself. People do this anyway. All we do is suggest you become aware of it.

2. Trust yourself.

Until you do this, you'll never be able to trust others and you'll put what trust you have in people who will hurt you.

3. Be Honest.

With yourself first because it makes it easier to be honest with others. Honesty will cost you and what it returns is worth it. Tell tall tales, lie with the best of them and exaggerate all you want when people know that's what you're doing. The rest of the time, be honest.

4. Respect people's boundaries and limits.

There's a difference between being selfish and being selfless. Realize what this means for you and you'll realize what it means for others.

5. Keep it Simple.

Because it's so much easier that way.

6. Take responsibility for your actions.

When you make a mistake and before anybody else knows the mistake has been made, raise your hand and say loud enough for others to hear you, "That one's mine. I did that." If the people around you are more interested in pointing their fingers at you and distancing themselves from you than helping you clean things up, you're standing around the wrong people. Let them distance themselves. They won't be around you when you succeed, and you will, because you'll have learned how to stand up tall, proud and free by recognizing, owning up to and cleaning up your own mistakes. From this you'll also learn compassion and dignity and how to help others clean up their mistakes, as well. Along with this …

7. *Mistakes are just that; You can reach again.*

So learn to stretch when you have to and to recognize when what you're reaching for isn't something you'd want to hold in your hands. You'll be better for it and so will those who love you.

8. *Innocence is not Naivety and vice-versa.*

Think of this as a self-recognition of " … wise as serpents and harmless as doves."

9. *Your rights end where your willingness to harm and hurt begin.*

If you need this one explained or you needed a moment to put this into a context you could get comfortable with, you are either intentionally ignorant (never a good plan) or hoping to excuse yourself for your. behavior towards others (also not a good plan)

10. *Language is a tool, like Maslow's Hammer.*

Some people think everything's a nail. Be neither. This is part 1.

11. *Language is a tool, and can be Eliadeian.*

Some people are or can become 2nd order thinkers. Be both. This is part 2.

12. *Faith is with the heart, but the confession of faith is with the lips.*

So until you can say it to at least two others, it ain't true and you and others will know it.

13. Everything is that simple.

As soon as you begin saying things are not quite that simple or that things aren't that easy, you've demonstrated you don't understand the true nature of the problem.

14. Be wary of those who only tell you of their successes.

They do not have a full view of life.

15. It is not easier to get forgiveness than permission.

Attempting to do so demonstrates a lack of concern and consideration for others.

16. Be thee not a respecter of men (or women).

Respect is earned through actions that are closely aligned with words, and both are externalizations of thoughts, beliefs and ideas, which brings us back to what you get when you squeeze an orange.

17. Do not go where you are not invited.

This, in all things, because being unwelcome can be a painful experience in more ways than one, and the corollary is that you'll always find your way to where you're wanted and loved.

18. Do not do what you are not asked to do.

Because until you are asked, you're doing it for yourself, not for them, and it may not be what they wanted in the first place.

19. People who don't ask for what they want deserve what they get.

So go ahead and ask. All a "no" means is that there must be other avenues you haven't explored yet.

20. Never, via your direct action or intentional inaction, allow

others to come to harm.

And the minute you begin debating what "harm" is, you've already allowed it to happen.

21. If someone is drowning don't ask them "How wet is the water?"

Make sure your questions are relevant to the situation you are asking about. Think before you speak, otherwise be prepared for those around you to care more about keeping themselves dry than helping you to safety.

22. You are not your brother's (or your sister's) keeper.

Show people enough respect to let them make their own mistakes. That way they'll be able to appreciate their own successes.

23. If you can't think outside the box then you'll spend your life as someone else's package.

And maybe you're comfortable with that. We're not.

24. Don't feed someone when you're hungry.

You'll be jealous of what they eat and there's no guarantee there'll be any left for you when they're done.

25. In the Game of Life, let the other person win once in a while.

You'll learn to be humble, they'll learn to be gracious. At some point in time they'll figure out what you did, then they'll learn to be humble and you'll learn to be gracious.

26. What is a Dark Mystery to you is Perfectly Obvious to someone else (and vice versa).

So when you explain something to somebody, explain the obvious. When you leave something out and they don't get it, you're the fool, not them.

27. Everybody knows there are classes in society, any society.
Wise people don't speak of it. The wisest people don't show it.

28. Respect people who know the name of their waiter or waitress.
It shows they value people.

29. Everything is possible.
When you decide something is impossible all you've done is demonstrate the limitations of your resources.

30. To each of us is given a measure, to some great and to some so small as not to be noticed in the light of day.
How can we know that the greatest measure, without the efforts of those barely noticed as foundation or support or crown, will be enough? Therefore never slight nor be jealous of those whose measure is greater or less than yours, because to each of us is given a measure. It's not the measure that makes us great, it's what we do with our measure that gives us greatness.

31. You don't always need a reason to get something done.
Sometimes things just have to be done, and that is reason enough.

32. Own your history. Don't be owned by it.
You are the only one who has the power to change the universe you live in.

33. Sometimes you just have to let the fool be slapped.
People know when they're not being upfront, honest, above board, ... , and nine times out of ten they want to be caught because it gives shape, form, and substance to the world around them. You honor them and yourself by catching them. Regarding that one out of ten that doesn't want to be caught? Put up walls between yourself and them. They will be a danger to both themselves and to you.

34. Never be afraid to appear a fool when asking a question.
It's the ones who won't ask questions who are truly the fools.

35. Be wary of people who enjoy casting large shadows.
It is better to be the light that allows shadows to exist, that lights the way for others, than to be in someone else's darkness.

36. Courage is not the absence of fear. Courage is what you do when you're afraid.
Be Courageous. It will cost you relationships, no doubt, but you'll be able to sleep at night.

37. When someone is hanging onto a cliff by their fingernails, don't ask them if they want to play catch.
Another example of making sure your questions are relevant to the situation. People in need, people under stress and strain, when distracted, suffer. Make sure you help rather than hurt.

38. Let your dreams create your capabilities.
Never believe that what you are now is all you ever shall be.

39. Some will ask, "What do you want?" Others with, "Who are you?" To answer either, you must first answer "Am I who I want to be?"
Whether known or not, spoken or not, it is the first question that must be answered.

40. Laws are the boundaries societies place upon the spirit.
Be boundless. You may be in a society of one, but being alone is often the price of freedom.

41. Never allow yourself to be blinded by those who lack

vision.

Surround yourself with those who encourage you to see, even if they can not. It is much to be preferred than to be around those who won't allow you to see because they themselves can not.

42. Shame is a gift given by someone who fears you.

This can be a hard lesson to learn. The only reason for someone to make you feel ashamed is to control you, and love has no need for control.

43. If you follow your path long enough, eventually you'll discover your dreams.

Therefore it is up to you to make sure your dreams are something you want to discover.

44. and in keeping with the above, Paths reveal themselves to you if you let them.

They are not always straight and often not obvious, therefore it's up to you to follow or not as you decide.

45. Acceptance is not Understanding.

Keep separate the things you accept and the things you understand. A few items will be in both camps, a lot of items won't. Knowing the difference means knowing what you're willing to change versus what you're willing to let change you, and the world of difference is there.

46. As with most things, if you're willing to go just a little bit further than you've ever gone before, an entirely new world 47. is opened onto you.

Explore to the limits of your abilities and willingness. It's the only way to know how big you really are.

48. Is it better to see the end, to hear its answer when you call

its name, or to be there?

Answer these and you'll know what eternity means to you.

49. *True Authority becomes such by acknowledging, understanding and incorporating all points of view, especially those that disagree.*

Authority can not exist without growth and change, and authority that can't include or disprove disagreement is no authority at all.

50. *Success is not synonymous with Achievement.*

People can have successful careers and have achieved nothing in their life, while people who've achieved but one thing are successful beyond measure. Success means you've grown (no small achievement, that). Achievement means you've helped someone else grow (and to be willing just to take on that task indicates you're a success).

51. *"Chaos, once defined, can be the most organized system there is." and "Don't burn your bridges before they hatch." are two orthogonal statements and their intersection is you.*

Take the time to realize that these two statements are equations of existence and that they define a universe of possibilities. Recognize that if they intersect you are the intersection and that if they don't intersect you're denying yourself a universe of possibilities.

52. *Always be willing to share your story and always be respectful of the stories of others.*

Tell people "I will tell you as much of my story as you wish to know, but I will never share your story with others nor will I share another's story with you." Understand this and you'll understand your own and other's boundaries, where you begin and end and how your words can heal and hurt others.

53. *If you can't clearly say "No" then nobody will know when*

you're saying "Yes".

So be clear and concise in all your communications when a "No" or a "Yes" will do. People will appreciate it and confusions will quickly melt away.

54. Handing over control is not giving up responsibility.

Hand over control of something to someone else and they become your responsibility as well as whatever you have control of. Consider this an opportunity to teach, yourself and them.

55. Never let your limitations be someone else's limitations.

You've probably worked long and hard to get the ones you have. Don't share them. Similarly, honor the ones others have that you don't. They worked just as hard to get theirs as you did to get yours.

56. Sometimes the best lesson is recognizing that someone is not your teacher.

It can save both of you a lot of pain and sorrow.

57. Paddle Plato's Life Boat with Ockham's Razor.

Find a theoretical structure that supports all data, even conflicting data, and find a theoretical structure that supports it all without resorting to unnecessary entities. This is where The Principle of Rich Observation meets The Principle of Parsimony. Live there. Be there. Be it.

58. You must be dancing yourself if you want to dance with somebody.

You can not find what you're looking for until and unless you're willing to first be it yourself.

59. Eliminate Variables, Remove Ambiguities.

You are going to make mistakes in life (see Principles 6, 7, and 22). It's possible to minimize those mistakes by eliminating as many unknowns as possible from the situation before you act. You can further minimize mistakes by removing all ambiguous information before you act. It isn't possible to ignore ambiguous information and it's usually possible to act in a way that doesn't require making use of the ambiguous data. Be patient. Ambiguous situations tend to resolve themselves given enough time. How do they resolve? By eliminating unknowns.

60. Be An Enemy of the People, point out the naked Emperor, protect The Old Man and tell people about The Rock.

You may be the only one who knows the truth and in truth, you're the only one who can know your own truth. However, that doesn't make the truth incorrect and your sharing it can possibly save lives. Even if it costs you yours.

61. It is perfectly useless to know the answer to the wrong question.

So before you answer another's question ask yourself if the question is worth answering at all.

62. Never cure a singer of their voice.

Sometimes people's gifts can frighten or disturb us, hence their gifts go unappreciated. Take a moment to make sure your goal is to be just and that your pursuit isn't just for yourself at the expense of others.

63. Choice is better than no choice.

This isn't Free Will versus Predestination, this is right here, right now, do you want to be in control of your life or give up control? The latter leads to victimization and can't be healthy for anyone involved. The former leads to opportunity and possible sacrifice, but it'll be your choice to sacrifice if you do.

64. Don't label people (for both your sakes).

It's sometimes helpful to assign labels to people so long as you remember that people are not objects, labels are like boxes and boxes can become coffins. For both of you.

65. Work honestly, accurately, and unbiasedly.

Doing so will be your testimony. And while some may despise you, the majority will recognize that you honor them through your work and return that honor a hundred-fold.

66. A worker is worthy of their wages.

Recognize that nothing is free. That's first. Somebody is paying some where at some time any time some thing is done. Directly paying the worker for work done demonstrates you value them and their work, that you recognize them as equals in a fair-exchange, and (perhaps most importantly) that you respect yourself enough to know your own value is not in question. That last one throw you? Then go elsewhere. The only time people want something for free is when they're not sure of the value of their own efforts because the price people are willing to pay is a measure of the value they place on their request. Want something for free? Then it has little value to you. Willing to pay? Then it's important to you. It's as simple as that.

The other side of this is that the worker can ask for wages in other than coin of the realm (and barter doesn't count. Barter is mutually agreed to coin of the realm). Recognize that the only commerce besides coin of the realm is with a piece of yourself — your time, your strength, your thoughts, your word, your knowledge, your wisdom, your friendship, your oath. Be careful with these. Coin is far cheaper than heart.

67. Act with kindness even though you don't know the outcome.

Never doubt that something you said or didn't say, did or didn't do, etc., changed the universe in some incredible way. The Universe's concept of the Butterfly Effect is "You said hello to someone walking down the street whom you didn't know therefore a lifeless planet is starting to form oceans."

68. Until you've gathered all the data available and understood its significance in the situation under study, your decisions regarding the situation are inherently flawed.

Even if they're the correct decisions, the decision process is flawed and outcomes are reproducible due more to luck than knowledge because you never know if the lacking data is contributing 1 or 99% to a complete solution. Explaining observed outcomes without complete knowledge of what's causing them is a fool's goal.

69. Forgive others so that you can be released from their grasp.

Forgiveness isn't done for others, it's done for yourself, to help you let go of the emotions that bind you to someone who wronged you. This does not mean you must love them, only that you may let them go.

70. Faith, until it is tested, is just an opinion.

It doesn't matter if faith takes the form of fealty to a friend, a place, a country, a product, an idea, a life-partner or a deity, until that faith is tested it is just opinion about your relationship to a friend, a place, et cetera. Tested, you know the limits of your faith and limits are just that, neither failure nor triumph, only today's boundaries and limits, only how far you'll go today in this particular test.

71. Technology is not how we make and keep relationships. We make and keep relationships because of who we are, not what tools we use to stay in touch.

Everybody's lives are hectic. If you can't get everything done you want to do and are missing appointments/meetings/friends/what-have-you, getting more technology won't organize your day because time isn't your problem, you are. You have as much time in your day as Michelangelo, Galileo, Newton, Einstein, Gandhi, Mother Teresa, Buddha, Socrates, ...

72. An individual can only receive a certain benefit if others are willing to take on a certain burden.

Remember, the Universe works in balance. From Principles 1, 4, 6, 9, 20, ... , remember that what you take you owe. Think you don't often enough, think this doesn't apply to you often enough and you'll find yourself on the long end of burden. Not a happy place.

73. When someone shares their success with you, focus on them, not you. There's no need to compare their success to yours. This is their moment, not yours.

Imagine your toddler or a friend's toddler taking their first step. Would you tell them about your first step? This Principle is a corollary to 14. Help people celebrate their successes. Especially those they struggled for. And earned.

74.Only teach those willing to be taught.

People demonstrate a real learning desire by how they ask and what they do with what you give them. Don't teach because you believe you have something to share. You may not teach what they want to learn, they may not want to learn what you want to teach.

Real teaching is about helping people discover their own way, their own doors, their own understanding. We teach best by our actions. Be careful with yours.

Coming Soon From Northern Lights Publishing

Stay up on early reads, special offers, and gift opportunities! Join our mailing list at http://nlb.pub/nlbmailings

March 2024: Tag

Two teenagers, Eric and Julia, seek tree grafts on the outskirts of their medieval village as a summer storm clouds the sky. Sullya, a witch hiding among the trees, grabs Julia. Eric swings his axe and severs Sullya's hand from her arm. Sullya seeks refuge in the deep bole of an old oak. Her hand falls onto the same oak and crawls up the trunk to join her.

Eric wants to flee but Julia, believing they are safe, torments the witch. Sullya curses them, their families, their crops, their livestock, and their eastern European village.

Crops wilt, livestock dies, and much of village falls ill. The village priest, Father Baillot, is often seems ignorant of church ways and proves ineffective against the curse.

The elders seek help elsewhere, specifically from a distant priest, Father Patreo, who knows the Old Ways as well as the New.

Patreo is out of favor with the Church because he makes no effort to hide his belief that progress comes from exploring all paths, not just those the Church decrees acceptable.

He and Verduan, one of the elders, investigate, and what they discover changes the face of Eastern Europe forever.

Ben Matthews and his son, Jiminy, are enjoying some bonding time together at New York City's South Street Seaport watching jugglers and other buskers on a warm late summer day, eating fried dough covered in brown sugar and cinnamon, and getting to know each other.

Suddenly the East River and beyond because a vast desert. A warm wind blows sand in people's faces. In the distance, three creatures walk towards the City.

Havoc ensues. People run, carts are overturned, mounted police work at crowd control to no avail, and Ben loses Jiminy in the chaos.

Ben grabs the leg of a mounted officer asking for help and is knocked down as the horse turns.

The three creatures walk up to him, stop, and peer down. The one in front says, "We are Healers from the Land of Barass." It points to the one on his right. "He is Cetaf, who cries for his own pain." It turns to the one on his left. "This is Jenreel, who tends to his own needs. I am Beriah. I will tell you how I feel. We are Healers from the Land of Barass."

THREE QUESTIONS FOR YOU

1. *Did you know most readers rely on other readers' reviews and comments to make their book buying decisions? Ongoing research begun in mid-2022 indicates reviews and comments are better decision drivers than video teasers, author interviews, author blogs, and everything else combined.*
2. *Did you know most on- and off-line bookstores - from the smallest indie to the largest megastore - rely on reader reviews and comments to decide which books to put on their shelves?*
3. *Did you enjoy* Search?

Help Northern Lights as a publisher and Joseph Carrabis as an author by reviewing Search *on Amazon http://nlb.pub/Search Goodreads http://nlb.pub/GSearch, Barnes&Noble, BookBub, NetGalley, your favorite reader Facebook and LinkedIn groups, TikTok, Instagram, anywhere and everywhere.*

Join Northern Lights Publishing's Journey
http://nlb.pub/JoinNorthernLights

Join Northern Lights Publishing's Journey
http://nlb.pub/JoinNorthernLights

About Northern Lights Publishing

Northern Lights Publishing/Press is an association of five professionals (one graphic artist, one marketer, one editor/book designer, one copyeditor, one editor/educator/author) and a rotating group of ten published authors and poets all of whom are passionate readers. Financial backing is provided by a small group of investors led by Susan and Joseph Carrabis through the NextStage Evolution Corporation. Everyone receives remuneration and owns an equal share of the company with the exception of Susan and Joseph Carrabis.

We're developing our publishing/marketing model so we're not accepting submissions at present.

We'll open our doors to submissions (and announce it through various social networks) once we're sure we can break even and preferably turn a profit. Until then, wish us well.

It's an exciting journey and one we'd love to share, but only after we're sure we can successfully navigate the publishing seas.

Join Northern Lights Publishing's Journey
http://nlb.pub/JoinNorthernLights

Also by Joseph Carrabis

Non-Fiction

That Th!nk You Do - http://nlb.pub/TTYDv1

That Th!nk You Do is based on a series of blog posts Joseph wrote between 2008 and 2016. They dealt with ways his research in fields as diverse as neuroscience, linguistics, psychology, sociology, anthropology and other disciplines could be put to practical use to help people better their lives.

If you ever wonder about how to think like an expert, the difference between your inner critic and the actor within, your ability to be heard, the value of being a musician, how to protect yourself from liars or how to overcome fears, you will find answers in this book..

Reading Virtual Minds Volume I: Science and History - http://nlb.pub/Minds1

The science and history behind NextStage Evolution's Evolution Technology

Reading Virtual Minds Volume II: Experience and Expectation - http://nlb.pub/Minds2

Learnings and Take-Aways from NextStage Evolution's research and studies

Reading Virtual Minds Volume III: Fair-Exchange and Social Networks - http://nlb.pub/Minds3

Learnings and Take-Aways from NextStage Evolution's research and studies applied specifically on on- and off-line social interactions

Fiction: Novels

Empty Sky - http://nlb.pub/EmptySky

What if you're a young boy, Jamie McPherson, whose mother has been missing for over a year and whose father starts falling in and out of coma? What if you hold onto your aging dog, Shem, who's always been with you and always protected you, because the world isn't safe anymore?

And what if in the midst all that's happening, The Moon asks you to help her save the world's dreams?

Earl Pangiosi's greatest desire, since childhood, has been to control and manipulate people. Working for the NSA, Earl learns that people's dreams - their nonconscious minds - guide their conscious decisions. Control their dreams - weaponize them - and you control people at an unprecedented level.

Jamie will not face Pangiosi alone. The Moon sends her Guardians, winged, shapeshifting wolves; and her children, The Oneiroi, little black silhouettes, shadows in the darkness of night, whose multicolored, multifaceted, crystalline eyes serve as kaleidoscopic Gates — little rainbow bridges allowing humans passage from one dream reality to the next, to help Jamie.

Pangiosi sends the Native American giant, Nighthorse, to stop Jamie. But Nighthorse's grandfather introduced him to Wovoka, the DreamWorld, as a child. Going after Jamie, Nighthorse finds one of the Oneiroi's Eye-Gates and realizes his grandfather may not have been such a fool after all.

Meanwhile the Moon brings together a team of "Dreamers" to help Jamie. One such Dreamer is ANN, a supercomputer who can blend dream and waking realities via Penrose Consciousnesses, quantum superpositions.

If they fail, Pangiosi and the NSA will control the world.

The Augmented Man - http://nlb.pub/Augmented
What do you do with a deadly weapon when it's no longer needed?

Nicholas Trailer is the last of The Augmented Men, beings created first by society and completed by a political group the public can't even imagine exists. Captain James Donaldson takes severely abused and traumatized children and modifies them into monsters capable of the most horrifying deeds without feeling any remorse or regret.

But the horrors of war never stay on the battlefield. They always come home.

Battling what society and science has made him, Nick Trailer discovers he is loved. From the horrors of childhood to the horrors of a war, what does it take for someone to find true love and peace? Especially when everyone has their own agenda, from the senators who sanctioned his making to the Governor of Maine who wants to use Nick's struggle to propel himself to the White House.

The Augmented Men were good at war, perhaps a little too good. Now they have to come home ... or do they? What do you do with man-made monsters?

Nick must decide if his friends are his friends and if his enemies are his enemies, all while protecting the woman he loves.

And are you truly the last of your kind?

What if you must remain a monster to defeat a monster? Will you sacrifice love to protect what you love?

Fiction: Anthologies
Tales Told 'Round Celestial Campfires - http://nlb.pub/TalesV1
Includes:
Binky (available separately at http://nlb.pub/Binky)
What if you run an inner-city health clinic and are tired of fighting budget cuts, politics, protestors, police, ... ? And what if you question your purpose because caring is no longer cost-effective? And what if

you meet a bright, beautiful child who leads you to a child who died sixty years ago? And what if that child asks you to save its life?

The Boy Who Loved Horses (available separately at http://nlb.pub/Horses)

What if you're born and raised Hill but got City educated and now you drivin a big state issue Buick back into Hill 'cause you gonna show them you something else? And what if one town you drive through's got secrets it don't want nobody to know? And what if you plan to tell City those secrets and those secrets got they own idea who you gonna tell?

Canis Major (available separately at http://nlb.pub/CanisMajor)

What if you're a WereMan, human when the moon is full, a beast when not, and your father died before explaining your gift to you? And what if your fully human mother did the best she could but couldn't really understand your needs? And what if you're tired of being alone and afraid and once, just once, you want to hold someone and not be afraid of their fear?

Cold War (available separately at http://nlb.pub/ColdWar)

What if your last deployment left you so damaged driving a school bus tops your employable skills? And what if the kids laugh at you because you can't talk right and twitch at nothing? And what if the military calls you back, says they can make you a man again. Or get close. And what if you're so lonely, angry and tired you say sure without realizing they plan to leave you out in the cold, forever?

Cymodoce (available separately at http://nlb.pub/Cymodoce)

What if the only man you've ever given yourself to isn't a man at all? And what if you gave birth to twins, the son wholly yours, the daughter wholly his? And what if your daughter needs to return to her father in order to survive? And what if her survival means never seeing her again, and her brother losing his sister forever?

Dancers in the Eye of Chronos (available separately at http://nlb.pub/Dancers)

What if your love so delights the Gods they grant you immortality. But you learn love is meant to age, to mature, to grow and change in ways the Gods can't imagine. After millennia, they strip their gift from you. But that's what you wanted; to hold your lover's face one last time before darkness falls. Or is your love so strong it outlives the Gods themselves?

The Goatmen of Aguirra (available separately at http://nlb.pub/Goatmen)

What if you've signed onto a deep space mission and left behind a wife and young son? And what if your mission takes to you a supposedly uninhabited planet that harbors intelligent life that values family above all else? And what if they take you into their family to heal you? And what if, finally healed, your shipmates abandon you when the mission is called home?

Mani He (available separately at http://nlb.pub/ManiHe)

What if you've acquired your dream job but destroyed another man's life and career to get it? And what if the president of your company hands you a rifle and the keys to his mountain cabin with the instructions "Bring me back something to make me proud"? And what if the spirits in the mountains have their own ideas of what it means to be proud?

Power Unlimited (available separately at http://nlb.pub/PowerUnlimited)

What if Eddie's kid brother Tommy idolizes you guys at the gym and wants to be like you but you know he's not really built for it. And what if he sends away for some "GET BIG FAST" Muscle Pill exercise programs? And what if he starts looking like The Hulk and King Kong had a baby? And what if the people who make those Pills want them back?

Sema (available separately at http://nlb.pub/Sema)

What if a beautiful woman discovers you and your friends are beings living side-by-side with humans since the beginning of time? And what if she discovers you have abilities beyond imagination and she, too, has gifts no mortal should possess? And what if, having no knowledge of your kind, has trained with a Darkness humans can't imagine, never suspecting a Light beyond mortals' dreams?

The Settlement (available separately at http://nlb.pub/Settlement)

What if you're a young, hotshot, wildly successful asteroid miner who hasn't seen your parents since you joined the corp underage? And what if your parents are getting divorced and each is laying claim to guardianship of your fortune? And what if your parents never knew why you joined the corp or what you had to give up to get a ship of your own?

Them Doore Girls (available separately at http://nlb.pub/Doore)

What if the woman you love is the mistress of something else, something so monstrous, so hideous its summoning her creates ocean storms? And what if she knows this entity will destroy her, you, your village and all those you know if she denies it? And what if you know she goes to it willingly because it threatened to kill you, her one love, if she doesn't yield to its wishes?

Those Wings Which Tire, They Have Upheld Me (available separately at http://nlb.pub/Wings)

What if you're a little boy with brain cancer whose doctors say they can cure you by replacing your eyes with an experimental device? And what if that experimental device lets you see your guardian angel? And what if seeing your guardian angel makes you best friends with the class trouble-maker? And what if the class bully finds out you talk to angels?

The Weight (available separately at http://nlb.pub/Weight)

What if you've been a success at everything you've done in your life and decide to retrace a hike you took when wishes were horses and beggars could ride? And what if you met one of your heroes on that long ago hike and - miracle of miracles - you meet him again? And what if your hero isn't your hero and says you took something from it way back when and now it wants it back?

Winter Winds (available separately at http://nlb.pub/Winds)
What if you're sitting in your favorite chair, your son on your lap, helping him with his homework when you see something in the fields outside your house? And what if you turn on the floodlights and see unimaginable creatures battling in your fields? And what if your son and wife tell you you're the strange one because those fantastical creatures battling in your field are as natural as natural can be?

Follow Joseph's work in magazines and other anthologies at https://josephcarrabis.com/tag/im-published-here/

You can find most of Joseph's work at http://nlb.pub/amazon

About The Author

Joseph Carrabis told stories to anyone who would listen starting in childhood, wrote his first stories in gradeschool, and started getting paid for his writing in 1978. His work history includes periods as a long-haul trucker, apprentice butcher, apprentice coffee buyer/broker, lumberjack, Cold Regions researcher, mathematician, semanticist, semioticist, physicist, educator, Chief Data Scientist, Chief Research Scientist, and Chief Research Officer. He was an original member of the NYAS/UN's Scientists Without Borders program and held patents covering mathematics, anthropology, neuroscience, and linguistics. After patenting a technology he created in his basement and creating an international company, he retired from corporate life. Now he spends his time writing fiction based on his experiences. His work appears regularly in anthologies and his own novels. You can often find him playing with his dog, Boo, and snuggling with his wife, Susan.

You can follow Joseph on BookBub, Facebook, Goodreads, Instagram, LinkedIn, Pinterest, or Twitter.

Become a member of Joseph's blog - http://nlb.pub/JoinJoseph